NOMAD

Matt Rubinstein is one of Australia's most promising young writers. His first novel, *Solstice*, was short-listed for the Australian/Vogel award in 1994 and was published to widespread acclaim. A novel-in-sonnets largely written when he was still in his teens, *Solstice* was later made into a stage musical and was one of the hits of the 1996 Adelaide Festival.

Nomad, is Matt's first prose work. Born and raised in Adelaide he now lives in Sydney, where he is working on a third novel, which features a gruesome and unusual murder.

By the same author:

Solstice

NOMAD

Matt Rubinstein

HYLAND HOUSE

> To all my travelling companions

First published in Australia in 1997 by
Hyland House Publishing Pty Limited
Hyland House
387–389 Clarendon Street
South Melbourne
Victoria 3205

© Matt Rubinstein 1997

This book is copyright. Apart from any fair dealing for the
purposes of private study, research, criticism or review, as
permitted under the Copyright Act, no part may be reproduced
by any process without written permission. Enquiries should be
addressed to the publisher.

Publication of this title was assisted by the Commonwealth
Government through the Australia Council, its arts funding and
advisory body.

National Library of Australia
Cataloguing-in-publication data:

Rubinstein, Matt, 1974–.
  Nomad.

   ISBN 1 86447 024 0.

   I. Title.

A823.3

Typeset in Times 11/12 by Hyland House Publishing Pty Limited
Printed in Victoria by Robertson Printing

1 Een

It was raining in Amsterdam. The square in front of the train station had disappeared beneath a broad rippling puddle, and the criss-crossing tram tracks glistened in the dull light like parallel slug-trails. Through an electric web of power cables, the unbroken slate-grey of the sky hid the sun and made guessing the time impossible, but it was about five in the afternoon.

Damon pushed a clump of sodden hair out of his eyes and peered over the top of his glasses. The world had retreated into a defocussed blur, colours leached away by the shadowy half-light, shapes eroded by rain and myopia. Streetcars jangled their bells impatiently as he stumbled across the Stationsplein, unbalanced by the weight of his backpack. He found an empty bus shelter, let his pack slide to the floor and collapsed on a folding seat, breathing heavily as the rain drummed against the roof.

On snapping open his backpack he found that the rain had seeped through the stitching and soaked the uppermost layer of his worldly possessions, including his new budget travel guidebook.

'Shit,' he said, trying to separate the waterlogged pages. Half the section on Salzburg came away in his hands. 'Shit!'

Most of the weather had penetrated only as far as Finland, and once he had carefully thumbed his way through to the Netherlands the pages were only damp around the edges. He skipped through the general information and scanned the accommodation section for somewhere dry to stay. The first few youth hostels in the listing were run by Christians and had midnight curfews, which seemed to defeat the whole purpose of Amsterdam. The next couple were out of town, and would have involved negotiating the public transport system. But there was one just down the road in the Red Light District, which seemed perfect. He heaved his backpack onto his shoulders and stepped out into the storm.

The city looked like a different planet through the rain, alien and impenetrable. Shop signs began in English and then dissolved into inscrutable Dutch, bewildering him. Strange creatures with umbrellas for heads scurried by occasionally. Everything was cold and grey. He tried to remember what it was like to be dry, but was unable to in this odd liquid world.

Eventually the youth hostel sign leered at him through the rain. He went inside, dripping apologetically across the floor to the counter. His glasses fogged up immediately and he spent a while looking for something dry to wipe them on before giving up and taking them off altogether. The receptionist told him that dorm beds were 23 guilders a night, which sounded expensive, but the hostel was warm and dry and desperately *immediate*. He handed over a fistful of cheery Monopoly-set notes and headed down the corridor towards his room.

The dormitory stretched hospital-white before him as he turned the key and swung the door open. Most of the beds had backpacks tipped against them, and some were occupied by prone figures who nodded at him as he walked down the aisle towards a vacant top bunk. His backpack crashed to the floor and he ran his hands through his dripping hair, closed his eyes and took a deep breath of warm, dry air.

Returning to himself, he rifled through the pockets of his leather jacket and removed the debris that had collected there. A tube ticket from Earl's Court to King's Cross. British Rail to Dover. A ferry ticket to Oostende. His Australian passport, and—thanks to immigrant parents—his EC passport as well. One pound seventy pence in coins which he would never spend and couldn't exchange. His wallet, which he transferred to the back pocket of his jeans. His glasses, which he wiped on his bedsheet and returned to his face.

He peeled off the empty jacket and hung it from a metal bedpost, where it sent tiny rivulets sliding towards the floor. His shirt was wet around the collar and the sleeves; he wriggled out of it and slung it over the jacket. His T-shirt was merely damp, clammy, but his jeans were soaked. He popped the catch on his backpack, loosened the drawstring and took a selection of clothes and toiletries into the communal bathroom further down the hall.

Having soaked himself under an inconstant shower long enough for his body to return to its normal temperature, he stood before a mirror, wrapped in a threadbare youth hostel towel, and rummaged through his toiletry bag.

'Who shall I be today?' he asked, looking up at his reflection.

The reflection stared back at him, trying on a variety of expressions and moods. Naive enthusiasm, brooding inscrutability, affable stupidity. Intense, indifferent, absorbed, distracted—his features were malleable, ambiguous. His eyes were an indeterminate blue-green colour, or perhaps hazel. His eyebrows, thin and dark, danced acrobatically across his forehead, mostly in unison but often independently. His mouth was either broad and voluptuous or small and thin-lipped, his cheeks slack and squirrel-like or taut and sinewed, depending on how he set his jaw. Only his nose was unchanging: rather narrow and turned up at the tip, and nothing he could do about it.

He took a comb from his kitbag and experimented with different ways of styling his hair. Black when wet, it would fade to a mid-brown as it dried unless he preserved the colour with gel. It hung almost to the end of his nose; long at the top, short at the back. He tried parting it to the left, then to the right, then slicked it back. It looked pretty good either way. He teased out a few strands and let them fall across his left eye. Even better. Then he dropped the comb into the basin and ruffled his hair vigorously with both hands until there was no style left but a drooping Beatles mop-top. Perfect for a city still lost in the hedonism of the sixties, he thought, nodding in satisfaction. He put on his auxiliary jeans, which were black, and a black rollneck sweater: his new personality was complete. He worked his face into a laid-back, glassy-eyed expression and strolled back to the dorm.

There was a skinhead in a trenchcoat and jackboots sitting on Damon's bed. Noticing Damon, he looked up from the porno he was reading and nodded at him.

'Hi,' said the skinhead. 'This your bed?'

'Sort of,' Damon said. 'You want it?'

The skinhead laughed. 'Nah, mate. Just want to sit on it, read my book.'

'Oh,' said Damon. 'Make yourself at home, then.'

'Ta.'

Damon looked closer: the skinhead seemed far less menacing than he had initially appeared. His face was young and cherubic, his eyes bright. His voice was high, the accent familiar.

'You from Australia?' Damon asked.

'Born there,' the skinhead said. 'Where are you from?'

Damon looked surprised. 'I'm from Australia too,' he said. 'Sydney.'

The skinhead raised his eyebrows. 'You don't sound Australian.'

'That's because we talk the same. We just sound normal to each other.'

The skinhead shook his head. 'You travel long enough, you can pick any accent—even your own. You sound more English, I dunno, kind of American too.'

'Really?'

'Yeah. You must watch too much TV.'

'No,' Damon said, taken aback. 'Not really. I've been in England for the past month, where there's nothing on except dismal soapies from back home.'

'Yeah, shocking, isn't it?' said the skinhead. 'Twice a day, in case you didn't get it the first time. How can they watch that shit?'

Damon shrugged. 'I couldn't believe it. But all they could ask me was what's going to happen on *Neighbours*, who's going to do what to who on *Home and Away*. I mean, I don't watch any of it, I had to make stuff up. Y'know, Ramsay Street gets demolished for a shopping mall, Summer Bay's hit by a tidal wave. And the scary thing is, people believed me.'

''Course they did,' the skinhead said. 'You're from Australia—even though you don't sound it. You're like some demigod to these people: some dopey, forthright, straight-toothed, speedo-wearing bronzed surf-lifesaver of a demigod. Why would you lie?'

Damon grinned. 'You ever actually met an Australian like that?'

The skinhead snorted. 'Saw one in a pub once. He was getting the shit kicked out of him.'

'But this is how the world sees us, man. This is our national identity.'

'Not mine, mate.'

Damon frowned. 'No,' he said. 'I guess it's not mine either.'

''Course it's not yours,' the skinhead said. 'You don't even have the accent. You're not anything. You're just a dispossessed cultural bastard of a nothing, that's what you are.'

'Oh?' Damon said. 'What are you, then?'

The skinhead grinned gleefully. 'I'm one too!' he said. 'It's great!'

'Well I'm not one,' Damon protested. 'I may not wear a blue singlet or drive a ute, but I'm still an Australian.'

'Sure, fine,' said the skinhead, suddenly weary. 'Be what you like, I don't care.'

'Well, I've got to be something.'

'Good luck.'

This annoyed Damon even more. 'So how would you classify yourself?'

The skinhead sat up abruptly and extended his hand. 'I'm James,' he said.

Damon shook it tentatively. 'Damon.'

'Good to meet you, Damon the Australian,' James said, eyes glinting. 'Good to meet you, true-blue Damon. G'day, I should say.'

'Likewise,' Damon said. His voice was faintly cold. 'G'day.'

Their exchange was prevented from becoming any more antagonistic by the interruption of a low moan from the next bunk.

'Mmroooaagh,' it said. 'Jeeeeesus Christ. I am soooooooo fuckin' SLAW-ered.'

James met Damon's gaze and smirked. 'Poor guy,' he said.

'Slaaaaww-errrred,' the moan repeated.

'What's he saying?' Damon asked.

'He's slaughtered,' James interpreted.

'In what language?'

'Northern England, sounds like. Harder to pick when they're stoned. Manchester, Sheffield maybe.'

'Daaaar,' said the moan. 'Daaaaaaar. Fuck. Derbyshire.'

James nodded. 'Close enough.'

'Is he okay?'

'Is he okay?' James laughed. 'He's cruising, mate. He's off with the dope fairies. He's whacked, he's wasted, he's baked, and he's toasted. So yeah, he's okay.'

'Hey,' said the moan, suddenly coherent. 'Hey, you up there. I can hear you, you know. Stop talking about me behind my back. Above my head. Wherever you are.'

'So come up here, mate,' James said. 'Come talk to us.'

'Gnnn.' From the adjacent bottom bunk came a faint shuffling, a groan of exertion, and then the sound of a heavy weight collapsing onto a sprung mattress. 'Fuck that. Come down here, man.'

'Forget it,' James said. 'I'm reading.'

He picked up his magazine and started leafing through the pages.

'What?' said the voice from the bottom bunk. 'What you reading?'

'Porno,' James said.

There was a brief rustle and a painful bump, and a spiky-haired, glassy-eyed and haggard face poked over Damon's mattress. It looked at James's magazine and said 'Bah, what's this shit?'

'*Penthouse*,' James said. 'I got it at the train station.'

'Soft-core bullshit,' the head complained. 'Haven't you been to a real skin shop yet?'

'I just got here.'

The owner of the head chuckled to himself. 'Just got here, he says. Listen, man, this place is insane. No—fuckin' amaaaazing, that's more like it, that's what it is. The drugs, the women, the alcohol, the sex, the, er—' He faltered—'The drugs... amazing. Get out while you still can, know what I'm saying? Been here a month now, I have. SLAW-ered I am.'

'Yeah,' Damon said. 'You said.'

James's eyes were aglow. 'Where?'

'Where? Where, he says. Look around you, man! Where? Fuckin' everywhere! That's where. Go downstairs and take a right. Or a left. Fuck, I gotta lie down again.'

The head disappeared and the moaning recommenced, softer this time. James threw down his *Penthouse* and turned to Damon with a diabolical flicker in his eye.

'Come on!' he said. 'You heard the man. We're wasting our time here, mate. There's a whole new world out there. A whole vile, disgusting, seedy cesspit of a world. Let's go!'

Night had fallen and the rain had stopped. Pools of red light glowed in the wet cobblestones further up the street, growing more crowded with distance. Automatic food dispensers held eerily backlit *frites* and *krokets*; street vendors hawked rollmops and chocolate-coated waffles. James and Damon walked up Warmoesstraat away from the train station, finding themselves in the adult literature section of the Nieuwmarkt.

'Hey, look at this.' James set off across the street, turning to beckon Damon over as well. 'This must be what Derbyshire was talking about. Come on.'

They stopped outside a magazine shop. It was closed, but its display window was still lit, crammed with hard-core. There were books, magazines, posters and pinups, videos, playing cards, calendars, even records and CDs, pressed against the glass in a crowded mosaic of naked flesh. Women with huge, doughy breasts pouted through the window, opening their mouths and legs for anonymous phalluses. Men buried themselves in the enveloping folds of flailing obesity. Pubescent teenagers wrapped their bodies around each other, probing experimentally with their fingers.

Wide-eyed, intrigued and revolted, James and Damon moved on to the next store, and the next—but they were all the same. Men, women, children, animals, food and electronics, hurled together in every possible combination. Every perversion, every obscure or socially unacceptable fetish, every Freudian misattachment of libido—all were captured by a dozen glossy quarto periodicals, filled to depraved capacity with half-focussed Polaroids of bored-looking models, doused in artificial sweat, faking innumerable orgasms. VHS cassettes with 'XXX' classifications pasted across their covers shouted vaguely appropriate English titles like 'Horny!' and 'Buttocks!' Calendars boasted a different position every month. Everywhere James and Damon looked, they were met with pure, unabashed pornography, running together in an insane Bosch-like pastiche of undifferentiated genitalia.

'Wow,' James said in delight. 'That's gross.'

'Look at the dick on that black guy!' Damon said. 'How can you live a normal life when your dong's two foot long?'

'Custom-made hipsters,' James suggested. 'Probably gets his underwear from the same place she does.'

'That's a *horse*, man,' Damon said, wincing. 'How can she even pretend to fuck a horse?'

'Relax, mate, that's not a horse,' James said. 'Just a Shetland pony.'

'I'll never be able to use a Mixmaster again.'

'Tried it, have you?'

'For cooking, dickhead.'

They found an open bookstore and James bought a magazine

called 'Siamese Twin Sex'. Inflatable dolls, pink or brown with surprised gaping mouths, hung from the ceiling. Dildos and vibrators in a wide variety of shapes and sizes lined shelves around the walls.

'Ouch,' said Damon, glancing at a large plastic penis. The price label underneath it drew attention to its bonus 'Anus Spike!'. He shuddered.

'Let's go,' he said to James. 'I feel kind of sick. Like that bit with the naked girl in *Clockwork Orange*. With the groodies. Let's go before they start playing Beethoven.'

'Yeah, okay,' said James. 'It's pretty disgusting, isn't it? Christ, my hard-on's even gone down.'

They found themselves looking the other way as they passed more porn shops. But as they walked, the stores were gradually replaced by cafes, coffeeshops and bars. The lights grew brighter, the noise increased and suddenly there were people everywhere: shadowy ambling shapes drifting sociably across the street with bottles in their hands and glowing cigarettes between their fingers. The air was laced with a sickly sweet smell.

'Mmm,' James said, inhaling deeply. 'Get a noseful of that, mate.'

Most of the buildings had large marijuana leaves painted on their windows or hung from their wooden pub signs. James and Damon found a cosy-looking bar and went inside. The interior was dark and warm, the ceiling slung low. Oak panelling muffled the drone of conversation that rolled around the room, and absorbed the dim light of a few hooded bulbs. A single barman wiped the same glass continuously, talking to a few of the loners crouched over the bar. Behind him, an extensive selection of spirits lined the wall, and above it a blackboard menu listing more varieties of marijuana than Damon, for one, knew existed.

'Check that out,' he said, nudging James. 'Thai grass? Jamaican stick? Indian bud? Haze? What's the difference?'

'Holy shit,' James said, reading down the menu. 'I can't believe they've got a blackboard. Look at this! Some of these I've never heard of. And the rest I've only heard about. Baby! I feel like a kid in a candystore.'

The barman came over to them and nodded in greeting, as if unsure what language to address them in.

'Hi!' James effused. 'Can we have a couple of joints?'

'Sure,' the barman said. 'What kind?'

James looked at Damon, who shrugged back at him.

'Uh, we don't really know,' James said. 'Something cheap, but good.'

The barman nodded. 'Nice crop just in from Rotterdam. Seven guilders each, guys.'

He reached under the counter and surfaced with two conically-rolled, foil-tipped joints. James and Damon gave him some bright blue money, got some tiny coins in change and took their rolls of dope over to a newly-vacated pool table.

'Here, use my lighter,' James said.

Damon flicked a few times until the flame stayed, then held it to the end of his joint and inhaled until the leafy tendrils began to curl up and glow. A combination of smoke, ash and grit poured down his throat and into his lungs. He began to cough violently, sending great explosions of smoke into the air until he had expelled all of it from his body. He kept coughing while James took a long, determined drag with his hand cupped over the glowing tip and an expression of deep concentration on his face. James rested his joint carefully in an ashtray and watched patiently as Damon continued to cough.

'Are you okay?' he finally said, exhaling a long, straight column of smoke.

Damon nodded emphatically and stopped coughing. His eyes were red and watery. 'Just a bit harsh,' he grated.

James looked at him thoughtfully. 'Have you done this before?' he asked.

'What, this?' Damon looked surprised. 'Of course. All the time. Just not for a while. Look, rack 'em up; let's have a game.'

'Yeah, sure.' James found a triangle, gathered up the balls and rearranged them in some personal configuration. Damon broke, and as they played they talked and smoked. The game became steadily more protracted and incompetent as the joints disappeared into ash.

'So what do you do in real life?' James asked. 'Back home, I mean.'

Damon looked up from lining up his shot and shrugged. He wondered if it were possible to have a conversation in which that question never came up. He supposed it was not, however much he would have preferred it. Fortunately, he was prepared.

'Not much,' he said. 'I did a year of Arts at uni, but it wasn't my scene. Spent the last eight months or so trying to set up this band.'

'Rock band?'

'Yeah, sort of sixties retro with a modern edge. Hendrix influence, I guess.'

James miscued and sent the white ball into a pocket. 'Fuck. Two shots. What instrument you play?'

Damon put the ball back on the table and missed it completely. 'Whoops,' he said. 'Try that one again. Six-string. Axe. Guitar is what I mean.'

James spent a long time aiming, and finally sent one of Damon's balls screaming into a pocket. 'Beautiful,' he said. 'Oh no, wait. Two shots. How many people in the band?'

'Let's see. Me on guitar. Jim on bass. Sam on drums. Jill—that's my sister—on keyboards. Barry plays, uh, the saxophone. That's, what, four. No, five.'

James frowned. 'You've got a sax in a Hendrix band?'

'Well, you know, that's the modern part. Jazz-Hendrix fusion.'

'What are you called?'

Damon hit the cue ball too low and sent it hurtling off the table. It hit a wall, bounced twice and rolled noisily across the wooden floor. 'Is that bad?' he said. 'How many shots you get for that?'

'Two shots,' James said, sauntering over to retrieve the ball. 'What's your band called?'

'I can't believe I just did that,' said Damon. 'I'm not usually this bad. Look, we're out of drugs. At least we won't get any worse.'

'Let's finish the game and go somewhere else, then,' James suggested. 'Why won't you tell me the name of your band, man?'

'What?' Damon said. He was becoming too stoned to think of anything. 'Oh, the band. Indian Night Stick. That's what we're called.'

James looked doubtful, but smiled wryly. 'Appropriate.'

He tried to sink the four sitting on the edge of the pocket, but the cue ball richocheted off a cushion and potted the eight ball.

'Fuck,' he said. 'Oh well, I guess you win. Let's go.'

As they left the squat, smoke-filled pub, James turned back to look up at the marijuana menu above the bar. He scanned a few lines, smirked knowingly and followed Damon through the door and into the street.

The world had become soft around the edges. A fine mist hung in the air, exploding against their faces as they walked through it. Damon felt quite removed from the whole scene, as if his head were a movie camera, lens smeared with vaseline, projecting images over a vast distance to where his mind was floating, watching. The rippling of neon in the inky canals, the slippery crowded streets, the yellow half-moon poking between the thinning clouds—all appeared as they would in a movie: more real than reality; more immediate, more intense. He felt detached, diffused, almost non-existent. But this time he didn't mind.

'That stuff was good!' he said. James nodded. His shoulders were hunched, hands deep in the pockets of his trenchcoat. He kept looking swiftly from side to side. A film of sweat had broken out across his forehead.

The scenery around them had changed; they were somewhere else. The streetlamps were further apart than before, and more of them had been smashed. The cobbles were grimier and less even, smoothed by the footsteps of fewer people. Buildings towered above them on both sides, digging ominous canyons. They walked for a long time without seeing a street sign; when one appeared, high on a stone wall, it told them they were on the Zeedijk. It was one of the streets the guidebook had warned was unsafe after dark. Damon felt a sensation of dread flooding through him. Suddenly he was aware of everything—furtive figures in the shadows which he hadn't seen before, sinister rustling sounds, the steady clop-clop-clop of stalking feet. Danger. He wished he could think straight, but the marijuana clouded his thoughts, leaving room only for irrational panic.

'We're not meant to be here,' he said, stopping and clutching James by the arm.

James turned and looked at him in incomprehension. His lips were twitching. 'Huh?' he said.

'We're not meant to be here,' Damon repeated. 'This place, this is a bad place. It said so, the book said so. It said so in the book.'

A broken neon sign buzzed on long enough to illuminate James's face. His eyes were wild, unblinking, like an animal's. 'The book!' he said. 'The Bible, you mean?'

Damon rubbed his eyes with the palms of his hands. 'No!' he cried. 'Not the fucking Bible! What are you talking about? The guide book, you crazy fuck.'

'Crazy,' James echoed. He mouthed the word a few times, as if tasting it. Then he threw back his head and let out a torrent of cold, inhuman laughter, echoing through the streets. Somebody howled in return, at a distance Damon couldn't judge. Then both voices faded into a silence broken only by the faint sound of running water.

Damon was instantly aware of someone standing behind him. A low voice hissed 'Crack cocaine! Crack cocaine!' in his ear. The tang of sweat, mingling with another, unidentifiable smell, filled his nostrils. He whirled around, almost tripping over, but there was nobody there. A shadow disappeared into an alley.

James was leaning on Damon's shoulder. He was sweating harder now; a thin trickle was running down the ridge of his cheekbone. But his eyes were lucid again, piercing. His breath was strained, his chest heaving.

'What the fuck was in those joints?' he said. 'Jesus, I'm spinning out. Must've been laced.'

Damon gaped at him. 'Someone just tried to sell me crack,' he said. 'We've got to get out of here.'

James nodded, jerking his head forward. 'Up ahead.'

Further down the street, a narrow alley branched off to the left. It seemed to be filled with a pinky-red glow which spilled out into the Zeedijk: a warm light, welcoming. The bass line of some loud but distant music thumped out of the alley, carrying above it the chatter of voices. A couple of scarlet-tinted figures stumbled out into the street and headed away from James and Damon. The colour dropped away from them as they disappeared into the darkness.

It seemed to Damon that they walked a long time without coming any closer to the warm brightness—but all of a sudden they were there. The music blared into full volume—heavy, primal, insistent—and an instant later they had rounded the corner.

The alley stretched before them, narrow walls receding until they were obscured by the crowds of people squeezed between them. Everything was bathed in a uniform crimson light. Doors and curtained bay windows were set at regular intervals along both walls, and above each of these a red neon strip bled into the alley. Some of the doors were closed, and thick red curtains were drawn across the adjoining windows. But where the curtains were open, so were the doors—and against these doorways, undressed women in red or white or black lingerie leaned seductively and winked come-ons at the passers-by.

James drew a sharp breath. 'My God,' he said reverentially. 'They're beautiful.'

Damon nodded mutely. A hooker to his right had caught his eye and was holding it, mouthing hello. She was tall, dark, slender, unbearably attractive. He started to grin goofily back, but tore his eyes away and kept walking. This time it was a voluptuous blonde who met his gaze, looking at him as though she had known him forever and smiling like she was in love. Further up the alley a Chinese woman tossed her head and tongued her upper lip so alluringly his legs almost gave. A girl in thigh-boots and a cowboy hat waved her riding crop at him. A Slavic giantess considered him haughtily. No sooner had he dragged his eyes away from one bewitching stare than he was entranced by another. He felt dizzy, high on beauty.

The figures sliding slowly past him had become transparent

and insubstantial; ill-defined trespassers in this dreamy blood-tinted land of beautiful women who had apparently elected him king. He was lost again, fragmented and divided among these sirens until there was nothing left of him. Nothing was important, nothing mattered, nothing existed apart from these divine creatures who looked deep into his eyes and told him with their faces that there was nothing, nothing they would rather do than lead him into their little red bedrooms and make ecstatic love to him for hours—and enjoy it immensely, and perhaps forget all about the money, insisting on it only as an afterthought, a tedious necessity to keep them in condoms and AIDS-tests.

He turned to look at James's face and saw an expression of deep hypnosis. He saw himself. He saw the lie. He saw that it was not just him who was king in this Amazonian idyll; it was James as well. And not just James either; it was every sorry slave-to-libido who walked these alleys. Every desperate, soulless sex-junkie, every dirty old man, every timid and wide-eyed teenager. Every sucker who fell for this ultimate sales-pitch and was dragged willingly beneath the flickering neon to part with his bodily fluids, his cash and his pride.

Damon slapped James on the shoulder with the back of his hand. 'Snap out of it!' he cried. 'Look at you, man, your tongue's hanging out!'

'Did you hear that?' James said, not looking at him. 'She loves me, mate. She said so!'

Damon hit him again. 'Listen to yourself!' he said. 'She doesn't love you, you gullible stoned wanker. She loves your wallet. She's a hooker, for Christ's sake!'

James shook his head groggily. 'No,' he said. 'I mean, sure, I know she's a hooker, mate. But this is different, she's really going for me. Not a trick this time; she wants to do it.'

He had stopped walking, and was standing directly in front of a diminutive olive-skinned woman in a black G-string and lace brassiere. She raised the corners of her mouth at him, batting sultry Latin eyelids, and took a step forward.

'*Buenas noches*,' she said. Her voice was soft and low, breathy.

James swallowed. '*Olé*,' he said.

A smile flickered across her lips and was gone. 'How you doing tonight?' she said.

James considered this, nodding. 'Pretty good,' he said. 'Amazing place you've got here. If I lived here I'd be dead by twenty-five.'

She raised her eyebrows. 'How old are you now, baby?'

'Seventeen,' James admitted. Damon turned and stared at him. James had seemed young, but not that young. Damon had picked him as closer to his own age; nineteen perhaps, or twenty.

'Don't worry, baby,' she said. 'I won't tell anyone. You look older, you know, you really do. I seen a lot of seventeen-year-olds, but none as old as you. None as sophisticated.'

James beamed. 'How old are you?'

She scowled in good-natured indignation. 'Now that ain't polite, baby, asking a lady her age. Where you from?'

'Tasmania,' James said.

She looked impressed. 'That so? You speak real good English, honey.'

Damon tried to stifle a giggle, and James shot an irritable look at him before turning to her and saying, 'Thanks.'

She looked suddenly coy. 'You know what, baby?' she said, slinking forward and running her index finger down James's chest. 'I like you, baby. I like you a lot.'

'Really?' James said, leaning towards her.

She looked up into his eyes and nodded slowly without breaking his gaze. 'Uh-huh.'

'I like you too,' he said. 'Listen, what time do you get off?'

She looked at him blankly for a second. Then her eyes glittered with recognition and she laughed breezily. 'Good one,' she tinkled.

James frowned. 'No, really,' he said.

She raised herself up on her toes and took the lapel of James's trenchcoat between her fingers, feeling the material. She parted her lips and made as if to kiss him, swerving at the last moment to whisper in his ear: 'Fifty guilders.' Her voice was different—emphatic, businesslike.

James took a step backwards. 'What?'

She advanced on him again. 'You heard me, baby. Fifty guilders.'

James appeared confused. 'But—I thought you liked me...'

She smiled. 'Sure I do, baby. But I got to eat, got to pay the rent.'

James looked as if someone had punched him in the stomach. His chest had slumped inward; his eyes were surprised, wounded. Damon took him by the elbow and propelled him away from the indignant senorita, telling her 'adios' over his shoulder as she kicked the doorway with her stilettoes and cursed under her breath before turning and smiling meltingly at a new stranger.

'Fuck,' James said, staggering along beside Damon. 'Don't I feel like a dickhead.'

'Forget it, man,' Damon said. 'Any consolation to know you're not the only one?'

James stuck his bottom lip out contemplatively. 'Some,' he decided. But he continued to look dejected as they walked further into the maze of alleys. His hands remained hidden deep in his pockets, and he scowled darkly at the women who approached him. His surliness inflamed them; they raised their arms and shouted abuse after him as he trudged past.

'This is all wrong,' he complained. 'Hookers are supposed to be these sad, pathetic victims of society, you know? It's a terrible thing to sell your body, mate. To a stranger. It must make you feel like shit. So why do they act like they enjoy it so much?'

'That's it, I guess,' Damon said. 'They're acting. You wouldn't want them if they were all sorry and wretched. You want them because they're powerful, they're confident, they're like a sexy girl hitting on you in a nightclub. So that's how they act.'

James was staring straight ahead. 'But look into their eyes, mate. There should be something there. Pain or something, or disgust—even if they were dead, empty eyes, that would make sense. But all there is is this I-want-you look, that's what does it. Eyes tell no lies, that's what my grandma used to say. I guess she never came here.'

Damon watched the prostitutes they were passing. He looked

at their bodies, their faces, looked into their eyes. 'There's this painting,' he said eventually. 'Called *Olympia*. By Manet, I think. This naked call-girl is sitting along a couch with her legs stretched out. And she's staring right at you, not like most paintings of nudes, where they're looking away, kind of demure. But she's not demure, she's more—I dunno—brazen. She's looking at you with a real fuck-you kind of expression. She's proud, man. She's in control. She's not taking any shit from anyone. All these women, they're just like that.'

James gave a wry smile. 'I just wish I had fifty guilders.'

'Really?' Damon said. 'You'd do it?'

'I dunno,' James said thoughtfully. 'I'd feel a bit weird about it. But they're so fucking sexy. And like you say, they seem like they're in control. I wouldn't feel like I was demeaning them or anything.'

'Well, yeah,' Damon said. 'But still...'

James shrugged in acknowledgement. 'It's not really an issue anyway. I don't have fifty guilders, so it's not my decision to make. By the time I have fifty guilders again I won't be stoned anymore and it's even less likely that I'd do it.'

'You still stoned?' Damon said. 'Come to think of it, yeah, I guess I am too.'

'Shit's sending me to sleep,' James said. 'Come on, let's go back to the hostel.'

'You go,' Damon said. 'I'm going to stay out a bit later.'

James looked at him suspiciously. 'What for, mate?'

Damon smiled. 'I have fifty guilders.'

She was even more stunning than he had remembered. Short, but well-proportioned and vivacious. Her lace bra had disappeared and she was wearing only a G-string; her small breasts stared at him with their dark nipples. She said her name was Juanita, from Rio de Janeiro.

'It means River of January,' she said.

She didn't appear to remember Damon from when she had broken James's heart earlier. She asked him where he was from, but didn't comment on his English. She knew where Sydney was.

'Koala bears!' she said. 'Vegemite, Mel Gibson. Sure, baby, I know Australia.'

She drew the curtains and the red room suddenly seemed very small; snug and warm and soft, like a womb. It wasn't much of a room, really; more of a bed with a roof. A lamp threw darkroom light through a heavy red shade. There was smoke in the air, swirling around the ceiling.

She kneeled on the bed, facing Damon where he stood uncomfortably on the small patch of carpet by the door.

'So, baby,' she said, playing with the folded neck of his sweater. 'What can I do for you?'

He grinned. 'What have you got?'

She moved closer, speaking directly into his face. 'Whatever you want, baby.'

'Do you kiss? I heard you girls don't like to kiss.'

She shrugged her narrow shoulders, jiggling her breasts. 'Sure, why not?'

He leaned forward and she deftly tilted her head upwards to meet his lips. Her tongue darted into his mouth, curling and running over his teeth, touching on his own tongue and disappearing as he tried to chase her around their mouths. She tasted faintly of cigarettes. He could feel her hands running through his hair, cradling the back of his head. He kept his own arms by his sides.

'Was that the kiss of a girl who doesn't like to kiss?' she said. Her lips brushed against his as she talked; he felt her words. 'Was it, baby?'

'I guess not,' Damon said. 'Is it just me, or is it getting hot in here?'

'It's not just you who's hot in here,' Juanita said. 'It's me too, hon.'

She licked her finger, held it to the curve of her breast and made a *tsss* sound with her tongue and her teeth.

'See?' she said.

Damon tugged at his rollneck. 'No argument there,' he said.

She smiled, satisfied. 'So, what do you want to do now?'

'Actually,' Damon said. 'There's a lot of things I'd like to do. But let's just talk for now, okay?'

He didn't know whether she would be relieved or disappointed by the proposition. But she didn't seem either; she just flopped back onto her bed and sat there with her back to the wall.

'Sure thing, baby,' she said. 'What you want to talk about? Girl troubles, maybe?'

Damon laughed. He wondered what Emily would say if she knew where he was. Something shrill, he supposed. *That's not like you, Damon*, as if she knew what he was like. As if she even cared. 'No, nothing like that.'

'Course not, no. Good-looking guy like you wouldn't be having girl troubles. You got a girlfriend?'

She seemed to be reading his mind. 'Actually I don't,' he said. 'I broke up with someone before I came over here. She's in Sydney hating me at the moment. But I don't want to talk about that.'

He thought about it, though. He supposed he wasn't lying. Leaving the country without a word could probably be construed as a break-up.

'How can we talk about anything when you're all the way up there, baby? Come down here and sit with me, then we can talk properly.'

Damon looked apprehensive, but climbed over and sat against the wall next to her. She turned and hoisted her knees over his outstretched legs. It was impossible to think about Emily anymore. About any of that.

'That's better,' she said. 'Now we're comfortable.'

'Good,' Damon said. 'So, let's talk about you.'

'Me?' Juanita laughed with her mouth, but her gaze was cold and still. 'What you want to talk about me for, baby?'

'I want to,' Damon said. 'Tell me about yourself.'

A sudden darkness passed behind her eyes, melting back into a playful twinkle before he noticed it. She let her hand slip from her leg onto his, sliding it up to his thigh. 'Nothing to tell,' she said.

He took her hand and dropped it back onto her own body—not roughly, but decisively. An indignant frown flashed across her face.

'What made you want to be a whore?' he asked.

She glared at him, genuinely incensed this time. 'That's an ugly word, baby. I'm not a whore, I'm just doing my job. I'm a professional; you'd know that, if you weren't wasting time talking like this.'

'I'm sorry,' he said. 'I didn't mean to insult you.'

'Forget it,' she said, suddenly compliant again. She raised herself up and sat with her knees straddling his legs, facing him. Her hand cupped his cheek. 'Now where were we?'

'Don't you find it demeaning to do this?' he said, looking only at her face.

Her expression was blank with intense control. 'Listen, baby,' she said, as if addressing a child. 'You can tell me your problems, if you like. Or we can screw for a while. Or I could give you the best blow job you ever heard of. But stay the fuck out of my head, okay?'

Now she was pinching his cheek, white between her fingers. Her hand was trembling slightly. He slapped it away and rubbed his injured flesh.

'Jesus!' he cried. 'What's your problem? You're out selling yourself in the street—how much privacy do you think you've got?'

'Selling myself?' she hissed. 'Selling myself?' Her mouth dropped open and an angry furrow drove its way between her eyebrows. 'I am *not* selling myself! This is what I sell—' She grabbed her breasts with both hands and thrust them in his face. 'And this—' She pulled down the crotch of her G-string for an instant. 'But if you think that's all I am, you're the sickest son of a bitch who ever came in here. This is not *me*—' She ran one hand from her collarbone to her hip and down her thigh. '*This* is me.' She struck her temple with the tips of her fingers. 'What I think, what I know, what I feel—*that* is who I am. And *I* am *not* for sale.'

Her eyes were glowing and her fists were clenched into angry knots, knuckles white with tension. She stopped and took several deep breaths, ribs seething beneath her olive skin.

'Get out,' she ordered, climbing off the bed and opening the door. 'I am no longer open for business.'

'But my fifty guilders—' Damon started.

'Fuck you,' she said simply.

He felt his face burning as he struggled to his feet and walked back out into the alley. He turned to say something to her but she shut the door in his face. He suddenly felt very tired, and a helpless, retarded, drugged feeling flooded over him. It was raining in a thin, steady drizzle. He stumbled a dozen metres along the alley before the delayed appreciation of what had happened flooded through him, leaving him winded and gasping.

Guiltily, he looked back the way he had come. Juanita was standing beneath her red neon strip again, talking to a short, balding man in a dishevelled suit. She oozed at the man seductively, playing with his collar. The man appeared a little taller, slightly more dynamic, as she led him by his tie into her red bedroom and closed the door defiantly.

Damon felt the world spinning around him like the end of a dream. He closed his eyes and tried to focus the mass of cottonwool that had once been his brain. His throat seemed to be closing up, still hurting from the joint he had smoked a lifetime ago. He looked around, not knowing where he was, and splashed down the street in what he hoped was the direction of the youth hostel.

That hadn't worked. His role as a dope-smoking musician and philosopher had landed him in more trouble than he cared to think about. And it had stirred up old memories, old insecurities he had hoped to have left behind.

He would have to try something else tomorrow.

2 Twee

Stacy returned to the hostel at about three in the morning to find someone asleep in her bed. Ordinarily this would not have been a problem; there were plenty of other beds. But tonight she was sailing on a tab of local acid, and it was of fundamental importance that she assert her right over the bunk usurped by the mop-haired lump who undulated softly before her.

'Hey,' she whispered. 'Hey, wake up.'

The sleeping man's face twitched, and he seemed to mutter something inaudible. Stacy bent down and pulled her backpack from underneath the lower bunk, digging around inside it until she found her torch. She lit this and flashed it around the room like a light saber, watching the beam it picked out against the darkness, the circle of light it flung against the walls. It looked like fire was flaming from its tiny bulb; impish figures danced in its yellow light.

She pointed the torch straight into the sleeper's eyes and ruffled his hair with her free hand.

'Excuse me,' she said. 'I think you should wake up now. Your face is on fire.'

He screwed his eyelids together, curling his upper lip. Then he opened his eyes a fraction. They were bloodshot and gummy; he had gone to sleep stoned. He stretched out an arm towards Stacy, shielding his face from the light. The shadow of his hand danced across his features.

'What?' he moaned. 'What do you want?'

'You're in my bed,' she told him.

He rolled onto his stomach and buried his face in his pillow. 'No,' he said, muffled. 'Go away.'

She reached up and snatched the pillow from under his head. His face sank into the mattress, and he flailed around ineffectually with one hand, trying to grab the pillow back.

'Come on,' he complained. 'Give it back.'

'My bed, my pillow,' she said. 'Go find your own bed.'

'You go find your own bed,' he said. 'There are plenty of beds.'

'That's not the point,' she said. 'This is my bed. I slept here last night. It smells like me. I left some of my hair here, a layer of my skin, my memories, my soul. I can't sleep anywhere else.'

He levered himself up with his arms and looked at her blearily. 'What are you on?' he said.

Stacy frowned. 'That's not important either,' she said. 'Don't judge me. Just get out of my bed and let me get some sleep; it's three o'clock in the morning.'

A weary voice came from halfway across the room. 'Just get out of her bed and let us all get some sleep,' it said. 'It's three o'clock in the morning.'

Stacy turned to her bed and grinned triumphantly at its occupant. 'See?' she said. 'Two against one. You're obliged by democracy to get out of my bed.'

'This is not your bed!' he protested. 'None of these beds is anyone's bed. They're all everyone's beds. We don't own them, we have to share them around.'

'Spare me the communist manifesto,' she said. 'You want me to hit you with this flashlight?'

'Oh God,' he said. 'You're American, aren't you?'

'I'm tired, is what I am,' she said. 'Do I have to ask you again?'

'Forget it,' he said. 'I'm not going to argue with an American.' He swung his legs over the side of the bed and slid down onto his feet. The bottom bunk was empty, so he collapsed onto that and fell asleep again immediately.

'Good,' said Stacy. 'Thank you.'

Someone started to clap slowly, and brief sarcastic applause broke out across the dorm.

'No, really, it was nothing,' Stacy said. She climbed up onto the top bunk, pulled off her hiking boots and let them drop to the floor. She couldn't be bothered taking off any more of her clothes, so she lay there in her shirt and jacket and leggings and socks, watching fascinating LSD patterns explode across the backs of her eyelids, until she fell asleep.

When she woke up the room was very bright and a short, hunched woman was running a roaring industrial vacuum cleaner over the floor. The walls vibrated with the din, but the woman wasn't hearing it. She had a walkman strapped to her belt; a pair of earphones pumped tinny music into her head. She was singing along, mouthing lyrics to the drone of the hoover, sweeping the nozzle across the floor to a private rhythm.

Stacy sat up and immediately regretted it. She felt very flat. Her limbs, normally thin but wiry, had become limp and heavy. Her hair, which was fine and usually fell to the middle of her back, had been teased into a wispy dark halo around her head. She fingered her puffy face and could hardly feel her cheekbones, gifts of a Slavic ancestry which usually protruded severely. Her lower lip was tender where she assumed she had bitten it, and now a hunchbacked harpie was riding a vacuum cleaner around the room like something out of a kids' joke.

'This place is going to kill me,' she said.

A man sitting on the bunk next to hers turned and looked at her, having somehow managed to hear her over the noise. With a start she realised that it was the unfortunate trespasser she had evicted from her bed. He looked different this morning. His ragged hair had been neatly styled in one direction, and his eyes seemed to be a different colour. He was also wearing small, round glasses.

'I suppose you're going to kick me out of this bed now,' he said.

Stacy raised a weak smile, which he cheerily returned before picking up the inaudible conversation he was having with the skinhead sitting on his bunk. They were the only other people in the room. She looked at her watch, which had printed itself red into the pale flesh of her wrist. One-thirty in the afternoon. Everybody else must have gone to make the most of the day— or, more likely, to find somewhere quiet to nurse their hangovers.

The vacuum cleaner whined into silence and the woman trundled it out into the hall. Stacy immediately heard two things: the cleaning lady singing 'Excuse me while I kiss this guy' as she disappeared, and the conversation taking place on the opposite bed.

'"Inga was so surprised to see such a man in her room, she dropped her trowel to the floor,"' the skinhead was saying.

His friend looked confused. 'Where'd she get a trowel from?' he asked. 'I thought she was having a shower. Was she gardening?'

'Towel, Damon,' the skinhead said. 'They mean towel. Now be quiet and listen. "The man, with a bulge in his overall, considered Inga's magnanimous breasts, and steaming damp slice of chocolate love cake."'

'Chocolate love cake?' Damon laughed. 'That's the most ridiculous thing I ever heard.'

'You kidding? I think it's worth a Pulitzer.'

'What are you guys reading?' Stacy called from her bed. 'Wait, let me guess. Faulkner? Hemingway? No, I've got it: Henry Miller.'

'*Horny Hotel*, actually,' the skinhead said. 'From the little-known Shakespeare tragedy.'

'Naturally,' Stacy said.

'James also has *Siamese Twin Sex*,' Damon said.

'Really?' said Stacy. 'How adventurous of him.'

'It's a magazine,' James explained. 'Total rip-off, too. They'd been separated.'

'How about *Zero-G-Spot*?' Damon suggested. 'That's about astronauts.'

Stacy made a pained expression. 'You guys are pathetic.'

'You just don't appreciate European literature,' James said. 'That's because you're from upstate New York.'

Stacy stared at him. 'How did you know?'

'How did I know?' James repeated, mimicking her accent expertly. 'It's written all over your voice. I knew a girl from Saratoga once, she sounded just like you.'

'Sure,' Stacy nodded. 'That's on the way to the city from me. I've been there a couple times.'

'Nice place?'

'Sure, I guess. Small, you know. Peaceful. Not like here.'

'Nowhere is like here,' Damon said. 'Here is just—' He made a circular waving gesture with his hand, trying to coax out a suitable word. 'Certifiable.'

Stacy grinned. 'I was in the bar downstairs yesterday, and this guy just came up and offered me a trip. I mean, as a gift, like he was buying me a drink.'

'Something for nothing in Amsterdam?' James said, looking sarcastically incredulous. 'That's a new one on me.'

He shot a sideways glance at Damon, who turned away looking uncomfortable.

'Yeah, it was powerful, too,' Stacy said. 'I got pretty wired on it.' She looked at Damon and said, 'Which I guess is my way of explaining last night. I'm not usually such a hoe.'

Damon looked at her over his glasses and smiled warmly. 'Don't worry about it,' he said. 'It was your bed, I was just too stoned to realise. Once I'd gotten comfortable, you know, I really didn't feel capable of moving.'

'Oh yeah,' she said. 'I remember my first night here. Some of it, anyway.'

'Just to change the subject,' James interjected. 'Can I ask you a personal question?'

He seemed very serious. Damon leant forwards, looking intrigued.

'I guess,' she said apprehensively.

'What's your name?' James said. He paused a second, then grinned.

'God, is that all?' she said. 'Stacy.'

'James,' he said.

'Damon,' Damon said, looking distracted.

The room grew instantly brighter as a sudden sunbeam picked out a window-shape against the floor. Swirling dust particles scurried through the light in a frenzied snowstorm. Through the window, a widening patch of blue sky dazzled in the distance.

'You know, this is really a beautiful city,' Stacy said. 'Away from all the sex museums and coffeeshops, it's meant to be very pleasant.'

'I dunno,' James said. 'I thought the coffeeshops were pleasant enough.'

Damon looked faintly distressed. 'I don't think I could face all that again just yet,' he admitted. 'Last time it was a little intense.'

'You want to check out the rest of the city?' Stacy said. 'Find somewhere nice?'

'Not me,' James said. 'Where's that sex museum you were talking about?'

Damon shot a disbelieving glance at him, then turned back to Stacy. 'That sounds good,' he said. 'Eat some cheese, maybe find a windmill or something. I could handle that.'

'Well, good then.' Stacy nodded in satisfaction, then turned and said to James: 'The sex museum's a few blocks up, on the next street across. Just by the hash museum, actually.'

James's eyes lit up. 'Baby!' he said. 'Have a charming time, guys. I'll see you tonight.'

By daylight, the city was completely different. The canals rippled sky-blue and stone-grey instead of the broken electric palette of the night. There were more waterways in Amsterdam than in Venice, spreading out in concentric horseshoes from the

Centrum: Singel, Herensgracht, Keizergracht, Prinsengracht, like a skipping chant. The Amstel river wound gently between the canals, bleeding into each of them until it disappeared completely. The ground was uniformly flat, raising itself lazily into gentle humps only where absolutely necessary to support a bridge or to let a drain flow past below. Cyclists effortlessly pedalled rusty one-speed bikes along the streets, dressed like eighteenth-century romantics, trousers tucked into their socks. The light was soft, the air body-temperature. Everything about the city seemed comfortable.

Damon and Stacy walked up the Damrak towards the Dam, the main square. It seemed like a pretty normal main street: hi-fi stores and bookshops and a McDonald's. There was some sort of renovation going on, so large portions of the pavement were missing and a makeshift boardwalk had been laid over the sodden exposed sand. A few cafes had burst out into the street, where people sat and drank coffee and looked European.

'So how long have you been travelling?' Damon asked.

Stacy looked at her watch. 'One hundred twelve hours,' she said. 'How about you?'

Damon examined his own watch and rolled his eyes back, mouthing soundless numbers to himself. 'Six months,' he finally said.

'That's a lot of hours,' Stacy said.

'I was in London the whole time until yesterday,' Damon said. 'Which wasn't really travelling, since I was staying in the same place for so long.'

'What were you doing in London for six months?'

Damon held up his thumb, moved it backwards and forwards between himself and Stacy and stared at it intently with one eye. 'Art school,' he said.

Stacy felt her stomach twist. But she swallowed and laughed at his thumb. 'They teach you that there?'

Damon opened his other eye and dropped his arm to his side. 'That and a few other things.'

'What do you do, draw, paint, what?'

'I'm an Impressionist,' Damon said.

'I thought they were all dead.'

'Okay, then I'm a Neo-Impressionist.'
'Aren't they dead as well?'
'Fine,' Damon said. 'So I'm a Neo-Neo-Impressionist.'
'Last of a dying breed, huh.'

They reached the end of the street and the Dam opened up before them. The tram-wires had gone crazy above them, stretching over the square like a tangled safety net. The old palace stood regally behind its stone columns.

'So what does a Neo-Neo-Impressionist do?' Stacy asked as they walked away from the square. A narrow flagstoned street carried them between towering old terrace-houses.

'Same as what the original Impressionists did,' Damon said. 'Pretty much.'

Stacy looked across at him for several steps, while he looked straight ahead.

'Which is what?' she eventually prompted.

'They captured essences,' he said. 'They recorded the feelings of a scene.'

He turned to the left and to the right, craning his neck to look up at the tops of the houses. Then he spun on his heel and started walking backwards, facing Stacy and the sharp vanishing-point perspective of the view behind her.

'Look at these buildings,' he said, spreading his arms out on either side. 'There's such an atmosphere about them, such a feeling of urban Dutchness. They're old, they're crowded, they're beautiful. They have so much history. Maybe Rembrandt lived in one of them, maybe there's a floor up there stained with blood from Van Gogh's ear. People survived wars in them, invasions. People hid from the Nazis here—one of these is Anne Frank's house. But how do you describe the feeling you get looking at these places? Do you talk about the chipping paint on the doorframes, the old mossy tiles on the roofs, the gargoyles and different kinds of gables, the way they all join up at the top, the way neighbours are separated by only one wall and not two? Or do you go closer? Do you talk about the texture of the bricks, the different curtains in the windows, the patterns of rust on the drainpipes, the style of the numbers on the doors? You can spend all day talking about a street, a house, a room, a wall, a brick, a wedge of mortar—'

'As you've just demonstrated,' Stacy interrupted, smiling.

'Exactly,' Damon said. 'But it doesn't get you anywhere, it's just overwhelming. There's too much information, too much to know. You can't describe everything in detail; you just want to convey the atmosphere, enough to make someone else feel what you felt. That's what an Impressionist does. Sees something, feels something, and puts it on canvas as fast as possible, *bam*.' He made an exploding gesture, bunching up his fingers and then splaying them as he snapped his hand forward.

'Bam?' Stacy said, imitating the motion.

'Bam,' he repeated.

'Yeah, but what about under the surface?' Stacy said. 'What about what's really there, behind the impression? Maybe it *was* Rembrandt's house. Maybe someone was murdered here; maybe some kid drew a flower on the wallpaper. Detail. History. Context.'

Damon shook his head. 'You can't know that,' he said. 'All you can see is what's on the surface. The rest you can only guess at; it's all interpretation. And interpretation's everybody's right, not just yours. So you paint what you see and let everyone make their own interpretation.'

'Sounds like taking a photo.'

Damon reached into his jacket and pulled out a compact Instamatic camera. Before Stacy could move, a flashbulb exploded in her face and the shutter snapped.

'Thanks,' she told the blue spots floating before her eyes.

'Two compositions in one,' Damon said, looking pleased. '*Old Dutch Houses* and *Surprised American Tourist*.'

'Traveller,' Stacy corrected.

'What?'

'American *tourists* wear shorts and knee-socks and baseball caps and travel around in Con-Tiki packs trying to tip people and complaining about the french fries—' She paused, and pointedly added: 'And taking photos of everything.'

'Hey,' Damon said. 'I'm not a tourist; I'm an Impressionist.'

'And I'm a traveller,' she said simply.

'Done.'

'So that's what you learned at art school?' she said. 'To take happy snaps with that piece of crap camera?'

'It's my portable canvas,' he said defensively. 'It has to be a crappy camera, or there'd be too much detail. There'd be composition; I'd be bringing myself into it. This way the shots are out of focus, they're underexposed, they're badly cropped, and there's no zoom lens so there's no detail. It's great.'

'I've been taking bad photos all my life,' Stacy mused. 'Nobody told me it was an art form.'

'Nobody knew tins of soup were an art form until Andy Warhol decided they were,' Damon said. 'But I can paint, it's not all Kodak moments. If a good photo comes out I'll do it big on canvas with watercolours.'

'Great,' she said. 'I could be the new Mona Lisa, standing with my mouth open in front of a bunch of old Dutch houses.'

'Perhaps.'

The houses dropped away as the street ended. A stone embankment followed one of the major canals as it drifted by; a ferry full of waving people churned past, honking its horn as it came to an intersection. The concrete broke into steps leading down to the water, and at the bottom of the steps a row of coloured paddle-boats queued behind a small white hut. Stacy and Damon selected a sleek purple number, paid the deposit and set sail down the Prinsengracht.

The station and the stairs disappeared behind them and the canal began to carve its way through the terraces. Above them, parallel rows of houses leaned crazily inward, threatening to topple into the water. The backs of the buildings seemed to have been designed with a maritime audience in mind: their roofs were ornate and individual, each gable a unique combination of fused geometric shapes. The canal lapped against half-submerged doors and windows. Stacy lay back and paddled lazily, trailing her hand through the green water as Damon steered. She felt like she might fall asleep, feeling the soft, still air against her face, listening to the gentle slap of the ripples against the banks.

'This is such an odd place,' she reflected quietly. 'Can you believe this is the same canal as the one that heads through the middle of the Red Light District? Over there it's filled with used condoms and syringes and God knows what else—' She took her hand out of the water and wiped it on her jeans. 'But here it's just ducks and waterbirds and people going about their business.'

'It's the whole city,' Damon said. 'One minute someone's offering to give you a blow job or sell you smack, and the next you're buying cheese off them. First you can't find anywhere to look without seeing something seedy or threatening or downright gross, and then suddenly you're in the middle of this idyllic Northern haven. And you're still walking on the one street; all it's done is turn a half-corner or go over a bridge. It's schizophrenic, that's what it is. It's a Jekyll and Hyde city.'

Stacy smiled. 'Like a werewolf,' she said. 'Only every night's a full moon. And we're all werewolves too, you know. When the sun goes down, we get transformed.'

'Yeah, but that happens everywhere,' Damon said. 'Don't you think?'

'Maybe.'

The deli, when they found it, was so quaintly Dutch they thought they had stepped into a picture postcard. Everything was wood and wicker. Pyramids of cheese lay piled in the middle of the room; shelves of pickled things lined the walls. There were quiches and tortes behind the glass of the counter, and big baskets of fresh-smelling bread on the floor.

Damon bought a quiche, and Stacy chose a couple of baguettes before getting the shopkeeper to cut her a hunk from a huge millstone of cheese. They left the shop and walked back towards the youth hostel. Damon ate happily from his paper bag. Stacy tucked her bread under her arm while she sliced her cheese with a pocket-knife, then snapped the blade closed, deftly split the rolls lengthways with her thumbs, and stuffed the cheese into the soft woolly bread.

'You've done this before,' Damon said.

Stacy grinned. 'Uh-huh,' she said through a mouthful of sandwich. 'It's about all I can afford. Tastes pretty good, too.'

'This is the life,' Damon said, tearing off a piece of quiche and considering it between his fingers. 'Eating and walking. Walking and eating. No time to sit down; too much to see. People don't do this at home. They sit down.'

'Where are we going to sit?' Stacy said. 'In the gutter?'

'Well, we could,' Damon said thoughtfully. 'But the edge of that canal looks nicer.'

Stacy shrugged. 'Sure,' she said. 'It's probably better for the digestion anyway.'

They walked to the water and sat on the stone embankment, dangling their legs over the side. A cold wind blew across the canal, shattering the orange reflection of the sunset. As they finished eating, the blue of the sky darkened to navy, and the night appeared over the horizon. The moon rose from behind a building, fatter than it had been the night before. A star twinkled into being.

The breeze lifted Stacy's hair and blew it into her mouth. She spat it out and pushed it around to the back of her head, where it flapped gently. Her pale skin glowed a warm gold, catching the last rays of the sun. She shivered slightly, feeling a sudden chill.

Damon turned to look at her. His eyes were shining, his face slack and contented.

'What a beautiful night,' he said. 'Stars, moon, sunset, water. Amsterdam. It couldn't be more romantic if it tried.'

'We should be getting back to the hostel,' said Stacy.

James was waiting for them when they arrived at the dorm. He was sitting on Stacy's bed, talking to a teenage-looking girl with long blonde hair tied in plaits. His porno magazines had vanished.

'What is it about my bed?' Stacy complained. 'Is there some ancient Dutch blessing on it or something?'

'Oh, hi, guys,' James said, turning around. 'Have a nice day?'

'Wonderful,' Stacy said. 'How was the sex museum?'

James frowned at her and shot a glance towards the blonde girl without moving his head.

'What sex museum?' he said.

'You know,' Damon joined. 'The sex museum you were going to check out. The one near the hash museum.'

James looked daggers at him. 'You must have misunderstood,' he explained. 'Astrid and I went to the Rijksmuseum. There are lots of Rembrandts there, and some Van Goghs. A magnificent collection.'

'Were there any Impressionists?' Stacy asked.

James made a face. 'Impressionists,' he said disparagingly. 'Not likely. These were artists in the finest classical tradition. Did you know that Rembrandt was his first name? Fascinating.'

'Actually, it was kind of boring,' Astrid said. 'I wanted to go to the sex museum; I hear they've got a great new exhibit on bondage.'

James turned and stared at her. 'Why didn't you say?'

Astrid shrugged. 'It doesn't matter. I'll see it next time.'

'Astrid's just up from Alkmaar,' James explained. 'It's only about an hour away.'

Stacy and Damon introduced themselves and Astrid smiled at them.

'I come here when I need to get away,' she said. 'When everything gets too much at home there's nothing better than hitting the Nieuwmarkt and getting completely out of it.'

James looked at her with something like reverence.

'That's a plan if I ever heard one,' he said. 'Have you guys had dinner?'

'Kind of,' Damon said.

'Good,' Astrid said, jumping down from the bed. 'I know a great place for dessert.'

Astrid led them back through the winding streets, which were just gearing up for the evening rush. The atmosphere had changed with the weather; the rain of the night before had washed the Nieuwmarkt clean, and it was now dry and sanitary. The red lights looked less seamy without their misty haloes; probing fingers of film-noir fog no longer twisted through the air. The waxing moon threw silver light across the city, illuminating the cobbled streets, casting faint shadows.

The Red Light District ended with one of the major canals linking the Amstel to the ocean. A final row of brothels lined the waterfront, further apart than before, and larger. Sex workers slouched against the doorways in groups of two or three, like lonely taxi drivers sharing a cab on a deserted rank. They seemed to have suffered from their fringe-dwelling status: they were older, paler and more haggard than their central sisters. They were either overweight or dangerously thin; bruised trackmarks peeked out from behind their elbow-length gloves.

'Jesus,' James said. 'See, this is what hookers are supposed to look like.'

Damon nodded soberly. 'She looks like my grandmother,' he said, passing a middle-aged woman in drooping black lingerie and garters. She followed him with her hollow, plaintive eyes and croaked 'Twenty guilders' after him.

'How can they do that?' Stacy wondered. 'I'm sorry, but that's just sad.'

'They're disgusting,' Astrid said. 'Out here they have sex without condoms, although they're not allowed to, and they don't even have regular check-ups, although they're supposed to. That's why they're sick all the time.'

The wail of a baby rang out from one of the red-lit buildings, and a gaunt skeletal woman rolled her eyes and disappeared inside. Stacy felt like crying with the pathos of it all. She looked away, watching the water instead of the wretched prostitutes until the red glow faded and the only light was warm and yellow and came from the cafes across the canal.

They crossed a humped stone bridge and Astrid said, 'Here we are.'

'Hard Rock Cafe?' Damon said. The familiar circular logo shone in white neon above the open front doors. It was a long, squat building, like a Viking hall. It looked much more low-key than its counterparts in New York, London, and everywhere else. But circular tables and red sixties bar-stools could be glimpsed through the wide doors, and there were guitars hanging on the walls, which seemed something to be obscurely thankful for.

'No,' Astrid said. 'Next door. Hard Rock Coffeeshop.'
James smiled. 'Even harder.'

Inside, the coffeeshop was a fifties dream of laminex. All of the surfaces were shiny red and blue, finished in polished metal. The booths were of a plush crimson vinyl, elevated by a curious architectural theory of split-level design. Below them, a rounded stainless steel counter sat futuristically before a row of swivelling stools like a milk bar from *The Jetsons*. Generous slices of technicolour cake lay beneath plastic bubbles, plastered with bright icing, studded with silver sugar balls. At seven or eight guilders each they were fairly expensive, but this was to be expected as they were also fairly narcotic.

Stacy bought some radioactive-green sponge cake and carried it upstairs to a booth while the others selected and ordered. James also bought a plate of space-biscuits, enough for everyone.

'See what I mean?' Astrid said as they munched contentedly on their hash cakes. 'Best dessert in the world. And unlike smoking, it's not carcinogenic.'

'It sure tastes good,' James said. 'But unlike smoking, it's also not getting me stoned. The cake may be baked, but I'm not.'

'It takes a little longer,' Astrid said. 'It has to get through your digestion. But it also lasts longer, and tastes better and doesn't leave you smelling like Amsterdam.'

'Right,' said James, collecting the crumbs from his plate and sucking them off his fingers. 'I guess we just wait then. Cookie, anyone?'

They each took a biscuit and ate in silence, ceremoniously breaking bits off and pushing them hungrily into their mouths. As they stared at each other across the table their faces slackened, their eyes glazed over and they began to grin spontaneously. Soon they were giggling uncontrollably at nothing, forgetting to breathe in their inexplicable hysteria.

The muscles in Stacy's cheeks began to ache, but she could do nothing but sit there grinning like a happy idiot. She felt the world contract into a tiny impenetrable sphere immediately around her head. Inside was her mind; wise, tranquil, lone god of a private universe. Outside, nothing mattered. There was no past, no future, hardly any present. A hidden undercurrent of pain, so constant she no longer felt it, was suddenly conspicuous by its absence: she felt empty without it, disoriented. She floated around her psyche, thinking about nothing, too relaxed to speak. Too relaxed even to listen, she realised. She strained her ears.

'This whole travel thing is just amazing,' Damon was saying, his voice drifting back into focus. 'Everything is just so new and fascinating.' He paused and stared into the middle distance, nodding and working his jaw as if chewing over the thought. 'Culture is like a smell,' he said. 'Everywhere has a different one, but if you live there you can't smell it because you're used to it. It just smells natural, like there's no other way it could possibly smell. But when you go somewhere else, you can smell *that* culture, because you've never smelled it before. It smells weird and unnatural, and you can't imagine how anyone could think it smells normal. And you notice everything about the smell, all the little idiosyncratic odours that waft around, all the things you never realised were there back home.'

'I realised they were there,' James said. 'I can smell the culture at home. It stinks.'

'You smell home?' Damon said. 'Really?'

'Sure,' said James. 'When you go home you'll smell it too, because you'll have forgotten what it smells like. For a while at least, your own culture will smell as weird as anyone else's. I've been travelling all my life, so that's how it is for me. I'm not used to any smell. Nowhere smells like home.'

'*Smell* is such a funny word,' Astrid reflected. 'Think about it.' She looked up at the ceiling and slowly formed the sound with her lips. 'Smell. Sssmmmeeelll. Smell. Smellsmellsmellsmellsmell. Smell! Smell?'

James looked at her and burst out laughing. 'Fuck, you're stoned,' he said.

'You have a weird language,' Astrid told him. 'Smell. Much. Knuckles. Asparagus. Bent.'

'Bent is right,' said James. 'We're all bent, my sexy young Dutch friend.'

'Why do stoned people always talk about how stoned they are?' Damon said. 'No-one ever says "Christ, I'm straight" or "I am *sooo* fucking clear-headed," do they? So why do we feel the need to broadcast the fact? It's not like we're doing anything brave or heroic or rebellious; it's legal here after all.'

'Decriminalised,' Astrid said, separating the syllables carefully.

'Yeah,' said James. 'That's a funny word too.'

'No,' Astrid said. 'I mean it's still illegal here, it's just that nobody cares.'

'Well, then it's legal,' Damon said. 'A law isn't a law unless it's enforced. That's the first thing they taught us.'

Something jarred in Stacy's mind, troubling her enough to pierce the drugged cocoon she had woven for herself. She had the feeling that two inconsistent ideas had run into each other and were sticking like mismatched pieces in a jigsaw puzzle. 'At art school?' she finally said.

'Art school?' James said. 'What are we talking about art school for? You're stoneder than anyone, strange upstate-New-York girl.'

'Am I?' Stacy said.

'And she's got a name, you know,' Damon said gallantly.

'Yeah, she does too,' James said. 'Something endearing and cutesy-American. Barbie or Buffy or Bimbo or something, I can't remember.'

'Stacy,' she said. 'And it's not cutesy-American. It's short for Anastasia. Anastasia Karayev, and you can't get much less American than that.'

'Stacy isn't short for Anastasia,' James argued.

'Sure it is,' Astrid said. 'It's much shorter.'

'Yeah, but "smell" is shorter as well, and she doesn't call herself that.'

'I know what my own name is short for,' Stacy said. 'This is a ridiculous argument.'

James began to sulk. 'You started it,' he said. 'You were the one talking about art school.'

Stacy looked exasperated. 'What's art school got to do with it?'

'Exactly,' James said smugly.

'I go to art school,' Astrid said helpfully. 'Alkmaar's a university town; they have quite a good art course.'

This appeared to stump James. 'Yeah,' he said. 'But how did Anastasia know that?'

Astrid ignored him. 'You guys should come when I go back in the morning. Tomorrow's the last cheese market day of the season; it's always huge. They fill the town square with piles and piles of the most amazing cheeses from all over the district. People come from miles around to bid for it.'

'Cheese,' James said, discarding the word. 'Do you have a Red Light District?'

'Sort of,' Astrid said. 'There's two streets on the wrong side of the canal where hookers hang out. It's a bit like the street we just came off.'

James grimaced sourly. 'That'd be enough to put you off your cheese.'

'If you're lucky you might find someone else,' Astrid said in a low voice, looking him meaningfully in the eye. 'And not even have to pay for it.'

James appeared to choke on the biscuit-crumbs he was poking into his mouth. 'Alkmaar!' he exclaimed, recovering. 'Sounds like a great idea. What do you think, guys?'

Stacy shook her head slowly. 'No,' she decided. 'I'm heading north tomorrow. I want to see Scandinavia before it gets too cold. It's September already; winter's coming and I'd rather be in the south of Italy when it happens.'

'Good plan,' Damon said. 'You catching the train?'

'Ten past eight tomorrow night. Want to come?'

Damon shrugged. 'Sure.'

'I was going to catch the early train home,' Astrid said. 'I want to go to sleep now. So sleepy...' She trailed off and dropped her head into her folded arms.

'Maybe we should go back to the hostel,' James suggested.

They spilled out into the street, feeling lighter on their feet than before. The chill night air roused them, brushing their faces with its clammy fingers. They swept through the alleyways, four abreast, arms linked, tripping on the pavement. Amsterdam was suddenly more amusing than it had been. Spruikers outside live sex theatres hurried over to shout 'Girls! Naked girls! Bondage act! Nude wrestling! Banana show!' at them, sending their imaginations spiralling into absurdity. Stunted figures scuttled towards them as if to hiss 'Crack cocaine!', but paused and drifted away from their maniacal laughter. The red lights dazzled with a friendly magic.

The bar next to the youth hostel seemed to be caught in the grip of a perpetual happy hour, and tonight was no exception. The street outside was thronging with the overflow of travellers, recognisable by their hiking boots, faded jeans, warm unfashionable walking jackets. They held a two-for-one mug of beer in each hand, clinking them together, drinking alternately from each. Stacy felt a comfortable sensation of belonging as she wound her way among them: these are my people; we are the same. She smiled at them, and they smiled back and toasted her with their mugs. She felt sorry to leave them behind as she led the others into the hostel. But she knew that they would be there again tomorrow, and the next day, and the next city, and the next country.

They crashed into the dormitory, and Stacy made sure she was the first one to her bed. She leapt on it territorially, baring her teeth and laughing into her cupped hands. Damon looked thoughtfully at an upper bunk for a while before deciding that the lower one would be easier. James and Astrid ended up in the same bed, where they curled up against each other and went to sleep, snoring in quiet harmony.

Stacy dreamed she was flying through the mountains. Jagged, snow-capped peaks slid past far below her, spreading in all directions like a vast, rugged carpet. She swooped downwards until she was hurtling between the outcrops, banking and weaving, avoiding the rocky walls by miraculous inches. The scenery rushed past in a blur, surrounding her like an I-Max movie. She felt the sting of the wind in her face, heard her hair flapping wildly against her ears like a loose sail in a storm. She pulled out of her descent, shot upwards and felt the sunlight strike her back as she broke through the clouds and floated above their puffy dreamscape.

Suddenly she felt heavy; too heavy. She scrabbled against the clouds as she began to sink, but they parted between her fingers, stretching into curling wisps and snapping as she fell flailing away. It was cold and wet for a moment, then grey, and there were no clouds below her but mountains. She plummetted, faster and faster, past terminal velocity and beyond, spinning into a death-spiral. The peaks shuddered and jolted, dancing around her in a jarring circuit. The blood roared in her ears, louder than the wind. Then there was white everywhere, filling her field of vision, so endless and unbroken that she could not tell how close it was until it hit her everywhere at once, flattening her into nothing, knocking the life out of her. And it was no longer white, but black.

She lay face-down in the blackness for a long time, knowing that she could not move. Paralysis had settled over her like a terrible weight, locking her body into its final, eternal position. She couldn't open her eyelids to see; couldn't work her lungs to breathe. Snow filled her mouth, cold and hard, unmelting.

Footsteps crunched towards her body, and she felt the pressure of a hand on her shoulder.

'See you later, upstate-New-York girl,' said a muffled voice. 'Anastasia.'

She tried to get up, pushing with all her might against the blanket of anaesthesia. The footsteps faded away again, leaving her in dark silence. She collapsed into the ground and felt it swallow her.

She woke up with her face in her pillow and wet, salty tears streaming down her cheeks. Her hands were shaking. She had not dreamed like that for as long as she had been travelling. And yet the dream was different; there was something new: footsteps, the voice. She sat up and saw that James and Astrid had gone. She shook her head and the dream-fragments vanished, melting away.

Damon was sitting on his bed, reading his guidebook. His eyes shone blue in the bright sunlight, and his face looked more vital than before. His hair was dark and parted in the middle.

He wore a white singlet, and Stacy saw for the first time that he was muscular and well-built.

He noticed her, smiled and said 'Morning!' to her.

'Hi,' Stacy said, rubbing the tears from her face and running her hands through her tangled hair. 'Do you look different every single day?'

'I try,' Damon said. 'Tell you what, this Copenhagen looks like an interesting place. What do you want to do today?'

'Nothing,' Stacy said. 'I want to find a respectable cafe outside the Red Light District, eat non-narcotic pastry, drink healthy fluids and write letters home all day.'

'Sounds okay,' Damon said. 'I guess my parents'll be wondering where I am, too.'

They found an underused coffeeshop in the old Jordaan district, and ate Danish and drank milkshakes at opposite ends of a long, polished-pine table while people bustled past the window. Stacy took a pad and some envelopes out of her day-pack and began to write. Most of her letters were similar: pleasantries and personal enquiries to open, travel updates, city descriptions and immediate plans, more pleasantries and missing-yous to close. She wrote all morning, addressing envelopes as she went: *Mam & Papa Karayev, Heidi O'Reilly, Beth Turner, Chet's Diner Staff & Customers*, all directed to Lake Placid, NY, USA. Lost in her reminiscences, she only stopped when her stomach started growling and her hand began to cramp.

She looked up and saw Damon frowning into a blank piece of paper. There were a few screwed-up sheets around him, littering the table like origami almond blossoms. His pen had dropped from his fingers. He picked up the paper and looked at it, turning it around before his eyes.

'Writing your folks?' Stacy said.

He put the paper down. 'Trying to,' he said.

'Hard to know what to say, isn't it?'

He nodded. 'Beats the hell out of me.'

'How long since you wrote them last?'

'I left them a note on the kitchen table before I caught a taxi to the airport.'

Stacy gaped at him. 'Six months ago?'
'Yeah.'
'Did you leave on bad terms, or something?'
Damon looked thoughtful. 'Not really.'
'Won't they be worried about you?'
'Probably.'

Stacy shrugged, tired of a conversation that wasn't going anywhere. She called a waitress over and ordered a basket of bread. When it came, she munched on it as she wrote her final letter. It took a long time: she wrote slowly, ponderously, weighing up each phrase in her mind, twisting it around to see how it fitted before she wrote it down. An expression of weary sadness crept over her face as she wrote, and her mind began to slip backwards into another, painful place. She brought the letter to a hurried close and stuffed it inside an envelope, which she addressed to *The Rogan Family*.

She felt tears pricking her eyes until she raised her head and saw Damon still staring blankly at his void piece of paper. He had folded and unfolded it several times in various directions, and was now absently tearing thin strips off it. He met Stacy's eyes and grinned warmly, forcing her to smile back.

'Oh well,' he said. 'Maybe I'll try again in another six months.'

He balled the paper up and threw it over his shoulder, looking relieved.

1 Een
2 Twee
3 **Tre**

When the train stopped grinding against the tracks and sighed to a halt, the new silence seemed louder than the past hours' clacking and rumbling. Damon lay on the top berth of the couchette and stared into the darkness. A few loud percussions, metal running into metal, came from further down the train, ringing out in the eerie quiet. He propped himself up and looked out the window, wondering where they were. There was nothing outside: no town, no station, not even a train signal.

The sound of Stacy's quiet breathing drifted up to him. He imagined her lying asleep, pale skin painted silver-blue in the starlight. Her dark, delicate lashes resting against her cheekbones; thin eyebrows arching above. Her hair spreading around her face like an aura, spilling over the edge of her bunk. Her sharply-defined lips, pursed into a somnolent pout. The slow rise and fall of her chest. So peaceful; so beautiful.

The train remained still. A few shapes faded into view outside the window as his eyes grew accustomed to the darkness. They didn't look like anything; just bulky shadows, blacker than the rest of the night. He lay down again and listened to Stacy's breathing, coordinating it with his own, realising how shallow and irregular it was.

'You're awake, aren't you?' he asked quietly.

'Haven't been to sleep yet,' she admitted. Her voice sounded thin and lonely, stifled by the immense dark silence.

'Why aren't we moving?'

'We are,' Stacy said. 'We're on a boat.'

'Uh, no,' Damon said. 'I'm pretty sure it's a train.'

'The train is on a boat. That's what all the banging noises were; all the carriages being loaded. Copenhagen's on an island.'

'So we're nearly there, then?'

'Must be.'

Damon searched his mind for any sensation of motion that would validate Stacy's assertion. He closed his eyes and concentrated, but was unable to feel anything resembling movement. The train was locked in limbo.

'I wonder what time it is.'

'When we left the last station it was four-thirty.'

'We're going to be tired today.'

He waited for a response but none came. He stared in the direction of the ceiling and tried to think of something to say, something that would connect them through the darkness. Floating in the warm air of the couchette, drifting on the black North Sea, he felt disconcertingly unattached. He needed something to anchor himself to: anything, even a lone voice in the night.

'Why do you have such a Russian name?' he asked.

There was silence below, and for a moment he was afraid she had finally gone to sleep.

'My parents are from Russia,' she said at last. 'They defected when defecting from the Soviet Union was still a big deal. My father was a scientist, a mathematician. He was professor at the university in Kiev until the government called him up.

He was developing codes for the military; you know, ciphers, cryptography. Then he found out something about one of their operations—I don't know what, exactly, something bad—and wanted to leave, to go back to his old job. But they didn't think that would be a good idea. Not safe. So he left the country with my mother.'

Her voice was rich with reminiscence and admiration. Damon felt its warmth and was reassured. It was as if they had shared something important. He wished he had something to offer in return.

'Just up and left everything,' he mused. 'Just like that.'

'Just like that,' Stacy repeated. 'Now they run a hardware store. Their prices are too low, but they still make a profit through some mathematical theory Papa invented.'

'Why'd they move to small-town America? Why not Washington DC, Silicon Valley, somewhere where he could still be a mathematician?'

'He was always afraid they'd find him,' she said. 'The KGB would find him and send him back home. He was paranoid; worse than McCarthy. Red under every bed. So they holed up in Lake Placid, had me, started a new, quiet life.'

'And now you're back in Europe.' he said. 'Are you going to go to Russia?'

'I probably couldn't get a visa,' she said. 'I expect we're still on record somewhere; if they let me in they wouldn't let me out again.'

'You have an interesting history,' Damon said, sounding envious.

'I didn't ask for it.'

There was a subtle change in the air, a strange reverse motion indicating that they had indeed been travelling and had now stopped. Shouts rang out in the distance, and there were more percussive noises. The train shuddered massively as the engines grumbled into action, and the carriage began to lurch uncertainly forward as the black of the night faded into the steel-grey of dawn.

By the time the train arrived in Copenhagen it was half past eight and reality had become somewhat twisted. A smeary veil of fatigue clouded Damon's vision, and everything simple was now difficult. He fumbled with the fasteners of his backpack, trying to hoist the straps onto his shoulders and almost crying with despair when he could not. None of his clothes seemed to fit properly; zippers jammed, pockets refused to open.

Stacy seemed to be having similar problems. Her movements were slow and leaden, mechanical. She kept making mistakes tying her shoelaces, pulling the loops too small, losing the ends, having to start resignedly again. Her eyes were dark and hollow, standing out starkly against her whiter-than-usual skin.

'We have to find somewhere to stay,' she said, finally tying her bootlaces and standing up.

'Stay?' Damon said, looking incredulous. 'We have to find our way off the train first.'

They left the couchette and trudged down the narrow corridor, knocking their backpacks against the walls as they made their way towards the exit. They climbed down onto the platform, smiling at each other in grim triumph, and walked down through the underpass.

It was surprisingly bright outside as they stepped out of the train station. The morning sunlight stabbed at their bodies, warming their skin but leaving their spirits more cold and tired by comparison. They walked past the Tivoli, a sprawling carnival complex which had closed for the off-season: padlocked wrought-iron gates imprisoned garish sideshows and silent rides. A block later, the road opened into the town square. Beautiful old brownstone buildings surrounded the Rådhuspladsen, faces disfigured by scaffolding and neon advertisements. Myriad bus stops dotted the square; somehow they found the one mentioned in the guide-book and waited for a bus to take them to the youth hostel.

The Københavns Vendrerhjem was a long way out of town, in the middle of a park. The bus driver told Damon and Stacy where to get off, and they followed the youth hostel signs down the street and into the wilderness. A gravel track wound between the trees, following the shore of a small lake, until a series of squat brick buildings appeared around a corner. They looked fairly modern and institutional, almost military; out of place in the idyllic surrounds. But Damon had never seen anything so welcoming in his life: after the long train trip, long bus ride and seemingly endless hike, he finally felt he was home.

They went into the largest of the buildings, found the office and were told the rooms had just closed for the morning.

'What?' said Damon, feeling faint.

'Closed for cleaning,' the receptionist repeated. 'You can put your gear in the storage room, and the common room's open all day. The dorms open again at one o'clock.'

Damon looked desperately at his watch. It had just gone ten, and the second hand hardly seemed to be moving. He shook his wrist, trying to make the time go faster. One o'clock seemed days away.

'At least the common room looks comfortable,' Stacy said, glancing around. The room was large and airy, with cushioned low-slung chairs arranged in airport-lounge rows. The decor was white and red, cheery. There were people everywhere, sleeping in the chairs, sitting around coffee-tables, talking to each other. Some of them looked like they had just been turned out of their rooms and didn't have anywhere else to go; others looked like Damon and Stacy felt: just in from another city and determined not to do anything until they had slept a few hours. All of them seemed restless, as if they were just waiting for something to happen so that they could go somewhere else. It was Casablanca in a common room.

Stacy and Damon limped over to the middle of the room and collapsed on a red couch, dumping their backpacks and sinking into the upholstery. Instant relief flooded over them.

'This is nice,' Damon said. 'Let's just wait here until the rooms open.'

Stacy nodded emphatically. 'I'm not going anywhere.'

Most of the people in the room seemed to have similar plans. They sat around patiently, reading, smoking, writing letters. A group of Canadians, maple leaves sewn to their backpacks and jackets, were playing poker around the opposite table.

'I'll bet a quarter,' one of them said, throwing a coin onto the table.

'I'll see your quarter,' said another, matching it. 'And I'll raise you fifty pence.'

'I'll see you,' said the next. 'And raise you a hundred lire.'

'See and raise two guilders.'

'Fifty pfennigs and some of these Polish things.'

'No way,' said the first one, a sandy-haired man with lively eyes. 'Hard currency only.'

'What about a franc, then?'

'A franc's good, Curt. I'll raise you five kroner.'

'Danish kroner? Local currency? Stuff we can actually spend?'

'A genuine, bona fide, hole-in-the-middle Danish five kroner bit.'

'Perry, man, what kind of hand do you have? I fold.'

The rest of the players threw their cards face-down on the table. Perry grinned at them and pulled the pile of assorted coins towards him, all different sizes and metals. Curt reached for Perry's cards, looked at them and threw them into his face in disgust.

'I don't believe it,' he said. 'You were bluffing!'

Complaining groans echoed around the table and Perry grinned harder, shielding his head from the barrage of cards and coins flying at him. He added the coins to his pile, collected the cards and dealt another hand.

The betting procedure repeated itself, cataloguing currencies: centimes, pesetas, rupees, pesos, all kinds of dollars and cents. The alien words worked themselves into a lullaby in Damon's head, running into each other as he drifted into a strange half-sleep, filled with images of money and banking and exchange bureaus. Krone, krona, lira, guilder, deutschmark, finn-mark, rand...

He was torn from his reverie by the high-pitched whine of Stacy zipping and unzipping the various compartments of her backpack. She pulled open one section, *zip*, shuffled through it for a while and closed it again, *zip*. She repeated this procedure for all of the pockets that hid between the canvas folds of her pack: zip, shuffle, zip, zip, shuffle, shuffle, zip. When she had finished she started again.

'What are you looking for?' Damon said irritably, opening his eyes.

'My Eurail map,' she said, still searching. 'It's in here somewhere.'

'Here,' Damon said, dipping into his own pack. 'Have a look at mine.'

Stacy took the map from his hand and studied it intently. Damon stretched his arms, feeling his shoulders crack in sleepy protest. The Canadians had silently disappeared, leaving behind them a few scattered coins. There was a shabby, unshaven man sitting where they had been, absently picking holes in a grey woollen jumper. His face was all deep creases and large pores clustered around a hook nose. He stared up at Damon from beneath his black, bushy eyebrows, and did not look away when Damon did.

Damon turned his attention back to Stacy. 'You going somewhere else already?'

'Just looking,' she said, tracing a finger along the red train routes of the map.

'Amazing freedom, isn't it?' he said. 'All these countries around us, all within reach. You can go anywhere, be anyone. Easy as filling in another date on the rail pass. We could wake up tomorrow and say "I think I'll go to Spain today" and do it. Or Greece. Or Austria. Or Russia.'

'Eurail doesn't cover Russia,' Stacy said without looking up.

'No, right, you're right,' Damon said. 'Pity, I'd really like to go there. But then there's the visa thing as well.'

The dishevelled man made a sudden gargling noise in his throat and said, 'Don't need one.'

Damon looked up at him. 'Excuse me?'

'Don't need a visa. For Russia,' said the man. A sly look crossed his face.

'I think you do,' Damon said. 'That's what the guidebook says. You need to do the whole thing through Intourist, or else get an invitation from someone who'll look after you and make sure you don't overthrow the government.'

'Guidebooks,' the man said disparagingly. 'What do they know?'

'All sorts of things, actually,' Damon said, feeling like an advertisement. 'How much a beer costs in Munich, for example. What to do if you overdose in Amsterdam. Where to get the biggest Wiener schnitzel in the free world. It's all here.' He pulled his guidebook out of his backpack and tapped it proudly.

The man ignored him. 'Go to Helsinki,' he said. 'Catch a boat to St Petersburg. Sleep on the boat, don't need a visa. Stay two, three days. Cost you less than a hundred dollars.'

'Really?' Damon said, curious but suspicious. 'How do you know all this?'

'I know everything,' the man replied sagely. A look of sadness passed behind his eyes. 'I worked at the Iraqi embassy here.'

Damon raised his eyebrows. 'That'd be a popular place.'

The man shook his head. 'They closed us down, kicked me out. Now I have nowhere to go. They just left me here.' He scowled like a Vietnam veteran, betrayed by his government.

'So you live here in the youth hostel?'

He nodded. 'I could tell you some stories. See that girl over there? She never goes out. Never leaves this place. Just buys cornflakes and Pepsi from the hostel shop and sits in the common room all day. Been here three weeks now. I been watching her.'

Stacy had stopped looking at her map and was staring at the man.

'Watching her?' she said.

'And that man asleep,' he continued. 'He sleeps all day, every day. In his room, or out here when that's being cleaned. He goes out every night after midnight, with a big bag, and comes back in the morning with no bag. Been doing that for a month. I been watching him.'

Damon shot a sideways glance at Stacy.

'Watching him,' he said.

'I see things,' the man went on. White flecks of dried spittle were forming around his lips. 'I know people. That receptionist woman? She's Moroccan. Late at night, behind the counter, she sings Elvis songs and makes sad faces in the mirror. She thinks there's nobody here, but I'm here. I been watching her.'

'Have you,' Stacy said. The man nodded wisely and said no more. Stacy turned to Damon and said, 'Want to go get something to eat? I'm even more hungry than tired.'

'Sure,' said Damon, frowning. They got up, dragged their backpacks into the storage room and walked out of the hostel. Damon turned around as he followed Stacy through the door, and saw that the strange man was still watching them with his hollow eyes.

'Creepy guy,' Stacy appraised as they left the bakery, clutching bags of Danish. 'He kept looking at you when you were asleep. He was sitting over the other side of the room until those people playing poker left. Then he came over.'

'He must have found me interesting,' Damon said, sounding pleased. 'Like I was a spy or a drug smuggler or something. He must have thought I was weird.'

Stacy frowned at him. 'You *are* weird if that sort of thing makes you feel good. I don't want him looking at *me*.'

Damon shrugged. 'There's only one thing worse than being looked at...' He trailed off rhetorically.

'Attention-seeker,' she said. 'And you're slipping: you look the same today as you did yesterday. Kind of scruffier and less shaven, but definitely the same.'

Damon felt uncomfortable at her scrutiny. He was feeling somewhat stale, suddenly trapped in himself: she had hit a nerve. He felt the need to shift again; his metamorphosis was overdue. But he excused himself by saying, 'I feel the same today as I did yesterday. Just a lot less awake. It's still the same day, really. Days aren't separated by nights anymore; they're separated by showers and changes of clothes.'

'If that's how it works, then that hostel guy must have been living the same day for weeks,' Stacy said, screwing up her nose. 'Did you see his clothes? Or breathe in near him? He should spend less time watching, more time washing.'

'Interesting what he said, though,' Damon said. 'About

Russia. We should look into it; I was going to go to Helsinki anyway.'

'I don't like to plan that far ahead,' Stacy said. She was walking in front of him now, staring up at the sky. She stopped and dug her hands into the pockets of her jacket, looking as if she was about to say something, then walked on.

'Just a thought,' said Damon.

The town square was much as they had left it: bus stops and disfigured buildings and skeletal autumn trees poking through brown holes in the concrete. The clock on the town hall registered two hours later than when they had first seen it, but Damon felt like he was returning to somewhere he had been in a former life. Everything was familiar but not quite recognisable.

The street they had followed in from the station crossed the square and turned into a paved pedestrian mall on the other side. The Strøget wound its ochre-bricked way between cafes and clothing stores; tributary arcades branched off it at regular intervals. Painted signs shouted through shop windows with their crossed and dotted vowels. Bone-coloured mannequins strutted marble catwalks behind the glass, torsos wrapped in fur coats, stoles encircling their jointed shoulders. Most of the shops offered 'Tax-free for tourists!' in friendly lettering.

Damon felt himself sink into the crowd as it surged around him, burying him. Europe had come to shop on the Strøget: the street was in chaos. There were people everywhere, bustling past hurriedly or wandering aimlessly while others bumped *tsk*ing into them. They laughed, talked, frowned at ensembles in shop windows. They walked alone, or in pairs or threes or larger groups; self-absorbed couples with resentful single tagalongs; dawdling shoppers with impatient husbands; power-dressing businessmen mobile-phoning absent others; slouching teenage gangs sharing walkman buds. Lawyers and bankers, accountants and nurses, students and poets and lovers.

Passage along the Strøget was obstructed by the outdoor cafes which scattered their tables across the pavestones. The air was crisply cold, but the sun was shining and enough people had been enticed outside to fill the available seating. A few wanderers circled the tables, searching for vacant spaces like aeroplanes in a landing pattern, steam rising from the cooling cups of coffee they were trying not to spill. A man and a woman, dressed in matching pinstriped suits, got up from a table just as Damon walked past. He caught Stacy's attention and sat firmly in one of the free seats, ignoring the glares of the indignant Danes who had begun to make their way towards the momentary vacancy.

Stacy sat down in the other chair and said, 'You can't still be hungry.'

'No,' Damon said. 'But take a look at this. Just watch.'

He turned his attention back to the crowd, appraising each person or couple or group, trying to determine who they were, where they had come from, what they were doing. A small boy pressed his face against a shop window. An old man hobbled gingerly along, propped between a walking stick and the arm of a teenage girl: probably his grand-daughter. A child sulked a few steps behind his mother or aunt or nanny. A couple in their early twenties stood in the middle of the crowd, oblivious as it surged around them. They kissed each other on the lips, briefly then deeply; then disengaged, wrapped their arms around each other, buried their heads in each other's necks. They tightened their embrace and swayed slightly back and forth as people bumped into them and walked off looking embarrassed or disapproving or envious.

'Look at them,' Damon said, quietly, without taking his eyes off the couple.

'Who?' Stacy said, staring blankly into the crowd.

'There,' Damon said, pointing. 'Those two; look at them. I wonder what their story is. Did they meet a week ago at a party? Or years ago, at high school? Or are they old friends who just realised they were in love? They're probably sleeping together; that looks like his shirt she's wearing. What do you think?'

'I don't know,' Stacy said. 'Why don't you go ask them?'

'That's no fun,' Damon said. 'It's more creative this way. Look how happy they are. Something great must have happened. Maybe they just won a holiday somewhere. Or they found out she's not pregnant. Or she is and they don't mind.'

'Who cares?' Stacy said, looking away. 'Leave them alone.'

'It's interesting,' Damon protested. 'Look at that. They don't care about anything that happens around them. They know exactly what they want. They know each other; you can tell. They really do. They're not just together because they've got nothing better to do. Or because he didn't know how to refuse her. As long as they've got each other they're going to be all right. See how they're holding onto each other? This is good stuff. Go on, you have a go.'

'I'm not interested,' Stacy said.

'Sure you are,' Damon persisted. 'Give it a try.'

'All right,' Stacy said suddenly, turning and narrowing her eyes at the couple. 'How's this? Those two are doomed. They've got a month, tops. Sure, she's white-knuckled holding onto him. But the tighter she holds him the faster he's slipping through her fingers. Look, she's lost him already. He's not even holding her; his hands are dead fish on her back. See him staring over her shoulder at that blonde? They're not going to be all right. They're going to scar each other emotionally, for life.'

Damon frowned, distressed, looking alternately between Stacy and the couple. 'You're good at this,' he finally admitted.

'No, I'm not,' Stacy said. 'You shouldn't spy on people. You're as bad as Saddam back at the hostel.'

'Saddam?' Damon said, looking confused.

'You know,' Stacy insisted. 'Iraqi Saddam. *I been watching you* Saddam.'

'God,' Damon said. 'You're such an American.'

Stacy glared at him and he turned away defensively, this time not out into the crowd but in towards the cafe. The shop window was a one-way mirror, reflecting the street and making it look doubly populated. The crowd shifted and his own reflection flashed into view. He saw himself, the brooding look on his face, the pout of his lips, Stacy frowning at him disapprovingly, arms folded. He wondered if anyone else was looking at them. What would they see? Petulant lovers, perhaps. Feuding friends, or sworn enemies forced together by prudence and protocol.

The prospect of being the focus of someone else's scrutiny sent a twinge of panic through him. He scanned the crowd to see who was watching, but was met only by a wall of faces oriented in other directions, people going about their business. He turned back to the mirrored window. Stacy's reflection had been eclipsed by a man with moussed hair and a trenchcoat, so that the only face Damon recognised in the mirror was his own. His image gazed back at him, gaunt, inquisitive, accusing. He needed a shave and his hair was all over the place. His clothes looked crumpled. He was ordinary, unremarkable. Nondescript. An onlooker might have woven any number of fictions around Stacy and himself, but there was nothing anyone could say about him alone. He realised this as he and his reflection stared each other out like squinting gunslingers. There was nothing about him. No distinguishing features. He looked awkward and uncomfortable, alone and out of place. Everyone else belonged. Everyone else looked like someone. He didn't look like anyone. He suddenly felt painfully empty, hollow. Nauseated. He was there but invisible; he was a mirror himself. People looking at him saw only themselves; if they squinted they would look straight through him. They were laughing at his nothingness.

'Hey, are you okay?' Stacy said, jerking him out of his self-absorption.

'Um,' Damon stammered, blinking. 'Claustrophobia. No, agoraphobia. Wait, which is it?'

Stacy looked at him with some concern. 'I have no idea what you're talking about.'

He shook his head briskly and smiled at her, weakly but reassuringly. 'Let's just get out of here.'

The pedestrian street split in several places near the middle, branching off towards the Vesterbro, Østerbro, Nørrebro and Christianshavn districts. Damon and Stacy headed north until they found themselves in the botanic gardens. A series of parks, linked by cinder and dirt tracks, crept towards the harbour. The grey buildings and domed cathedrals of the city were lost from view as the path wound its way through the lakes, gravel-ringed flowerbeds, bronze statues, bridges and tunnels of the gardens. Clouds started to roll over the sky, darkening as they came. The sun disappeared and it was suddenly much colder.

The gardens ended at the waterfront, where a narrow esplanade followed the edge of the land around the harbour. Cranes and gantries poked at the sky on the opposite side of the inlet, and the faint shouts of dock workers drifted across the grey water. The wind picked up, buffeting the seagulls flying above the rocks.

Damon and Stacy rounded a corner and found a thick cluster of people gathered around a pile of boulders on the shore. They were tourists, popping flashbulbs and talking too loudly to each other and wearing inappropriate hats. Most of them just stood around, facing different directions, wondering how much longer they had to stay in order to have *done* whatever it was they were doing. Damon pushed through them, trying to get to the front of their irritating semicircle.

A large rock sat balanced on a few others at the water's edge; wavelets lapped against the base of the structure. There was a bronze statue reclining on top of the upper rock: a mermaid, legs melting into a tail, arms draped across her knees. She stared out over the water, towards the Øresund, ignoring the jagged clutter of the derricks against the skyline, gazing forlornly at the ships chugging into the harbour as if waiting for the one that would never come.

'She's beautiful,' Stacy said at his shoulder. Cameras were still clicking in the background, harsh accents still grating, but they seemed to belong to some other reality.

'Who is she?' Damon asked, not turning around.

'*Den Lille Havefrue*,' Stacy said. 'It's the little mermaid. From Hans Christian Andersen.'

Damon nodded appreciatively at the statue. 'She's a babe.'

Stacy ignored him. 'She gave up three hundred years of happiness and sold her tongue to a sea witch, just so she could follow some guy around. And he went off with someone else and it killed her. Now there's a lesson for the modern woman.'

Damon turned and stared at her. 'You're quite cynical, aren't you?'

Stacy smiled grimly and said nothing.

'She looks like you,' Damon said. 'Tell you what. Go and kneel on the rock next to her, in the same position. I'll get a photo.'

Stacy raised an eyebrow at him. 'I don't know,' she said. 'Posing? That doesn't sound very Neo-Neo-Impressionist to me.'

'So what?' he said, shrugging. 'So maybe today I'm a Neo-Neo-Neo-Classicist.'

Stacy looked dubious, but clambered down to the rocks and made her way towards the statue. She climbed onto the boulder next to the mermaid and leaned over her bronze shoulder to check her exact posture.

'Why'd you do it, sister?' she whispered into her sculpted ear. 'Really, where was your self-esteem? They're not worth it.'

She kneeled in roughly the same position as the mermaid, folding her legs under her and letting her forearms rest on her thighs. She slumped forward slightly and stared out towards the horizon. An expression of hopeless anticipation lingered in her eyes. She drifted through the mermaid's pain, transported, feeling in flesh what had been moulded in metal. Sympathetic tears teased her eyelashes.

Damon stood on the rocks with his legs apart, balancing. He held his camera up to one eye, tilting it for composition, wishing he had a zoom lens. The square of the viewfinder refracted a reduced but perfect picture of Stacy. Her hair was blowing backwards, away from her ivory skin, her pale cheekbones. The choppy water mirrored the colour of her half-closed eyes. Her gaze was distant, as if she were intently watching things that were not there. She looked like something out of a fairytale herself; a princess, Snow White perhaps.

Snow.

An image flashed into his mind. She was lying motionless in the snow; skin as white as the icy background, as white as nothing; hair and eyebrows and downturned lashes as black as nothing: a photograph of black and white and infinite contrast except for her lips, lips red as blood, red as everything.

He drew in a sharp breath, wondering where the image had

come from. His finger trembled against the shutter button as he frowned and looked through the camera again. She was beautiful, he thought. She really was. He reinvented himself every day, but she was constant, every day the same. And every day he found her beautiful. That was something, at least.

Stacy and the mermaid were suddenly bathed in a flash of electronic lightning, and a click-whirr sounded behind his shoulder. He spun around to be blinded by another explosion of light, and another, and soon the air was buzzing with mechanical percussions and the strobing of flashbulbs.

'Hey, fuck off!' he shouted angrily, blinking away the afterimages. 'All of you! This is my picture! Go find your own picture!'

A few of the tourists looked sheepish and lowered their cameras, letting them hang against their paunches. The rest appeared—or chose—not to understand Damon and continued to line up their shots. Some paused to smile at him reassuringly before carrying on.

'Just take the photo,' Stacy pleaded. 'My leg's going to sleep.'

Damon turned back towards the water, aimed the camera at Stacy and pressed the release button without looking, without caring. He stuffed the camera back into his jacket in disgust and strode through the crowd, away from the statue.

'Fucking tourists,' he fumed once Stacy had caught up with him. 'They ruin everything. What are they doing here anyway? They don't see anything in the mermaid. They don't see beauty. All they see is something they can tell their friends about when they get home, something to help them in their quest to bore their relatives with crappy slideshows and mispronounce foreign names and wear dicky berets and pretend to be interesting, worthwhile, cosmopolitan people-of-the-world instead of fat, ignorant, camera-clicking leeches like they really are.'

'Come on,' Stacy said. 'They just wanted to take a picture of the mermaid. You were doing the same thing; what's the difference?'

'I wasn't taking a picture of the mermaid,' Damon said. 'I was taking a picture of you.'

'Oh,' Stacy said, looking at him quizzically. 'Well, don't, okay?'

By the time they got back to the hostel they were exhausted. They dragged their feet against the dirt track, which seemed to be stretching further and further in front of them. The bushes by the side of the path began to look remarkably comfortable. Damon wondered what would happen if he just curled up in the shadows of the undergrowth and went to sleep. Probably he would freeze to death, he realised. But at least he'd die well-rested.

The hostel finally loomed around the corner, light glittering through its windows. They staggered inside, found the storage room and pulled their backpacks along the floor behind them. As they crossed the common room they passed the shabby man from the Iraqi embassy, sitting where Damon had sat before.

'Ah,' he said, looking up at them. 'I knew you'd come back.'

'Of course,' Damon said. 'We just got here; we haven't even slept yet.'

The man turned his attention to Stacy. 'This the guy you're in love with?' he said.

Damon froze, feeling something move in his stomach. Stacy frowned and said, 'What?'

'I been watching you,' the man said. 'You're in love; I can see it in your eyes. But no,' he said, looking more closely. 'It's not this guy,' he said, pointing at Damon. 'It's someone else. Someone far away. Someone who's gone? Who?'

Stacy's cheeks, flushed with the indoor heat, drained to white again. 'What are you talking about?' she stammered.

The man nodded and raised a finger to the side of his nose. 'Ah,' he said. 'Fine. Play it your way, then.'

'What's he talking about?' Damon demanded.

Stacy ignored him. 'You don't know anything!' she shouted at the man. 'You don't even know me! You don't know anything about me!'

'I been watching you,' the man maintained. 'I see things. I know you.'

'You're full of shit,' Stacy said.

'Am I?' the man challenged. 'Tell me I'm wrong, then.'

'Fine,' Stacy said defiantly. 'You're wrong.' She let out a deep breath and blinked furiously. 'I'm going to bed,' she mumbled before turning and dragging her backpack towards the women's dorm.

Damon stared after her in confusion, then turned back to the man angrily.

'I'm not wrong,' the man said before Damon could speak. 'I see things. I see things in her. You I'm not sure about; I can't see you. Are you in love with her?'

'Look, fuck off,' Damon told him. His heart was pounding.

'Too bad if you are,' said the man.

In the morning she was gone. Damon sat in the common room as window-shaped patches of sunlight crept towards the walls and a grumbling string of hostellers shuffled out of the closing dorms. He sat there, waiting for her to emerge, as the red padded chairs filled and emptied, faster than life like a demonstration of stop-motion cinema. Outside it was warm and bright; puffy cumulus clouds drifted across the sky. Everyone had gone outside to enjoy the fickle weather while it lasted. Even the observant Iraqi ambassador had vanished, presumably having trailed some interesting subject out of the hostel. Stacy was nowhere to be seen.

Damon approached the receptionist, who was flicking through a tourist information brochure and absently humming *Love Me Tender* under her breath. Sensing his presence, she stopped and looked up at him questioningly.

'Listen,' Damon said, leaning against the counter. 'I need to know which dorm Anastasia Karayev is in.'

The receptionist looked at him sternly. 'I can't give out that information.'

'Sure you can,' Damon said. 'She's my girlfriend, and she forgot to tell me which room was hers. I need to find her. It's—' He stumbled—'It's our anniversary.'

A sympathetic smile crossed her face for a second before collapsing into another frown. 'It's ten-thirty,' she said, looking at her watch. 'The dorms have been closed for half an hour.'

'I know,' Damon said. 'But she's a really heavy sleeper. She wouldn't have heard the announcement; she won't wake up until the cleaners try to fluff the pillow under her head. Tell me which dorm and I'll go get her.'

'Can't you just wait for her?'

'I've been waiting an hour,' Damon pleaded. 'Come on—do it for a fellow Elvis fan?'

Her expression melted into resigned submission. She sighed and said, 'What was the name?'

'Karayev,' Damon pronounced carefully. 'Anastasia.'

She pushed aside a pile of brochures to reveal a gigantic ledger book lying open on the counter. As she ran her finger down the columns she shrugged intermittently and looked discouraged. Then she turned back to the previous page and brightened momentarily before frowning again.

'Oh,' she said. 'She checked out this morning.'

'That can't be right,' Damon protested. 'We only got here yesterday.'

'Her card's gone,' she said, checking the rack on the wall behind her. 'And that means she's gone, too.'

'Oh,' Damon said, crestfallen. 'Did—did she leave any messages?'

'Sorry,' she said, shaking her head sadly. 'And on your anniversary, too.'

'What?' Damon said. 'Oh. Yeah.'

He turned and walked back to his seat, mind racing. Slumping deep into the red upholstery, he stared at the ceiling, not seeing. He felt his mind chasing itself into a confused whirlpool, a hurricane of colliding emotions. His thoughts fell flailing into its vortex and were sucked into its slowly-spinning core; crushed and compacted into one bewildered expression of feeling: *what?*

'Hey.'

The syllable sank into the turbulence of his mind and dispersed it, scattering thoughts in all directions. He raised his head and opened his eyes; dark patterns melted from his field of vision. There was a man standing over him; young, tall, a mass of sandy hair falling into his eyes. He wore jeans, scuffed hiking boots, and a green windbreaker with a Canadian flag sewn to its shoulder. Damon recognised him as the card shark of the previous morning.

'Cool ceiling, eh?' His eyes twinkled with ironic enthusiasm.

Damon shifted his weight and struggled to sit higher in the sagging seat. 'Huh?'

'You were looking at the ceiling,' the Canadian said. 'And why not? It's a nice ceiling.' He glanced up and nodded appreciatively. 'White.'

Damon looked at him in despair. 'What do you want?'

The Canadian gazed upwards for a while longer before appearing to register Damon's question. 'Oh,' he said, looking down. 'I left a pack of cards here—where you're sitting, actually. Have you seen them?'

'No,' Damon said grumpily, then repented and added, 'Sorry.'

The Canadian looked distressed. 'Well, could you have a look? Maybe they fell down the side of your chair.'

Damon exhaled irritably and stuck his hand between the red cushions, groping unenthusiastically until his fingers closed around a flat cardboard packet. He pulled it out and held it up to the Canadian, whose eyes lit up when he saw it.

'Thanks, man,' he said, taking the cards. 'Hey, I'm Perry.'

'Hi,' Damon said.

'You okay there?'

A note of genuine interest had infected the flippancy of his voice. Surprised, Damon looked up and found a similar concern in his face: his eyebrows were raised slightly, eyes wide with human curiosity. Damon paused in the middle of the brush-off he had reflexively begun, closed his mouth and thought for a second.

'I've lost something,' he finally admitted.

Perry looked sympathetic. 'Maybe it fell down the other side of your chair?' he suggested.

Damon smiled weakly at him. 'No.'

'What was it?'

'I don't know,' Damon said, voice quavering with creeping

desperation. 'Did you ever see something out of the corner of your eye, and then have it disappear? Like, a word or an image'll jump into your mind, and you wonder where it's come from so you stop and look around for it, but it's gone—and you know you'll go crazy unless you can find it again. Because out of all the chaos of things in the world, this one thing is interesting enough to catch your attention, and it'll eat away at you until you can track it down and have a better look at it.'

Perry looked introspective and began to nod slowly. 'Yeah...' he said, doubtfully.

'That's how I feel,' Damon said.

'Where did you see it last?' Perry said thoughtfully.

'Here.'

'But it's not here now?'

'No.'

'You'd better look for it somewhere else, then.'

Damon raised his hands in exasperation. 'It could be anywhere!'

'Anywhere?'

'Well,' Damon said, reconsidering. 'Anywhere in Europe.'

Perry brightened. 'Fortunately, that's where we are,' he said. 'You're bound to find it sooner or later. You know how it is. You always find what you're looking for when you've given up searching, or you're looking for something else.'

'Needle in a haystack,' Damon said, pressing the ball of his hand into his forehead. 'Needle in a fucking haystack.'

'You'll be all right,' Perry said, unexpectedly placing his hand on Damon's shoulder. The contact was surprising but reassuring.

'I need a drink,' Damon said. 'Is anything open?'

'The Carlsberg factory is,' Perry said, looking pleased. 'My buddies and I were just on our way there when we realised we forgot the cards. They're waiting at the train station for me. Why don't you come? They give free samples.'

An uneasy familiarity crept over Damon as he trailed the guided tour around the brewery. He and the Canadians were led between imposing rows of aluminium fermenting vats, empty and echoing, ripe with the overpowering stench of stale alcohol. The spirits of departed spirits lingered in the booming metal drums, silently recalling the gallons that had been patiently nurtured there. The tour guide's voice reverberated through the vacant tanks, sombre as a valediction.

The rest of the tour was a cacophony of production: mixers, distillers, purifiers, filters, centrifuges. Industry everywhere. An interminable stream of brown-tinted bottles filed past him to be filled, capped, labelled, stacked, packed and crated by an army of mechanical slaves, whisked along by conveyor belts and fate. He felt a certain empathy for the hapless bottles. They were victims: passive, powerless, controlled by greater forces. Hurled through a series of improving processes which would gradually mould them to a predestined design. Shaped by the production line of the system. He knew the feeling. He was the same, he realised: a product of external influences, of parents and friends and Emily. Slapped with their labels, capped with their bottletops, and empty on the inside.

'Sometimes I feel like a beer,' he told Perry.

'Me too,' the Canadian said. 'I wish they'd hurry up and give us some.'

'That's not what I meant,' Damon started, before the tour guide interrupted him to tell the group something about shipping and distribution.

They were shown into a large tasting room furnished with polished wooden benches and long Viking tables. Clusters of bottles stood in molecular patterns at various points along the lacquered pine. The Canadians burst past the tour guide and arranged themselves around one of the tables, seizing bottles and beer steins, pouring, clinking, drinking. Damon sat down opposite Perry and helped himself to something chill-filtered.

The Canadians had been ignoring Damon in the friendliest way since he and Perry had caught up with them at the train station. As far as he could make out, they were all recent graduates of Western in Ontario. They all seemed to have names out of American frat movies: Bud, Curt, Jay, Chuck, Tobe, one which sounded like 'Tonsil'. They talked at length about lecturers and co-eds and extra-curricular hell-raising, laughing uproariously at each other and back-slapping everyone in reach, Damon included. He grinned vacantly where appropriate, nodding and feeling extraneous.

'So I'm standing, minding my own business at the forty-yard line, doing nothing, having a scratch maybe, and Jerry Lobeck comes out of nowhere, built like a goddamn refrigerator, runs straight into me,' Chuck reminisced. Five empty bottles raised a glass barrier between him and the world.

'I remember that!' Tobe said. 'Sent you flying. Right off the field; right out of bounds.'

'Right into the cheerleaders,' Jay added. 'Legs and pom-poms everywhere. Carnage.'

'I wouldn't have minded so much, except he was on my team,' Chuck lamented. 'And we were playing touch.'

'You didn't seem to mind anyway,' Jay said. 'You ended up lying sprawled across Marla Peterson and that brunette, and you wouldn't get up.'

'I was stunned,' Chuck protested.

'Marla's tits would stun anyone,' Tonsil said with feeling. 'And you were using them as an orthopaedic pillow.'

'She didn't seem to mind,' Chuck said. 'We went out for six weeks after that. Then she dumped me for Rocky goddamn Harris.' He scowled and reached for another beer.

'What happened to him, anyway?' Curt said. 'I didn't see him all semester.'

'Maybe he killed himself over Marla,' Chuck said, brightening. Then he looked resentful again and growled, 'But more likely she fucked him to death.'

Scattered empties formed a crude mosaic across the table, now the only table with anything on it. Nobody was really drunk, but everyone was speaking loudly, slurring perceptibly, gesturing widely. Damon was buzzing.

'Toilet break!' Tonsil announced, standing up too quickly and swaying uncertainly.

'Piss comp!' Tobe cried with gusto. The other Canadians cheered and leapt out of their seats, seizing each other by the shoulders as they followed Tonsil out of the room. Perry poured the rest of his bottle into a mug and raised it calmly to his lips.

'Aren't you joining in?' Damon asked.

Perry peered at him over the rim of his glass. 'I don't know the rules.'

Damon looked surprised. 'Why not?' he said. 'Were you sick for that lecture on Macho Watersports 101?' He raised his bottle by its neck and took a brief swig, breaking off to add: '...At Asshole U.?' His lips tripped over themselves as he talked: *let-shur*, *ash-hole*. He became vaguely aware that he was more drunk than he had realised. The alcohol intermingled with the bad mood that had emerged from Stacy's disappearance, culminating in a cocktail of dark cynicism. He savoured his surliness with smug pleasure, letting it drip from his tongue like a sweet poison.

'What?' Perry said, propping up the side of his face and staring across the room.

'I'm just surprised you're not off being homoerotic with your college buddies,' Damon said. He formed the words carefully, but still skidded over occasional syllables. *Homer-rotic.*

'They're not my college buddies,' Perry said. 'I never even went to college.'

Damon raised his hands, palms upwards, imploring. 'What are you doing with them, then?'

'I met them at the hostel the other day. They wanted to play with my cards.'

Damon stared at him. 'But they're assholes! All-American quarterback jock assholes to the man! Were you listening to them?'

Perry shrugged. 'They're all right. They're on holiday; they're having fun. Besides, they're Canadian.'

'Doesn't change anything.'

'They're not hurting anybody.'

The Canadians piled back into the room and collapsed along the benches. Their faces were ruddy with alcohol, eyes slightly glazed.

'Who won?' Perry asked.

'Curt for height, Bud for duration.'

Damon folded his arms in front of him and buried his head in the crook of his elbow.

The sky was marbled grey and black with heavy clouds when they emerged from the brewery, and by the time their bus arrived at the town square the rain was lashing everything with thick ropes of icy water. The streets were awash with radiating ripples, and the few patches of earth showing through the concrete had become pools of mud. The buildings had lost their focus, edges blurring, bleeding into the mist. The Canadians got off the bus and roared in disgust at the disintegrating weather before splashing across the square to the nearest shelter.

Damon and Perry followed them through a series of saturating dashes until they found the covered entrance to a huge, domed cathedral. Romanesque statues struck classical poses around the green copper hemisphere of the roof. Shallow steps led up to a broad portico supported by columns. The Canadians sat on the stairs, dripping miserably, and watched the rain cascading around them. Damon zipped his leather jacket all the way to the top, hiding the grey collared shirt he wore underneath it. His black slacks had become even blacker where the rain had soaked into them. His hair had been smoothed back into a slight quiff, but now hung in clinging strands over his face. Beads of water rolled across the polish of his leather shoes.

'Perry, man,' Jay said. 'Break out the cards. This rain looks like it's here to stay.'

'Hey, wait,' Tobe protested. 'Playing cards outside a church? There's something in the Bible about that. It's, like, against God, isn't it?'

As if in response, a flash of sheet lightning flicked across the sky and a clap of thunder boomed over the city. The wind blew the rain into tiny tornadoes, spinning chaotically around the courtyard.

'Bullshit,' Chuck said. 'That's just gambling. We won't gamble. We'll play Asshole.'

Damon stifled a blast of dark laughter. The Canadians turned to him, seeming to notice for the first time that he was not one of them.

'You know how to play?' Chuck asked him. 'Basically, you

have to get rid of all your cards, and avoid ending up as the asshole.'

'I know how to play,' Damon said. 'Here, let me deal.'

He took the cards from Perry, slipped them out of the box and shuffled them expertly, splitting the deck in two with a swift motion, recombining the piles by bending them and letting the cards flip back one by one, and arching them together with a satisfying snap. He repeated this procedure several times, working entirely off the ground as he had spent half a day in an Edinburgh train station practising. Then he performed a one-handed cut and began to distribute the cards.

The Canadians were looking at his hands with appreciative awe.

'Where'd you learn to do that, man?' Tonsil asked. He sounded genuinely impressed.

'Back home I'm a dealer,' Damon explained. 'I work at a casino on the Gold Coast.'

'No kidding?' Tobe said. 'I've been there. Surfers Paradise. Which casino are you at?'

'The new one,' Damon said. 'The, er, the Golden Dollar.'

'Cool,' Tobe said. 'They got great surfing there, man. You surf?'

'Sure,' Damon said. 'I mean, not all the time. That's why I'm not blond. But, sure, I like to get my board wet now and again.'

'Cool,' Tobe said again, nodding.

'It's the sea, man,' Damon said, warming to his subject. 'It's just—out there. All of it. So powerful, so huge, bigger than anything. But, it's friendly. You can surf on it. Greatest force on the planet and it's there for you, man. And you're on top of it, and you ride it, and it's the greatest feeling in the universe. When you and the sea are one.'

'Yeah!' Tobe said. His eyes were wild, inspired. 'And that's just exactly how I feel about grass. Turf, I mean. Like on a football field. A football field is just like a big, flat wave, and you surf it all the way to a touchdown.'

Damon looked doubtful. 'Yeah, whatever,' he said. 'Let's play some cards!'

The rain thinned to a drizzle towards the end of the afternoon and dried up completely as night fell. Damon had been playing some pretty reasonable Asshole. He had been President for over an hour straight, and hadn't fallen far below Citizen. He had become the designated shuffler, despite the rules. He enjoyed it, flourishing the cards and making up casino stories. He felt his shell growing back, creeping over the transparent albumen laid bare the day before. There might have been nothing inside, but this facade was entertaining enough. Nobody would mind.

Orange streetlights flickered on, bathing the city in an artificial sunset. Stars began to appear through the gaps in the clouds, shimmering in the damp air. Tight groups of people scurried past, pulling their clothes close to their bodies, breathing billows of mist into the night. Blinding headlights swept the cathedral like beams from a lighthouse.

The Canadians gave up straining to see in the dark and threw their cards down. Damon tried to zip his jacket higher but was already at the top. The temperature was dropping rapidly; the stone steps sucked the heat from his body.

'It's stopped raining,' he said. 'Let's get out of here; it's freezing.'

The Canadians looked at him. 'Freezing?' Chuck said. 'Back home we go swimming in this kind of weather!'

'Give him a break,' Tobe said. 'He's from Surfers Paradise; he probably doesn't know what cold is.'

'Sure I do,' Damon said. 'It's something you go inside to avoid.'

'The man has a point,' Perry said. 'Let's go find somewhere warm. There might be something to drink.'

The Canadians, persuaded, clambered to their feet. There was music coming from somewhere, so they tracked it through the streets. As they neared its source, more layers attached themselves to the sound: first a trembling bass line which they felt more than heard, then a grunge guitar groaning through low notes, the electronic hum of a keyboard on reverb, the metallic twang of strings, and finally a wandering vocal line. As they got closer still they realised that the singing was painfully off-key.

'Jesus,' Jay said, screwing up his face. 'What is it, cat strangling night at the local?'

'Worse,' Perry said as they rounded the corner and found themselves in an alley painted red and blue with the neon of a nightclub. 'Karaoke.'

Inside, the club was thronging with frenzied Danes. A crazy-looking blond man was singing *Justify My Love* on a small circular stage while the lyrics rolled across a screen behind him. The floor was alive with people dancing completely out of time with the music, throwing their arms and legs in all directions. The rest of the venue was filled with chairs and tables and raucous groups of back-slapping, belly-laughing, fist-thumping Scandinavians.

'Chaos!' Damon cried gleefully as they ploughed through the mass of bodies towards an emptier part of the club. 'What are all these people *on*?'

'Denmark's got one of the highest alcohol consumptions in the world,' Perry said. 'People come from all over Scandinavia to drink here.'

'I love this city!' Damon said. 'There's just something about it! Maybe there's nothing much to see; no major attractions or anything. But it's a great place to *be*. To sit and watch the world go by. Everyone's busy, restless, doing something, going somewhere. It's alive!'

'It's a rest stop,' Perry said. 'It's a transit lounge. There's Northern Europe above us, the rest of Europe below, and the only way to get from one to the other is through here. That's why everyone is so agitated; most of them *are* on their way somewhere, or they've just been somewhere else. It's the middle of an hourglass, only sand is rushing in both directions. And you can't keep still for long. Sooner or later you get swept along with it. You get caught up in the movement and you can't stay any longer; you have to take off again. So you love it, and then you leave it. And every day it's different. Every day is like the first day.'

Damon's eyes flashed wildly in the strobing neon. Blurred circles of light floated across the world in a spinning universe, reflected off a mirror-ball. He stood in the centre of this dizzying cosmos, in the middle of this seething city, and felt a sudden stillness within him, a complete peace. As if he were in the eye of a tornado, bobbing in a calm created by the forces raging all around.

'My kind of town!' he said.

1   Een
2   Twee
3   Tre

4   Fire

Stacy was in Hell.

Hell, Norway, a tiny hamlet a few degrees below the Arctic Circle. A speck on the map, nestled above the fjords, whose main export was picture postcards with 'Greetings from Hell!' printed across their faces. During the summer months, anyway: as the temperature dropped, so did the enthusiasm of the occasional travellers who made the day-trip from nearby Trondheim to visit the town made famous by its accidental namesake. But for the warmer part of the year, at least, messages from Hell radiated across the globe in a minor, but significant, international joke.

Now, in October, autumn was sliding into a long and bitter winter. The trickle of tourists had fallen away, the youth hostel had closed for the season, and the town had gone back to being a town again, no longer a destination. The sun's zenith was dropping lower every day, lingering above the horizon through interminable twilights, seldom more than a luminous patch in the cloud cover. The temperature rarely crept above zero. Sometimes it rained, freezing rain that left a slippery coat of ice where it fell. Snow covered the world like a torn eiderdown, frosty feathers settling over the village, whipped by the wind into lunar drifts. The main roads were still being ploughed, but with decreasing frequency, and the minor streets were left to suffocate beneath the deepening layers. Winter was falling over the town, muffling its sounds, insulating it against the world.

Stacy was in Hell, and Hell had frozen over.

She had seen a lot of winter over the past few days. It began soon after the train left Oslo and climbed towards Bergen, tracing a hairline track across the white tundra. A blank infinity stretched forever on either side. Stacy stared out of the window as the train ploughed resolutely along, skidding on the powdered rails. She lost herself in the immensity of the scene, becoming absorbed into it until there was no carriage, no train, and she was nothing but a mind hurtling through the void, following the twin tracks like a lifeline through the white vacuum, spurred by the roar of phantom diesel engines.

She thought about what she had left behind: the crazed Iraqi who seemed to see through her, and Damon. Damon seemed to have seen something as well, which was strange. He himself was curiously opaque, as though he bent the light around him. She wondered what made him so elusive and felt a twinge of regret at having left him. But there were other things to think about, and things about which she could not yet think. And the snow whipped away these thoughts and half-thoughts, settling over her mind with its blanket of emptiness, of peace.

Then the train had dropped below the snowline, below the treeline, and suddenly the mountains were raising their snowy ramparts impossibly high above, thrusting their reflections deep into the clear water of the fjords. The rocky walls plunged directly downwards, doffing their white caps and bristling with fir trees as they sank into the lakes formed between them. The sky was leaden, heavy with the promise of bad weather, remaining menacingly quiet as the train gathered speed for its final descent into coastal Bergen.

Stacy spent an hour in the new city; long enough to eat a cheese sandwich in the town square and decide that all she really wanted was to be back in the snow again, if just for a moment, to feel as she had felt crossing the tundra: free, insignificant, unencumbered. She caught the next train back to Oslo: dusk fell around her as she crossed the fjords, and the snow-covered steppe glowed with an eerie light as her mind darted through it once again.

After a single night in the Oslo youth hostel, which was brand new and sat on top of a hill in the middle of a park, the urban environment began to close in on her. A suffocating, industrial odour laced the air. There were people everywhere, too many people, wandering the cold streets like zombies, eyes dead in the blue-black skin of their faces. People and memories, flashes of familiarity in every cadaver's expression, jolting through her like an electric shock, more than she could stand.

As the morning train slid northward from the station, she realised she had gathered only one clear memory of Oslo. Wandering desolately through the streets, she had stumbled on an enormous metal fist, taller than she was, punching through the pavement and towards the sky, leaving piles of rubble and broken bricks around its iron forearm. There was a sculpted rose between its clenched fingers, held high, silhouetted black against the grey sky as she walked staring past it. That image and nothing else. Light flakes of snow drifted towards the speckled ground as the train left the city on its way towards Trondheim.

Hell had opened up before her like a blank slate when she arrived early in the pale morning. The information bureau at the train station was closed, and looked like it had been for days, weeks, possibly months. A faded sign curled against the window, 'Bed and breakfast accommodation' written across it in felt-tip. There was an address scrawled in the lower half of the notice, and a crude map with arrows leading from the train station. About five kilometres out of town, in the bottom corner of the page, a child-like sketch of a house blew cheery smoke from its chimney.

The actual house looked remarkably like its picture when Stacy finally found it: big and square with a triangular roof and large windows. The road on the map turned out to be less than a track, identifiable only by the wire fence running along it. It soon took her out of view of the train station; for several kilometres there was only the fence guiding her across the fields, nothing else to confirm that anyone had been that way before. The snow crunched beneath her boots, leaving footprints deepened by the weight of her backpack; yeti footprints. Everything was very still. Then the clouds in one particular part of the sky merged into a column of billowing white smoke and disappeared down a brick chimney as she passed through a cluster of snow-dusted fir trees and came upon the house.

An old woman answered the door. Her skin was pale and choked with deep wrinkles, stretched unevenly over her swollen joints. Her hands were frail and withered, blemished with liver spots. She carried herself carefully, deliberating over every movement. She reminded Stacy of her grandmother, of everyone's grandmother. The only unusual things about her were her hair, which was fiery red and fell to her waist, and her eyes, which were dark and intense and piercing, remaining steady when the rest of her body trembled. She didn't seem surprised to see Stacy.

'You stay with me,' she said.

The house was much smaller on the inside than it had appeared from the outside. There was clutter everywhere; a lifetime of collectibles, things too precious to throw away. The walls were hung with a startlingly incongruous array of posters, prints, paintings and tapestries. Furniture abandoned by each of a dozen decades sat in unaccustomed proximity: tables and chairs, chests, writing desks, tallboys, hatracks, umbrella stands. Books filled the forgotten spaces: lining the walls in stained oak shelves, stacked on tables, piled on the floor, wedged between things, propping up uneven legs. Millions of words of knowledge, information, opinion, stagnant beneath half a centimetre of dust. The old woman walked around the house with reverence, greeting each item with a comfortable familiarity, running her hands along the surfaces as she walked past.

'My life,' she said.

There were photographs, too, arranged in yellowing albums, propped up in frames, piled haphazardly on tabletops. Most of them were old and sepia-toned; some were crisp, black-and-white. A few had been hand-tinted in flat, unnatural colours. A handful of faces reappeared in many of the pictures, providing a continuity, a link through the chaos of images. A young girl, with dirty knees and hair tinted red, who grew into a fresh-faced teenager, nervous white-gowned bride, proud mother, and disappeared just as the old woman's features began to creep over her face. The groom from the wedding photograph, shrinking in one direction into a clean-shaven military cadet, a boy with a tennis racket, a solemn baby; ageing in the other to become an office-worker, a husband, a father. Brothers and sisters, recognisable from rigid family portraits. Children growing old and vanishing. There was a single colour photo floating in the sea of brown and grey: a polaroid, showing a woman who could almost have been one of the black-and-white children, surrounded by children of her own. They were standing on a beach in front of some palm trees, wearing hula skirts, laughing.

'All I have left,' the old woman said.

Grand picture windows stretched along the outer walls. The world flooded through the double glass and into the house, blurring the division between inner and outer, here and there. Drifts of snow piled against the bookshelves, melting in front of the fire. Tree branches scratched the light fittings. At night the world retreated, vanishing into the darkness, and the old woman drew the curtains and dropped quarter-logs into the fireplace and denied the wasteland stretching to the horizon. But during the day she sat in an armchair facing the windows and welcomed the bleak elements inside to gather around her like fawning pets. Sometimes she would sit there for hours, watching the wind blow and the storm-clouds hurtle past.

'Stories in the snow,' she said.

There were no clocks in the house; no time passing but the slow pulse of day and night fading into each other. Stacy found herself looking at her watch with decreasing regularity. Eventually she left it in the bottom of her backpack, where it ticked silently to itself, muffled by socks.

Each morning she put on as many of her clothes as she could and stepped out into the new snow, following the fence for direction, dragging a fresh trail of footprints behind her. When the sun shone, a few hours at most, she wore sunglasses to keep the blinding reflections from burning away her sanity. When it snowed, gently as if pieces of cloud were falling to the ground or violently like the collapse of Valhalla, she clung tightly to the wire and walked on through the weather, losing herself in it, feeling it close behind her.

The whirling snowflakes confounded her vision, dashing randomly about like television static, like chaos. Her mind found patterns in the storm; shapes and pictures and even sounds rising above the howl of the wind. Images flashed before her, floating out of the blizzard and then dissolving back into it. She saw mountains like the ones she had seen above the fjords. A tent, safety-yellow with a camp-stove beside it. The crater-edged print of a body in the snow. A dark shadow falling, falling before her eyes, hidden by flurries of white, gone. A creeping sunset, washing over the ground like blood. And then a scream which tore the air and sent flocks of birds flapping from the trees.

When the dusk began to fall she returned to the house and told the old woman what she had seen. The woman, sitting stock-still as Stacy talked rapidly and emotionally and without caring whether or not the Norwegian understood, nodded calmly and said nothing for some time. Then when she spoke it was in her own language, modulated in a lilting, lyrical accent, and although Stacy knew none of the words she understood by the reflective tone that the woman was recalling experiences of her own. She talked for a long time, swallowing the hours with the tenderness of her voice, forging delicate music out of the foreign sentences. Then, when her libretto had faded into silence, she turned to Stacy, smiled wanly, and lapsed back into her sparse English.

'You see them too,' she said.

Once she had come to terms with the general weirdness of it all, Stacy grew to enjoy these mutually incomprehensible exchanges. She began to relate long and complicated excerpts of her life to her host. She rambled, unaware of her rambling, darting from one idea to the next, following tangents which never returned her to her original train of thought.

'I guess it was always in my blood. Whoever heard of Lake Placid? How could I stay there, in this nowhere? Mam and Papa would sit and talk for hours; they never went out, never met anyone new, just talked to each other about places I couldn't imagine, people I'd never meet. They weren't sorry to have moved; they love America, but it was never their home, so it was never mine either. I always knew I'd leave. I couldn't imagine it any other way...'

And the old woman just sat there, smiling, savouring the words. Sometimes she looked at Stacy, but more often she stared into the fire, gazing at the flames as if they were alive. Reflected in her eyes, the fireplace became a stage where dancing furies acted out the stories hanging richly in the air.

'I'd known him all my life, really. We grew up together, though we didn't have much to do with each other at first, just saw each other around. He was a year above me. We had different friends. I think I was in the Christmas parade with his sister once. She was a raccoon. I only discovered after we left school how different he was. My friends just wanted to find someone to marry who would give them a joint account and not beat them too often. Little dreams. But he was like me. All he wanted was to get out, to see the world. We were going to do it together. There was so much we were going to do...'

She tended not to look at the old woman while she was talking. She looked into the fire, mesmerised by the twisting light, or stared through the crack in the curtains where a narrow strip of snowflakes fell. The Norwegian disappeared from her contemplation and was replaced by a succession of characters from her memories. Attentive phantoms sat at the edge of her consciousness and listened silently as she talked, shouted, cried with the same words she had hurled at the apparitions in the snow.

'You said we'd go together. I counted on it. You son of a bitch! How could you leave me behind? Alone! We would have made it! How could you betray me? You knew I loved you. I love you! Didn't you think about me at all? You were the only thing that kept me going. I hate you. I hate you!'

When she turned her head she saw momentary figures, sitting in the old woman's place, disappearing from the corners of her eyes. Familiar faces staring at her with sad, empty eyes, arms raised in characteristic gestures. They opened their mouths but never spoke. As their images faded away her mind invented fragments of speech for them: apologies, explanations, answers to the questions which plagued her. But the words jumbled against each other, not fitting, making no sense together. She was left alone with her questions, questions jabbing at her like tiny circling demons until the fire was sucked beneath its glowing coals and the old woman creaked out of her armchair and silently vanished from the room.

For the first time since she had left the United States, she felt alone. She had expected this of her travels: an isolation, a separation from the familiar, a bitter, glorious loneliness. But she had not found it. Instead she had met travellers, stayed in youth hostels, lost herself in a continuous cycle of conversation. Where are you from? How long since you left? Where have you been? Where are you going? Wherever she went she was embraced by a throng of people eager to know her and be known to her. Strangers became soulmates in the space of minutes. She travelled alone, but was never alone.

Until now. Now, with no companion but an old woman who asked no questions and would not have understood the answers, with no backdrop but the empty canvas of white sky and whiter snow, with nothing to do but think and nothing to see but herself; now, she felt alone. Trudging through the buried fields, bulging like a Michelin woman through jumpers and jackets, she hugged her body tightly and imagined she was the only thing in the universe. Sometimes she would squat in the snow, locking her limbs into a foetal position, feeling like an atom in a vacuum. Or she would raise her arms to the sky, taunting the infinity as the wind stung her streaming eyes and sent her hair spiralling around her head. She felt powerful and insignificant, alternately, simultaneously. As sole inhabitant of the cosmos she was its ruler and its slave.

Feelings were crystallising inside her, focussing from an amorphous mass into a few discrete and identifiable emotions, separating out like elements in a centrifuge. The more she thought, the clearer everything became. Like an instant photograph freshly exposed, a new understanding was fading into existence, gradually sharpening, gaining definition. She no longer saw pictures in the snow: now the pictures were in her mind, more vibrant than before. Things were becoming simpler.

There was pain. The pain had long been there, buried in a shallow and temporary grave, leaving a treacherous ridge in the surface. She had not tried seriously to escape the pain: she had learned to recognise futility. Instead she had accepted it, allowing it to become a part of her. But now it was emerging, exhumed, rejected by her body like a failed transplant. Tearing away from her like an escaping parasite, flopping onto the snow in a steaming mass of cancerous tissue, scarred organs, afterbirth. And it was smaller than she had remembered.

Loss, too. An immense loss, almost physical, as if the pain-abomination had taken some of her own organs with it as it exited her body. Nothing so cliched as a heart, but perhaps an intestine or a piece of lung. Something crucial, anyway: a chunk of flesh torn from her torso, leaving her to haemorrhage. A missing arm which still itched unreachably.

And, growing out of these, bitterness. Cynicism spreading like scar tissue over her wounds; severed nerves, dead skin. A sensation of numbness, an unwillingness to feel when the only thing to feel was pain. She welcomed this desensitisation, this healing. It felt comfortable, durable. Invulnerable.

Something else was emerging as well, too new to accurately discern. Something to do with danger, apprehension, anticipation tinged with a cold and unnamed feeling. It crept around stealthily, largely submerged, frightening in its novelty. She ignored this unknown emotion and concentrated on the others, the old familiar feelings. These were becoming manipulable in their clarity: she could not hide them or abandon them, but she could move them around, looking at each of their facets in turn. She held them up to the light, dusting them off, chipping away at them like an archaeologist.

She saw herself, lone actor on an empty set, and understood herself completely.

She knew that she would always be alone.

1	Een
2	Twee
3	Tre
4	Fire

5 Viisi

Forty years after the Olympic games, Helsinki had long moved out of the international spotlight, and seemed a colder place as a result. November was looming, vanguard of the approaching winter. A dense mist had rolled in from the harbour; low clouds scraped the treetops. The upper half of the Olympic tower disappeared into the fog like a concrete beanstalk. The air was thick with floating water particles and tumbling threads of drizzle. Far from the warm huddle of the city, the Olympic quarters had fallen into disuse, except for the section which had been turned into a youth hostel.

Damon and Perry sat in the shelter of the doorway and watched the rain slide down the concrete walls. The world looked very grey.

'What is it now?' Damon asked.

Perry tugged back the sleeve of his jacket to look at his watch. 'It's ten twenty-eight.'

Damon ran a hand through his still-damp hair. Checked. 'I make it ten thirty-one.'

'The optimism of youth,' Perry said, sitting back and tipping his head against the wall. 'Whatever. It's still a fucking long time.'

'I can't believe the place doesn't open until four,' Damon complained. 'I can't believe we can't even get inside where it's dry.'

'We could go back into town,' Perry suggested. 'But town's a half-hour away.'

'I'm not lugging this bloody thing another inch,' Damon said, indicating his backpack. 'I swear it weighs twice as much as it did yesterday. Some prick on the ferry's stolen all my clothes and put rocks there instead, I know it. I'm afraid to look.'

Perry ignored his ranting. He angled his backpack against the wall and leaned against it, stretching his legs. 'Wake me up at four, okay?'

Damon stood up and walked a few feet away from the doorway. A squall of wind blew rain into his face, fogging his glasses. He turned back towards the shelter, vision blurry.

'What are we doing here?' he demanded. 'What the fuck are we doing here?'

'We're going to Russia,' Perry said sleepily. 'Just think about that. It's going to be great.'

'Yeah, if we don't freeze to death first.'

The wind howled around the building, gusting into the doorway. Outside, the clouds were darkening, distended underbellies sagging. Damon felt the cold creep through his clothes and nestle against his skin, coaxing gooseplmples from his flesh. He hugged himself miserably. The worst thing about travelling, he decided, was arriving somewhere. The ferry had been luxurious, the train at least heated. Transit was comfortable. But now he was here, and here was wet and lonely and miles from the world. Melodrama took over. He was huddling against an arctic ruin, lost, abandoned, half-sheltered by a glacier while the wind and rain and nothing else raged around him. Perry was slipping away, drifting into comfortable sleep. The bastard.

'How can you sleep?' Damon asked. 'How can you possibly sleep? It's cold, it's wet, the floor is hard—'

'And it's noisy,' Perry complained. 'What, you don't want me to sleep? Why not? Why can't I sleep?'

'You're no good to me asleep,' Damon said.

'I don't want to be good to you,' Perry said. 'I want to be nasty to you, and poke you with sharp things until you shut up and let me get some shut-eye.'

'Fine,' Damon said. 'Go to sleep then. I didn't want to talk to you anyway.'

'As long as you're sure,' Perry mumbled, trailing off into oblivion.

A pair of shadows faded out of the fog and drifted towards the doorway. Colours crept over them as they drew closer, purple and green. Soft clicking noises, like the chirp of a miserable cicada, hid behind their splashing footsteps. One was a man and the other a woman, but they wore identical hair, matted and black and tied in matching ponytails. They wheeled mountain bikes beside them, tyres dribbling winding tracks across the concrete as they reached the shelter of the entrance.

They clicked past Damon and Perry, regarding their prone forms with an expression of curiosity which faded to disappointment as they arrived at the door. The man tried the handle without too much hope; it rattled ineffectually in his hands.

'*Nein...*' the woman moaned behind him.

''Fraid so,' Damon said, knowing how she felt.

'The youth hostel is closed?' the man asked in a moderate German accent.

'Until four o'clock,' Damon told him.

'*Scheizen*,' the man said.

They leaned their bikes against the wall and sat on the crossbars. The woman untied one of her pannier-bags and shuffled through it until she found a towel. She wiped the rain from her face and tried to dry her hair. The two Germans looked remarkably similar. Their faces were fresh and healthy, their eyes dark but sparkling. They had the same nose, a sharp triangular wedge.

'I am Max,' the man said, extending his hand. 'This is Martina.'

Damon shook Max's hand and nodded at Martina, who was towelling behind her ears.

'Damon,' he said. 'And this lump here is Perry.'

Martina paused and looked at Perry's dozing figure. 'What's the matter with him?' she asked.

'He's just asleep,' Damon explained. 'We stayed up most of the night on the ferry.'

She looked down disapprovingly. 'No time to sleep,' she said, throwing her towel gleefully at Perry's head. 'Wake up!'

Damon stared at her in disbelief; Max rolled his eyes. Perry found his face full of wet towel and spluttered into lucidity.

'Hey!' he protested. 'What? What was that for?'

'*Guten morgen*,' Martina chirped playfully. 'Good morning. Rise and shine. I am Martina. He is Max. That is Damon.'

'Pleased to meet you,' Perry said, looking bewildered. 'Is this your towel?'

'*Danke*,' she said, snatching the towel from Perry's outstretched hand. 'You are a gentleman.'

'Thanks,' Perry said. 'You're very, er, psychotic yourself.'

'Excuse her,' Max entreated. 'We've been cycling through nowhere for three weeks. We haven't been near people for a while.'

'Good plan,' Perry said, looking at Martina. 'Hi, I'm Perry.'

'I already introduced you,' Damon told him.

A splashing, pounding noise filled the air and a large wet figure burst out of the mist, skidding to a halt at the doorway. He was covered in a bright red jacket and a thick, dark beard. His eyes glittered beneath bushy eyebrows.

'Why are you all sitting out here?' he boomed. American.

'Fresh air is good for the soul,' Martina said. 'You're very big.'

'Yes, I am,' he agreed. 'This air isn't fresh, it's wet. Wet air is bad for everything.'

'The door's locked,' Damon offered, feeling slightly nervous. 'Until four o'clock.'

'Goddamn!' the American shouted. 'That's four hours away!'

'Four and a half,' Damon corrected.

'Goddamn!'

He dropped his backpack to the ground and sat on it disconsolately, looking out at the weather and back towards the other travellers. 'You brought bikes?'

'Yes,' Max said. 'We've been cycling up north.'

'North?' he cried. 'I didn't think there was any more north. You two must be crazy!'

'At least one of them is,' Perry said. Martina brandished her towel threateningly.

'I am Martina,' she said. 'These are Max and Perry and Damon.'

'I'm Denis,' the American boomed. 'I know it doesn't suit me, but don't laugh or I'll hit you.'

Damon and Perry looked deadly serious. Max and Martina just looked confused.

'Which of the States are you from?' Damon asked, changing the subject.

'Vermont,' Denis said. 'So I get this kind of climate at home.'

'So what are you doing here?'

Denis threw up his hands. 'I don't know!' he shouted. 'I wanted to see what a socialist democracy was like. I didn't think it would be so depressing.'

'Highest suicide rate in the world,' Perry said.

'I'm not surprised, if nobody's allowed inside until four in the afternoon,' Denis said. 'Suicide doesn't seem like such a bad option. Why are you guys here?'

'We're going to Russia,' Perry said.

'Russia!' Denis exclaimed. 'I'd love to see what a collapsed communist dictatorship is like. Isn't it, like, really hard to get a visa?'

'It probably would be, if we needed one,' Perry said enigmatically.

'What? Don't need a visa?' Denis said. Max and Martina leaned forward, interested.

'This crazy Iraqi in Denmark told me there are boats from

here to St Petersburg which you don't need a visa for,' Damon explained. 'You sleep on the boat. There's some loophole.'

Denis looked suspicious. 'And you trusted a crazy Iraqi? I mean, Bush was an asshole over the whole Gulf War thing, but I still wouldn't go around putting my travel plans in the hands of a crazed Iraqi. No matter how much of a victim he was.'

'That's what we thought,' Damon said. 'So we went to the Intourist agency in Stockholm on the way here, just to make sure. The woman said we needed visas, of course, and that we'd have to book the whole thing through them and pay a hundred dollars a night for hotels. But there were pamphlets on the counter about these no-visa cruise things, so we took one while she wasn't looking.'

'It's all true,' Perry corroborated.

Their attention was distracted by a shuffling sound, and a dishevelled man in a blue raincoat appeared in the doorway. His black hair, short but in need of a cut, hung limply over his forehead. Dark stubble dotted his face, stark against his pale skin. He looked generally wet and miserable.

'Hello,' he said quietly. 'I'm Roger. I'm from England.'

'This is beginning to sound like some kind of joke,' Perry mused. 'Stop me if you've heard this one. An Englishman, an American, a Canadian, two Germans and an Australian are sitting in a doorway in Helsinki...'

'Which one's the Australian?' Denis asked, looking puzzled.

'I am,' Damon volunteered.

Denis frowned. 'You don't sound Australian,' he said. 'I thought you were English.'

'No, I'm English,' Roger said helpfully. 'Did I hear you talking about Russia?'

Damon repeated the story of the crazed Iraqi and the disobliging Intourist woman. Everyone seemed instantly fascinated. Enthusiasm crackled like electricity, charging the air. The next boat to St Petersburg was a Baltic Shipping Lines ferry, the *Konstantin Simonov*, leaving Helsinki harbour in three days. A four-day cruise in ultra-economy class cost 355 local markka; the travellers spent some time translating this into their native currencies and Damon came up with about $120 Australian.

The conversation moved on, energised. They listed and compared the places they had been, exchanged horror stories, shared discoveries. Denis's powerful voice echoed off the concrete. Martina continued to perplex everyone except Perry, who now seemed to be taking her in his stride. Roger kept rubbing his stubble. Time began to pass, gathering momentum.

Damon retreated from the conversation and watched it from an epistemological distance. There was something comforting about their huddle: a unity in separation. They were cut off from everything: the hostel, the city, the world. Their square of dry concrete, raft on a shallow ocean, held all that was relevant in the universe; the rest had been washed away by the rain. They were sitting under a bubble on a lunar colony, hidden in the only bunker to have survived the apocalypse.

Four o'clock came before anyone expected it. It wandered out of the rain in the shape of a short, balding man who dripped across the concrete, unlocked the door and disappeared inside. The moment seemed strangely empty. The travellers stared at each other for a few anti-climactic seconds, then nervously picked up their luggage and followed the man into the youth hostel.

The rain had cleared up during the night, and downtown Helsinki was glittering. Leviathan shopping centres clustered together, reaching skywards with stubby fingers. Polished marble and terracotta walkways linked townships of hi-fi and clothing stores, radiating around food halls. Auto-teller machines stood sentry at each corner. Everything was clean, modern and expensive.

From the distance the hinterland was advancing, creeping towards the coast. Out of sight, frozen Finland stretched towards the North Pole. There was something heartening about the huddle of shiny buildings, teetering on the edge of the wilderness. Civilisation was making little progress in the war against geography, but at least it was holding its ground. A well-placed glacier could nudge the whole city into the gulf, but it seemed intent on clinging to the coastline at least until the next Ice Age.

Grey wavelets lapped the harbour, white-tipped with tiny crests and seagulls. Blunt-nosed tankers and ocean liners nuzzled each other along the docks, bellowing with massive combustion or shunted by cheerful chugging tugboats. The sea breeze collected sounds and whipped them along the waterfront: clanging equipment, moaning klaxons, seabirds crying. The air was stale but freshening, a battlefield of odours. Salt and salted fish and rotting fish and fresh fish, freshwater fish, saltwater fish, salt water.

Makeshift market stalls perched on the harbourside, selling herring and squid and mackerel from the morning. Suspended schools of fish hung from hooks or lay in baskets, caught in a moment of surprise, dead eyes staring, throats grinning. Fishermen in boots and beanies stood behind the stalls, shifting restlessly, gripping cigarettes between white, wet fingers. The travellers wandered past, delighted by the local flavour, wishing they could indulge in the experience of buying fresh Finnish fish without having to lug the slimy things through Helsinki all day.

They left the stalls for the more permanent market, housed beneath a broad tin roof. Here were more portable and disposable foodstuffs: nuts, dried fruit, cakes and pastries, soup in steaming saucepans. Clothes, too, wool and fur, blending European fashion and Scandinavian insulation. Martina kept snatching hats from nearby racks and jumping up to slam-dunk them onto Denis's head, winding dancing scarves around his neck. Max watched her with some amusement; Damon noticed his smirk.

'So, you and Martina—you're not, like, together,' he said. 'I mean, you don't mind that she's flirting so outrageously with everyone?'

Max looked shocked. 'Of course not,' he said. 'She's my sister.'

Damon raised his eyebrows. 'Really?' he said. 'I didn't know that; I just assumed—still, you do look alike. It's just that I can't imagine travelling around Europe with my sister.'

'You have a sister?' Max asked.

'No,' Damon said. 'But if I had one, I mean.'

'She's good for hitch-hiking,' Max confided. 'But bad for

nightclubs: other women think she's my girlfriend.' He smiled to himself, amused by the prospect. 'Not that there are many nightclubs up north.'

'That's another thing,' Damon said. 'If I had a sister, I wouldn't want to spend three weeks with her and nobody else. We'd end up killing each other.'

'You're wrong,' Max said. 'With Martina it can be like being alone. Anybody else, you're always aware of them. But someone you've known all your life, you can ignore them and they won't be offended. If you want to go off into your own world they're happy to let you. We only saw three other people while we were up there, people through car windows for half a second. You get to know yourself.'

Damon looked thoughtful. Up ahead, Martina was getting Denis to try on a fur cap which made him look even more like a grizzly bear. Roger was in the grip of an uncharacteristic enthusiasm, gesturing wildly as Perry punctuated his expatiation with interested nods. A happy murmur reverberated through the market. Damon felt good. New friends around him, and the promise of adventure hanging in the air. Only one thing missing: if only—but he censored his thoughts, unwilling to compromise his contentedness. To keep himself cheerful he bought an icecream from a skinny bald man who seemed not to care about the temperature. The chocolate chip sent shivers through him like tiny frigid orgasms.

Roger was proving to be full of surprises. Something seemed to have happened to him overnight, some new chemical slowly slipping into his bloodstream. At the market he had grown increasingly vocal, drawing the rest of the travellers and a few of the locals around him to witness his exposition on what turned out to be a new breakthrough in rail-signal technology. He had blazed a fervent path through the city, darting between museums and monuments like a tour-guide on amphetamines. Finally, after a Big Mac dinner, he had suggested they celebrate the fact that they were alive and in Helsinki by going to a nightclub. And so here they were.

The alluringly-named KY-Exit club was a happy, colourful

place full of beautiful people and music that had been in the Top 40 when Damon left Australia. Only he and Roger had made it all the way to the club. Denis said he was too big for dancing; Martina agreed and volunteered to console him over his awkwardness. Max and Perry just wanted to find a quiet bar where they could talk about mountain bikes. So Damon had wound up stagging with Roger.

It hadn't looked promising. Upon paying the cover charge and being stamped with a smiley face, Roger had rolled up his sleeves, flipped his collar and announced that he would see Damon later.

'Let's split up,' he had said, raising his voice as it lost itself in the music. 'We're on the pull tonight, eh, mate.'

Then he had vanished.

Damon sat in a booth with a glass of bourbon and watched the video wall behind the dancefloor. A Japanese animation was screaming along with the music; wide-eyed figures shot each other in a bloodthirsty dance. Teenagers mirrored their jerking movements on the floor, cartoon-like in the strobing light. A couple were necking in the next booth, breathing in frantic snatches. Damon turned his attention back to his glass.

He had spent a lot of time in places like this, but now he couldn't think why. Emily and his friends had told him he was a nightclub person. He supposed he was, as much as anything. He had always tried to be what people wanted. His parents wanted a successful son; Emily wanted a presentable boyfriend; his friends wanted a compliant friend. He had been all things to all people, or tried. Now they were gone; he had shaken them off in desperation. Which meant that he could be anything. Which meant that he was nothing.

Roger slipped in beside him and wiped his forehead with the back of his arm. His face was glistening with sweat; his eyes wide.

'Oh, mate,' he gasped. 'That was harsh. I was talking to this girl for twenty minutes, bought her three drinks all at once— stunning she was, blonde, tits like you wouldn't believe. She was going for me, really, she really was. But then this guy comes over, hand on her arse, and she's straight down his throat. Then she gives him one of my drinks and introduces us—boyfriend—and they disappear, probably for a bonk in the toilet for all I know. Bitch.'

He paused for breath and took a belt of Damon's bourbon. Damon looked at him pityingly, examining his face in the neon. He was ugly, in a tragic way which made Damon feel guilty for thinking so. He obviously had no hope of scoring until at least four in the morning, by which time one of the beautiful people might be drunk and desperate enough to settle for a scrawny tourist from England, not far away enough to be exotic. It was only half past twelve, and the youth hostel had a curfew of two. Roger was out of luck.

'Ah,' Roger said, brightening and gazing across the room. 'My next target.'

Damon followed him with his eyes as he disappeared into the darkness. He felt sorry for the hapless Englishman, at the same time angry at himself for the ugliness of his condescension. He was no-one to judge, he reflected as a waitress brought him another glass. He was sitting in a strange nightclub, alone with a tumbler of 80 proof. Nobody loved him either; at least Roger was trying. He leaned on his elbows and stared at the tabletop. Nobody loved him. He couldn't remember how many drinks he'd had; barpeople kept coming and whisking away his telltale empties. He slumped lower. His eyebrows felt heavy, falling over his face.

'Bloody hell, everybody here's got a boyfriend,' Roger complained at his ear. Damon heard the noise but didn't register it; when he finally shook himself into looking up, he was alone again.

The music stopped for a second and a slow song began to ooze from the speakers. Bryan Adams. Couples rushed to the dance floor and drifted in circles, buried in each other. The strobe shut off and a rosy glow filled the room. Damon scanned the mass of interlocked faces. They were less Scandinavian than the faces of Sweden and Denmark; the proximity of the Russian border had left its mark in the gene pool. Dark hair. Grey eyes. Cheekbones. Pieces of Stacy everywhere. She was behind the bar, collecting glasses, dancing to the theme from

Robin Hood, kissing a male version of herself. Everywhere Stacy.

Damon realised he was obsessing. Obsession. An ugly word. Neurosis, fixation, compulsion—ugly words all. He was sure he hadn't drunk enough to justify these psychopathic symptoms. He resolved to snap out of it. Roger had the right idea; Roger had his heart broken every twenty minutes and thought nothing of it. Roger was a champion, a hero of modern times. Damon caught sight of him on the floor, slow-dancing by himself. Jesus.

Bryan Adams faded into silence and the techno surged up again, heavier than before, industrial-strength. Dry ice hissed from unseen nozzles and curled across the floor in a rising fog. Roger appeared out of the haze, strobing as if electrified. He staggered towards Damon's booth and collapsed in the seat.

'Well, that's it for me,' he said, raising his hands in a gesture of despair. 'Jesus, these girls are like ice. No luck either, huh?'

'I haven't even tried,' Damon said. 'How do you go about picking someone up in another language? I can't see how you can make a good impression with an opener like "Do you speak English?" It just doesn't work.'

'So don't ask!' Roger advised. 'Mate, everyone here speaks English. They've been learning it since they started school, which is over ten years for most of these girls. Just jump straight in, use one of your regular lines.'

'Sure,' Damon said. 'I'll just select a few from my forthcoming book, *Damon's Sure-fire Nightclub Lines for Paedophiles of All Ages.*'

Roger looked hurt. 'Don't be like that,' he said. 'Okay, so they're a bit young, but this is Europe. Things are different here. Any of these girls have had as much sex as I've had. Maybe even more.'

'Surely not,' Damon said without too much sarcasm.

'No, really,' Roger insisted. 'They're ready to go. All you need is the right line. You can borrow one of mine, if you like. I've developed a few especially for the Continent. Like, "You're Claudia Schiffer's sister, aren't you?"—that's a good one. Or "Your eyes are like morning sunlight on a field of snow." But you can't use this one, this is my favourite: "I need you to model as an angel for my ice sculpture." If that doesn't hook them, then nothing will.'

Damon looked at him disbelievingly. 'Roger, I hate to break this to you,' he said evenly. 'But your lines, wonderful as they are, have got you precisely as far as I have got with no lines. And the advantage of my position is that nobody in Finland thinks I'm a dickhead yet.'

Roger grinned sadly. 'Listen,' he said, appearing to melt into another character entirely. 'I know how this all sounds. I'm not stupid. I know I haven't really got what it takes to pull these lines off like some kind of movie star. But this is all I can do. And women, you know, they appreciate the effort. And so sometimes they respond—maybe not because they think I'm cool, but maybe because they think I'm funny, or nice, or so simple that they trust me. Whatever, it's all the same in the end. Who cares how you get there, as long as you do—right?'

Damon considered this wisdom. He had never heard of anyone using their own ineptitude as an angle. But perhaps everyone did without realising. Perhaps any solid belief in cause and effect was pure superstition anyway. Intriguing questions. But the throbbing air of the nightclub was not conducive to metaphysics—and besides, Roger had started talking again.

'I have this theory,' he said. 'People are basically repressed, right. The thing they're most afraid of is embarrassment. Everyone's like that, so they spend all their time looking as cool as possible. But my theory is, not being afraid to make a complete idiot of yourself can actually be quite attractive. It's different, refreshing maybe. Real.'

'You're a very strange character,' Damon told him. 'But you may be on to something. Come back when you've picked up a few of these girls; then I'll be keen to discuss your method further.'

Roger gazed lustfully around the room, eyes landing on occasional bodies. His period of self-awareness seemed to be over, and inertia was dragging him back into his old self. He dissolved into a picture of forlorn desire, spellbound by the sight of some distant Scandinavian siren. He muttered goodbye to Damon and disappeared across the dance floor, to loose a few volleys of pathos before being dashed against the rocks. The sea of writhing bodies parted and closed behind him as he half-walked, half-danced towards his doom, strutting like a turkey.

Damon pondered Roger's philosophy. He felt a new respect for the hapless Englishman. At least he knew who he was, and was happy with it. Damon looked around and realised he had been sitting in the same seat since arriving at the club. He had worn a contour in the upholstery, inverted buttocks of boredom. It was all wrong. Nightclubs weren't about nursing drinks and feeling dark. Nightclubs were about dancing and flirting and happy idiocy. He felt like an interloper, traitor to the cause.

The invisible disc jockey scratched in a Kylie Minogue track, boppy and bubblegum. Damon identified its synthesised strains with a rush of recognition. An Australian; a home gal. It was a pretty bad song, but it was a sign. He drained his glass, mostly meltwater, crunched an ice cube and launched himself onto the parquetry.

He had been watching long enough to work out the general style of dance favoured by the patrons of KY-Exit. It was high-energy and involved a lot of complicated footwork, moves seen on MTV and practised in front of mirrors. No problem: Damon had seen MTV too. For a while he watched his feet to make sure they were doing sufficiently interesting things; then, feeling the rhythm, he let himself go, blazing like a dervish across the floor. It had gone midnight; he was due for a change. Now he was a dancer and patron of nightclubs, losing himself in the music. Soon he was sweating.

His attention shifted outward. The other dancers were mostly female; obviously underage but in a strange way older than anyone he knew. They moved like professionals, all hips and swaying shoulders, acting sexy, being sexy. A blonde girl was squirming alone under a cone of red light, looking like she was trying to wriggle out of her dress. Her head was tipped back, eyes closed, lips parted as she bathed in the scarlet glow cascading like a warm shower over her throat and chest.

Damon watched her as she twisted in the light, oblivious,

running her hands across her body, touching her own skin. He winced and shook his head briskly, dispersing the desire that was accumulating. His mouth pursed itself into an involuntary O, which he exhaled through like a goldfish. He scoured his mind for an appropriate opener. He had seen this done before, successfully, a hundred times in movies.

Excuse me. Would you like to dance?

She was already dancing.

All right, then. Would you like to dance with me?

She was a better dancer than he was. Considerably. Bad idea. Not cool.

You don't belong here. You're too real for a place like this.

Interesting, but dodgy. What if she wanted to belong? And questions of realness in people made him uncomfortable.

Let's go somewhere and talk.

But where? He didn't know anywhere. And what would they talk about?

Let's go somewhere and fuck.

He had waited a long time for the nerve and opportunity to say that. And he would probably wait a lot longer.

Where are you from?

Actually not a bad one for a train station or a youth hostel. But weird for a nightclub. After all, most of the people in Finland were from Finland. It wasn't a Club Med.

I need you to model as an angel for my ice sculpture.

Sadly unavailable.

What's your sign?

Jesus.

Eventually he settled on a simple 'Hi,' drawing a deep breath and forcing his fears to the pit of his stomach before taking the plunge.

The girl stopped dancing and opened her eyes. 'Who are you?' she demanded.

'I'm Damon,' he said. 'And you are?'

She sneered at him. 'What do you want?'

Damon looked baffled. This wasn't going well. 'Well, nothing, I just thought—'

She marched up to him and drew herself up to her full

height. 'I know what you thought,' she said. 'You thought that just because I'm blonde, that means I'm easy. You think all northern girls are easy! Well, it's not true! That's just a stereotype. That stereotype is not true!'

'Look, I'm sorry,' Damon faltered. 'I didn't—'

'You're sorry? You ought to be sorry! You'll be sorry all right!'

She balanced on her toes and pushed him hard in the chest with both hands. His centre of gravity disappeared and he stumbled backwards, surprised. A sensation of deja vu flooded through him as he fell: make a note, he told himself. European women don't like you. His flailing arm caught someone's drink in its circumference and sent an arc of champagne through the air. He saw the beads of liquid fall in slow motion, twisting and wobbling, and almost had time to reach for the flute before it hit the ground and, thankfully, bounced. Plastic. He took a desperate step and slipped on the puddle he had created, crashing to the floor at the feet of a girl dripping with champagne.

Oh, God, he thought. Not again. But the girl dropped her hands, which had been raised in sodden disbelief, and clutched her stomach, laughing. People around them shook the alcohol from their clothes and kept dancing. Kylie was singing something about the Bus Stop, but the dancers ignored her suggestion and continued with their MTV steps. Damon's victim kept laughing as he climbed to his feet.

'Sorry about your drink,' he mumbled. 'I'll—I'll get you another one.'

She looked at him incredulously, sweeping a lock of dark hair away from her face. Her eyes glistened with lingering tears of laughter. 'You mean all this is a line?'

Damon rolled his eyes. 'Not on your life. No lines for me.'

'Good,' she said, smiling wryly. 'I'm Katja.' She touched her breastbone in a gesture of self-identification.

'I'm Damon,' he said, offering his hand. She took it and gripped it firmly, pumping it once. Her skin was cool.

'You're shaking,' she said. 'Maybe I'd better get you a drink.'

She led him towards the bar, pushing through clumps of people who occasionally waved to her and smirked evaluatively at Damon. The barman greeted her by name.

'What do you want?' she asked Damon.

'Bourbon rocks. But—'

The barman poured a couple of glasses, one with a straw and one without. Katja paid for both of them, drew the straw through her lips and threw it away.

'Damn Stefan,' she complained. 'He's such a chauvinist.' She gave the first syllable a hard edge: *tcho-vinist.*

'Listen, I was going to—'

Katja waved away his offer. 'Next time. Where are you from?'

It was cold outside. Damon clenched his teeth to stop them chattering, breathing fog through them like an asthmatic. The sky was clear and packed with stars; the aurora borealis clawed the horizon. The streets were deserted, lights extinguished, houses asleep. Katja had him by the arm, propelling him onward.

'Where are we going?' he demanded. He was growing cold beyond the capacity for rational thought: paranoid delusions bombarded his consciousness. This was a bad idea. He was being led again; he didn't want to be here. He had fallen into the clutches of a Scandinavian serial-killer. The papers might call her the Ice Queen. She would let him freeze to death and make a sculpture out of him. He'd be an angel...

'My place. We're almost there.'

They turned into another silent street. Squat, matching houses faced each other in dozing rows, blind with blinds. Katja led him up a few steps to the front door of one of them and fumbled with the lock, hands made clumsy by gloves.

'Shh,' she whispered, putting a finger to her lips. 'Don't wake my parents.'

'Your parents?' Damon hissed. 'Jesus Christ.'

The door clicked open. Damon shuddered in a momentary combination of guilt and panic before biting his lip and following her inside.

Inside was like a tropical glasshouse. Warmth engulfed him, confusing his frozen nerve endings. His shivering subsided slowly. They tiptoed down the hall, past doors sealed with slumber, into Katja's room.

She had a fireplace, radiating fierce heat from its tiny metropolis of cinders. She tossed a few fresh logs into it; when they had caught, she stood up and took off her clothes. Jacket, shirt, skirt, bra, stockings and panties surrounded her feet like the base of a statue. Her nipples, erect from the cold, gradually softened against her breasts. Damon thought: aureoles. Her body glowed orange as the flames leapt; the shadow of her pubic hair played across her thigh in a dark, dancing tuft. She was slim, almost skinny, almost angular. But stunning. She came towards him.

Damon thought: what am I doing? She pushed off his jacket, unbuttoned his shirt, slid her fingers across his chest. His jeans were shrinking, too tight; she unzipped them and let them fall to the ground. Underpants, jockey-style, too. She cupped his balls in her hand. Cold.

Damon felt his objectivity slip away. This was going too fast. He tried to understand what was happening. They were kissing. Lips. Teeth. Tongue. Words darted around his head, triggered like the nerves that were firing all over his body. Metallic tang of saliva. Muscles struggling to be free. Fragments, images: everything had become narration. Her mouth detached from his and sank down to his—what? Penis. Prick. Cock. Whang. So many words; a thesaurus. Some guys had pet names for theirs. One-eyed Jake. Old Feller. Clovis. It was his dick when he pissed through it; that was easy, no problem. But now it was transformed; a different thing entirely. He looked down at it, buried in Katja's mouth. He could feel her tongue teasing it. It was all he could feel; his entire being that single sensation, concentrated life.

He stepped backwards, back from the brink. Something was different; a subtle pressure. He was wearing a condom; somehow, she had managed to slip it on. Damon gaped at the prophylactic: she was good, a professional; he was out of his depth. No matter. She sat back on the rug and let her legs fall outward. He knelt on the ground, held her around the thighs and slipped his tongue into the cleft of her—this was even harder. This wasn't even his; he didn't know how to name it, couldn't think about it without a name. Not a vagina, medical, clinical, cold. Too warm for a vagina; too warm and wet. Too definite for abstracts like her womanhood, her sex. Too real. Not a pussy, stupid word, insulting. By no means a steaming damp slice of chocolate love cake. Perhaps a cunt, base word, no beating around the bush: frank, brutal, but at least not coy. Call a cunt a cunt. Break the taboo, diffuse its power. Right on. But these were all his words, English words: she might know them, but privately she would use her own. For something so intimate she would surely think in Finnish, or possibly Swedish, the other official language. She would probably even contemplate him with the same vocabulary, he realised. Sex had no single language. He had been transformed again. What was once his dick had become something else, something he couldn't even pronounce, bursting with umlauts and double consonants.

He broke off thinking about foreign tongues and concentrated on his own as it massaged her clitoris—not many words for that. She squirmed around him, clutching his hair, driving him into her, drowning him in gushing fluid. She came, gasping, giggling, pulling his head away and dragging him by the ears until their faces were level. They kissed again, desperate, angry, forgetting to breathe. Pubic hair tickled his—whatever it was—and, unable to wait longer, he slid it into her—whatever *that* was, skidding on the water-based lubricant and her own ejaculate.

Again he thought: what am I doing? What, exactly? He would have liked to be making love, loving, lovemaking. Lovers. But he hardly knew the girl; love was out of the question. Screwing sounded bad, euphemistic and at the same time distasteful. Bonking, shagging, rooting—merely comical. Maybe fucking, plain and simple. Again the taboo. Sex had never been so semantically confusing. But whatever they were doing, they did it completely, rolling over each other, thrusting, pausing and thrusting again with a rhythm that could have got them on MTV. At last Damon's body convulsed with orgasm and he collapsed against Katja, losing himself in her, thoughts finally laid to rest, mind filled with nothing. The world disappeared.

He woke to footsteps in the hallway. The fire had burned down to a dull glow, orange coals the only colour in the room. Grey light carved a windowframe out of the fading darkness. Katja was sleeping on his arm, clutching blankets around her. The door cracked open, spilling light across the floor; there was a sudden snap and he found himself blinking against an electric blaze, white-hot against his eyes.

A middle-aged woman, hair the colour of Katja's but flecked with grey, appeared in the doorway. She looked at Damon and frowned, more apologetic than outraged. She acknowledged him with what he hoped was a friendly nod.

'Hello,' he offered nervously.

'Ah! English! How are you?' she said amiably, then barked '*Katja!*' and let forth a stream of impenetrable Finnish. Katja stirred, buried her head in Damon's armpit and moaned incoherently, waving towards the door with one groping hand. Her mother gave a warning look and disappeared.

'What did she say?' Damon asked.

Katja looked up at him through blurry slits of eyes. 'She said I'd be late for school.'

Damon stared at her, then at the ceiling. 'Jesus Christ.'

Damon's spirits were high enough to survive even breakfast with Katja's parents. They were pleasant people, given the circumstances. Instead of chasing him out of their house with a meat cleaver, they had served him kippers. Damon sensed he was far from the first unexpected guest at Katja's breakfast table, and this was strangely comforting. While Katja was collecting her schoolbooks, her father gave his views on the European Union and Damon tried to follow the cartoon adventures of a boy and his stuffed tiger called *Lassi & Leevi* in the morning paper. He felt exhausted and elated: pleased with himself, enchanted with the world. Something had been exorcised from him, and he was at peace.

'What do you do for a living?' Katja's mother asked, making a friendly effort.

'I'm an actor,' he replied: a dangerously honest answer, though not to the question which had been asked. He ruminated on this consideration with a new clarity, a clarity which seemed to extend to everything. Yes, an actor. He was searching for the perfect role, one which he could make his own and become stereotyped in. He had not been assigned one yet, as most people had, but there was still time. Europe was his stage now. He smiled to himself.

His mood remained elevated as their paths diverged and she disappeared towards a cluster of her friends, schoolbag bouncing on her back. He felt a certain sadness at her departure, but he had her number and address in case of emotional emergency. He examined the scrawled note with some sentiment, turning it between his fingers for a minute before filing it in his wallet.

Fatigue began to take over as he reached the youth hostel. Gradually, all his thoughts became bogged down in exhaustion, sinking into a confused mire. The hostel was closing for the day. People drifted out of the stadium like aliens from a spaceship, blinking in the unfamiliar terrain. He almost ran into Roger.

'Mate, what happened to you last night?' the Englishman demanded.

Damon prepared to boast, to say something impressive about his conquest, but he couldn't find the words. 'I don't know,' he admitted.

Perry bounced through the doorway and stopped before Damon. 'Hey, Australian buddy!' he said. 'We're being tourists today. You coming?'

Damon had the sensation of waking from a dream and finding a bleak reality. A cold emptiness was emerging from the fatigue. Something hard was building in his chest, something bewildering settling over his senses. 'Sure, whatever,' he said uncertainly.

Tourist tram 3T rattled the scenic route through a crumbling world. Damon watched Helsinki slide past the windows and felt a growing depression stifle the spirits from him. The weather had turned again, flicking angry clouds across the sky. Grey light lingered like a half-completed dawn. She was out there, somewhere in the city—and *she* was out there, further away, somewhere on the continent. He would never see either of them again—a reflection which filled him with equal degrees but varying strains of pain. He had done each of them a disservice; each of them, and himself as well. The old uncertainty was resurfacing, asserting its dominance, forgotten for less than a day and then not entirely. He wondered what he had been thinking. He wondered what he was thinking now. Losing it.

Roger dragged them off the tram outside the Temppeliaukio church, a modern cathedral rough-hewn into the rock. The interior walls were hidden in shadow and scarred with the efforts of excavation. Candles glittered across the sprawling cavern, flickering in the air-conditioning. An immense silence stifled the footsteps of visitors and the sound of outside traffic, insulating the church with a combination of reverence and rock. The faint strains of piped choral music wafted through the foyer, fading away before they reached the main chamber.

Penitents and tourists alike dotted the pews, sitting in quiet awe of God or architect. Damon stood in the aisle, watching the blazing altar, and felt memories stirring within him. Memories of Sunday School, imposed by parents doing the right thing, as always. Hypocritical faith, abandoned but never entirely forgotten. Predisposed to guilt, he seized upon these primordial anxieties, rejecting them too late. Forgive me, Father, for I have—no, fuck *off*. He felt momentarily uncomfortable about swearing in a church, blaspheming mentally, but once he had started he couldn't stop. Fuck fuck fuck. Jesus fucking Christ. Dickhead. Fucking dickhead. Cheap. Nasty. Empty. Fuck. Empty fuck. Head-fuck. Fuck fuck fuck. The word was losing its meaning. It was no more than a sound, a syllable, the bark of an animal. Its perverse pleasure was vanishing; the pleasure of the word and the deed and the memory of the deed were tarnishing and turning to shit in front of him. Father forgive me.

There was no sunset, only a gradual darkening of the murky air. Distant rumblings rolled across the sky, and the stiff breeze disintegrated into a turmoil of wind and rain, lashing the Olympic tower until its walls bled with chaotic rivulets. The clouds swirled like oil paints in water.

'Is this safe?' Damon shouted, panting as the last few steps sucked the breath from his lungs.

'Safe?' Perry cried back at him. 'It's spectacular!'

'What about lightning?'

'Count on it!'

They reached the top of the tower and slumped against the concrete barrier. The world was closing in again. Clouds crept towards the blind lighthouse and heaved massively past, trailing thunderous wakes. Damon and Perry looked out onto nothing: the city was buried in mist, suburbs in muddy greenery. The rain was thick and heavy, exploding where it hit the concrete. Soon they were soaked.

'I don't understand you, man,' Perry said, dripping back into the tower. 'It's like, every five minutes you're a different person. You're happy, then you're miserable, and now you're just plain weird. What's with you?'

'I'm in a transitional period,' Damon said, joining him in the shelter.

'Life is a transitional period,' Perry said. 'Deal with it.'

'I'm dealing with it,' Damon said. 'At least, I'm trying. It's just—'

A flashbulb of lightning blinked through the darkness. The wind howled for a few seconds before the thunder came. Damon closed his mouth.

'Yesterday you were dealing with it,' Perry said. 'Today you're a mess. What happened?'

'I fucked up,' Damon said, tipping his head against the wall. 'Big time. Jesus, I hate one-night stands. They're like drugs, you know: you feel good for a while, forget your worries, but when you come down it's worse than before.'

Perry frowned. 'What exactly are your worries?'

Damon stared at the ceiling. 'You know that thing I lost back in Copenhagen?'

Perry nodded.

'I can't get it out of my head.'

A double flash exploded around them as a fork of lightning twisted across the sky. The earth was booming sheet metal, fading away in a slow decay.

'I'll tell you this,' Perry said thoughtfully. 'Life moves fast. It fucking rips along. You know how fast the planet's spinning? Fast. Atoms, electrons, they're not just sitting there. They're spinning too, vibrating; they're all over the place. Everything is moving, all the time—your life is a runaway train, man. So what you're trying to do is bad shit. You're trying hold onto something, trying your hardest. But life carries you along so fast, if you hold onto anything, *anything*, it'll tear you in two. That's the only thing that can happen. Rip your fucking arms off. You're on the train, bleeding, and your arms are left dangling on the station, gripping this thing because you were too stubborn to let go. Not a pretty picture, is it?'

'No,' said Damon, clutching his shoulders unhappily.

'No,' Perry agreed. 'It's a girl, right?'

'Yeah,' Damon admitted.

'Of course it is. You dumb asshole. What are you doing to yourself? You're travelling, man! You're supposed to be having the time of your life. What's with this moping teenage shit?'

Damon shrugged. 'I dunno, man. This girl is just—'

Perry waved him into silence. 'I'm sure she is. But you can't be concerned about this shit at this time in your life. This could be a period of great personal development for you; you could be on the way to sanity. Don't fuck yourself up like this.'

Damon scowled at him. 'When did you get so preachy? Didn't you ever get messed up over a woman?'

'Plenty of times, back home. But we're beyond all that now. There's more to life.'

'It's hard for me, you know,' Damon said. 'Maybe I'm not fucking perfect in all situations. Maybe I don't ever know what I should be doing. Maybe I'm sick of people telling me who I am. Maybe I want to figure it out for myself.'

'Now you're talking,' Perry said. 'That's what you should be doing.'

'But maybe I don't want to,' Damon said. 'Maybe I don't even want to look. What if there's nothing there?'

'Whatever,' Perry said. 'Either way. It's not about whether you get laid or find some girl or another. Like I'm telling you, there's more to life.'

'More to life,' Damon repeated. 'Well, sure, I suppose.'

Night had fallen, but the sky was flashing in the electric storm. Perry's face strobed into occasional view, frozen in momentary illumination. Its pale afterimage floated before Damon's eyes like a sacred vision, omniscient, wise. An oracle. The thunder was continuous, too loud to talk over. Wind tore at the tower as if trying to teach it a lesson about hubris. And the rain kept falling, hurling itself towards the ground, a deluge to douse the flames of hell.

'More to life!' Damon cried through the chaos. A bolt of fire reached down and grasped the tower's lightning rod in its electric fist, holding on for a split second, connecting earth and sky in a white-hot thread. The air crackled and Damon felt his hair separate. The tower exploded in a deafening clamour, walls shaking with the din. The discharge tore its way towards the ground and earthed itself; the lightning released its grip and disappeared. Damon grinned in the afterglow, baring his teeth, holding his hands above his head.

'More!' he shouted, then: 'To life!'

The *Konstantin Simonov* dominated Helsinki harbour in the late afternoon. A few rays of early sunset stabbed through the clouds, catching the hammer and sickle painted on the turret and igniting it against its crimson background. Semi-trailers and petrol tankers clustered around the ship like soldier ants servicing their queen. Radio gear jangled above the deck in a cat's cradle of technology, and red lifeboats hung reassuringly from the sides. It was a normal sea-going vessel, sharp-hulled and broad-beamed, with nothing to distinguish it but the old Russian insignia not yet repainted. But it carried with it enough psychology to transform it into a kind of alien craft, conduit to another world.

The travellers filed past an inattentive official and waved their tickets at him: Denis first, Martina and Max, Perry, Damon, and finally Roger. The Germans carried a pannier bag in each hand, having left their bikes in storage at the terminal. The others lugged their backpacks up the gangplank and into the space between East and West.

Some time travel was evidently involved in the transition: the interior of the ship seemed to have settled firmly in the seventies and saw no reason to budge from those happy, tasteless days. There was zebra-printed carpet over the walls and floor, and everything else was mirrors and dull brass. A man in a tuxedo was wending his wide-lapelled way through the overstuffed lounge bar with a tray full of champaska flutes, whispered to be complimentary. Each of the travellers took one, grumbling about the surprise fifteen-markka gratuity but paying it anyway before descending into the cabins in the belly of the ship.

The sleeping quarters were small but comfortable. The zebra print stopped at the door, and the bunks were dressed in a more restful beige. Each room had three beds and an ensuite, ample wardrobe space and a list of emergency procedures translated humorously into eight languages. Damon dropped his pack onto the floor of the cabin he was sharing with Perry and Roger. Home.

They passed a few other passengers on the way back up to the lounge, but the boat was obviously underfilled. A few middle-aged couples, fat and American, pushed past them. A frail-looking old woman smiled charmingly as she dragged her suitcase behind her. There were a few youths in college football jackets, variations on the Tonsil theme.

Damon's stomach turned over at the sight of the face he had been seeing everywhere. A dark figure appeared in his peripheral vision, an outline of fine black hair. He turned, startled, and saw again the same pale eyes, fair skin, chiselled cheeks, features he had seen a thousand times wherever he went, wherever he looked. She was here again, following him, wouldn't leave him alone.

But this time it really was Stacy.

1	Een
2	Twee
3	Tre
4	Fire
5	Viisi
6	**Шесть**

Stacy stared at him. She had more than half-expected to see him, but she had never stopped to consider what she would say to him, and now she had no idea. He looked different—but then he always did. His hair was ruffled and dull, and he was wearing a ridiculous green arctic jacket made of some space-age fabric, something-*tex*™. Daggy, in a word. But appealing with it, perhaps less contrived than before. He stood there looking shocked and daggy, surrounded by people who were apparently his friends. She searched for the right thing to say, something that would ease them back into a rapport more comfortable than this strange silence.

Eventually he saved her the trouble. 'Where have you been?' he said.

'Me?' She laughed airily. 'Hell and back.'

Damon frowned. 'What?'

She smiled, groped for an explanation, and finally waved it away. 'Forget it,' she said. 'I'm sorry to disappear so suddenly. I just had some things to work out.'

Damon remained unsatisfied. 'What sort of things?' he demanded.

'Just things.'

'But—'

'You know, Damon,' one of his friends interrupted, diverting his attention. 'Things.'

Stacy turned gratefully to her new ally. He was tall and tanned, with hair that clung loosely to his scalp without any attempt at style. His eyes were clear and blue: honest eyes. There was a red maple leaf on his shoulder.

'Things,' she agreed.

He grinned and shot her an expression of instant understanding. She lowered her eyes, taken aback. There was something about him, revealed in that glance, something she didn't even want to start thinking about.

Instead she asked, 'Why do all Canadians wear flags on themselves?'

He smirked. 'So people don't mistake us for Americans.'

A large and slightly scary-looking man turned to him and boomed 'Hey! Watch it!' through a thick black beard.

The Canadian looked contrite. 'No offence, Denis, man. Vermonters are pretty cool. You're almost on the right side of the border, after all. Texans are the ones you have to look out for—anyone from the south, really. Californians, too—if I hear any more deadbeats saying they left the States to come find themselves, *man*, I'll smack their hippy heads in.'

Damon winced.

'What about New Yorkers?' Stacy asked.

'New York New Yorkers? Apart from being completely fucking insane, they're quite funny. It's the way they talk. Any psychosis is hilarious in a Brooklyn accent.'

'Upstate New Yorkers?'

'Never met one.'

'You have now.' Stacy extended her hand. 'I'm Stacy.'

'Perry,' said the Canadian. A strange warmth flowed from his hand as it enclosed hers.

Damon jerked out of his stasis and introduced the others. A klaxon blared and a crackling voice on the PA announced that they were pulling away from the wharf. The floor trembled beneath them as the ship's engines geared massively into action. The vibration subsided and the boat slid away from the harbour and into the Baltic Sea, ambassador to a disintegrating empire.

The crew of the *Konstantin Simonov* had evidently been selected for more than their ability to batten down hatches and swab things. Economic rationalisation and necessary multi-skilling had bred a unique race of deckhand-entertainers. As the ship ploughed through the choppy grey waters, the director of entertainment—a roly-poly Swede by the name of Stig who was probably also the captain—compered a gala evening of variety acts in the club lounge. Stig aside, the crew were entirely Russian, and their traditions shaped the performances. The stewards hurled themselves into an energetic Cossack dance, kicking their red-booted feet beneath folded arms with a gusto not normally found in cabin personnel. Stewardesses and waitresses danced in ethereal circles, dressed in white gowns and pointed hats. The cook sang ballads from his homeland, clutching his ample gut and wailing the pain of a country lost. Someone in a white uniform—three stripes, whatever that meant in Russian: possibly a radio operator, equally likely a meatball-taster—plucked an acoustic guitar. But the highlight of the evening was when Stig himself swapped his emcee's microphone for that of silver-tongued crooner. The band—mechanics and technicians—struck up a seductive Russian waltz, sliding from beat to beat with the slick rhythm of a conductor's baton between peaks.

Stacy felt the music draw her into its enchanting folds. She felt something unfamiliar about it, her Western ears unaccustomed to its peculiar system of tension and resolution, its differing treatment of majors and minors. But it reached out to her with the stretching fingers of its staves, gripping her imagination with a strange sense of fellowship. Perhaps this was the music of her blood, buried by a lifetime of rock and roll but somehow embedded in her genes. Perhaps her mother, mourning the forgotten sounds of her country, had sung these plaintive tunes over her cradle. Or perhaps music transcended culture; perhaps it was universal. Perhaps what she saw as a familiar difference was merely unexpected similarity.

Stig began to sing in Russian, breaking off in English to urge everyone to get up and dance to his accompaniment. Stony-faced middle-agers responded to his encouragement by looking in the other direction. Stacy felt a nudge at her shoulder.

'How about it?' Damon said, gesturing towards the dance floor. Stig noticed his invitation and nodded persuasively at her. She relented, drawn by the music. Damon took her hand—his was slightly clammy—and led her onto the linoleum. Stig sang with additional fervour, inspired by their response. Damon lay his hand delicately on her hip and seemed surprised when she directed him backwards.

'I'll lead,' he offered.

'Sorry,' Stacy said, realising her presumption. 'I never danced with a guy who could dance before.'

He smiled at her, pleased. With some effort she relinquished her control and allowed herself to be led: not so much by him—his direction was subtle, unobtrusive—but by the rhythm, which slowed and lulled the fever pitch of her mind.

One, two, three...

She stared past him, feeling his breath on her neck. His hand was growing more confident on her waist, reaching further, spreading his fingers, adjusting the pressure. His other hand was warm in hers, a little sweaty. She wondered: could he be...

Een, twee, drie...

She thought back to the last time they had been together. Canal. Train. Mermaid. Photographs: he'd said he was an artist, a good excuse, but she didn't really believe it. And if not, then why did he seem so...

En, to, tre...

Her mind shied away. He was just friendly, a friendly traveller who took photos of people because photos without people were dull as a tourist map. Friendly, nothing more. And if there was more then she would ignore it; she had to ignore it, it was too soon, too soon...

Yksi, kaksi, kolme...

But the music kept playing, dragging her thoughts away from her, carrying them on its trills and flourishes. Stig sang on, filling her mind with a language she knew everything about except for the words, replacing her English worries with Russian peace. And Damon kept dancing, guiding her without her realising until their bodies moved together as one, dancing like a graceful four-legged creature: a stag, a fleet gazelle, a prowling leopard. Or—more likely—Misha the Russian bear, lumbering on all fours...

Один, два, три...

She drew back and looked at his face. An expression of deep concentration had embedded itself into his features, and his mouth moved fractionally. He was counting too, flicking his tongue against his teeth in half-formed consonants. She smiled at him, feeling confident. He noticed her stare, looked puzzled and said, 'What?'

One, two, three...

'Nothing,' she said. 'Thank you, this is nice.'

He beamed at her. 'Yes. Thank *you*.'

Dum, da, da...

She returned her head to his shoulder; their bodies nestled together, dovetailed perfectly as they swayed in circles. He tipped his face against hers, cheek to cheek, mouth to ear.

'Where did you disappear to?' he asked softly.

Hell and back...

She tensed only slightly. Unexpectedly, the words were coming—coming easily, easily as the music flowing through her body, no longer sticking in her throat.

'I went to Norway,' she said. 'Right up north. Then through the top of Sweden, along the Arctic circle, over the Gulf and back down again. There wasn't much there. Just ice and snow and...'

*Mem*ory...

'...And little towns boarded up for the winter. But it was nice, you know. Beautiful, unbelievably beautiful, in a lonely sort of way. And there were a few things I had to sort out, things to think about...'

Death.

The rhythm vanished in mid-beat and she found her feet tripping over each other. Damon trod on her misplaced toes and sent a wake-up bolt of pain through her spinal cord and into her brain. She struggled to regain her poise.

One, two, three...

'Coming back was the weird part. You know, after so long in the middle of nowhere, Helsinki's an incredible place. It's like this ice palace on the edge of the wasteland, big and glittery and hi-tech. It's totally unexpected when you find it; you're never sure whether it's Vegas in the desert or just a mirage.'

Xanadu...

'Well, it's good to see you again,' Damon said, too nonchalant. The music finished with a single percussion and the audience clapped. Stacy turned and bowed; Damon saw her and curtsied obligingly.

'Can you also dance a polka?' Stig asked them as the band tore into a new tune. Damon shook his head in defeat and sloped back to his seat, where Roger slapped him on the back. Perry looked at Stacy with that twinkle of recognition. She wondered what he knew. Stig started singing again and a few of the older couples got up to polka. Stacy felt the boat crashing through black waves, felt Russia looming ever nearer, and felt the expectation of tomorrow overwhelm the experience of tonight.

The asphalt of Morskoi Vokzal tingled beneath her feet as she stepped off the gangway and into Russia. She felt like saying something momentous before touching down on this alien terrain: *one small step for a woman,* something like that. But there was nobody around to hear her. The wharf was deserted, an empty expanse with an entry terminal in one distant corner. Sleeping gantries snagged the low clouds drifting up the gulf, and an early hydrofoil skipped across the grey water. A few distant fishermen dangled lines off the embankment, stick figures in the morning light. Apart from that, nothing. No fanfare. No

Welcome home, Anastasia—welcome to the fatherland. Curious. She tried to evaluate her relationship with the country. It wasn't home, of course, but then where was? It was surely as much her home as anywhere. And yet she saw immediately that in this place she was a stranger. Even with nobody around, she felt conspicuous. She was, after all, an American in Russia, historically not a popular thing to be. She wore expensive jeans and air-cushioned shoes, and at home she watched cable TV. She felt like a visitor from Disneyland. There would be no welcoming committee—why should she expect to be welcomed here?

As it turned out, the welcoming committee was hidden on the other side of the terminal. Having exchanged ten dollars for a ridiculous number of rubles and getting her passport stamped unnecessarily, she led the ship's passengers out of the building and towards the tour bus. Immediately she was surrounded by a throng of entrepreneurial locals, mostly children, thrusting rabbit hats and Babushka dolls and military badges in her face, shouting 'One dollar! Two dollar! Five dollar!' in their strange, familiar accents, tugging at her clothes. She struggled through them, bewildered, and clambered onto the minibus. When the other travellers arrived, Denis was wearing a rabbit hat and grinning like Rasputin. Martina smiled with an air of satisfaction, as if she had won some ongoing competition.

Damon and Perry were the last to get onto the bus. Damon climbed on backwards, looking around him with an expression of profound awe. Stacy felt faintly irritated that someone else should be as affected by the experience as she was. What right did he have? But he seemed keen to share his enthusiasm with her; as he walked past on his way to an empty seat, he smiled at her with such glowing and involuntary excitement that she forgot her resentment.

A young man with pale skin and dark hair stood up beside the driver as the bus ploughed its way through the receding group of black-marketeers.

'Good morning!' he shouted cheerily. 'My name is Alex! I am a student here in St Petersburg. I am also your tour guide. Here is a tip! The most useful words you can know as tourists here are the words: *nyet, sbaceba.* That means, *no, thank you!* When someone tries to sell you a hat and you don't want a hat, say to them: *nyet, sbaceba!* If anyone offers to exchange money for you, you should always say *nyet, sbaceba!* Or they will rip you off. If a beggar asks you for money, it may sound a little strange to say *nyet, sbaceba!* But he will know what you mean. If you are in a bad mood, you may simply say *nyet! No!* But it is best to be polite.'

Nobody was listening much to Alex. Everyone was too busy looking out of the windows, catching their first glimpses of the new world. Autumn trees lined the roads, speckling the grey morning with red and golden leaves. Metal statues flicked past: proud rulers, rearing horses, proud rulers on rearing horses. Many of the buildings were predictably grey, but more of them were painted in pastel colours, red and blue and green. Russians jaywalked and rode bicycles and drove Skodas along the streets, looking like ordinary people.

'I will tell you a story!' Alex promised. 'There is a story people used to tell here. An old man lived in the same city for all of his life. People asked him: where were you born? He said: I was born in St Petersburg. They asked him: where did you grow up? He said: I grew up in Petrograd. They asked: where do you live now? He said: I live in Leningrad. Then the people asked him: where would you like to die? And the old man replied: more than anything, I would like to die in St Petersburg.'

A few of the tourists looked confused, but a ripple of appreciative laughter made its way through the bus nonetheless. Stacy thought she had never heard anything so beautiful.

'The old man got his wish!' Alex continued triumphantly. 'We have our name back!'

A number of people cheered. The bus wheezed to a halt outside the St Isaac's cathedral, and the passengers filed out to look dutifully at the huge stone church. Saints and angels teetered along the roof, blessing the tourists below. A bas-relief engraving sprawled across the portico, balanced on thick columns. The gold-plated dome shone dully beneath the thinning clouds.

'The view from the dome is wonderful!' Alex advised.

'Climb up and look out over the city. Keep an eye out for Nevsky Prospekt, the main street, and the River Neva.'

Stacy hung back as the others disappeared into the cathedral.

'Coming?' Perry prompted.

'I don't like heights,' she said, stepping nervously back from the entrance as if afraid the gaping hole would suck her in like a tornado and whisk her high into the air.

Perry raised his eyebrows and said, 'Well, okay, if you're sure.'

'I'm sure,' Stacy said. She turned and walked away from the church, striding through a park and across a road, coming to a halt beside the statue of someone sitting straight-backed on a charging horse, frozen in mid-gallop. Opaque streetlights clustered together, four to a pole like wrought-iron Hydras.

Stacy turned back towards the cathedral. Three more tour buses had arrived: serious ones this time, like Greyhound coaches. They looked faintly ridiculous, dwarfed by the imposing architecture. The tourists who piled out of them looked even sillier as they milled around the daunting structure, searing it with flashbulbs too feeble to illuminate even a quarter of its sombre face. The black-marketeers were also out in force, arriving out of nowhere. A lot of the tourists seemed to be biting. Damon appeared between the columns and stopped when he saw the tour buses. His scowl of disapproval was discernible even from Stacy's distance.

'This sucks,' he complained as the minibus clattered away again. 'I didn't come here to see fat tourists with bum-bags and Nikons. I can see them at home.'

Alex seemed to recognise his complaint. 'I will tell you a secret!' he confided loudly. 'As you well know, it is officially illegal for you to leave the tour group! But if you were to somehow get lost and miss the bus—I can tell you that the next stop would be the best place to do it! As long as you promise me not to overthrow the Russian government, I will tell nobody. And the authorities are usually too busy trying to stop the economy from collapsing to worry if you wander around on your own. Of course, if you get caught, you heard none of this from me!'

They needed no more encouragement.

Nevsky Prospekt carved a wide canyon through downtown St Petersburg. Nothing in the city was allowed to be taller than the spire of the St Peter and Paul Fortress, so the buildings tended to reach communally towards this respectful ceiling and level off at the same height. There were no skyscrapers; everything was squat and broad, oversized bricks lining the streets. Distinction was maintained by the unique variation of colour schemes: here a pale blue building, there a pastel green, and over there a facade as red as a pun about communism.

The street was packed with people, jamming the sidewalks, stopping in shop doorways, waiting to brave the traffic and cross the road. No tourists here: the tourists were off being whisked between monuments. The only tourists were Stacy and Damon and his friends. Everyone else was a Russian. The distinction slapped Stacy in the face wherever she looked. Everyone else had the same shaggy haircut, the same ill-fitting clothes, the same sombre expression. She felt herself being picked out by a social spotlight, blinking against its stark glare. Her clothes were new and not grey. Max wore shorts despite the cold. Perry had a moderate tan. They were all looking at things other than their own feet. Irreconcilable differences.

Electric buses crawled up the street, groping their power cables like lumbering blind giants. Rusty cars wove between them, functional Skodas with no mufflers. And crumbling trucks jarred from pothole to pothole, wheels bare of hubcaps and suspension, looking like they belonged on a farm or army barracks but somehow appearing right at home on this, the city's busiest street. Everything was old and run-down. Nothing mechanical worked properly; every artifact was defective. Nothing existed in its own right: all were mere imitations, failed attempts to duplicate something efficient and capitalist. It was the West through a shadowy mirror, confusing what it reflected, getting everything the wrong way around. Only the buildings retained their perfection: breathtaking structures, remnants of a prosperous, other Russia which had erected ornate monuments to itself and maintained them while its people starved. But even the buildings seemed ethereal, insubstantial, mirages which could disappear at any moment. The Russia they represented no longer existed. They were not real. Real were the fake Levi's, disguised behind names like *Live's* or *Livins*. Real in their own way. The bottles of Russian Pepsi, Пепси , mixed with the bacterial local water—they were real. The factories spewing out thousands of shoes with the heels on the wrong end: real. Real were the hairline fractures splitting the country apart minutely but surely.

'Goddamn!' Denis cried, emerging from a department store. 'Look what I just bought!'

He pulled the brown paper off the package he was holding. It was a clock, about the size of his substantial head. A spinning pendulum twisted frantically in its glass cabinet, and the hands ticked lazily. It was beautiful, ornate, marble and gold. The numbers were Roman.

'Five bucks!' he shouted. 'I paid five bucks for this thing. It would take a Russian a month to save up for this. It was the only thing left in the shop!'

'Bloody hell,' Roger said. 'I want one. We'll have to find another shop.'

None of the other stores seemed to carry clocks. Some had a few coats and shoes which looked second-hand. One had a fair assortment of stationery sets. Quite a few sold a lot of things nobody could quite identify. It was probable that the storeowners didn't know what they were either; they stocked them because they were available, and people would buy them because there wasn't anything else to buy. There didn't seem to be much food anywhere; probably the food was sold in occasional markets away from the city centre. Today potatoes, tomorrow turnips, perhaps next week a surprise shipment of bananas. From the look of the shops it appeared that the three-year siege of World War II had returned. And yet the people seemed adequately nourished. Somehow they got by. Their existence would never be as simple as dropping in to the corner store for milk or strawberries or oven-cleaner or frozen Coke at three in the morning. But with a little foresight, the right contacts and a certain degree of luck, they seemed to do all right.

The travellers stopped at a bookshop selling posters of communist propaganda and what looked like MiG blueprints, a few cents each. One depicted a space shuttle with the CCCP emblem on its wing. Stacy wondered if NASA knew anything about it. The poster probably counted as a military secret which she wouldn't be able to take out of the country. She bought it anyway.

They spent a while longer browsing the blank shelves of State department stores. But the strength of St Petersburg was clearly not in its shopping opportunities. There wasn't even a duty-free. Rodeo Drive, yes. Champs-Elysees, *oui*. Nevsky Prospekt, *nyet, sbaceba.*

Museums were what the city did well, and the Hermitage was probably the finest anywhere. It sprawled by the top end of Nevsky Prospekt, in the Winter Palace, beyond the concrete wasteland of the Palace Square. *Square* was probably the wrong word; it was more a vast rectangle, pregnant with a bulging pentagon. *Square* also understated the immensity of the area between the palace's opposite facades—one green, one yellow, both three storeys high and immeasurably wide, defying perspective as they stretched along what was not a square but something more awe-inspiring, a *ploschad.* The *ploschad* was like an abandoned carpark for aeroplanes, cross-hatched in white; without the Nelsonesque column in the middle it would have made an ideal landing spot for the apocryphal Russian space shuttle whose image lay curled in Stacy's daypack.

The buildings themselves were equally gigantic, perforated with grand windows and ridged with columns. An army of statues stood sentinel along the main roof, gazing into the square as if their awe had frozen them in green copper. Half-buried windows peeked out onto the concrete; there was no telling how deep the gargantuan foundations lay. Such opulence; such baroque excess. An enduring display of wealth in a bankrupt country. Stacy wondered what stopped the hungry citizens from hacking gold from the roof, now that the czars had gone. Civic pride or fear. The hypocrisy sickened her. She hadn't seen a city of such glaring contradictions since—well, since New York.

'This is incredible,' Roger said, spinning around as if unable to decide where to look. 'Look at this! Are you looking at this?'

'Trying,' Damon said. 'It's just... huge. Imagine living here.'

Denis whistled. 'That's monarchy for you,' he said. 'Love it or hate it, it leaves behind damn big buildings.'

The interior of the Hermitage was no less impressive. Acres of floor, tiled with intricate designs, stretched through a thousand lavish rooms. Chandeliers clung to the ceiling; burnished staircases linked the levels. It was a place to get lost in, lost among two *million* of the world's finest artworks: framed landscapes like magic windows, statues like Medusa's victims, a cluttered pawn shop of assorted still-lifes, a city's population in portraits. The group quickly fragmented, following their individual tastes through the glittering labyrinth. Occasionally they spotted each other from opposite ends of corridors, catching glimpses as they disappeared between statues. Roger and Damon tended to adopt the classic art-gallery pose, one foot forward, arms crossed, expression serious and intense. Perry stood with his hands in his pockets, rocking on the balls of his feet as he admired a painting. Denis, Max and Martina went straight for volume, cruising the halls in a swift triad, glancing at everything, halted by nothing.

Stacy wandered between paintings until she found a picture of herself. She stopped, intrigued, and peered at the canvas. A young girl sat under a tree in a snowfield, knees drawn up in a foetal position. A plate on the wall identified the piece as *Winter Death* by Vlad Androvitch. The title sent a chill through her—but it was the image that had claimed her, not the name. She looked closer. The girl was ten, maybe twelve, but her hair was grey. Closer. The hair was made of clouds, pearling and eddying around her head in tiny detail. The tree was a black skeleton, stripped by the winter. Closer. Darker patches for eyes, a grinning jaw: hooded Death. Death reached for the grey-haired girl, clutching at her with its gnarled branches, clasping her to its crippled trunk. Pools of sunset flooded the snow, red as blood. Closer. The sun was red, but not setting: it was still high in the sky, cold, old, a sun near death. Most of the painting was rough, sketchy, painted in broad and apparently careless strokes. But areas of intricate rendering focussed the chaos in places: the cloudy hair, the cold sun, the bony face in the tree. And the girl was definitely Stacy, huddled by a pool of blood in the cold shadow of Death.

She looked back to the information plate. Oil on canvas. A Russian artist, active during the 1920s and working mostly in Minsk. Part of a narrow revivalist movement calling itself...

'Hey, Damon,' she called. 'Take a look at this.'

Damon melted out of his art-critic's posture and detached himself from the reclining nude who had been staring at him. He wandered across the hall and looked at the picture of Stacy.

'Creepy,' he evaluated. 'Still, Russia's probably not the cheeriest place in winter.'

'Do you know this guy?' Stacy asked. 'He's a Neo-Neo-Impressionist. Just like you.'

'Just like me,' Damon echoed distantly as he scanned the placard. 'Well, no, I don't know him individually, only as part of the movement.'

'But this isn't what you said,' Stacy protested. The emotion of the painting had infected her. 'This is what *I* said. You said, don't look beneath the surface, just give an impression. But look at this—this is all wrong. This is deep; it's layered. She's got a cloud on her head! And look at the tree!'

'Yes,' Damon agreed, frowning. 'You know what? I don't think this is Neo-Neo-Impressionism at all. That must be a mistranslation: what we've got here is actually Post-Post-Impressionism.'

Stacy looked at him. 'What? What's the difference?'

'All the difference in the world,' Damon said sagely.

'But look at this, in the original Russian,' Stacy said, indicating the top half of the information plate. 'I know what Cyrillic sounds like. This word, this means Impressionist. And before that, that definitely means Neo-Neo. It can't be Post-Post; there's no P in it. Pi means P, everyone knows that. And there's no pi.'

Damon ignored her. 'This is really interesting. A Post-Post-Impressionist!' He took a piece of paper from his wallet and a ball-point pen from his pocket. 'Androvitch,' he mused, writing down the name. 'Vlad Androvitch.'

'You're making all this up, aren't you?'

'Of course I'm not. Look, it's clearly Impressionist at its heart. Look at the brushwork, there, and—there.'

He pointed the pen at various parts of the canvas by way of illustration. An explosion of angry Russian sounded behind him: a roar studded with nasal vowels and guttural consonants. Damon kept pointing.

'And there, see? The only difference is these bits here, the symbolism.'

He waved the pen in a quick arc. The Russian roar soared to a hysterical pitch and swooped upon him like a squealing tornado. A squat woman with angry eyebrows and an official-looking badge seized him by the elbow and spun him around to face her so she could shout at him some more. She stuck her hands indignantly into her hips, removing them only to wave emphatically with outstretched palms and clenched fists. Damon stood there looking utterly confused as she continued her incomprehensible tirade. She pointed at his pen and reached up to snatch it from him; he snapped it away from her grasp and clumsily stuffed it back into his pocket. For some reason she seemed satisfied by this gesture; her ferocity gradually abated and she walked harrumphing back to her attendant's chair, looking over her shoulder to glare at him. Damon turned to Stacy in dismay.

'What?' he said. 'Can't you write down the names of painters here? What's the big deal?'

Stacy looked bewildered. A young man with white-blond hair and a Slavic face approached them with a helpful expression.

'She thought you would draw on the painting,' he explained in a Russian accent which, curiously, had a tinge of Brooklyn to it.

'Draw on the painting?' Damon protested. 'Why would I draw on the painting? What sort of Philistine does she think I am?'

The man shrugged. 'People here are suspicious of foreigners. Where are you from?'

Damon and Stacy introduced themselves.

'Ah, New York,' the man said. 'I have studied there, in Manhattan. I like it very much. I am Andrei.'

'Hi,' they told him.

'But—Stasi,' he said. 'A Russian name, yes?'

Stacy nodded. 'My parents are from Kiev.'

Andrei beamed. 'Wonderful Kiev! I have never been there. But this is a large country.'

'It's incredible,' Damon said. 'I've never seen anything like it. I love it here.'

Andrei looked at Stacy. 'And you? This is your country. How do you find it?'

Stacy frowned. 'It's not my country,' she said. 'Not really. I thought it might be. But it isn't. And, I don't know, it's a strange place. I mean, all this is beautiful, mind-blowing, but outside there's so much ugliness. So many poor people.'

Andrei nodded thoughtfully. 'We have our problems. But it is the same everywhere. The strong are strong and the weak are not. It is the same in America: I have seen it. And the small people survive. If you know your way around, life is not too uncomfortable. We have art, as you can see. Great writers, poets. Our food is simple but there is usually enough. If you know where to look.'

'Maybe you can help us, then,' Damon suggested. 'Where should we go to eat?'

Andrei clutched his elbow and stroked his chin. 'You might have some trouble finding a place. Many people are resentful of foreigners; you are so much richer than we are. You may go to an empty restaurant and find that there are no seats available.'

'Damn,' Damon said. 'We've accidentally lost our tour group, so we don't really know what to do.'

Andrei looked thoughtful, flicking his eyes from side to side as if evaluating possibilities visible only to him. 'I will take you,' he decided. 'Yes?'

'Great!' Damon blurted. 'Thanks! Oh, man, lucky we found you.'

Stacy nodded her agreement. 'We have some friends,' she said. 'We'll have to wait for them.'

'Yes,' Andrei said. 'I have a friend too. Sergei. We will all go together.'

Sergei was as solid as Denis and had a blond crew-cut. He contrasted curiously with Andrei, who was thin and wiry with soft features. They were like a Soviet Abbott and Costello. Sergei understood a fair amount of English but spoke none.

'I am like a dog,' he said, translated through Andrei. 'I understand but cannot speak.'

The Russians led the travellers through the darkened streets—they had missed the White Nights by half a year—until they arrived at a nondescript door with some cyrillic characters carved above it. Andrei knocked loudly, then turned to smile reassuringly.

The door opened a fraction and a face appeared. Andrei greeted it in Russian and a brief exchange ensued. The face kept looking at the motley group and shaking its head. Andrei raised his voice and insisted. The face shouted back. The capitalists shuffled their feet and felt the precariousness of their future.

Eventually Andrei broke off and turned back to the group, huddling them together like a football team.

'He will feed us,' he said. 'But we will have to give him ten US dollars. I am afraid Sergei and I have none. Do you have ten dollars you can give?'

'Wait a minute,' Damon said. 'We have to bribe the guy, just so he'll let us into his restaurant? What sort of business sense does that make?'

Andrei shrugged. 'The food is good.'

The food was good. Nobody knew quite what it was: a soup of some kind, something with fish and potatoes in it, a dessert made of rice. Simple, solid, filling and flavoursome. The decor was rustic, wooden beams and candelabras, warm orange light flooding the restaurant. Cold, throat-burning vodka flowed freely, served in shot-glasses continuously replaced. There was no Pepsi.

'This is a nice place,' Martina evaluated. Andrei nodded appreciatively.

'It's very exclusive,' he said. 'The food is expensive. This meal will cost each of us half a week's salary.'

Roger looked particularly concerned. 'Half a week! I'm on a budget!'

'A Russian's salary,' Andrei reassured him. 'I believe that

comes to about a dollar with the current exchange rate. Less on the black market.'

'Unbelievable!' Denis said, raising his shot glass. 'Here's to socialism, that's what I say!'

Andrei and Sergei scowled. 'We have never had a socialist government in Russia. Not even true communism, true as Karl Marx intended. Here as everywhere we have the oppression of the weak by the strong, the poor by the rich. But here the strong and the rich are the State, which is supposed to be for the benefit of all we Russians, but is not and has never been. And the State's—what is the word?—instrumentalities grow as fat on our suffering as any Western tycoon. No, there has been no socialism. Only oppression.'

Andrei reached for his own glass and downed its contents angrily, grimacing as the vodka hit his dissident's throat. Denis looked apologetic.

'Well,' he said. 'Welcome to capitalism.'

Andrei's scowl deepened. 'We do not welcome capitalism!' he said fiercely. 'Not in the way it has been given to us. In the West you think Gorbachev is hero of the people, with his glasnost and his perestroika. But to many of us he is a villain, a despot. Now the queues are longer, inflation runs riot, there is less of everything and what there is we cannot afford. Have you seen the political babushka dolls they sell in the market? You will notice that it is Yeltsin, not Gorbachev but Boris Yeltsin, who is the biggest and outermost doll. Yeltsin covering and obscuring Gorbachev as he covers Brezhnev, Khrushchev, Stalin, Lenin. Our hero Misha has thrown the country into chaos, and it is Yeltsin who will lead us out. Or perhaps not even him, for in some circles even he is losing favour. Perhaps someone new will arrive to solve our problems and add another layer to the babushka doll. We have seen many false prophets here in Russia. You will forgive us if we do not fall at the feet of every new Messiah who comes our way.'

'Hey, we forgive you,' Perry said appeasingly. 'We might even go you one better. Guys, how about we thank Andrei and Sergei for finding us this place by paying for their meals? It's the least we can do.'

Everyone agreed instantly. Stacy looked at Perry in admiration.

'Good,' Perry said. 'Now let's quit talking politics and have some fun.'

Andrei and Sergei were so grateful that they called over the manager and persuaded him to sell them part of his store of vodka. The unlabelled bottles cost a dollar each and smelled like industrial solvent but were cold enough for it not to matter. The temperature outside was such that the alcohol had no chance to warm up as the group marched through the empty streets like a band of drunks.

The scenery ran together as they turned countless corners, ducked through unexpected alleys. Everywhere were balding trees, circled by fallen leaves like dandruff in the moonlight. Sharp iron railings guarding gardens, spears without sentries. Squares of grass bursting through the concrete. Statues and stern busts frowning with disapproval on vandalised pedestals. Streetlights far apart, blind or blinking, only a few orbs gazing steadily like the full moon peeking through the silver-edged clouds. Sidewalk cracks like a metaphor.

The city felt like a ruin. Stacy had no idea where they were, but they were the only ones there. She had a momentary vision of a Soviet ghost town, monuments toppled, pastel paint peeling, tumbleweeds rolling across the *ploschads*. It wasn't hard to imagine. The first sign of a crumbling empire, the deterioration of its nightlife. At one time the sun never set on the Soviet Union, but that was probably because there was nothing for it to do after dark. And now the night was seeping through the country's fissures, leaving its inhabitants and visitors cold and restless. Now is the winter of our discotheque.

But even empty streets come alive with friends and vodka. They walked, strode, lunged through the clammy night, sending the thin fog into confused spirals in their wake. They held the eerie silence at bay by shouting, laughing, shrieking at the top of their voices. They passed the vodka between them, swigging from the bottle and breaking off to roar silently, teary-eyed, breathing invisible fire from their throats.

Fairly soon they were singing. Sergei may have spoken no English but he sang it beautifully, chanting in a resounding baritone. Andrei harmonised in his reedy voice. They each sang their national anthems, stumbled through their repertoire of Beatles and Bob Dylan tunes, and knew they were drunk when they started to slur *The Rainbow Connection* from the Muppet Movie.

Stacy felt happy. Her singing voice improved with alcohol, although her sense of rhythm was becoming somewhat hobbled. She and Damon were working out some euphonic harmonies together, walking behind everyone else, trading mouthfuls from a bottle of vodka. He had a pleasant voice, steady if unadventurous. She wasn't surprised that he could sing. She imagined he could do almost anything passably: sing, dance, paint, change a tyre, make pasta, recite capital cities, juggle oranges, walk on his hands. Lacking focus, he had mastered a hundred superficialities. He was jack of all trades: competent at everything, excellent at nothing. She was surprised by the clarity of her analysis. No sooner had she thought it than she knew it to be true. She saw everything with absolute certainty. She was wise, a mind-reader. She was a psycho, psychothingy, psychoenamelist. Whatever. She stumbled sideways, forgetting for a moment to keep tabs on which way was up. The bottle clinked against the asphalt but she managed to right herself before any of its precious firewater was lost.

'Here, give me that,' Damon commanded. He snatched the bottle from her grip just as the ground leapt up at her.

'Ouch,' she said, sitting heavily. Damon stooped and tried to help her up, but she slumped deliberately, dead weight in his arms. He let go and she sagged against a wall.

'Hang on,' she said. 'Just a minute. Where have my feet gone?'

'Fuck, you're drunk,' he said. 'And on vodka, too. I thought this piss was supposed to be in your blood. You're meant to have some sort of resistance.'

'I have,' she said. 'I have resistance. I just need assistance!'

She giggled. Good one. Up ahead, a group of shadowy figures danced without moving their legs. She focussed and their numbers halved.

'Are you okay back there?' one of them shouted. It was Perry, gorgeous Perry, the one with the maple leaf.

'Perry!' she cried. 'Gorgeous Perry! I'm fine. I was just talking to gorgeous Damon here. How are you?'

'We're fine,' Perry said. 'But we've run out of songs and it's after midnight. Andrei's going to find us a taxi. Come on, we're going home.'

'What?' Stacy protested. 'But this is lovely. Look at us, we're singing with Russians. Harmonising with the enemy! What could be better than that? If only they sang *Rainbow Connection* at the UN, there'd be no more wars! Think about it! Singing will save us. It's a small world after all...'

'The enemy has to get up early in the morning,' one of them said, the Russian one, the one who talked. Andrei. 'But we will meet you tomorrow. Now let us get you back to the ship.'

'Noooo,' she wailed. 'I don't want to go! Stay here with me! Damon will stay here, won't you, Damon? Lovely Damon. Damon of all trades. Yes?'

'Sure,' Damon said gallantly. He looked at her and winked. She smiled broadly at him, stretching her cheeks in a prolonged rictus.

'You know how to get back?' Perry called. 'The address is on your boarding pass. Andrei says it's about half an hour's walk. Go straight across that bridge, that bridge there, you see the one I'm pointing to? And it's on the other side of the island.'

'Right,' Damon assured him, feeling less confident than he sounded. Woah. Confusing. 'We'll just wait until Stacy can stand up, and then we'll follow you,' he said. 'We'll see you in a while.'

'Bosh!' Stacy said, giggling at the word. 'I can stand up. Watch!'

She stood up awkwardly. Fine, good start. And suddenly the scenery was flashing past her, skipping frames like a sloppy animation. Trees, poles, fences appeared in her field of vision and were gone. And then there was nothing in front of her, nothing but a wobbling blackness alive with slivers of light.

She teetered on the river bank and retreated from the edge.

'Woah,' she said. 'Nearly went for a swim there.' She turned around and saw that she had crossed a wide but fortunately empty road. Scary. Behind the road loomed the Winter Palace, white columns bony in the moonlight, green walls black. She staggered back across the bitumen, making sure to use the zebra crossing. The palace towered high above her, confusing her mind as she leant against two of its walls, huddled in a baroque alcove. Damon came and sat beside her.

She looked out across the river. The moon was there, full but fractured, swimming. The bridge paddled in the water. The sky was a bright black; the outline of the city spread across the horizon in a darker shade of nothing, needling the stars. The river flowed slowly, oozing like tar between the banks. She looked up. Focussed. Her mind returned from its drunken meanderings, stopped and looked around.

'You know, it's funny,' she murmured to herself.

'What is?' Damon asked. The words snagged her thoughts like an anchor, dragging them down, tugging on her mind. Careful.

'Nothing,' she said. Sadness. Private misery. Not to be shared.

'No, really, what?' Damon persisted. Her thoughts rallied together, buoyant in their masses, struggling to be free. Fine. Let them bounce, flow, surge. But not out. She raised the bottle to her lips and felt its warmth flow into her.

'It's just...' she started, wary, wary.

'Yes...?' he prompted.

'Nothing,' she said, clamping. Drowning in another gulp of surly vodka.

'No, what?'

'No, *nothing*. No nothing.'

'Christ!' He jumped up and spun around, hands clutching at his head. 'What is it with you? You're so damn secretive!'

'You don't...'

'What?'

She paused, pondered. Her thoughts burned, volatile: she had to translate them into innocuous words. Package them for public release. Thought and speech, cleft, heading in separate directions. Think this, say that: even the alcohol could not penetrate this, the most intuitive of defences.

Secrets. Hidden. No-one may know. Too awful, too awful.

'I'm a private person.'

'No, it's more than that. There's something there. I don't know what. That crazy fuck saw it in Denmark, that Iraqi, he saw it. What?'

Bastard. Bastard for bringing that up. Too close to the bone, too close.

'He didn't see anything. Why are you busting my shoes like this?'

'Busting your...? I'm not busting your anything. It's just, why are you so evasive? Are you like this to everyone? Doesn't anybody get to know you?'

One. Only one, ever and forever. One...

'Maybe I don't trust many people, that's all.'

'Why not?'

Because one tore my heart from my chest, froze it in ice, smashed it against a rock, shattered it into a thousand shards, sharp, sharp as cold glass.

'You learn not to.'

'Learn? Where do you learn that?'

Where? From every breath that stabs my lungs like icicles, every thought that sticks in my brain like a throbbing aneurysm, every memory clouding my vision in a blood cataract, blind spots like a haemorrhage. Every razor stripe of experience.

'From... experience. You learn from experience.'

'What experience? What, you've been hurt or something?'

How much pain can there be? Flaying alive, giving birth, sting of a scorpion: can anything compare? Betrayal. Smashed hopes. Dreams run aground, hulls torn. Yes.

'Hasn't everyone?'

'I guess. But people get over it.'

People? People live in a world of averages. Little dreams, tiny successes, negligible setbacks. People don't know what it's like to lose yourself, completely, all traces gone. I do. I know.

'No. I won't get over it.'
'What's so bad that you'll never get over it?'
'If only you knew.'
'Well, I'm asking.'

Many have asked. How I have wished to tell, wished for the words. Even you, stranger, I wish I could tell you.

'I wish I could tell you.'
'You can, you can tell me.'

Get back. There is nothing here for you. Go!

'Forget it.'

'No! Jesus! You don't know what I've been through! I searched, I searched for you! Everywhere I went, every corner, every youth hostel, I looked for you. I scoured! I scoured fucking Scandinavia! If you knew where I've been, just looking for you—there was this girl—Jesus Christ, I don't even want to think about it. But now I've found you again, but I still don't even know you, but I want to, I feel it, I think, I know I can. So don't give me this shit, please. I'm begging you.'

'You don't know what you're doing. You don't.'
'But I want to, can't you see? Tell me! Let me know!'
'You should never have found me. Really. You can't reach me. No-one can. I'm sorry.'

She looked out over the water. Strange things were happening. Her thoughts and her words were dancing around each other, dodging and weaving, moving closer together. Thoughts were diverted to her mouth, erupting into sound. Words lost themselves in her head. Everything was swimming in vodka, enveloped in a distant haze. Losing direction. Mind and mouth confused, stumbling in decreasing circles. If they were to collide, to move as one—that would be like acids and bases, nitro and glycerine, a chemical reaction, unpredictable but terrifying. What explosion of emotion would ensue from their union? Only one way to find out, and that too dangerous to contemplate. Better not to know.

A low moan sounded, studded by the clanking of chains. The Dvortosovy Bridge split in two and opened with a pained rumble. Its halves separated massively and rose to the sky like a pair of reaching hands. Tiny ripples spread across the river, driven by the vibration. The grinding stopped and the pieces of bridge froze into their upright positions, timeless monuments to engineering.

'Wow,' Stacy said. 'That's beautiful.'

A snub-nosed cargo ship slid through the bridge, dragging its wake in an expanding V, engine chugging in a low gear. Further down the river, another bridge was opening with a rusty gate's distant squeal.

'Yes,' Damon agreed. 'But... isn't that the bridge we were supposed to go over?'

'Bridge?' Stacy said. She thought furiously back through the clouds of her memory. 'Yes! Bridge! That's the bridge we were supposed to go over!'

'Fuck,' Damon said earnestly. 'What are we going to do?'

'I don't know,' Stacy said, waving her arms in dismay. 'Wait, yes I do! Let's have some more to drink.'

She sucked oblivion from the bottle. A wave of nausea flooded over her as she swallowed; bile rose to the back of her throat. Saliva was filling her mouth, cheeks flowing like walls dripping blood. She suppressed the urge to spit, afraid she would vomit. Her forehead tingled, sweating coldly. She blinked.

'Are you all right?' Damon asked.

She nodded and stared straight forward, not confident to speak. Blackness was creeping from the edges of her vision. She blew stale air through her pursed lips. Too much to drink, too much. No more.

'Stacy?' Damon persisted. 'Hey.'

She shook her head as the blackness surged and disappeared. Her stomach settled and breath came easier.

'I'm okay,' she said uncertainly. 'You know that one drink too many?'

Damon nodded.

'Well, that was it.'

He took a mouthful from the bottle and swallowed carefully.

'Tastes all right to me,' he said, grinning.

'Smartass.'

She leaned heavily against the wall, still shaking, vulnerable. Feelings rose and fell within her like speeding biorhythms. She wished she was not so drunk, or drunker. She wished she could say more, wished she had kept her mouth shut. Wished that her life was simple, that memory was short, that the past was over.

'What happened to you?' Damon asked gently. His voice was soft, smooth as a liqueur.

'I'm scarred,' Stacy said blankly. 'Scarred, scarred for life.' She was somewhere else, looking down, talking through her mouth by remote control.

'By what?' Damon prompted.

'I knew this guy,' she started, head spinning, unsure now where the words were coming from. They seemed to string themselves together, bursting out of nothing like the Big Bang. Clumsy and unformed, but there.

'No, I'll go back,' she decided. 'First you have to understand something about the place I live.'

'Upstate New York,' Damon said.

'Right,' Stacy nodded. 'Lake Placid. I know you've never heard of it.'

'Sure I have,' Damon said. 'You told me before.'

'Right,' Stacy said. 'No. Wait, I'll go back. First you have to understand something about my parents.'

'From Russia,' Damon said. 'Your father's a scientist of some sort.'

Stacy frowned at him. 'Who's telling this story?'

Damon looked contrite. 'I'll be quiet.'

'Good. Yes. They're from Russia. Russia—*this* is Russia! I can't believe it. My parents are from here. God. Parents, you know, they can fuck you up. Or not. So much depends. If it wasn't—then—you know?'

Damon shook his head. 'Sorry—what?'

She tried to remember what she had just said. No good. Usually she was quite a lucid drunk, articulate. But now she couldn't keep track of sentences. She stumbled, overlapping her words, slurring them to boot.

'Forget it. Place. Lake Placid, New York, US-fucking-A. 12946. Doesn't have the same ring as 90210, does it? There's a reason. No Hollywood Boulevard where I come from. Still, there's a lake.'

'Lake Placid,' Damon prompted her.

She sighed. 'I'm not getting anywhere. Let me—let me surmise, summarise. Okay. Parents—from Russia. Outcasts, outlaws, out—outsiders. Didn't fit in. Fitted out. Outfits. But. Place—small. Teensy tiny little place. Three thousand people on a good day, max. Where is Max? Max!?'

'He's gone back to the boat,' Damon said wearily.

'Damn,' she lamented. 'Still. Tiny place, one horse town. Mom and Pop store, little school, bait and tackle shop. Did I mention the lake? Yes. Good. Tiny, stifling place. Suffocating. Everyone was dead, but nobody realised. Their lives didn't *mean* anything. It was just, go to school, fuck on prom night, get married to same prom-night fuck, send kids to same school, buy a pickup truck. Cook brownies every now and again. Which is fine if that's what you want; the world needs people to fuck and cook brownies. Backbone of society. Salt of the earth. Whatever. But if your parents come from Russia—anywhere—you realise that the world is bigger. Big place. Full of life and experience and art and culture and nobody really gives a fuck about brownies. And you want out. You want it more than anything. You feel the whole thing—the smell of diesel from the truck stop, the old guys whittling, young guys rebuilding their engines, the Order of the Caribou with their stupid fucking hats—you feel it all closing in on you, ramming its happy hometown horseshit down your throat. And you have to get out.'

She paused for breath. The words were coming back, tumbling easily from her mouth, warming up. Damon was watching her with a fierce intensity, staring too deep into her eyes. She looked away. More boats were slipping under the broken bridge, greeting each other with foghorn blasts as they passed, hulls slapping in each other's wakes.

'So you look around for a way out, for someone to help you. But nobody wants to help; they're all busy going about their tiny lives, deciding what prom dress they should have ripped off of them, whether they'll let Tony bone them in his station wagon or make him pay for a room at the Best Western. It's like Invasion of the fucking Body Snatchers; everyone's walking around with dead expressions, eyes that can't see. You're running all over the place, tugging at people's arms, trying to tell them something's wrong, there's more to life. But they're just, like, "Oh, hiiiiii *Sta*-cy, are you going to Buffy's hay-baling on the weekend, Rod's going to be there, I think he thinks you're cute, and can I eat your brain?" And you just want to tear their heads off, but you can't, so you go home and Mam and Papa are still talking about the old country, wars, sieges, famines, politics, reform, real things. And you can't stand *that* so you leave again, go hang out down at the truck stop where the men are fat and smelly and wired to the eyeballs with amphetamines but at least they've been places, they've got stories to tell, they know what it's like to travel even though all they see is truck stops. But they just want you to take a look at the inside of their cabs and *that* can get pretty ugly. So basically you spend a lot of time wandering around, though there's nowhere you can go, and you get depressed and despondent and you have the feeling that you're not really emotionally involved in your life, you're just going through the motions. And you're too bored even to drink or do drugs anymore, and it's—it's just *bad*.'

She drank some more vodka, didn't feel sick. She was beyond all that, in a zone.

'But then you meet somebody, a guy, and somehow he's escaped the mind-numbing curse of Smallville, USA, and you wonder why you've never heard of him before. Why he hasn't been in all the papers: Backwoods Boy Has Grand Ambition, Locals Baffled. Because you've given up hoping that in a town of three thousand max there's somebody like you. But there he is. And he's beautiful, beautiful and different, and he has this intensity you've never seen before except on TV or maybe in a mirror. He wants out. He's burning with the desire to do something, make something of his life. And so you're inseparable. You make plans, talk about how you're going to do it. You plan the Great Escape. And you have angry sex, desperate sex, fucking on mountaintops. You cling together, you two against the world. Ready or not, here we come. Here we fucking come! But because he has this great passion he gets into terrible moods, not violent, never violent, but gloomy, filled with despair that he won't ever get out, won't ever do anything. And you thought you had it bad, but him, he's got it worse. And sometimes it's frightening, and sometimes you feel so helpless. But you stick by him and cheer him up as much as you can, because, well, because you love him. You're in love, and that's the scariest fucking word there is. Love...'

A single sob ruptured her throat, bursting into the night like a tennis ball regurgitated. Her face felt like it was shrinking, hot and cold at once. She raised her hand and felt tacky moisture beneath her fingertips. Fresh tears sluiced over the contour of her cheeks. Damon breathed 'Hey...' and put his arm around her shoulders. She leaned into him, snuffling her nose with one fist. He was warm, comfortable. Taut muscles beneath layers of arctic clothing. For an instant she felt his hand curled against her stomach, nudging her breast—and then it was gone, expunged from her consciousness, no longer part of her personal reality.

'And then one weekend, one winter weekend, the two of you go camping in the mountains. In the Adirondacks, as far away as you can go with no money and no way of getting any. But it's beautiful. Snow, snow everywhere. Everything so peaceful, pure, covered in white like an empty page. The air is so clear it's like there's nothing there, no air. It's like you don't need air, you don't need anything. Fresh, divine. And it was almost like, yes, this is the first step. We're on our way. This is the beginning. The initiation.'

She shivered, voice drowning in a sudden tremolo: *initi-iti-ati-ation.* Her body shuddered, every muscle collapsing into spasm. She felt like she was being sucked into a whirlpool, a black hole, drawn inexorably inward, unable to escape. No turning back. The tears were flowing more freely, now; she made no attempt to wipe them away. Damon held her tighter, tipped his head against the side of hers. She closed her eyes, staring at the vortex behind her eyelids, steeling herself against the pain.

'So you think everything's going fine; it looks like you may have a future. Hell, you might even be close to happy. It's your turn to cook dinner so you're boiling something up on the camp stove. Noodles. He's gone off for a walk. He's late. The sun's getting lower. It's snowing, just a little. Tiny flakes. You get up and walk the way he went, following his footprints. But the footprints get shallower, filled with new snow, disappearing. You're lost, blundering, trees in the way. The sun's already set down on the plain, but it's still shining in the mountains. Everything's going orange, pink, red. The snow picks up the colours. Then you see him, and it's like, Thank God. But he hasn't seen you. And you notice where he is. He's standing on the edge of a peak, a cliff, a hundred feet down at least. He's standing there staring, and the posture of his body is enough to make you freeze. You fucking freeze. And you call to him, call Hey! Be careful! And the snow's picking up, swirling around, but you can still see him as he turns and looks at you, dead in the eye, and his eyes, too, they're dead. Dead with pain, miserable as death. And he shrugs. As if to say, Oh well. Too bad. Everything's slow motion. He picks up one of his feet. Steps forward. There's nothing there, nothing under his foot. You lunge but he's thirty feet away, soon forty, fifty before you can blink. Plummeting. Jesus God! Falling, falling before your eyes! And you hear a scream—ripping, tearing the air—but it isn't him, it's you. And the scream lasts forever, and he's still falling, just a sack, like he's already dead. He disappears from view and you don't hear him hit the ground but the sound you imagine is far worse, far worse. The sound you imagine knocks your eardrums out, wipes your mind, pushes you to the ground, fills your mouth with snow. And the screaming stops, there's silence, dead silence, and it's all over. All over. All over...'

Too much. She rammed her palms into her eyes, trying to stem her anguish. Tears flooded her face, clogged her nose. Her ears rang like a Chinese torture. Her throat convulsed, choking on strangled cries. She wailed tremulously at the falling moon, forgetting herself, crushed by the vortex until she ceased to exist and there was only pain, confusion, debilitating emotion whipping itself into a storm around her.

'Fuck,' she moaned. 'Fuck. Oh fuck.'

Damon was still holding her, trying to calm the spasms that wracked her body. His skin felt cool. She looked at his face, couldn't tell whether the tears there were his or hers.

1 Een
2 Twee
3 Tre
4 Fire
5 Viisi
6 Шесть

7 Семь

She finally fell asleep. He looked down at her, lying silent in his arms. Her eyes were puffy and circled with dark rings, raccoon eyes. White tracks forged their way through the accumulated city grime of her face. Her nose was red. Tears drying. He could no longer feel her body under his hands. His knuckles grazed the buried curve of her breast, contact which would have generated sparks but did not. His longing had vanished, shocked into a confused retreat. Her personal associations were clinging to him, creeping over his own world-view: love and pain, sex and death.

    The magnitude of her experience buried him. He felt almost jealous, wished he had known such extremes. He thought back across the chasm of his own life. Stockpiles of trivia. Property Law exam failed. Dead grandparents never known. Arguments with his parents. Leg broken in a football game. Nose broken in a pub brawl, reconstructed expertly. Friends coping with low self-esteem, bulimia, dyslexia, public transport. Overall, a comfortable life. Happy hometown horseshit.

He wanted Stacy's pain; he would gladly have taken it off her hands. To have something like that, something so constant—that would be something. To feel the same thing every day, to think: this is me. She knew who she was, unquestionably, irrevocably. She was a feeler of pain. Perhaps it was a bad thing to be, but it was something. He looked around and felt emptier than ever, felt the night pressing against him, wafting through him.

The bridge heaved into its level position, grumbling as the strained hydraulics fought restless gravity. He nudged her, tried to jiggle her into consciousness. His initial efforts prompted a low moan which no amount of perseverance could improve upon or even reproduce. She was out cold, buried in a sleep deeper than sleep. He wondered what she was dreaming of. Whether she had any demons left after this, Mephisto of them all. Her eyes were dead in their sockets. No rapid eye movement; no eye movement at all. So, probably no dreams. Nothing but random neurons firing in isolation, too confused to form images.

He gave up trying to rouse her and let her slump against him, manoeuvring into a position comfortable for them both. The walls were getting harder, prickling with new obstructions. The temperature of the concrete was dropping away, dragging his body heat down with it. He shivered, shifted his weight. Held her tight, burying his face in her neck. Her hair was cold, cascading like icy water over her shoulders. Smelled of coconut. Tasted like hair. He spat out the errant strands and arranged a nest with his chin. Almost sensual. Almost comfortable.

The moon snagged itself on the fortress spire and, punctured, sank below the skyline. The stars were clear and still, twinkling only occasionally. Cold stars, stars through a telescope. Clouds wisped across the sky like dark ghosts. The world seemed full of phantoms. Wandering spirits, itinerant spectres, homeless harpies, cramming the night air with the memories of unhappy deaths. Stacy felt warmer against his body. She was still with him, clinging to the world despite the temptation to rejoin her destiny on the other side. She was here, after all. She had chosen.

And maybe there was something for him here. She had told him, even if it had nearly killed her. He was a listener, now, a guardian of secrets. And now he was a watcher, a sentry. That was his role. Tonight, at least. And, if tomorrow, then forever.

He sat there, alone with her ghosts, as time passed without trace. He waited for what must have been hours until the bridge opened again, then waited another hour for it to bellyflop once more into the water. He waited as the first trucks clattered along the riverfront, waited as the night faded imperceptibly and the sky graduated through subtle increments of grey. He waited as the morning seagulls squawked tinnily at each other and somewhere, crazily, a rooster crowed. Waited until, shortly after dawn, she stirred, pried her eyes open and sat up stiffly.

'Damn,' she said. 'Where am I?'

'Just where you left yourself,' Damon told her.

She leaned forward, twisted her head around to look at him. His arms slid away from her body. Her hair was sticking in all directions, sculpted into a bulletproof bouffant. She ran her fingers through it, flattening it, wincing at the knots.

'We'd better get back to the boat,' she said. 'They've probably got the KGB onto us already.'

She sprang to her feet like a faith-healer's bogus cripple and strode across the concrete. Digging through her back pocket, she unearthed her boarding pass and looked for the address of the ship. An unusual concept. Damon pushed himself to his feet and followed her away from the palace.

'How you feeling this morning?' he asked.

She glanced at him briefly. 'Fine. I guess vodka does run in my veins after all. See? No hangover.'

'I don't mean that. I mean the other stuff.'

'What other stuff?'

He frowned at her. Surely she couldn't have...

'You look like hell,' she interrupted. 'What were you, awake all night?'

'Kind of.'

'Why?'

'I figured someone should be.'

'How gallant.' Her voice stung with an uncharacteristic sarcasm.

'And I was feeling a little shaken.'

'Something wrong?'

'With me? No.'

'Good. Let's make some time, okay?'

She forged ahead of him, wavering only slightly from side to morning-after side. He followed in her wake, rubbing his forehead. His life felt like it had turned out to be a dream, a rumour unsupported by anyone else's experience. What had last night been? He wished he had some kind of witness to corroborate his version of the facts—I saw it all, your Honour. It happened like he said. Let this be entered on the record as the truth, the whole truth, something like the truth. So help me God.

Perry was waiting on the tarmac with a bagful of Swedish meatballs.

'Hoped you guys'd make it back,' he said. 'Have some breakfast. Stig said we could take a doggy bag from the buffet. No wonder they can't afford anyone to sing but the cook.'

Stacy lunged at him, seemed about to fall into his arms. Instead she squeezed his shoulder and took a meatball.

'Perry,' she said, gazing into his eyes. 'You are a god. You're the god of inappropriate breakfast foods.'

'You should have seen some of the other stuff,' Perry said. 'This was the closest thing to breakfast I could find. I just wanted some toast, cornflakes maybe, but everything was, like, goulash and segments of boiled fish.'

'I can't believe I drank a bottle of vodka last night and I'm eating meatballs in cheese sauce for breakfast,' Stacy said, chewing proudly. 'People would kill for my constitution.' The end of her sentence lost itself in her breakfast, muffled by meatballs. *Comfatoofun.*

'You're an inspiration,' Perry told her. 'You want a meatball, Damon? Breakfast of champions.'

Damon shook his head. 'I generally have to sleep before I can consider breakfast.'

Perry raised his eyebrows. 'You guys were up all night?'

'Not me,' Stacy said. 'I slept like a log. Couldn't have made it back to the boat. I was asleep as soon as you left, just about.'

'What kept you up, then?' Perry asked Damon.

'I had a bad dream.'

'But—I thought you hadn't slept.'

'I didn't.'

'What have you done to Damon?' Perry demanded of Stacy. 'Looks like you broke his brain.'

'Don't blame me,' she said. 'It was like that when I got here.'

'He needs a meatball,' Perry suggested. 'Here, have one, Damon. Brain food. Do you good.'

Giving up, Damon terminated the conversation with a full stop dripping cheese. He chewed it thoughtfully. Dry and solid. The meatball felt like it would sit in his stomach all day, bouncing around until dinner time when his metabolism would be more accommodating. The strange breakfast seemed appropriate to the surrealism of everything.

'Where are the others?' he asked.

'They didn't want to wait,' Perry said. 'We're meeting outside the Hermitage at lunchtime; the Russians should be there too.'

They found a bustling outdoor market, teetering on the brink of legality. Vendors of paintings, sculptures, souvenirs and military paraphernalia voiced their preference for hard currency but would trade grudgingly in rubles. Police officers browsed the stalls, poking through the junk without apparent concern about the illicit nature of the black market. Some even bought badges to stick to their uniforms, promoting themselves to generals, secret service agents, submarine commanders. They glanced at Damon as they walked past. A wave of paranoia splashed him into alertness: he didn't have a visa, had been AWOL 24 hours, hadn't checked back with the boat. Off to Siberia for him. But the only people interested in him were the hordes of traders who shouted all the English they knew at him as he walked past.

'Rabbit hat! Buy rabbit hat! Fifteen dollar!'

'*Nyet, sbaceba,*' he snapped, smiling at his own canniness.

'Yeltsin doll! See? Six doll, ten dollar. Take home!'

Andrei had been right: Yeltsin generally had pride of place in the babushka hierarchy, waving the new Russian tricolour with a caricatured scowl of pride. Red, white and blue—just like everybody else. Some of the dolls still bore Gorbachev's face, frowning beneath hammer-and-sickle birthmark. Perhaps they had been hard to shift, manufactured too late; perhaps an underground band of hardline painters were trying to reassert the former leader's position. Or perhaps 'Gorby doll' just had a more appealing ring to it. The Russians were learning a lot about marketing.

'*Nyet, sbaceba,*' Damon decided.

'Army badges! Whole sheet, two dollars. Genuine original!'

Metal clinked as a square of foam studded with heraldry appeared in his field of vision, held aloft by a tiny hawker. Military badges, perhaps. Or train-conductors' pips, ice hockey emblems, *Have a nice day* buttons. Or *Kick me, I'm a stupid tourist* printed on plastic. No way of knowing. Better if the trinkets were fake, in a way: sad to see the genuine insignia of a proud culture traded like baubles; beads and mirrors to encourage the invaders.

'*Nyet, sbaceba,*' Damon said regardless.

'Original artworks, one of a kind. You buy. Unique!'

Racks of paintings stood like paned windows refracting different views of the same scene. A wall of watercolours, seabirds settling on lonely rock formations in the middle of choppy oceans, strips of sunset washing the sky. Charcoal sketches of the city in a kaleidoscope of angles: Nevsky gate, Winter Palace, St Peter and Paul Fortress, monuments, gardens, buildings—all streaked with lines of bouncing rain, scarred with the artist's world-view. Snowscapes in a white blanket flecked with black silhouettes. Little figurines like a disorganised chess set.

One painting caught his attention. It was fairly small, five by eight like an upright photo, framed in dull metal. Watercolour. An intersection sat in the middle of a plain, spreading paths in all directions like a geographic octopus. Empty signs clustered around a single pole, blank fingers pointing unhelpfully. A man was standing in the middle of the crossroad, standing with his back to Damon. He wasn't looking along any of the paths, wasn't trying to see where they led. Instead he stared at the tangle of signs, hypnotised by options, unable to move. Stared at the signpost, frozen by indecision.

Damon asked the man behind the stall what the piece was called.

'What else could it be called?' the artist said. '*Untitled.*'

Perry and Stacy were poking through a pile of coloured rubble which had reportedly been part of the Berlin wall.

'Must have been a big fucking wall,' Perry said. 'If there's enough to go around all over Europe.'

'Is real, is real,' the pedlar assured him, sensing his doubt. 'Two dollar this, five dollar this.' He pointed out a few chunks of various sizes.

'*Nyet, sbaceba!*' they chorused gleefully, joined by Damon as he arrived behind them.

'Look what I got,' he said, showing them the painting. 'The guy wanted ten dollars, but I beat him down to seven. I think I'm getting the hang of this.'

'Nice,' Perry said. 'It suits you.'

'What movement is this part of?' Stacy asked acidly.

Damon flipped the painting and looked it over. 'I don't know,' he admitted.

'No,' she said. 'I don't suppose you would.'

She looked at him pointedly, eyebrows raised in challenge. As if calling his bluff. He stared back at her, not knowing what to say. He had started the day thinking he had something on her, some privileged knowledge guarded carefully and known to few. But perhaps it was the other way around. A sudden chill coursed through him. Spluttering through vodka, had he blurted out more than he could remember? She apparently had. There seemed to be no holes in his recollection. But there was always doubt. What did she know?

'Now, now,' Perry admonished. 'Let's travel friendly, okay? Come on; we're almost due at the Hermitage.'

A battered trailer sat on the *ploschad*, dwarfed by the Winter Palace like a dinghy bobbing alongside a destroyer. A gnome-like Russian woman sat behind smeared glass, poking limp hamburgers through a ticket-booth hole. Ten rubles a pop; exorbitant by local standards but pitched perfectly at the tourists visiting the Hermitage. Denis was sitting on the kerb with a stack of five burgers beside him, peeling off layers of waxed paper and devouring each slab of meat between soggy white slices in a few bites.

'Goddamn,' he shouted as he spotted Damon. 'These must be the worst hamburgers I've ever eaten. You can taste the communism! But they're cheap!'

Max appeared in the door of the Hermitage, framed by pillars. Andrei and Sergei flanked him, walking in loose formation as they approached the hamburger stand. They smiled calmly in greeting.

'Andrei! Sergei!' Stacy called, starting towards them. 'And Max! Three thousand Max!'

The words echoed through Damon's head, reverberating like a movie flashback. Three thousand max. Hurling through his memory like three cars on a rollercoaster, ducking and turning, looking for a context. Finding one. Three thousand max. A number; an upper limit. A population. An explanation.

He seized her by the arm, stopping her. She turned and looked at him angrily.

'You *do* remember,' he said, ears ringing.

She glared at him, fire flashing in her eyes. 'Of course,' she hissed. 'I remember *everything*. That's the whole problem.'

She tugged free of his grasp and lunged towards Max and the Russians, leaving him to stutter 'But—' like a goldfish drowning in air. Thoughts flew from their positions, losing themselves in a chaos of rearrangement, whirling through his head like coconut in a glass snowstorm. He followed her, tagged her shoulder, swiped air behind her, snatched at her clothing, finding nothing beneath his fingers. Finding her gone.

'Not now,' she snapped, ducking out of reach. 'Not now,' she said with her voice. But with her eyes she told him: *not ever.*

Damon's mood darkened as he trudged through the city streets. She was ignoring him; that much was obvious. She always managed to be where he was not; dawdling behind him, forging ahead, separated by Denis or Martina or, most frequently, Perry. She talked to Perry as she always had, Perry who knew nothing about her, Perry who would be shocked to hear half of what *he* had heard. Perry who captured her attention too completely, saving her eyes from wandering. She laughed with him, pointed at things, acted as if everything was normal. Damon dug his hands deep into his pockets, felt his shoulders curl into a defensive hunch, and kicked the pavement as he walked.

Roger was sidling up to him, irritating in his friendliness. 'Out all night!' he said, elbowing him playfully in the ribs. 'And after that waltz. Mate, you're smoother than I gave you credit for. Fast work! She's cute, too. If you like cheekbones.'

Rage pressed Damon's eyeballs like captured steam in a boiler. 'Fuck off!' exploded in his throat. He clamped it between his jaws and released it in an angry hiss.

Roger slapped him infuriatingly on the shoulder. 'What, you bombed out? Well, too bad, mate. Some of these Russian women are all right, I tell you what. The young ones, I mean. When they get older they seem to go, I dunno, all rectangular...'

Damon shrugged Roger's arm away. The surroundings had altered in character; everything was cold and grey, dank and depressing. Tainted by his frustration. He felt a headache building at the base of his skull, pulling at his temples with octopus straps. The afternoon was tumbling into a quagmire of dissatisfaction. Monuments drifted past him, redolent with sombre arrogance; scowling, he brushed away their demands for admiration. Museums crowded around like suffocating vaults of time, cementing the hands of his wristwatch while speeding his impatience into a maelstrom. Russians selling Pepsi T-shirts were unable to drag a single *nyet* from him, shouting guttural abuse at him as he shouldered them aside. Everyone was an arsehole.

An underpass dipped below Nevsky Prospect, dodging the traffic. Nearby, the metro plunged deep into the rock. Acrid smells wafted through the sluggish air: sweat, diesel, urine. A tramp sat against one wall, buried in a pile of rags like a child in rotting leaves. He held a grimy palm in front of him, stub-nailed fingers poking through a half-glove. Beggar in Russia: not a lucrative career.

'Wait, I've always wanted to do this,' Perry said. He dug through his pockets and pressed fifty rubles into the outstretched hand. The bum closed his fingers by reflex, then looked at the notes protruding from his clenched fist. Counted them twice. An expression of disbelief flooded his face as he stared between Perry and the money. Fifty rubles: nothing to them, everything to him. Food for a fortnight. He leapt to his feet, laughing with sudden affluence, seized Perry by the arms and then dusted him off apologetically. His eyes sparkled with happy tears. Damon felt nauseated.

'Damn, that felt good,' Perry said as they walked on.

Wanker.

Muffled music rose through the empty floor of the White Nights discotheque: a deck below, the cossack-dancing crew were at it again. Brief silence, then a slowing of the rhythm, tripping into triplets. Stig's honeyed voice waltzing on its own melody. Damon stood up, shuffled across the dance floor. He closed his eyes and let his hands hang in the air, embracing an imaginary partner. Waltzing blind and alone: *one*, two, three. He tipped his head back, felt everything slip to the rear of his skull. Safer there; unobtrusive. His sneakers dragged against the lino as he swung in expanding circles. He felt comfortably tragic, wallowing in his misery. The world had let him down and he was reacting, sensibly, by withdrawing from it. It was the only way.

After a few circuits he felt a twinge of dissatisfaction, too alert—and, crucially, too sober—to completely accept the self-portrait he was trying to draw. His mind's eye, ever watchful, hung high above him and looked down with disapproval. Cold light fell on a snaking vein of self-indulgence, igniting it like fool's gold. Disconcerting lucidity. He felt faintly embarrassed. But he shook away the feeling, let it fall to the ground, and continued to dance.

Pressure on his waist and again on his palm; an immovable obstruction in his path. He levelled his head and opened his eyes. Stacy stood in front of him like a frozen dancer, holding him with the grip of a waltzing mannequin. He halted and dropped his arms to his sides—but she insisted, guiding him back into position and into the dance. She looked at his shoulder, eyes sinking leadenly, never rising.

'This is all your fault,' she said. 'You just had to push, didn't you?'

'I—' Damon started. Off balance. 'I didn't know you'd freak out like that.'

'I was drunk. Vodka's a maudlin drink.'

'Yeah,' Damon said, shaking his head. 'But no. You may have been drunk, but you didn't just make all that stuff up.'

'No, I didn't. I didn't make it up. But if I hadn't been drunk, I would *never* have told you any of it. Do you understand that? I don't tell *anybody*. I never even think about it.'

'You must think about it. If it was me I'd think about it all the time.'

'But it's not you. It's *me*. And maybe I do think about it, not all the time but pretty damn much of it. And maybe I'm *trying* to think about it as little as I can—and maybe you're not helping any.'

He shook his head. 'Running away...'

She stopped dancing; took a step forward and clutched at the throat of his jacket. 'What am I supposed to do? Stay? What good's that going to do? He's gone, isn't he? It's over! There's nothing left! So, damn *straight* I'm running away! I'm going to run as far and as fast as I can, and I'm going to keep running until it's safe for me to go back. Because it's not safe now, no it isn't, and what you saw last night was nothing, *nothing* compared to what I felt back home. And I'll be *damned* if I'm going back to *that*.'

Her grip was tightening, gathering more material, choking him. He took her by the wrist and detached her from his jacket. Fire vanished from her eyes as she looked up at him. She patted his chest apologetically and dropped her gaze.

'Sorry,' she said. 'You see? See what this does to me? So it's either, forget about what happened, or check into a padded room with my jacket on backwards. I can't go on like this.'

She raised a hand to her tortured face, thumb propping up her cheekbone, fingers pressed into her forehead. Chin dropping. Damon melted, involuntarily pulling her towards him and cradling her in his arms.

'No,' she said, pushing him away and wiping her eyes with a defiant thumb. 'I'm not done being mad at you yet. Don't touch me.'

'But I didn't do anything!' he protested. 'You started off all by yourself. I could tell you wanted to talk. You *needed* to! All I did was sit there; once you got going, there was nothing I could do.'

She took a step backward, looked at the floor for a moment. Then, quietly: 'I know. You're right. It wasn't your fault.'

'Then why were you such a cow to me all day?'

She turned and drifted off the dance floor. 'It felt weird, I guess,' she said, sitting down and drawing her knees up to her chin. 'Now you know more about me than I want to know myself. I don't know how to feel about that. I hardly know you at all, not well enough to trust you.'

'You can trust me,' he said, realising how convincing he sounded.

Stacy laughed darkly. 'Damon,' she said deliberately, leaning forward and looking up at him through her eyebrows. 'Everything you have told me about yourself has been a lie.'

'Everything?' he said indignantly. 'Not everything. I mean— nothing!'

She raised a single eyebrow at him. angling into a circumflex.

'Well, like what?' he challenged. Shovelling mud from his own grave.

'Well, like "I'm a neo-neo-gee-how-many-neos-is-that?- impressionist",' she said, voice Mongoloid with imitation. 'Gimme a break.'

'Well,' Damon said, struggling.

'Don't bother,' she advised wearily. 'Let me tell you something else. Jake was an artist. He was a painter, a real one. And so even if you hadn't shot yourself in the foot at the museum and every other time, I would have known you were a fraud. I knew. Because Jake had passion and he had intensity. He was driven. And you need that to be an artist. Without it you're directionless, you're diffuse. You're—you're like you.'

'Jake...?' Damon repeated unnecessarily.

'You know who I'm talking about.'

'I don't think you ever used his name before.'

She shrugged and folded her arms around her knees, hiding half her face in the crook of her elbow. The buried sound she made was too short to be a word.

'Okay,' Damon said, sighing heavily. 'So maybe the artist bit wasn't entirely true.'

She stared at him steadily.

'Okay,' he admitted. 'It wasn't true at all. You want to know the truth? Truth is, I'm not an artist—but I've always *wanted* to be. Well, maybe not an artist—but something. Something cool; something interesting, romantic, passionate, intense—all those things. And surely the wanting is the main part—if you're mentally all of these things, then that's enough, isn't it? Even if you don't do anything. It's a state of mind!'

Her face morphed into a blend of scepticism and pity. The eyebrow rose again.

'Maybe not,' he said wearily. 'Okay. Until I left Australia, I was a law student. Pretty exciting. Third year. I'd nailed or failed most of the compulsory subjects, you know, contracts, torts, property, criminal. Had to choose electives to finish the degree. See, but the trouble was, I had no idea what I wanted to do. Well, really, I didn't want to do any of it. Boring bullshit as far as I could see, if we're being honest. My parents wanted me to be a lawyer, God knows why. But there you go.'

He smiled a flat smile and raised his palms in a gesture of surrender. Stacy narrowed her eyes at him.

'That I can believe,' she decided. 'That's way too boring to be made up.'

'My point exactly.'

She nodded, smiling to herself. 'So, that's your big secret. You're not an undercover agent. You don't have a multiple-personality disorder. You're not even a pathological liar; you're just a lawyer. If there's a difference.'

'Hey, I'm not a lawyer yet. It's not like I even want to be one. I don't know if anyone really wants that. It's not your childhood dream; it's just something that happens.'

She listened to his protest with some amusement. 'So now you're busy acting out your childhood dreams,' she said. 'Let me guess. You're—an artist. A musician. A game-show host, movie star, astronaut. That the sort of shit that appeals to you?'

A few direct hits. But he shook his head. 'I dunno. Maybe. No, I really don't know. That's the thing; I'm just trying a few things on for size, see who I like being. I'm in a different country every other day, why not be a different person?'

'Well,' she said, considering. 'For one, other people find it... inconsistent. And they don't like being lied to.'

'I can't help that. This is a personal journey. I'm trying to find myself.'

'Trying to find yourself.' She laughed, soft laughter which rose up and mixed with the atmosphere, altering its chemistry. 'That's such a cliche. I mean, I see where you're coming from, but that's a *really* B-grade way of saying it.'

Damon grinned. The expression felt strange on his face, pushing his cheeks in an unaccustomed direction. Something had changed. The room felt like the aftermath of a storm: battered and shaken, but washed clean, pressure systems dispersed.

'Go figure,' he said, not even sure what it meant.

She laughed again. Their words seemed to have been exhausted. He looked silently at her and was surprised when she returned his gaze directly. Time passed comfortably.

'So,' he said, punctuating the silence with a nervous hand on her waist. 'Is everything okay now?'

'Yeah,' she said, smiling. 'Well, you know. Everything's bearable.'

'Bearable. Well, I guess that's about as good as it gets.'

Tears of something shone. 'Seems like.'

It was strange to be back. Helsinki seemed like a frozen Eden, lush with consumer abundance. A hidden El Dorado, Vegas in a desert of ice and water and Russia. There was something faintly repulsive about the sudden opulence, a decadence Damon hadn't seen before. Across the gulf people were queuing for potatoes; here they were buying slices of pizza in cardboard boxes and banking from home. But the contrast wore off as his elastic memory snapped back, and soon he was almost the same capitalist again.

'You know,' Perry said. 'I'm beginning to suspect that Eastern Europe is by far the most interesting half. I mean, all this is nice, but really what have we got here apart from McDonalds and shopping malls? Not much. And with everyone speaking English, it's just like being at home except your clothes smell worse.'

'What are you thinking of?' Damon said.

Perry shrugged. 'Poland, Hungary, whatever they're calling Czechoslovakia these days,' he said. 'Wherever.'

'I'm staying put for a while,' Denis said. 'Martina and Max are coming back in a few days; we're going to go hiking.'

'And I wanted to go to Sweden,' Stacy said. 'Can we stop there on the way?'

'We don't have much choice,' Perry said. 'The ferry leaves tonight; we'll be in Stockholm by the morning.'

'We don't have to stay there, though,' Damon said. 'We could just go straight to Berlin, use the same date on the Eurailpass. Save a flexi-day, look around the city for a while. That's almost East; the Eastern part at least.'

'It's thirty-six hours to Berlin,' Perry said. 'You're going to have to fill two days of spaces one way or another.'

'Oh,' Damon said, disheartened. He thought for a minute and brightened again. 'Okay, but tomorrow's the twenty-fifth, right? And a five turns into a six so easily. One stroke of the pen and we can travel an extra day!'

'You're a genius,' Perry said, gripping his shoulder. 'You go put your plan into action, and I'll go to Stockholm with Stacy. I've already been to Berlin.'

'You've already been to Stockholm!'

'True,' Perry said. 'But you were in such a mad rush to get out of there, I didn't see it properly.'

'It was awful,' Damon said. 'Don't you remember? Cold and wet and windy and too expensive to do anything. I couldn't go back there.'

'Come on, Damon,' Stacy said. 'We'll only be there a few days. A week, tops.'

'I can't afford a week in Stockholm. I'm *way* over budget already. Max gave me the key to his apartment in Berlin, said I could stay there as long as I like.'

'Do it,' Perry said. 'Check out the Ku'damm, it's great. Go to Checkpoint Charlie; get your picture taken with the sign that says *You are Leaving the American Sector*. Buy a T-shirt. Eat some sauerkraut. We'll see you in a week.'

Damon tried not to sulk. The Silja Lines ferry was everything the *Konstantin Simonov* was not. Its blue-striped, rhomboid bulk had dwarfed the Russian ship at the harbour, friendly blue seal towering over the humbled hammer and sickle. Now, ploughing the Gulf of Bothnia towards Stockholm, the boat was even more impressive. There was a duty-free store the size of a supermarket. The tables of the buffet diner bristled with food like a tropical jungle, fit to get lost in. Nightclubs, casinos, restaurants without number. A colony of cabins, hospital of bunk beds. Submerged cargo holds sinking into the ocean. All filled to capacity with tourists, backpackers—and Scandinavians on weekend benders, soaked in duty-free alcohol.

He had given up trying to read Stacy's signs. Every positive indication was offset by a negative of equal magnitude. She had wanted him to go to Stockholm with her, but was equally happy to let him go off to Germany. She had let him buy her a drink but he had ended up shouting Perry and Roger as well. She was sitting next to him, but she was talking to Perry.

He looked across at her. It was dark in the lounge bar. A cabaret show was unfolding on the stage; round tables and silver-piped chairs dotted the carpet around it. Stacy flickered orange and blue with the lights, pale skin picking up every nuance of colour. She had been a mess for the past couple of days: drunk, emotional, dishevelled— eminently human. But now she was beautiful again, skin perfect in the murky light, features striking in their definition, eyes pale and clear. Confident and animated, again unreachable. Damon bit his lip and stared. She was leaning into Perry, shouting something into his ear. His arm rode the back of her chair almost territorially. He answered her; she laughed.

Damon leaned closer, trying to make out what Perry and Stacy were saying. No good: their conversation hid furtively in the background noise, shutting him out. He sat back and looked around the room, bored. Jealousy curled in the pit of his stomach, fattening like a parasite.

The dancers left the stage and the band swung into a rock and roll medley, brassy and up-tempo. Couples sprang to their feet and bebopped onto the newly-cleared dance floor, twisting as the lights swirled around them. No MTV steps here: Top of the Pops, more likely. American Bandstand. Moves that demanded puff skirts and shiny shoes. Damon smirked at the anachronism.

Perry and Stacy nodded to each other and strode up to the stage. Damon watched in disbelief as they began to dance together, waving their arms like fifties idiots. Perry took Stacy's hand and spun her around, then pulled her into him and dipped her slowly, smooth as Brylcreem. They skipped in dizzying circles, arms extended in the caricature of a waltz. Stepping together and apart, raising their elbows like chickens, slapping their knees in a hayseed barn dance. Jitterbugging as Damon had never seen outside the movies. And laughing, laughing like there was nobody in the world but the two of them. Grinning as they made unselfconscious fools of themselves, not caring.

Damon choked on his ice cubes. It was all right for them, intoxicated by the rhythm, too self-absorbed to realise the spectacle they were presenting. But there was only so much he could stand. He lurched to his feet and wove uncertainly between the tables, tripping on chair legs, knocking his shoulders against pillars. The boat felt like it was rocking despite its unassailable bulk. Stormy weather and no sea legs. People swayed as he stumbled through them, desperate to get out of the room before he exploded. Angry fire coursed through his veins.

He crashed through a pair of double saloon doors, raged up a few flights of stairs, and burst into an outside he had forgotten was there.

The wind tore at his clothes, pushing his jacket back over his arms. His eyes streamed, hair flapping against his temples, ears roaring. He stumbled to the front of the deck, leant over the guardrail and felt his scream hurl back down his throat before it could sound. He was cooling down rapidly in the chilled air. Black water churned far below him, eight floors down. The ferry tore through the sea like scissors through velvet, leaving frayed white threads in its wake, floating impossibly like a pumice brick.

He looked up, trying to find the horizon. The sky was crammed with stars, and the moon shed a patch of silver on the water. Solitary red lights bobbed in the distance, bouncing on buoys. An island drifted past, lit like a squat Christmas tree. Darkness everywhere else. The deck was too high for the salt spray to reach. He stood awhile, leaning outward like a figurehead and feeling nothing but the buffeting gale and the immutable motion of the boat.

His face was becoming numb, nerve endings lashed by the cold and the wind. The anaesthetic sank through his skin and closed around his brain, locking it into frigid indifference. He felt a calm wisdom suffuse his consciousness. He'd been foolish, fixating on the wrong things. Nothing was important enough to compromise his enjoyment of this, the greatest experience of his life. Perhaps a defining experience. Perry had been right: there was more to life. Plenty more. It was time to cast aside trivial things. If he was going to be travelling around Eastern Europe with both of them, he would have to accept whatever relationship the three of them worked out together. And if he ended up the loser, as seemed to be happening, what of it? The adventure was what mattered; the romantic subplot was negligible. Fuck her. Or not. Who cared anyway?

He gritted his teeth and turned back towards the stairs, heart of stone weighing heavily in his chest.

1 Een
2 Twee
3 Tre
4 Fire
5 Viisi
6 Шесть
7 Семь
8 Åtta

Stacy and Perry ate pastry on a bridge while Stockholm undulated around them. Cobbled streets twisted through the archipelago city, winding among the islands like a yellow brick road only grey. Water rippled against the embankments; liquid steel.

Perry reached into his bag and pulled out a cherry Danish. It seemed to sparkle as he held it up to the light, glinting like a cartoon smile.

'This must be some kind of super-Danish,' he said. 'Look at it; it's like a work of art. It's so beautiful I don't think I can eat it.'

'Sure you can,' Stacy said. 'You've still got twelve more in your bag.'

She took a pastry from her own daypack and bit into it, reflecting that life moved in circles. Danish in the morning.

Sitting by the water, getting acquainted. Cobblestones and copper rooftops and things to explore, cities and personalities. Everything familiar but relocated. Different guy, same breakfast. Danish deja vu.

'True,' Perry said. 'I always think that the true sign of a good buffet breakfast is that it lasts all day. All it takes is a plastic bag and some sleight of hand.'

'I always feel kind of bad,' she said. 'But imagine how expensive travelling would be if we played by the rules.'

Perry chewed thoughtfully. 'It's not like we're actually *breaking* any rules,' he said. 'We're just *reinterpreting* the rules—in ways that the people who made them wouldn't have thought of.' He smiled contentedly, conscience set at ease.

'I guess you're right,' she said. 'I guess whoever invented all-you-can-eat may have meant in-one-sitting, not over-the-next-two-days. But how are we supposed to know that?'

'We don't,' he said. 'We interpret it as all-you-can-carry. Ignorance can be powerful. That's why I always assume that you only have to pay for the subway if there happens to be an inspector checking tickets.'

'Right. Like you just assume that nobody tips anywhere.'

'And that you never *ever* have to pay to use the bathroom. Ridiculous idea.'

'See this?' Stacy said, digging a plastic rectangle from her wallet. 'I got this student card from a friend of mine. She looks a bit like me, see? It expired last year, but nobody seems to notice. And if they do, you can just say that "expires" means "good from".'

'Nice,' he said. 'And I expect you've got one of those erasable pens for filling in temporary dates on your railpass—just in case they don't clip you that day?'

'Naturally,' she said. 'They say you're not allowed to use pencil, but is it our fault if they're not up with the technology?'

'Of course not. Hey, you know how sometimes in supermarkets or food halls they've got little sample trays, bits of food on toothpicks?'

'Do I ever,' Stacy said. 'You can get a free twelve-course meal out of those places. Frankfurters, cheese and biscuits,

Szechuan chicken, beef vindaloo. All on a little everything-kebab. Just one of those things you pick up.'

'We should write a book. Europe on no dollars a day.'

'Yeah,' she said. 'Feign ignorance of local custom—and save!'

They became increasingly glad of their pastry reserves as they travelled through the city. Stockholm was a beautiful place, carved from old stone and austere elegance. Modern and ancient buildings melted seamlessly together: spires and high-rises, domes and glass storefronts, courtyards and cobbles and concrete. Everyone was good-looking and better-dressed; the shops were well-stocked and tasteful. Socialism was working. Government subsidies, social welfare, public utilities and minimal unemployment propped up the standard of living, elevating it close to utopia. But utopia came with a price, in this case a literal one. Taxes were high and retail was higher, crippling any interloper launched on the city without the benefit of the social safety-net or the soaring salaries.

Stacy felt her Danish accruing value, weighing down her daypack as it turned to gold. It had been free; now it was expensive. Stockholm had the Midas touch, tinting everything with its economic alchemy. Except Stacy. She felt like a vagrant, stealing through paradise with dirty feet. She belonged here no more than she had in Russia. There, she had been conspicuously affluent; here, she was poorer than anyone else. She was a guest in the White House, looking but not touching and never close to owning. The city began to look like a museum, cold and ornate from its baroque town hall to the crown jewels buried deep in its palace.

'What else did you score from the buffet?' Perry asked.

'Three jam sandwiches, a bread roll and an orange,' she counted off.

'Better ration them,' he said. 'Looks like it's that and supermarket food until we hit Berlin. Have you seen the prices in these restaurants?'

'I saw them,' she said. 'But I thought I must be doing something wrong with the exchange rate.'

'Interesting approach,' he said. 'Unfortunately, with that kind of ignorance the only person you're fooling is yourself.'

'Yeah, but it works,' she said. 'Come on, I'll buy you a hamburger.'

The grey of the city faded to green as they crossed the bridge to the tree-lined island of Djurgården. The sky was as blue as a filtered photo, dotted with cottonwool clouds. A hot air balloon drifted away, dwindling into a striped speck. The air was fresh and cool. As they walked across a shaded park, the grass sprang back behind them, hiding their footprints.

The sudden hill of the Skansen loomed above them, fenced with stone and iron and wrapped in terraced paths spiralling like a helter-skelter. A cable car struggled up the incline, angles awry with compensation. Stacy thought of San Francisco. Trees of various kinds clung to the hill: evergreens and a fiery patchwork of deciduous death-leaves, as if the foliage had been spattered with the first half of a rainbow.

'That looks nice,' Stacy said. 'I don't want to sound too back-to-nature, but it'd be good to get away from cities for an afternoon. Let's go up.'

'I thought you didn't like heights,' Perry said.

'It's more the depths that worry me, actually,' Stacy said. 'But you call that a height? You're wimpier than I thought.'

'That so?' Perry said. 'Come on then; I'll race you.'

The height turned out to be more considerable than she had thought, and by the time she reached the top of the hill she was panting. Stockholm sprawled below her in a mountain range of rooftops: squat apartment blocks, copper domes and steeples, pitching gables, ochre shingles, emerging from the trees as the islands themselves rose dripping from the water. She breathed in tortured gasps, air burning her throat as she looked out over the city. Her legs throbbed beneath her, buckling as she collapsed on a nearby bench. Perry stood further off, gazing over the panorama and looking quite composed.

'Goddamn,' Stacy wheezed. 'Trust you to be fit as well.'

'What do I win?' he asked cheerfully.

She caught her breath and followed him across the hill. The Skansen was quite crowded. The visitors were mostly tourists, different from her: they were idiots; she was streetwise. Roadwise. Railwise. Different from Perry, too—he was like she was. Possibly even more so. Such an air about him, as if his whole life were an adventure which sustained him without ever dominating him—an adventure of his own creation. An intriguing character.

'So, listen,' she said. 'I never found out—what do you, like, do?'

He ducked a low-hanging doorframe. 'Mostly this. I travel; I see things.'

'No, I mean what you do normally.'

He smiled. 'So do I.'

'But travelling can't be what you *do*. Travelling is what you do in between doing what you do. When you're not doing what you do, you do that.'

'That's not how it works for me. Travelling is what I do. It's my life.'

'But what do you do when you're at home? You can't travel when you're... at...'

She trailed off, noticing his raised eyebrows.

'You do have a home, don't you?' she said.

'Not as such,' he admitted.

'But everybody has a home. Of some kind, anyway. What's so special about you?'

'Let me put it this way,' he said. 'I grew up in a place called Edmonton. Edmonton, Alberta. Do you know what Edmonton, Alberta is famous for?'

Stacy searched her memory, shaking her head slowly. 'Wait, I do!' she said. 'There's a shopping mall there, isn't there?'

He nodded. 'Right. The world's biggest shopping mall is in Edmonton. Ask anyone you like; if they've heard of the place, it's because of the mall. Which is a pretty lame claim to fame, if you ask me. Not that there's anything wrong with shopping malls, of course—it's quite a nice shopping mall, and it sure is big, there's no denying that. But it's not the sort of thing you want on your numberplate, is it?'

'Well,' Stacy said.

'No. So it's pretty safe to say I come from nowhere. Shopping mall, big fucking deal—the place is a big nowhere. Which would be fine, generally—no reason why your home can't be nowhere, if it's anywhere. The difficulty arises when you leave the nowhere and actually go somewhere. Which I've done. I first left the shopping mall about six years ago, went to Montreal. Which is somewhere. Then I went somewhere else, and somewhere else again, and although I'm a long way from having been everywhere, I've sure seen a lot of somewheres. And when you've got so many somewheres to choose from, the nowhere you came from seems pretty far from your contemplation—it's just eclipsed by all the somewheres. You really can't go back. Not without realising just how much of a nowhere the place really is—so much of a nowhere that it really isn't anywhere. And that can't be your home anymore. No way.'

'No,' Stacy said, thoughts hurtling back across the Atlantic. 'I guess not.'

'No,' Perry agreed. 'That's why the only time I feel homesick is when I'm at home.'

The youth hostel on Skeppsholmen was a fully-rigged clipper which had finally found the harbour after a century of wandering. Its masts swayed in the evening breeze as the sun sank between the islands. Below decks, Stacy and Perry sat in the galley and listened to the sound of groaning wood.

'Just can't seem to get away from boats,' Stacy said.

'No,' Perry agreed. 'Still, we're certainly building up those frequent sailor miles. Nautical miles, that is. Good thing we don't get seasick.'

He was busily addressing postcards, directing them all over the globe. A hot air balloon to Zaire, town hall to Brazil, raised shipwreck to Scotland. A surreal picture of many gumboots went to Algeria. Stacy noticed that nothing was going anywhere near Edmonton, Alberta. She thought of sending a note back home. But home was fading, fading into nothing, into nowhere. Perhaps another day.

A few other travellers occupied the room's wooden benches. They were talking to each other, reading guidebooks, sending curls of smoke towards the low ceiling. A black man in his mid-twenties wandered in and sat down at a nearby table. His hair was short and tightly curled, eyes wide and nervous behind big red-framed glasses. Horizontal furrows clawed his forehead.

'I like pineapples,' he announced to the room. 'But I wouldn't pay twelve dollars for one.'

His accent was American but nasal and effeminate. He gestured fluidly as he talked. The girl sitting across from him looked up and frowned, then turned back to her book.

'No, ten dollars for a cantaloupe is too much,' he continued. 'Like I told them at the hardware store. But everything is too expensive here, for the most part.'

The girl nodded at him, smiling uneasily. 'You're right,' she said. 'It is.'

'It is,' he echoed. 'I'm from New Jersey. Brooklyn, yes, that's right, Los Angeles. But I was born in Phoenix, for the most part. Born and raised in Arkansas. My grandmother was a wonderful woman.'

'Good,' said the girl, perplexed but intent on making an effort. 'What's your name?'

'You won't get an answer out of him, love,' an English man called from the other side of the room. 'That's Marvin; he's not the full quid. But you needn't worry about him, love; he's, you know, he's gay. Fucking arse bandit for the most part, aren't you, Marvin?'

Marvin turned and glared at the Englishman, who looked back defiantly and stubbed out his cigarette. 'You should listen to the Beatles,' Marvin said. 'Strawberry Fields for the most part, yes, I am the walrus. John Lennon was a genius, yes, blowing in the wind. My grandmother listened to them all.'

'Fuck off, Marvin,' the man said good-naturedly. 'Faggot.'

Perry looked up from his postcards and shot a warning glance across the room. The man missed it, reaching for another cigarette. But Stacy caught the glint of antagonism in Perry's eyes—and Marvin appeared to notice as well, spinning on his bench and turning to face their table.

'No man e'er went, nor e'er will go,' he explained. 'Who welcomed what he did not know.'

Perry and Stacy stared at him. The Englishman looked surly and said, 'What the fuck was that? John Lennon, or your grandmother?'

'Such a pity,' Marvin lamented. 'Such a pity my grandmother is dead. And Mozart. And the Beatles. For the most part. A tragedy. No, four ninety-five for a rutabaga is unthinkable.'

'Come and sit over here, Marvin,' Perry said. 'Come tell us about your grandmother.'

Marvin leapt to his feet and crossed the floor to their table. He brought a blue exercise book with him, hiding it under the bench as he sat down.

'I don't have a grandmother,' he said. 'No, never had one. She was born in Detroit to a family of Indians. I'm the last of my family. All the rest aren't related to me.'

Stacy watched Perry with increasing wonder as his conversation with Marvin progressed. Marvin made no sense, talking circles in his fractured way and punctuating his ramblings with 'for the most part'. Perry talked to him without humouring him, picking up on repetitions and deftly confronting him with them, so that their exchange began to follow a path of some logic—or at least some symmetry. She searched his face for some hint of sarcasm, some sign that it was all a rather amusing game. There was none. Maybe Perry was crazy too, or maybe a faggot, an arse-bandit—she laughed at the expression and was surprised at how much the possibility worried her. Strange emotion.

'He was a genius all right,' Perry was saying. '*Imagine* is possibly the most beautiful song ever written. The man was a visionary. Such a tragedy.'

'Prophets of past and future time are always cut down in their prime,' Marvin said. 'But though their bodies may be dead, their souls live on in what they said.'

'There's another thing,' Perry said. 'How do you do that? I know those aren't Beatles lyrics. Are they yours?'

Marvin smiled coyly at him. 'My grandmother said some amazing things. Before she died, for the most part. Before she lived, too, I imagine. Imagine there's no heaven...'

Perry peered over the table and pointed at Marvin's bench. 'That book you've got there,' he said. 'What's that?'

Marvin snatched his exercise book from the floor and clutched it to his chest, rocking like a baby with a security blanket. 'Lucy in the sky with diamonds,' he said.

'No, really,' Perry coaxed. 'What is it, poetry? Stuff you've written? Yeah, give me a look.'

Marvin frowned, but unfolded his arms and handed the book to Perry. He kept talking as Perry flicked through the pages. Anxiety drifted across his face and a panicked note crept into his voice, fuelled by desperation. His eyes never left the exercise book.

'I've been to the city, you know. New York City, the cityingest city of them all. And London, Paris, Cairo, that's where I've been. Never left Texas. There are places I remember, oh yes. In my life. And I've never paid more than five dollars for a banana split, but there's cafe on Broadway where they play Chopin. Divine. Kennedy, King, Kennedy. John Lennon and Malcolm X. Tragic, tragic. And Bob Dylan's old....'

Perry closed the book and slipped it across the table to Stacy. She flipped it open as he and Marvin continued to talk. The handwriting was small and compact, filling the pages from margin to margin, two lines of text for every pale blue stripe. Snatches leapt into her mind, hurtling out of the page like KAPOWIE in a Batman episode. Words and phrases, images effortlessly painting themselves. *The city draws asthmatic breath. Choking. The streets are broken mirrors, shards of life. I'm inside out, and chaos is the one religion. Why do the buildings laugh and stamp their feet? There's nothing worse than loneliness when other people are around. Fear is death. Love is loss. My soul is in the mountains, eating snow. Black and white make red, not grey. I lied and felt my tongue drip blood. I walked the street, and kicked a dog, and ate some dirt, and felt alone. But when I learned that all was gone and nothing could be counted on, I saw the world dissolve like salt in water. And from the fire the phoenix rose and spread its wings, and in its feathers was the world. And people called it resurrection, revolution, evolution, life from death. Like steam from snow. And only this new world had colour. I see you in my dreams and you mistake me for yourself.*

She emerged from the book, blinking. Perry and Marvin had stopped talking about music and vegetables, and were both watching her—Marvin with an air of nervous expectancy, and Perry with a calm and steady gaze of secrets shared. She wondered what they had been talking about. Meaningful exchange, or just word association?

'You're as crazy as each other,' she said. Both of them grinned, as if agreeing. She closed the book and left it lying on the table in front of her, blank cover as inscrutable as Marvin himself. For the most part.

1	Een
2	Twee
3	Tre
4	Fire
5	Viisi
6	Шесть
7	Семь
8	Åtta

9 **Neun**

Splitting headache, fevers and chills, sore throat, blocked nose: a catalogue of symptoms. Caused by—what?—freezing air, wet clothes, poor diet, misfortune. Cured by paracetamol and patience. Damon was running fairly low on both. He rifled through the medicine cabinet Max shared with Martina. Aftershave and tampons, cotton buds and anti-plaque mouthwash. Mint-flavoured dental floss. Closing the cabinet, he caught sight of his reflection. His face was white. He thought: white as paper. His eyes were puffy and ringed with black like tear-smudged mascara. There was a doleful frown etched into his forehead. He looked miserable. Worse, he couldn't concentrate, couldn't think through his throbbing sinuses and head full of snot. He stumbled back into the kitchen and made himself a cup of coffee. It didn't help.

Max and Martina's apartment was compact but stylish.

Everything was red and black and perfectly organised, each piece of furniture arranged as if influenced by some oriental philosophy. The stereo, always an informative social barometer, was matt black and had one button. The speakers were invisible. There was a dishwasher and a microwave, a VCR and a wide-screen TV screaming German-dubbed programmes into Damon's aching brain. The CD tower contained a lot of classical music, and an entire discography of Andrew Lloyd-Webber musicals—a sole concession to bad taste. Overall, the place was meticulous.

Emerging from this refined luxury, Damon was surprised to stumble out of the apartment and find himself in battered East Berlin. Apart from the actual apartments, the tenement block was sombre and old. Unlit staircases led from the flat to the gaunt antechamber where he had searched for Max and Martina's nameplate the night before. From there, heavy gates opened into the pock-marked streets. The half-city looked like an undernourished child—or one with Methuselah's syndrome, old beyond its years but stunted. Many of the buildings had been destroyed in the war and rebuilt exactly as they had stood; the rest had simply been allowed to dilapidate. There were no colours, not even the pastels of Russia. There was only grey. Off-white and faded black and a dirty yellow at best. A gloomy landscape of iron and stone and glass thick with grime.

Trudging for some time through identical streets, Damon finally came across a supermarket—in a manner of speaking. It was a squat, low-roofed room, flickering neon reflecting dully off the linoleum floor. Disgruntled German housewives carried rusty wire baskets around the aisles. Damon searched the shelves for something to make him feel better. The supermarket stocked a little of everything, which amounted to not much of anything. Spaghetti sauce and oven fries, suntan lotion and peanut butter and garden trowels. Spatulas and golf balls and plastic toys. He found a rack of shampoos and conditioners and thought he must be on the right track. But the pharmaceuticals, such as they were, were over by the rolls of toilet paper. Perhaps the goods were arranged alphabetically. In German.

The labels were certainly printed in German. That wasn't

helpful. If pressed by the Gestapo he could probably count to three and order beer, but beyond that his grasp of the language was fairly loose. One packet of tablets showed the silhouette of a man's head being attacked by a lightning bolt—either a cure for headaches or protection from thunderstorms. He took the package from the shelf, along with a few other remedies which he hoped wouldn't alter his heart rate or make him grow breasts, and headed for the lone checkout.

Back at the apartment, he realised that all of the medication's dosage directions were written in German as well. He wondered where the stuff had come from—or when. He scanned the text for cognates. English and German were both supposed to be Teutonic languages—he'd heard that somewhere. But it didn't seem to help. The digits were plain enough, but their context was hazy. Was it 1-2 tablets every 3-4 hours, or vice versa? Or 5-6 tablets for 7-8 year olds? As for before meals, after meals, during meals, with water, without water, upon waking up, before going to bed—he was completely lost. One of the pillboxes had a skull and crossbones on it: not wanting to find out whether it cured poison or *was* poison, he put it directly in the medicine cabinet. He took two tablets or capsules from each of the others and dry-swallowed them, one after the other in a chain of chemicals. Something had to work.

He wandered into the other room and turned on the TV. Donahue was talking German, which in itself was not as strange as the fact that it still sounded exactly like him. The Germans were clearly experts at dubbing. He switched channels. A local band was singing about the Winds of Change. Many gratuitous shots of the Berlin wall and people waving cigarette lighters. The picture was becoming blurry; he got up to adjust the antenna, but that was blurry too. He sat down again, flicking through the channels with the remote control. There were no more pictures, only flashes of colour and snatches of sound as he lurched from station to station. *Ein— hab—kann—mochte—fahr—ich—auf—atsch—gür—zie*, each syllable cut short by a snap of static. The nonsense German sounded like nonsense English.

He threw down the remote control, leaving Herr Donahue to wander the set. The room was swaying around him, and his eyes were squeezing shut like disturbed bivalves. He couldn't tell whether it was the disease or the cure affecting him so disorientingly. His headache was gone, though. Blackness crept across him. Heaving to his feet, he drifted to the nearest bedroom and fell asleep just before collapsing on Martina's bed.

When he woke up, the luminous digits of a bedside alarm clock were towering above him. It was four o'clock already; he would have to think about fixing something for dinner. But it was completely dark around him: had the sun set so early? Surely not. He realised that he hadn't opened his eyes yet; no wonder it was so dark. He tried to prise his eyelids apart but could not. The red numbers were still glowing in front of him. How bright must they have been, to shine straight through his eyelids like that? He shook his head. There was a small red dot by the digits; as he focussed it resolved into the letters 'AM'. It was four in the morning. His eyes were open but it was night outside. Things made more sense. He'd slept sixteen hours—maybe more. Maybe a day and sixteen hours. Maybe a hundred years, like that guy who slept for a hundred years.

A headache was creeping from the back of his skull again, stalking his brain. His throat had closed up; he felt like he was breathing through a straw. And everything seemed distant, as if his sense of perspective had been infected. The apartment was suddenly huge: ceilings towered above him; corridors stretched to infinity. He trekked out into the living room, where the TV set was spewing static. Staring into the snowstorm, he found patterns in the chaos. Circles and triangles and whirling helixes. He willed the shapes to move in various directions and they did, obeying his eyes. Cool. An angel appeared in the static, flapping its wings like a hummingbird. Or it could have been a demon, really—hard to tell with its wings flapping like that. He hit the off button and the world collapsed into a dot.

He put his hand to his forehead, then whipped it away, cursing. He was burning up; too hot to touch. He floated over to the medicine cabinet and took out his smorgasbord of pills. This time he varied the dosage to see what difference it would make: three of these, but only one of those. And no more of those, at least until daylight. He scooped them into his mouth and threw them down with a glass of water. Then he returned to the TV.

The dot had vanished and there was only his curved reflection staring darkly back at him, huge knees and a tiny head. He slumped in a black beanbag and wondered whether he was going to fall asleep again. Apparently not. The more he thought about it, the more improbable sleep seemed. Impossible even. And the apartment was heating up, growing too stuffy to breathe. The walls had returned from their outward journey and were now closing in on him, like the universe was supposed to do in a few million billion years. Surely he hadn't slept that long...

The cool air soothed his skin and tasted delicious. Dim pools of light ran across the flagstones at distant intervals, dripping from lonely streetlamps. He scuttled between their weak haloes, crossing vast tracts of unlit concrete. The moon had set and the night had reached its darkest ebb. Away from the streetlights, buildings loomed above him like great blocks of starless sky. He moved quickly, nervously, like a hunted animal. His eyes darted from side to side as his hunched shoulders propelled him onwards. There was something frightening about this part of the city. It was too much like it had been fifty years ago, too much like the set of a movie about the holocaust. He heard the roar of Hitler's rallies, the echoing clack of jackboots on stone. There were Jews hiding in the attics above him, hiding in mattresses and behind bookshelves. Stormtroopers and gunfire. He looked up and saw only darkness, heard nothing but silence. Just his imagination. But the truth was even more chilling, for in truth there were no Jews nearby, no Jews at all. They had all gone and most of them were dead. And no further need for stormtroopers: they had done their job too well.

Another streetlight. He lingered in its protective glow, leaning against its iron stalk. Catching his breath. Then away again: another stretch of darkness. The fear was disappearing—nothing to fear in a ghost town—but his feeling of unease remained.

There was too much history here. The past clung jealously to the city, refusing to relinquish its hold. It wasn't necessary. It was important not to forget, of course—but, really, life went on. Except in East Berlin at half-past four in the morning, where not much was going on at all. Just a lonely figure darting between streetlamps, trying to avoid being stomped on by restless ghosts.

The sky was beginning to lighten by the time he arrived at the end of the road and found himself dwarfed by the Brandenburger Tor. Massive columns towered against a sky no longer black. The old bronze of Schadow's horse-and-chariot *Quadriga* grew greener as Damon and the sun approached it gradually. He craned his neck as he walked through the gate—for a moment he was nowhere, and then he was in West Berlin.

East and West had been integrated, of course. Damon had simply strolled between the columns, feeling a momentary weirdness but not having to negotiate sentries with guard dogs and machine guns. There was no sign of the wall; it had been broken up and spread across Europe, then sold to tourists and distributed around the world. Berlin was officially one. But reality didn't quite correspond with the official version. Even Damon, wandering over the obsolete boundary in the empty pre-dawn, could see the difference. Immediately the roads were better, the lights more regular—and there was neon, scarring buildings with its luminous blood, flickering red, green, blue and white. Colour. He felt like he had left cold Kansas and stepped into Oz. Since the division they had called this the American Sector. It was an appropriate label: here was a billboard for Levi's, there a Coke sign. And over there the mighty golden arches, brighter than the columns of the Gate—and a Nike more famous than the goddess in the chariot. There was so much comfort in tackiness. Damon felt at home, walking down the street to the rhythm of distant music, desperate dawn stylings from underground clubs nearby. At a certain time of night all cities became indistinguishable.

The sun peeked over the horizon as Damon circled the

Siegessäule, Frederick the Great's victory column, at the hub of five roads in the middle of the Tiergarten. Seventy feet up, the angel raised her sceptre towards Paris, frozen in a triumphant step. Damon stared at her, dumbfounded. There was nothing more beautiful. The figure was too exquisite to exist in real life; too powerful to be anything but a symbol. But there it was. Tears of wonder filled his eyes, cold in the morning air. Immediately his nose began to run. He dug into his inside pocket and popped a few more pills, no longer caring what exactly he was ingesting, which neurotransmitters he was confusing. Then he sat on the concrete and gazed to the top of the column.

The angel was talking to him. That was weird. Weird that the statue was speaking at all, and weird that he could hear her all the way from the ground. But he could—straining his ears, he could catch her words as they tumbled down upon him like autumn leaves.

'Seek beauty in all things,' she said. The line seemed to hang in the air before his eyes, carving itself into the statue's base.

'What?' Damon said. 'What do you mean? When?'

The angel remained silent. Damon pondered her advice.

'Beauty?' he said. 'I thought it was supposed to be love. Love makes the world go round. Look at the Top 40; that's all there is.'

She fluttered her metal wings. 'Love is your greatest enemy,' she said.

'Right,' Damon said, nodding. 'Yeah, I thought so. So, beauty's the way to go?'

The angel dipped her head in a single nod. Her sceptre seemed to have swapped hands—and what was it in her other hand? A ring, crown, donut, what? Probably too ceremonious to be a donut. He suddenly felt hungry.

'Yeah, thanks,' he muttered, glancing upwards. 'I'm glad we had this chat. I was beginning to feel, you know, sane. But I'm going to stop talking to you now.'

'See you sometime,' the angel said, freezing into a deeper stillness. Damon sat back against the base of the column. The pillar pulled its shadow closer and the angel's silhouette flickered across the asphalt, fading in and out as clouds swept the rising sun. It was a pity she hadn't been more talkative. There must have been all sorts of useful things she could have told him. The meaning of life, maybe. The nature of God, the size of the universe, the sound of one hand clapping, some good jokes, where to eat in Berlin, and what the hell was in these pills...

'*Achtung*!'

A guard nudged him in the ribs with a steel-capped toe.

Damon shifted his weight and stared up at the guard. 'What?' he said.

'You can't sleep here,' the guard said, shifting into English. 'The monument is about to open.'

Damon looked across the square. A loose cluster of tourists had gathered around the column and stood loading their cameras, checking their watches. Damon glanced at his own wrist: it was two in the afternoon. The sky was patchy with clouds, blue and white like a warped checkerboard.

'We can go up?' Damon asked. 'Up to the angel?'

'For a deutschmark a great many things are possible,' the guard told him. 'Even talking with angels.'

Who needs a deutschmark, Damon thought. A few capsules of dioxy-metha-whatever-it-was does the trick nicely. But he handed over a silver coin, noticing the wings of the imperial eagle embossed on its obverse. Wings for an angel. The guard opened a door in the foot of the monument, and he followed the tourists to the top.

The angel was bigger than she had looked. She towered over the wire-grilled observation deck; he stared up at her golden legs, looking for signs of animation. But she had gone back to sleep—or else she was busy at her post, vigilant over the city. Damon circled the crows-nest, gazing down with his angel's-eye view. The Brandenburg Gate sat solidly across one road; beside it, the remains of the wall cut the city in half. Where the wall had gone there were piles of rubble; where the rubble had gone, a conspicuously empty strip of no-man's-land. The elevated rails of the S-Bahn teased the boundary, snaking along the old border and darting impudently from one side to the other.

He had the image of Siamese twins grown curiously non-identical. Ost and West: the Berlin twins. One, flamboyant, confident, handsome and good at sport, was invited to all the right parties. The other, earnest, homely and somewhat stunted, stayed at home working on tractors. People came up to talk to West, ignoring poor Ost. For thirty years they had grown apart. But while twins were separated, Berlin had been unified, though clumsily and incompletely. A botched operation whose scars still remained.

He spent the next few days wandering the city, crossing the border many times, dipping into East and West. The sleek U-Bahn and rattling S-Bahn trains sped him between destinations, fairly ripping through his guidebook's list of Things to Do. Berlin was certainly full of beauty. From the startling architecture to the haunting sadness of memory, the city provided countless opportunities for fulfilling the angel's directive. And Damon was determined to savour every one of them. He continued to take his unknown medication; his symptoms gradually alleviated, but things got considerably weirder as the week progressed. Still he went on, sometimes wandering like a zombie with little awareness of his surroundings, sometimes speeding through the streets while sensory messages beyond comprehension crammed his consciousness. East to West; West to East: beauty, beauty, beauty.

Then he was nowhere. Or everywhere. On a narrow strip of asphalt by Checkpoint Charlie, past the sign warning him in four languages that he was leaving the American Sector, a few paces before the old East. He stood for a while, reflecting that such hesitation would once have been fatal, hearing phantom gunfire and the echo of shouts finally dead.

Hawkers were selling chunks of the wall here as everywhere, but here a section was still standing. It looked fairly unimpressive, some twenty metres long and two high, ridged with concrete piping and covered with countless layers of graffiti. *Save our Planet* and *Anthrax* and *Kris Was Here 1991* and giant malformed faces. Damon stared at the wall, reading deeper as his eyes found smaller and older inscriptions hiding in the jungle of spray-paint. He stepped backwards, losing his balance.

Something clicked in his mind. The patterns began to spiral outward and suddenly the wall was full of tiny pictures of his life, his own life—thumbnail sketches painted in negative space, scenes built entirely of letters. Almost everything was there; everything he could remember. *This is Your Life* on a wall. Staring at the display, he was surprised at how interesting some of the scenes were to him—some even approaching beauty. Plenty of boring and ugly exhibits, of course: sitting in a lecture theatre, driving in peak traffic, throwing up in a parking lot, waiting in line for a nightclub. Being pushed this way and that, bumping between friends and family, never noticing what was happening to him until it was too late. There was much to be ashamed of, or simply to forget. But there he was standing on a hill in a thunderstorm, spinning in soaked circles; and, later, swimming underwater and watching the sunset ripple through the surface of the ocean. And there he was at five in the morning, drunk with a heartbroken friend, wondering only in passing how he was going to get up in two hours' time. Speeding on a country road with his head out the window and the stereo screaming in the wind. Saying *I love you* and *This is what you mean to me.*

There was beauty in his life, he saw. Not the kind he had been looking for, perhaps. Not monumental tragedies or aching poignancies. Nothing earth-shattering. But fragments here and there, subtle tinges. He remembered how he had felt, all those fleeting times. A flash of warmth, a chill: a spreading smile. The impression that the world was well. He had shaken the feeling off every time; or it had become drowned in his dissatisfaction, his confusion. But each scrap was a piece of him, he realised. And all the scraps together—perhaps they were him, after all.

There he was: Damon the lover. Not in bed with Katja, but taking her phone number and placing it tenderly in his wallet, where it still lay. And there, Damon the artist. Not holding his thumb against Dutch terraces, but noticing Stacy's distracted pain through his viewfinder and realising he could never capture it. There, Damon the musician: not spinning shit in a bar with James, but singing his drunken heart out on a street with Russians. Damon the actor did not impress strangers with a new role every day; instead, he was lost, searching, looking for resonances within himself. Even Damon the lawyer was there, in the wall: not learning how to trick juries or discredit witnesses, but looking around him, seeing injustice and turmoil in every country, and wishing it were otherwise.

He blinked as the wall shimmered subtly and reverted back to its simpler state, hidden images lost like a stereogram before untrained eyes, a 3D movie with no glasses. And like both of these things, the shifting wall left him with a killer headache, an icy spike which lodged in his forebrain and sent him staggering back to the apartment, marvelling at his life's newfound richness but equally happy to end it all by leaping beneath the S-Bahn.

The Kurfürstendamm stretched a glowing thread across West Berlin, pulsing with the neon of billboards and display windows. By the Zoo Station, the street was crammed with clothing, electronics and duty free stores; further away the lights grew less colourful and walls of sound from underground nightclubs ran into each other. Downstairs, Damon leant on a wooden bar and ordered a stein of German beer.

'*Ein bier, bitte,*' he shouted at the barman. Through a glass door, shadowy figures writhed to a muffled beat, flashing red and green. Whenever the door was heaved open, the music snapped into focus, blasting the bar area with its deafening punctuation. The barman returned and slid a glass of beer across the teak.

'*Danke schoen*,' Damon said gratefully. He lifted the mug to his lips and swallowed in satisfaction, reflecting that as long as he could order beer he could get by in any language. '*Merci beaucoups. Sbaceba.* Thanks a bunch.'

The skinhead slouching next to him turned and scowled. He wore a trenchcoat and heavy boots, and let forth a stream of guttural German which was not about beer and was thus beyond Damon's comprehension.

Damon started with recognition. 'James!' he cried. 'James from Amsterdam! James, my horny mate. How's it going?'

James raised a clenched fist. There was a swastika tattooed on each of his knuckles. But James hadn't had any tattoos. And he had been a lot more friendly. And he didn't speak German either. Damon realised his mistake.

'Sorry,' he said. '*Pardon. Bitte.* Sorry. I thought you were someone else.'

The German leered up at him. There was a mark on his forehead, obscured by his hair and too blurry to make out. His eyes flashed dangerously.

'Where are you from?' he demanded.

'Australia,' Damon stammered.

The German looked suspicious. 'Not from Russia?'

'No—not Russia. Australia.'

'Australian?'

'Yes. *Ja.*'

'Not Russian?'

'No.'

'Good,' the German said. 'Russia is dead.'

'Oh?' Damon said politely. 'Is it?'

The German nodded emphatically. 'Russia has fucked our country. But the revolution is at hand. Soon Russia is dead. We will bury her.'

'Will you?' Damon said. 'Who are you?'

'We,' the German said, pointing along the bar. There were a few more skinheads propped against the counter, scraping studded leather sleeves across the teak. They were all decorated with clumsy jailhouse tattoos and wore swastika armbands. They all looked unrelentingly mean. 'We will teach Russia a lesson she will not forget.'

'Oh,' Damon said. 'Listen, you're not—you're not Neo-Nazis, by any chance?'

The German laughed deeply at him, then turned to his friends and shouted something at them. They all raised their arms and cried 'Sieg Heil!' in unison, which Damon interpreted as an affirmative response.

'Neo-Nazis,' he mused. 'How interesting.'

The nearest Neo-Nazi suddenly stood up and thrust his face in Damon's. A beery stench wafted from his mouth, and his eyes swam pink in their sockets. He scooped up his forelock and pressed it against his scalp, baring his forehead.

'See that?' he hissed.

The tattoo danced before Damon's eyes. The initials scrawled across the Neo-Nazi's forehead in a spidery script, blue-green against his skin. Damon nodded.

'DM,' he read aloud.

'Know what that means?'

Damon shook his head. 'Deutschmark?' he hazarded.

The skinhead frowned. 'A clue. Enjoy the silence.'

'What?'

The skinhead looked impatient. 'Black celebration,' he prompted.

'Sounds familiar,' Damon offered appeasingly.

The skinhead stepped back and reached into his jacket, holding something inside it with an air of menace. 'I just can't get enough,' he warned.

Recognition. 'Oh!' Damon finally said, relief flooding through him. 'Wait, no—you're... you're Depeche Mode fans?'

The German flashed a serrated grin. 'You are a fan also?'

'A fan?' Damon said tentatively; then, seeing the German's expression change: 'Of course! Sure, why not? The eighties were a fantastic decade. Wham! should never have split up; that was a tragedy. And Depeche Mode—well, what can I say?'

The German turned once more to his Neo-Nazi friends. This time their salutes were accompanied by a rousing chorus of 'I just can't get enough!'

'But I don't understand,' Damon said. He sensed he was heading into possibly dangerous and certainly bizarre territory. 'What's Depeche Mode got to do with Russia?'

'Russia is dead!' the German shouted. 'The revolution is at hand! We will rise against Russia and crush her!'

'Hey, that rhymed,' Damon said. 'Depeche Mode could never write lyrics like that.'

'November eleventh,' the skinhead said menacingly. 'On the eleventh of November Russia will be no more.'

Remembrance Day, Damon mused. And something to do with Gough Whitlam. He pondered the significance of the date. But there were other things bothering him.

'So, let's recap,' he said. 'You—sorry, what's your name?'

The German saluted him and barked, 'Adolf.'

Damon looked pained. 'Come on,' he said. 'That's not your real name.'

'*Ja, ja*, yes, it is,' the German persisted.

'Your parents called you Adolf?'

'I gave myself that name,' Adolf said defensively.

'So what did your parents call you?'

Adolf looked uncomfortable. 'Errol,' he admitted. 'My parents called me Errol. But if you call me that I will cut out your tongue and use it for bratwurst.'

'Fair enough,' Damon said. 'Well, what I was saying was: you, Adolf, you and your Neo-Nazi friends, are going to invade Russia—all six of you against the biggest country in the world, armed only with your 12" remixes of Depeche Mode classics?'

'Yes.' Adolf nodded enthusiastically. 'Russia is dead.'

'Goddamn,' Damon said. 'You're crazier than I am.'

Adolf guffawed in delight and slapped him on the back. He shouted something at the rest of the Depeche Mode fan club and they all started to laugh and signal appreciatively at Damon. One of them bought him another beer and they all began to sing again, swaying on their barstools like drunken sailors bellowing shanties. They were becoming far too ridiculous to be sinister or even threatening, but Damon nonetheless filed the proposed date of the revolution in his memory. If it came to anything he could say: I told you so. And it was less than a week away.

He left the Neo-Nazis to their retrospective and turned towards the other end of the bar. The doors opened and closed a few more times, floodgates releasing waves of sound. His head pulsed as the music tore through his brain, disorienting him. The world performed a quick pirouette and the bar flew up to meet his forehead.

'That hurt,' he said, resting his head on the teak. Everything was sideways. The bar was a desert highway, stretching away from him and blurring into haze as it drew too close to focus on. Glasses and bottles ploughed towards him like motionless 18-wheelers. The babble of voices sounded like crickets chirping far away.

'Are you okay?'

A face appeared before him, circled by a blonde halo. It was an androgynous face, rugged but tender, with thick-set features which were nonetheless soft. A broad mouth, lips like an afterthought. Eyes red with bulging blood vessels, drunken eyes etched with crow's feet.

Damon raised his head as the room rotated. Androgynous, but certainly a woman's face. And most definitely a woman's body, curving towards the ground with contours which defied gravity. He looked back up to her face and was surprised that such clumsy features could belong to a body so elegant. He wondered whether he had miscounted, whether there were really two people sitting on the same barstool.

'I'm all right,' he said to both of them. 'Well, I don't know, actually. I just met some Neo-Nazi Depeche Mode fans, and earlier today an angel told me to seek beauty in all things.'

'That's good advice,' she said. Her face lit up with the warmth of a gentle smile. Suddenly it was a beautiful face; there was only one of her after all.

'Yeah,' Damon said. 'You're quite beautiful, you know that?'

She smiled again. 'I know. Thank you.'

Damon nodded appreciatively. 'It's good that you know. That's very good. I might fall in love with you, but the angel told me that love was my greatest enemy.'

'Love *is* your greatest enemy,' she agreed. 'Don't fall in love with me. But you're welcome to find me beautiful.'

'I'm not sure I understand completely,' Damon admitted. 'I mean, if an angel said it I suppose it must be true, but I never really thought of beauty as the thing to go for.'

'To find beauty in something, to let it touch you, is to recognise what is beautiful in yourself. Beauty is a mirror. Ugly people live in an ugly world, but the better the world looks to you, the more you unearth the perfection of your soul.'

Damon stared at her. 'Are you an angel too?'

'No,' she said. 'I'm a waitress. But to me, many things are beautiful.'

'What about love? When something is beautiful, you fall in love with it, right?'

She shook her head. 'That's the last thing you want to do. Oh, it's hard to avoid. The seduction of beauty is great. But you have to resist. Beauty strengthens you, but love will sap your energy. Love debases the soul, subjugates it to the object of love. Beauty is about the self, but love is about the other. Love is self-effacement and slavery. That's why it's your greatest enemy.'

'Oh,' Damon said. 'But isn't it good to, like, put other people before yourself?'

'Why is that good?'

'I dunno,' Damon said. 'It's Zen or something.'

She made a disparaging face. 'Self-denial is for people who find themselves repulsive. These are the people who fall in love. In beauty you will see yourself, but in love you will lose yourself. The choice is obvious.'

Damon chewed this over. 'How about sex?' he said.

She looked him up and down. 'No thanks,' she said. 'You're too young for me.'

'I didn't mean—'

His shoulder exploded with sudden impact and he turned to find Errol the Neo-Nazi leering up at him.

'Come on!' the skinhead shouted. 'Let's go!'

'Adolf!' Damon said. 'Jesus, you scared the shit out of me!'

'Come on!' he repeated. 'We're going. Come on!'

'You go,' Damon said. 'I'm talking to—'

He turned around to indicate the beautiful waitress, but she had vanished. Damon shook his head. Had she really...?

'Let's go!' Adolf persisted, dragging Damon to his feet.

'Where are we going?' Damon cried as the gang stampeded up the stairs.

'Run amuck!' the skinhead cried. 'What the fuck! Run amuck!'

The bellowed chorus of a Depeche Mode song was already ringing through the streets.

They charged along the Ku'damm, eight or ten skinheads in studded leather with amateur tattoos, swastikas, jackboots— and Damon, caught in the middle, borne by the current of their insanity. He looked frantically around, wondering how he could manage to sneak off unnoticed. He was too sick for this shit. And the group had changed, tempered by adrenaline and mass hysteria. The humour was vanishing, drained like blood from a fainter's face. They were working themselves into a destructive frenzy, choking in a cloud of menace and volatility. They jumped against walls, battered street signs, smashed lights, sent dazed pedestrians sprawling. They had stopped singing Depeche Mode; reborn Nazi slogans stabbed at the night, carried on voices hoarse with exhilaration.

'Woah,' he panted at Adolf. 'This is my stop. I'll just get off here.'

But Adolf ignored him, picked up a bottle and hurled it through the window of a duty-free shop. Damon saw everything at once. Long splinters of glass fell jangling in slow motion, blue light spilled into the street and a wailing alarm sounded like an air raid. A security guard broke into a sprint, hand on his holster, barking in German. One of the skinheads tripped on the glass and struggled to his feet, knees tattered and bloody. There were eyes everywhere, angled in his direction, wide with interest.

Adolf shouted and took off down the street, dragging a trail of skinheads. In a split-second Damon considered just blending into the crowd, then felt the gaze of a hundred witnesses and lurched after the Nazis, pounding the pavement as his heart and head and throat pounded the walls of his body.

He caught up with them quickly, air-cushioned sneakers more suited to getaway than their steel-capped boots. The world jarred around him, bouncing each time his feet struck the pavement. His body seemed to be working on its own, legs pinwheeling in blurred cartoon circles. He felt nothing but the wind in his face, felt like he was running on air. The Neo-Nazis whooped around him, laughing insanely. He felt their delirium envelop him. His temples throbbed with boiling blood; he let his arms trail behind him and hurled himself forward, exhilarated.

He thought: what the fuck? I'm bonding with fascists. But the coursing adrenaline snatched his thoughts away and sped him faster down the street, waste paper spiralling in his wake.

He felt a tug at his shoulder, wrenching his neck. He stopped, panting, and looked around. The Ku'damm had disappeared, and with it the streetlights and neon. A dim alley stretched into darkness. The skinheads were there, doubled over with exhaustion, breathing heavily. Laughter emerged from their heaving; they high-fived each other and slapped triumphant backs. Damon joined them in their rough-housing, high on an unthinking camaraderie.

'You're fucking nuts!' he shouted. 'We're fucking nuts! What the hell was that?'

'Run amuck!' the skinheads cried. 'What the—'

'What the fuck!' Damon shouted over them. 'Yeah, I know. What the fuck! Run amuck! You crazy fuckers!'

Adolf took Damon by the shoulder and and grinned into his face. 'You're okay!' he blasted. 'This guy's okay! One of us! One of us crazy fuckers!'

'And *you*!' Damon said, grabbing Adolf by the collar. 'You threw a bottle through the fucking window! You—'

There was a sudden percussion and the sound of breaking glass. Damon stopped and looked down. At his feet, shards like ice crystals spread across the asphalt. In the middle of the pattern lay his painting, the one from the black market, empty signs and a traveller caught in a hub of roads. *Untitled*. He stared at it. He had no idea where it had come from; one of his pockets, obviously—probably his jacket. He couldn't remember putting it there. But there it was, leaping out like a divine symbol. Choices.

Adolf reached down and picked it up. He brushed the remaining splinters of glass from the metal frame and threw it to one of the other skinheads.

'Hey, give that back,' Damon protested. 'That's mine.'

The skinhead threw the painting on. 'You're one of us now,' he said. 'What's yours is ours.'

'I'm not one of you,' Damon said. 'Come on, give it back.'

The painting danced between the Neo-Nazis, leaping from

hand to tattooed hand. They were staring at him, looking less friendly than before.

'It's just a painting,' one of them said.

'It's special,' Damon said. 'I got it in Russia.'

Big mistake.

'Russia?' Adolf screeched at him. 'You're from Russia?'

Damon backed away. 'No! I'm not from Russia, I—'

'You're from fucking *Russia*?'

'I'm not from Russia! I was just visiting. Two days! I bought this there.'

'How much did you pay?'

'What—'

'*How much did you pay?*'

'Seven dollars.'

Adolf was turning red, veins bulging. '*Seven dollars?* In Russia seven dollars will buy an AK-47 assault rifle!'

'It's not a fucking rifle! It's a painting!'

'You gave American money to the Russians? Russia is dead! You bought guns for our enemies! *Communist! Fucking communist!*'

'Capitalist!' Damon shouted. 'Capitalist! It was the black market! It was—'

He only felt the impact, sudden as a jackhammer against his jaw. His head snapped backwards as Adolf's fist completed its arc. He looked at him, confused, and wondered where the pain had gone. Then it arrived, flooded through him, exploding from his mouth, sending shock waves through his body. He tasted blood, felt like his teeth had impaled his lips. But that was all there was. He felt nothing as the other skinheads laid into him, punching him in the face, kicking him in the ribs, pummelling his kidneys. There was no pain as he lay on the ground, hunched into a foetal position, wondering when the rain of blows would stop. All he felt was concern that he couldn't breathe and a distant panic at the clouds of blackness settling over his eyes. Then there was only noise, angry German cries filling his head like his own thoughts.

He woke up in Max's bed. The pillow had been red to start

with; now, drying blood was fading into view like invisible ink, sketching the dark map of a new continent. His entire body was wrapped in a dull ache punctuated by stabbing pains. He staggered to the bathroom, rinsed his mouth and spat bloody water like a consumptive. The face in the mirror was an alien's, the face of a mutant. Blackened eyes, split lip, cheeks like Marlon Brando. At least nothing felt broken; the damage was superficial. And all the pain was on the surface: his skin and flesh felt like they were on fire, but deep down he was fine. He realised with a start that his headache and twisted throat had vanished. He was the right temperature, and there was blood, but no mucus, blocking his nose. His mind felt clear, alert, uncluttered. Life was livable.

He looked around the apartment for some time, but the painting had gone.

1 Een
2 Twee
3 Tre
4 Fire
5 Viisi
6 Шесть
7 Семь
8 Åtta
9 Neun

10   Deset

He looked awful, but seemed happy to see them.

'You look like hell,' Stacy told him.

'Thanks,' he said. 'I guess we've both been there now.'

He stepped backwards and let the door open into the apartment. She and Perry followed him inside. The flat looked cold but felt warm.

'What happened to you, man?' Perry asked.

Damon turned and looked at them. His face was bruised, skin punctured above the eye and lip, but he seemed unaware of his injuries. Expressions darted across his face without treading gingerly. Strange, new expressions as well: happiness, humour. He was wearing his glasses again, lenses catching the light.

'I talked with an angel and some Neo-Nazis beat me up,' he said. 'How are you two?'

He knew already. He was thinking: lovebirds? Sweethearts?

Treacherous fuck-monsters? Or just her guilty conscience. She looked across at Perry, who met her eyes briefly, then turned away. No lingering stares, no gazing at infinite reflections. Careful, careful. As they had agreed.

'Oh, man, you should have come with us,' Perry said. 'You should have given Stockholm another chance. It was beautiful; the weather was perfect and the youth hostel was on this boat...'

'Oh, I've had quite a time of it here,' Damon said. 'Wouldn't have missed it for the world.'

There was something different about his tone—and about his expression. Beneath the healing scars and fading bruises there was something missing from his face. She couldn't figure out what it was.

She reached out and brushed his cheek with the back of her hand.

'Are you all right?' she said.

He took her hand and removed it from his face. His fingers were warm, confident. He looked into her eyes, and again his expression was almost unrecognisable.

'I'm all right,' he said. 'Thanks.'

And for an instant she almost knew.

The train's origins clearly leaned closer to Prague than to Germany. Everything was hard and cold, uncomfortable. The carriages shuddered as iron pounded steel. A narrow wedge of frozen air hissed through the unsealable window, curling through the cabin in cold convection. Nothing short of an oxy-welder would persuade the seats to recline, so they sat bolt upright and tried to convince their bodies that gravity had turned horizontal. Stacy dozed for a while, slipping unsatisfactorily in and out of sleep, finally contenting herself with sitting in the dark with her eyes closed. Objectively no difference.

Damon and Perry had given up altogether and were talking softly.

'Look, she's asleep,' Damon said. His voice was so gentle that she almost believed him.

'Half her luck,' Perry said.

She felt a twinge of guilt, felt like she should leap up and show them she was awake. But it was too much effort; she couldn't even open her eyes. Perhaps she really was asleep, dreaming of insomnia.

'I understand what you were talking about in Finland,' Damon said. 'On the tower. I mean, I understood it then, but now I know it.'

'Good.' That was Perry. Of course. 'That's good to hear.'

'How long have you been travelling?'

'Six years.'

'That long? No wonder you're so together.'

'I'm not so together.'

'She likes you.'

'Maybe.'

'No, she does. Maybe when I've been travelling for six years I'll be together enough for her to like me too.'

'She likes you already.'

'What, did she say something?'

'No.'

'Well, that's okay. I don't really mind. I'm still getting the hang of this, but I realise the thing to do isn't to get all worked up over her. It's just—to appreciate her, for who she is, for how beautiful she is. Because she's so beautiful.'

'She sure is.'

'I wonder if you know just how beautiful she is. No, I can tell you don't. Maybe she'll tell you. I'm not supposed to know, myself... and I kind of wish I didn't, because it's unbearable, really. What she's been through. There's so much sadness, so much sad beauty. She's like a burning funeral boat cast off in a sea of icebergs. That's how beautiful she is; how beautiful and... tragic.'

'I wish I knew.'

'I can't tell you.'

'I know.'

'So... look after her, okay?'

'She's not mine to look after.'

'No, I know. But she's more yours than mine. I mean, you guys seem to have some sort of thing going... of some sort.'

'You shouldn't go making assumptions.'

'Then I'm wrong?'

Perry didn't say anything for a while. Then his voice rose again. 'You don't think she's awake, do you?'

Even with her eyes closed, even through the darkness, she could see Damon smiling wryly. 'I know she is.'

Of course, it was all a dream. Dream voices in the night, dream tears trapped behind her eyelids. And dream emotions coursing through her mind, nebulous and expansive and unsure of who had given them life.

Now Damon was awake, and alone. Prague was less than 300 kilometres distant, but the antique train was taking the scenic route and had spent all night tracing a hesitant path along the various rivers of Moravia, distant Carpathians rising gothic over the horizon. Five-thirty was the darkest time, dawn just a flicker in the near-winter blackness. A few silhouettes rose against the darkness, and occasionally a sliver of rippling starlight marked the river.

Perry and Stacy were asleep opposite him, leaning against each other. He stared at them until he could discern their outlines in the dim light. A cozy huddle, pyramid of warmth. He wondered what they had between them. It had seemed sexual, a while ago, a lifetime. In Scandinavia he was certain that they were on the brink, a conversation or maybe three beers away from consummation. When they arrived in Berlin it looked like they were in full swing; he had thought his prophecy fulfilled. But since then, nothing. Just this tactile, almost supportive friendship. Like the tail end of passion, the aftermath.

Outside was greying, and a pale light drifted through the windows. Stacy and Perry were faintly illuminated, lying together like lovers in a suicide pact. Did Romeo and Juliet have sex? Another mystery. They looked incongruous together. But somehow they worked; yin and yang, opposites. Damon felt a twinge of jealousy; stifled it. Not now. Not anymore.

The north arm of the metro carved through the bedrock of suburban Prague. Stations whisked past, walls studded with art-deco adornments, shapes and colours which once looked futuristic but now dated the infrastructure. Indiscernible names crackled over the intercom, and Perry was still trying to negotiate with the landlord.

'First you said 500 a night for the room,' he argued. 'Then you said that was 200 each. Two hundred each is 600; that's wrong. Five hundred is all you get.'

The Czech shook his head. He had approached them as soon as they had arrived in the central station. Keen: it wasn't seven o'clock yet. 'Is not per room, is per person,' he said. 'Five hundred koruny for one person, 300 for two, each, 200 each for three. Nice place, best in town.'

'It's not *in* town,' Perry said. 'It's in an outer suburb. We'll work it out between us and give you 500 a night.'

'Five hundred, your friends find somewhere else to stay.'

'Look, don't be an asshole, okay? Don't perpetuate cultural stereotypes. Be fair now. You're already charging us double because we're from out of town.'

'You American?'

'North American, yeah. She's American.'

'American dollars?'

'We have some, yes.'

'Pay in American dollars, 150 koruny each. That is... seven dollars.'

Perry performed a quick calculation. 'Gimme a break. That's *six* dollars, at the most, and you can get a better rate on the black market. We'll give you six.'

The landlord looked thoughtful, then held out his hand. 'Okay. Deal. Shake, yes?'

Perry snatched his own hand away. 'Noooosir. First we look at the apartment.'

The apartment was fairly basic: a bedroom, a spacious living room and a kitchen. A few rickety beds and a pile of mattresses which looked like the most comfortable option. There was pale green lino on the floor, geometric wallpaper on the walls. But it seemed to be all that was going, so they took it. The landlord collected their greenbacks and promised to come back tomorrow for some more.

Prague was a city of chaos, five historic towns fused into a recent whole. Wenceslas Square protected the Old Town of Staré Mestro from the upstart New Town, a mere architectural infant at 650 years. Across the river the castles at Hradcany loomed, and the Lesser Town of Malá Strana felt wrongly inferior. Nearby sprawled Josefov, known as the Jewish quarter but actually only a fifth. Everywhere streets led nowhere, alleys collided with each other, and narrow thoroughfares tied themselves in knots. It was a place to get lost in, walls reaching baroquely skyward, everything at angles, confounding direction. And people crowding together, shopping, talking, eating with their fingers as they walked. Selling crepes through holes in the wall, shining shoes, hawking clothes and the military paraphernalia all of Europe seemed desperate to get rid of. Cathedral spires stretched towards wispy cirrus clouds in the too-blue sky.

Damon and Perry watched as Stacy carried her waffle towards them, dripping chocolate onto the cobbles. It was hard to tell who in the crowd was a tourist.

'That looks pretty good,' Damon said.

Stacy nodded, licking syrup from between her fingers. 'What have you got?'

'These cute little sandwich-things. They came from that shop around the corner; I got a whole stack of them for a dollar. It's a great idea; just these little bits of bread with stuff on them. They're like hors d'oeuvres—this entire city, all they've got is finger foods. It's like being at a party the whole time. Mate!'

Perry smiled. 'Mate!' he echoed. 'You know, I'm really starting to hear your accent now. Maybe I just know you better, but it sure sounds stronger than before.'

'You're right,' Stacy said. 'I hear it too. It's funny.'

'It's cool,' Perry said. 'Ger-*dye*, mite. Hev yer *seen* me king-ger-*reuh*?'

'Yeer mite,' Stacy said. 'Out boi yer bell-a-bang.'

'That's awful,' Damon winced. 'You guys are terrible.'

'Tirrabull,' Perry mimicked.

The Charles Bridge pulled the old cities together, shallow

arches tracing a skipping-stone's path across the Vltava. Dark statues blessed each other at intervals. The bridge was broad and solid, built from old stone, closed to traffic. Cars and trucks chugged across newer structures further up and down the river, but Karluv was reserved for pedestrians. Market stalls and buskers lined the walls and entrenched themselves in alcoves. There were hippy clothes and jewellery and, of course, apocryphal bits of the Berlin wall. Guitarists playing Bob Dylan, The Doors, Nirvana, more.

'I love this song!' Damon exclaimed. 'Oh, man, this is the best Australian pop song ever.'

Perry and Stacy drew up beside him as he stopped and listened to the singer belting out the lyrics. *Throw your arms around me.* An audience had gathered round. Damon felt a surge of patriotism warm him. An Australian tune. And it wasn't Kylie Minogue this time; this was actually a good song. He looked over to the musician, glimpsed his shaved head and trenchcoat through the crowd. Unbelievable. A Neo-Nazi singing so beautifully? He turned away, face twitching. The music stopped.

'Like to thank Mark Seymour for that one,' the skinhead said. 'A dear friend who I've never met. From a country I lived in once.'

That voice. Damon turned back and strode around the crowd, watching them swing around his periphery as he locked his gaze on the singer's position. The figures dropped away and there he was: James, definitely James this time, sitting on the edge of the bridge and picking random notes from a beat-up guitar.

'Mate, I keep running into you,' Damon said. 'Only last time you beat the shit out of me.'

James looked up. Recognition took a while coming. Then he grinned. 'I can't have been myself that day,' he said. 'Damon! My expatriate compatriot! What's happened to your voice?'

'What?'

'You old bugger, don't come the raw prawn with me,' James twanged. 'Your voice, mate, it's gone all Ocker on you.'

'People keep saying that,' Damon said. 'But I can't hear it.'

'You're a very strange guy,' James told him. 'Most people lose their accents when they travel.'

'You'd think so. But apparently I've got mine back.'

'Yeah, well, that's the other thing that can happen.'

'But—what are you doing here?'

'Here?' James slapped the stone affectionately. 'Here is the only place to be. I've been here three weeks and I don't think I'll be leaving. It's fantastic.'

'Looks pretty good,' Damon agreed. 'We just got here this morning.'

'Mate, you'll love it here. I mean, just feel it. Feel the atmosphere. This is Bohemian country—literally! Everyone's an artist, or a poet, or a musician, and they're *all on drugs*. You should come jam with some of us; you're in a band, right? What do you play again?'

Damon stared at James's guitar. 'Drums,' he said.

'Really?' James looked surprised. 'Oh. Well, grab some sticks and belt shit out of whatever you can find. Hey, you see that big red thing down the river?'

He pointed across the bridge to a hill by the river's bend. A distant red speck bounced from side to side. Damon adjusted his glasses, trying to see.

'It's a giant metronome,' James said. 'Mick Jagger or someone donated it to the city. Drugged wanker. It's been going for years. Tick-tick-tick-tick-tick. He must have had a bloody good time here.'

He absently rolled a cigarette, tongued it swiftly and lit it. Glowing worms twisted at its tip.

'I didn't know you smoked,' Damon said. 'Tobacco, I mean.'

James shrugged. 'Seems the thing to do here.'

He puffed again and surveyed the crowd. Damon looked at him critically.

'You don't seem very surprised to see me,' he said.

'Figured you'd be around sooner or later,' James said, billowing smoke. 'I reckon if you sat on this bridge long enough you'd see almost the whole world pass by. And the same faces turn up over and over, you'd be surprised. What happened to that girl you left with?'

'She's over there,' Damon said.

James looked impressed. 'You've stuck together all this time? Good man!'

'It's not like that,' Damon protested.

'Pity,' James said. 'Anastasia! Hey! Anastasia!'

She turned, looking confused for a moment, and finally spotted him.

'My God!' she said, striding over. 'James! I never expected to see you again.'

'Yeah, it's this whole reunion thing. You're looking great, haven't changed a bit, what are you doing with yourself?'

'Same old same old,' she said. 'How's—um—blonde, pretty, easy virtue... Astrid?'

'She's spectacular,' James said wistfully. 'But still in Alkmaar gorging herself on cheese. Amazing how she keeps her figure.'

'Some girls have all the luck,' Stacy said.

'I'll say,' James said, looking her up and down. 'I can't believe you're still with this guy.'

'It's not—' she started, then changed direction and looked towards Damon. 'Well, you know, he grows on you.'

James smiled. 'Like fungus?'

'I like it okay.' She paused, grinned, laughed.

James looked pained. 'Jesus. That the sort of thing they find funny in New York State?'

She nodded. 'Good to see you again, James. You know your way around here?'

'Yeah. Daytime's a bit confusing. But come sundown I'm home.'

'Great. Show us a good time?'

'Of course. If you're good I might even let you touch one.'

Prague after dark was pretty much like Prague during the day. The main streets of the Old and New Towns were still full of people, still full of life, still full of chocolate waffles. Wrought-iron streetlamps drooped towards the flagstones, and lights set into the old buildings sprayed the stone orange. Along the bridge, most of the market stalls had been replaced by new buskers, musicians and jugglers and people playing with fire. The statues glowed in an eerie light.

On the far side of the river, in the backstreets away from the bridge, the buildings were sombre and rectangular and looked like buildings were supposed to look in Eastern Europe. But they didn't sound like they were supposed to sound. Instead of tapping typewriters and the other vague rumblings of political unrest, there was heavy grunge guitar, thumping drums, lyrics distorted by language or volume.

James led them into a narrow three-storey terrace and up some flights of stairs. Each landing had a few people in it, resting against the walls or sitting in corners. Doorways opened into rooms crowded with bodies and music. The only things resembling furniture were stools for the musicians and tables full of mixing equipment. Everybody else sat on the floor or not at all. A different flavour of music blasted through each level: hard rock on one, bluesy guitar on another, squealing sax from the basement. The stairwells echoed with the fusion of sounds bleeding into each other, combining into undiscovered genres. Naked bulbs and candles threw dim light as far as they could, spreading auras which never intersected. Smoke and noise crammed the air, thickening it.

'Praha means threshold,' James shouted back at them. 'Remember that.'

The top floor was almost quiet; no music but the ripple of conversation. There were paintings, murals on the walls: peace symbols and yin-yangs, portraits of Buddha and Jim Morrison, uncompleted sketches of utopia. James found a group of friends in a corner and huddled with them for a while. When he came back he was carrying a Coke can and a small block of something hard and black.

'Any of you guys got a Swiss Army Knife?' he said.

All three of them reached for their pockets.

'Sure,' Damon said.

'Of course,' Stacy said.

'Never leave home without it,' Perry said.

'Good,' James said. 'One'll do.'

He took Damon's, which was the biggest and had scissors

and even a pair of pliers in it. He unfolded the leather punch, dented the Coke can and drove a cluster of tiny holes through the aluminium. 'Perfect,' he said.

'Modern art?' Damon hazarded.

'Hash pipe,' James said. 'Who's first?'

He crumbled the dark block and balanced a little cairn of hash-pebbles over the holes. Sparks jabbed with tiny claws until the fluid caught and an uncertain flame wafted from the lighter.

'Me,' Perry said. He sucked through the drinking hole, dragging the flame into the hashish until it glowed like a pile of sauna bricks. He nodded and passed the can back.

'Me,' Stacy said. She took the Bic from James and lit herself, inhaling for a long time, then nodding too.

'Me,' Damon said. As he breathed in, Perry exhaled, then Stacy, twin columns of smoke billowing like a pair of searchlights. He felt the drug catch on his throat, tiny particles of ash on its breath. Then down to his lungs, diffusing through the membranes of his cells, carried with his blood to his brain. He expelled the smoke but something remained, spreading through him still, turning him inside out as he passed the can and the lighter back to James.

'Me, me, me,' James said. 'That's all it is with you people.'

Damon laughed silently and hysterically as James puffed, skinhead's face dancing with the flame.

'Don't say that,' Stacy said. 'You don't even know us.'

'I know you,' James replied through smoke. 'All except this guy, I mean. Who the hell are you anyway?'

'We introduced you on the bridge,' Stacy said. 'It's Perry, you remember.'

'Hey,' James said. 'Sorry, shocking memory.'

'You remembered my name,' Stacy said. 'My full name, I mean. Which nobody calls me.'

'I'm okay with names,' James said. 'It's just faces are a problem. But pretty faces I never forget. Or pretty names.'

'Perry has a pretty name,' Stacy said.

'Perry isn't a pretty name.'

'Peregrine,' Stacy said.

Damon looked at both of them. 'Is that true?'

'It's true,' Perry said, looking at Stacy with disapproval. 'But it's not something I tell many people.'

Damon took the freshly-loaded can from James and sucked glowing distraction through the holes. More secrets brought to light. He wondered if she had told him hers. Maybe he knew everything, the whole deal. Perry special, Damon redundant. Jealousy swept across his forehead in a cold sweat, pinpricks of poison. But no. She hadn't told. He was just being paranoid. It was a symptom, like the munchies and losing track of time and not being able to follow the thread of your own train of...

'Peregrine,' James mused. 'I guess that's a pretty name. It doesn't suit you.'

'Thanks,' Perry said.

The can wandered around their circle a few more times, losing momentum as their faculties slipped away.

'Coke,' Stacy said. 'Look. Coke.'

She tried to say something else but her mouth was seized by laughter, twisting her lips in the wrong directions. 'You can't—' she giggled. 'Can't—'. She tipped her head forward and let her hair cascade over her legs.

'What's her problem?' James said. 'What's she trying to say?'

'Coke,' Perry said, stifling a chuckle himself. 'You can't—'. Laughter erupted from his own throat, snatching away his own words, and he leaned into Stacy and quaked silently with her.

'What the fuck's going on?' James demanded. 'What's wrong with you people?'

'Coke,' Damon said calmly. 'You can't beat the real thing.'

James furrowed his brow in disbelief. 'That's the joke? Fuck, I hate stoned people.'

Damon shrugged. Weird things were happening in his peripheral vision. Flickering shapes crept into his focus whenever he looked at the same thing for too long, which was often. He closed his eyes and watched the geometry unfold before him, diamonds and squares and triangles and whatsits, whatweretheycalleds, terrariums. No, trapeziums. Rhombuses or was it rhombi? Parallellallellograms with infinite L's stretching into nothing. He felt his head tip forwards and snatched open his eyes. Perry and Stacy were still laughing, and James was looking increasingly impatient.

'Get up, you two,' he said. 'And you, you look like you're falling asleep. Get up, all of you; we're going for a walk.'

'More,' Stacy said. 'Please, sir. More. More Coke.'

'Coke adds life,' Perry said, and they started laughing again.

'Listen, guys,' James said. 'If I had some real coke I'd give it to you and you could fry your brains all you wanted. But you're not wired, you're only stoned, and you're getting silly and intolerable. Let's go. You can have some more once we get there, but if we stay here any longer we're going to implode or I will kill you. Besides... things... by the river... frogs purple... my sister Annie likes frzlghrmplnn... hzzz... wrtzmnorrphl... thnthnwake *up* Damon, you wanker. Christ, I should have known this stuff'd be too intense for you guys. Come on, let's *go*!'

They staggered through the empty streets, away from the music. It was dark in the backstreets of Malá Strana, which were broad and dimly lit. There was no moon, but the mackerel clouds rippled with a dull light, reflected from somewhere. Gaunt trees lined the footpaths, reaching up to claw the stern facades of silent palaces. Distant figures scurried out of view. Everywhere were the hints of monuments: the bases of statues, clean shadows instead of plaques, courtyards conspicuously empty.

'There's the pink tank,' James said.

They looked around. 'I don't know what *you're* smoking,' Perry said. 'But it must be better than the shit you gave us if you're seeing pink tanks.'

'I thought it was supposed to be elephants,' Stacy said.

'That's drunk,' Damon said. 'Stoned, you see tanks. If you're lucky.'

'It's not here anymore, dickheads,' James said. 'They took it away like all the communist monuments. It was over there.' He pointed to a large block built from concrete bricks. It looked like it should have had something on it, something impressive. But there was nothing except a hammer and sickle spraypainted against its flank. 'Guy told me the story. It was the first Russian tank to hit Prague at the end of the war. They thought it was a good tank, a tank to save them from the Nazis. So they welcomed it in. But of course they were just trading oppressors; it was a bad tank too. Which they realised later in the Prague Spring when the tanks came back to stomp on their uprising. So as soon as they could they painted it pink, and then they tore it down.'

'Pity,' Damon said. 'There's something missing now. The place could really use a pink tank.'

'I wonder where it is,' Stacy mused. 'Did they strip it for pink parts, or is it sitting on the roof of some roadhouse out by the highway?'

'I think you're missing the point,' James said.

The air was cold but not bitterly so. They were staving off the winter, fleeing south as the earth twisted inexorably away from the sun. And they were warmed from within, burning with the forgotten fire they had breathed, now billowing only condensation as they drifted through the streets with their hands out of their pockets.

Further along the riverfront, an archipelago of tiny islands hung to the shore from a series of footbridges. The ground was carpeted by autumn leaves, naked trees stretching above. Perry and James sat in a pile of red and orange.

'Which of our current cultural icons do you think have long-term relevance?' Perry asked. 'I mean, look at the past. Even the last few decades. We've got *Star Wars*, *Happy Days*, the Flintstones, Jimi Hendrix, Marlon Brando, *Saturday Night Fever*. They all still have meaning. Which of today's icons will last? Will REM? Will the Simpsons? Will Bret Easton Ellis? Will *Jurassic Park*, or the *Fisher King*? You just can't tell, can you?'

'Look at this leaf,' James said. 'It's so perfect. There's infinity in this leaf.'

Damon left them to their stoned musings and walked to the edge of the island. The leaves under his feet were soggy, glued to the ground by mud. Tiny ripples lapped at the bank. The Charles bridge loomed in the middle distance, lit orange. The faint sounds of music and speech skipped across the water. He felt distant from everything.

Leaves rustled behind him and Stacy appeared through the trees. She hummed something slow and unrecognisable as she walked to the water's edge.

'People talk about weird things when they're stoned,' she commented.

'Yeah,' Damon said, staring out across the river.

'Them back there, Perry and James. They're totally out of it.'

'Yeah.'

'Talking about trees now. When to plant them and such.'

'They're stoned.'

'I feel like it myself; like talking. I just feel like saying anything.'

'So talk.'

'You're not a talker, so much, are you? When you're stoned. You just clam up and listen to things. Only I can never tell if you're actually listening or just distracted. But you don't say much.'

'It depends.'

'Oh, it's okay, it's fine. I'll just ramble on, that's fine, you don't even have to listen. Sometimes I get to talking and I just can't stop; I can go on for hours and I'm likely to say anything. Not often; often I don't say much at all, but sometimes I do and once I start, forget it, you know, that's all.'

Damon turned to face her. 'I know.'

She smiled, suddenly bashful, and looked away. 'Yeah, you do, don't you. You know, I was thinking—I think, I actually think you might know me.'

'I think I do too,' Damon said. 'Stacy, right?'

She grinned. 'Right. But you don't understand what that means. I mean, nobody knows me, not anybody. Not even Perry, not even he knows me like that, although in another way—' She covered her mouth with her hand and smiled guiltily. 'Whoops. That's over, anyway; that was just—just a thing. But—oh, I'm not explaining this very well.'

'It's okay,' Damon said slowly. 'I know what you mean.'

'Yeah, I think you do. And you know what? I think I know

you, too. Now. I didn't think I could, but now, all of a sudden, I do. Before you seemed like a different person all the time, like not a person at all—but now there's something underneath all that and it's a person after all, and I know who it is. At least you look the same most of the time now. And I like your hair like that, like you've got it now. Falling into your eyes like that.'

She reached up and brushed a few strands of his hair to one side. Her hand was cool against his cheek, cool and refreshing as the underside of a pillow. For a moment he was sure he would kiss her, take her in his arms and kiss her for hours, sure as the first move in a film romance. But he wrenched his mind away and found another inevitability: of course, he would not. He would do no such thing. He would simply stand there until she looked away and started talking again; then, he would listen. And soon enough Perry and James would come over, and they would go back to the apartment and he would fall asleep next to her on the floor, and perhaps lean against her in the night, and they might brush and perhaps clasp fingers during a half-dream, and that would be all. And in the morning they would wake up and eat breakfast and feel like closer friends—close, and yet so far.

The Nazis had wanted to destroy Prague in 1945, to level it in a final act of spite. After the fall of Berlin they had planned to show the world what it meant to wipe out a country's heritage. Were it not for the efforts of the Czech nationals and the timely arrival of the pink tank, they would have bombed it to rubble, as their own capital had been blitzed by the allies, as Warsaw had been flattened, London burned. Surprising that there was any of Europe left, really, after a history of war as old as history.

Damon cast a final gaze over the city, trying to memorise everything. The place had survived unscathed for so many centuries that the odds were bound to catch up with it, likelier sooner than later. He didn't know how long it would be there.

James was still at the apartment when Damon returned. It was getting towards evening, and Stacy was cooking dinner.

'This place was amazing,' she said. 'There were, like, three people in the entire supermarket, and about three hundred *waiting* to get in. I stood waiting too until I realised what was going on. See, the place was empty, but they were all waiting to get hold of a shopping trolley, and there were three of them, I swear. So I figured, this must be some Czech custom or something; you don't go shopping until you've got a trolley. But I couldn't wait so I just barged through and bought all I could carry. Then all I had to do was pay four cents for the paper bag to lug it all home.'

'Good work,' Perry said. 'I tell you, these oppressed post-communist countries are just ripe for exploitation.'

'Yeah.' She grinned. 'There wasn't much to buy, though. All I could manage was a few bags of macaroni and some chili sauce.'

'So what's for dinner?' Damon said, draping his jacket.

'Macaroni and chili sauce,' Stacy said.

She poured the macaroni into a saucepan of water and lit the gas, then uncapped the chili bottle.

'Right,' she said. 'I'm done.'

'That wasn't much of an effort,' Perry said.

'Well, it's not easy to feed a family of four for a dollar and still have change.'

James was rigging a complex arrangement of glass, chewing gum, pins and hashish. He held his tongue between his teeth as the water bubbled.

'You know, we've probably got a Coke can somewhere,' Damon said.

James shook his head. 'Too much waste,' he said. 'This way you don't lose anything. Allow me to demonstrate.'

Smoke was curling to the top of the overturned glass. He inhaled through the gap between the lip of the table and the rim of the glass, sucking the trapped air clean. As he stopped, the glass began to cloud again. He slid it across to Stacy.

'How'd your mission go, anyway?' he asked Perry.

'Got 'em,' Perry said. 'Eight-thirty tonight. Cost me four bucks each. But I got caught without a ticket on the subway, and the guy fined me five dollars.'

'That'll learn you.'

'International Jazz Festival in Prague,' Stacy said, passing the glass. 'That sounds so cool.'

'I'd buy that for four dollars,' Perry said.

Damon was stoned again. There were people all around him, rushing towards him in a tidal wave of bodies. All he wanted was to get to the ticket machine, three metres of train station concrete away. But everyone was stampeding *from* the ticket machine, pressing against him in their haste like clawing skeletons. He couldn't breathe. The machine was fading away, dwindling into the distance. He struggled against the tide, flailing desperately. He had to get a ticket. Had to get a ticket or he'd be fined, fined *five dollars*. And worse: the ticket guy, the inspector guy, would know he was stoned, he would *know*. Panic seized him, dipping bony fingers down his throat.

'Come *on*!' they were shouting behind him. 'The train's about to leave!'

'Ticket!' he cried back at them. 'Need a ticket! Inspector...'

'Fuck the ticket!' they shouted. 'Forget it! There's no inspector! Let's go!'

He lunged towards the machine, shoving stubborn commuters aside. He reached into his pocket, jammed coins into the slot, tore away the ticket as the machine spewed it out. The tide had turned and he had to fight through still more people to get back to the others as they thundered downstairs to the platform.

The feeling of utter disorientation clung to him as they rode the metro line to the concert hall, slapped down their tickets and found their door, section, aisle, row, seats. The place was huge. The lights went down.

People were clapping so Damon joined in. A bunch of black guys sauntered onto the stage. Everyone applauded especially loudly for the last one, a tall guy in a mustard suit carrying a trumpet. There was silence, and then it began.

Two hours disappeared. All he could remember was music, wonderful music wafting silkily from trumpets, saxophones, drums, piano, double bass. He saw the melodies and harmonies weaving together, stretching across the auditorium like hurled streamers. He closed his eyes and tasted the chord changes in the back of his throat. His body was swaying involuntarily; he was a snake, charmed, writhing. He was a pair of quavers, perfection in their association. A semibreve, curled into an eternal circle. A string, plucked, vibrating uniquely. The bell of a saxophone, honking low B-flat, squealing altissimo, resonating in between. Jazz. T-*tsh*-tuh, t-*tsh*-tuh. Plunk plunk plunk. Awayawayawaya. Smoooooth.

Then there was no more music, only light and people going crazy, clapping, screaming, whistling. Onstage, bowing. Damon hammered his hands together until they stung. He looked at Stacy applauding beside him. She was beautiful—dressed up, kind of. Sophisticated. Sexy. He looked at Perry on the other side. He was sexy too, grinning broadly. Even James, further along, bald head bristling with stubble, even he was sexy. Jazz made everyone sexy.

'Who was that?' Damon shouted. 'Who was that guy?'

'Marsalis,' Perry said. 'From the family of jazz gods. Jazz gods, man!'

'You know what?' Damon cried. 'I love—I *love* jazz!'

'I *love* jazz!' he cried, upside-down.

They hung from the bars of the train carriage, hair drooping towards the floor. The motion rocked them from side to side. Perry was hanging from his feet alone, which looked kind of impossible but seemed to work.

'You keep saying that,' Perry said.

'It's *true*!' Damon reiterated. 'I'm not making this up, not this time.'

'It's all right,' Stacy said. 'We believe you.'

'Oh, man,' Damon said. 'If you knew how I feel right now...'

'I feel it!' Perry said. 'It's this whole city! James has the right idea, you guys. I'm not leaving this place, no sir. I'm staying *forever.*'

Damon hung limply from his knees and looked down at Perry. 'Oh, no,' he said seriously. 'No, you can't stay. I mean, *I* can't stay. Not another day. I can't stay here and wait for it to get boring. I'm going to remember Prague like this, and I'm leaving tomorrow, and this will always be the most amazing place in the world to me—until the next place, I mean.'

'It never gets boring,' James said, hanging from an arm and a leg. 'Every day can be like this!'

'Everything gets boring,' Damon said. 'There's always a peak, and this is it. We've got to move on. Always.'

'You do what you've got to do,' Perry advised. 'I'm staying put. This is too good to leave. Stacy'll stay here with me—won't you?'

'Stacy'll come with me,' Damon said. 'She's still searching—isn't that right?'

Stacy clambered down from the bar and sat down looking anguished.

'I'm torn,' she complained. 'I love it here, but Damon's right; I have to keep going, keep seeing more... but I don't want to leave you guys behind.'

'Someone always gets left behind,' Perry said.

'You guys seen *Casablanca*?' James interjected.

'This isn't *Casablanca*,' Stacy said.

'Maybe not,' James said. 'But if you don't get on that train, you'll—'

'Don't even say it.'

'I can't believe this is it,' Stacy said.

But it was. Praha Hlavní Nádrazi, the international rail terminal. People were loading their bags onto trains, spending the last of their koruny, effecting lingering farewells. The engines were firing up, and last-minute carriages clanked into place. Definitely it.

'It's okay,' Perry soothed. 'We'll all see each other again.'

'When?'

'I don't know,' he admitted. 'Never, I guess. But that's kind of depressing.'

'Yeah,' Stacy said unhappily. 'Lock, maybe we should stay a bit longer.'

'You'll meet other people,' Perry said.

'Not like you.'

'Plenty like us. It's the scene. Travellers are the best people.

Drop in on any youth hostel and you'll meet a dozen new best friends. I guarantee it. Then you'll lose them and have to make more. You get used to it.'

'Do you?'

'No.'

Stacy threw her arms around him, looking over his shoulder as he whispered something in her ear. She nodded, drew back, and they clasped hands.

'You've got my address,' she said. 'Write me when I get home. I don't know when I'll be there, or for how long... but somebody should know where I am. And if you ever get yourself an address... well, let me know what it is.'

'Of course,' Perry said.

'Just get going,' James growled. 'It's getting way too emotional around here.'

'Take care of yourselves, guys,' Damon said. He took both of their hands and shook them solemnly. 'You've—you've both taught me things.'

'Go easy out there, young Damon,' James said. 'It's a big world. Maybe I'll see you back home.'

'So long,' Stacy said, backing into the train carriage.

'Bye, mates,' Damon said, following her.

'Happy rails,' James called.

Perry raised his hand to them, then turned and walked into the station complex. He didn't look back.

The train rattled through the afternoon, heading West as if defecting. Bohemia slid past, glowing gold with the falling sun. Nobody was talking.

'Well, that's it,' Stacy finally said. She looked out of the window, arm wedged between the sill and her cheek. Her eyes flicked from side to side as she followed the rushing view. Then stared directly ahead, shining.

'That isn't *it*,' Damon said. 'This is only the beginning.'

She turned and smiled at him. 'Maybe it is,' she said. 'But it's the end, too.'

Her eyes were heavy with sadness. She seemed to be looking backwards—back to Prague, back into the past.

'What did you guys *do*, anyway?'

His voice refused to inflect properly at the last moment, unresolved. The question dangled its tail in his throat as the train ground against the rails, beating an iron rhythm.

'It's not what you think,' she said.

'It isn't?'

'No,' she said. 'We only had sex.'

Damon laughed. 'That all?'

'Yes.'

Seeing she was serious, he dropped his smile. 'How is that different from what I was thinking?'

'It's different. It was just—sex. Nice sex. Sex with Perry is like a hug from a friend. It makes you feel good, picks you up when you need it. It's almost, I dunno, like a favour. He's gentle; he's giving. It's almost not like sex at all. Normally everybody wants something out of it. They're desperate, they're reaching, clinging; they have this emotional *need* to satisfy. That's what you're thinking of.'

'Angry sex.'

She nodded. 'Desperate sex.'

'Fucking on mountaintops.'

She winced, and her eyes seemed to reflect something distant. 'Yeah.'

'Sorry,' he said.

She shook her head. 'It's okay,' she said. 'You know what? It's okay. Well, more so.'

She looked at him for a long time, silent.

The sun set over the hills of Southern Germany, and the lights in the compartment flickered on. A strip of orange stretched along the horizon, melting into the darkening sky. Venus popped into view, steady and green.

'Star light, star bright,' Stacy said.

'It's a planet.'

She grinned. 'Who asked you?'

His eyes found a star, real this time. Soon, another. For a while he could still count them: five, eight, thirteen. Then there were too many. And the moon, almost full again, drifting. He flicked the lightswitch into darkness. A fluorescent glow found its way along the passageway and cracked into the compartment; apart from that, only the moonlight.

She came out of nowhere. Through the darkness, a hand on his knee. He froze, surprised. The hand moved up, down, up again. He took it, lifted it, wrapped it in his own hand. She gripped him back, moving beneath his touch. Wonderful fingers: tactile, clasping, unclasping. He lifted her hand to his mouth, pressed his lips again her knuckles. Closing his eyes, he thought: no. But pulled on her arm. A single tug, and she was there, kneeling above him, a thigh on either side of his body. The train tore through a nameless town with streetlights flashing. Her face flickered: white skin, dark eyes, moist lips. He reached for her, cradled her cheek. She rested her wrists on his shoulders, touching her fingers behind his neck, bringing his head forward. The town passed and the moon painted her blue and black. Twin spheres danced in her eyes. His hands found her hips and moved up her sides, dragging material. Her ribs rippled beneath his fingers, undulating laterals tensing. She was trembling, slightly, slightly. Her bra strap dipped into her flesh; he followed the curve in and out. Reaching her underarms he changed direction, brushing fingers behind her shoulders. Hair tickled his hands as he searched for the back of her neck, reading her vertebrae like braille. Then her head darted forward and she kissed him, quickly, on the lips. She looked into his eyes and smiled. He brought her closer, kissed her smile. And again. And too many times to count; as many as the multiplying stars. Lips, teeth, tongue: slow, gentle, delicious. The sound of the train, the trees hurling past, the clouds and the moon, and Stacy with him, cradling his head, drawing noisy breath. Mouth against mouth, tongue teasing tongue, crotches heaving together.

Damon felt something slipping away from him, drawn out through his mouth and into hers, exhaled into the night like a snakebite sucked. He felt himself losing it, entranced, falling into a soft, warm pit. His resolve flew from him like a flock of flapping doves, whirring in an upward snowstorm, carrying his convictions on their wings. And he was left alone, alone with his failings and Stacy, beautiful Stacy; and he felt himself sinking further, felt the surface close over him, burying him, and he was *gone*—but it was all okay, because the angel had been wrong, wrong...

She rolled off him and wrapped his arm around her shoulders, hoisting her knees onto the seat and leaning into him. She felt very warm, trembling no longer.

'Listen—' he started, but she reached up and touched a finger to his lips.

'No,' she said quietly. 'Don't say anything.'

'I was just wondering where we were going,' he said.

The train rumbled onward, gathering speed.

'Let's work it out as we go,' she said.

1 Een
2 Twee
3 Tre
4 Fire
5 Viisi
6 Шесть
7 Семь
8 Åtta
9 Neun
10 Deset

11 Onze

'God, Paris,' she said. 'This is such a cliche.'

She reached over and kissed him. They sat on the concrete banks of the Seine, legs dangling. The river rippled past them, cold and grey. The Notre Dame turned its gothic back on them while tour buses filed past its more familiar face. A bridge they didn't know the name of—not one of the famous ones—arched across to an island they didn't know the name of either. The Hotel de Ville loomed on the Right Bank. Everything seemed right; everything appropriate. As if things had reached their natural fulfilment. There was Paris all around and love was in the air, circling, looking for a spot to land. Coffee and baguettes and wine and berets and B-grade perfection everywhere.

He put his arm around her as someone rode behind them on a scooter.

Later, further along the Left Bank, they ate croissants in a street cafe. Waiters whisked properly past, and a trio played jazz on the sidewalk. Nothing like Prague, of course, but pleasant enough. The sun was setting.

'Croissants for dinner?' Damon said, poking.

'It's all we can afford,' Stacy said. 'Hotels don't come cheap, you know.'

'Well, you get what you pay for.'

Stacy smiled. She suddenly saw the two of them from a distance; propped together at their table-for-two, leaning towards each other as if sharing a milkshake from the fifties. Looking for all the world like a couple. She turned the idea around in her mind for a while, seeing how well it fitted. Then kept watching. The whole cafe was couples, looking the same as them, scattered at different angles across the pavement. Variations on a theme. She wondered if two people could be in Paris and not be a couple, or at least look like one.

The music wafted between them, wrapping its tendrils around them, pulling them together. Cigarette smoke curled towards the moon, and smooth French conversation wove music of its own in the background. She felt happy, warm with memory and anticipation and whatever lay in between. This was going to work.

Damon looked bewitched. He raised his wine glass with one hand, traced her fingers with the other. The glass hovered an inch from his lips, red liquid swaying in a miniature tide.

'You know,' he said dreamily. 'I'm going to fall in love with you any time now.'

Her fingers clenched involuntarily and a cold wave shuddered through her. For a second she felt as if she had ignored all advice and looked down, down into the abyss. She managed to raise a shaking glass to her mouth. Damon took her hand, untwisted her fingers and kissed her palm.

She smiled.

The hotel room was small and kind of dingy but it didn't matter. There was a box of emergency candles in the cupboard, so they melted them to saucers and set them around the room. They turned out the lights and all the world's defects, including the hideous wallpaper, retreated into the shadows. There was music playing down the street, plaintive and lingering, valium jazz.

It had begun.

She stood before him and began to undress. Sitting on the bed, out of reach, he looked steadily at her. She shrugged her jacket off and felt it brush her calves. The corners of his mouth twitched in a half-smile. Their gaze was broken by her T-shirt as she pulled it over her head: a flash of white and there he was again, watching the shirt as it fell, no longer sure where to look. His eyes darted around the room as she unbuttoned her jeans and slid them to the floor. Straightening up and stepping out, she tried to catch his gaze but couldn't hold it; couldn't keep it from slipping down her body. She told him with her eyes: *now you*, then turned her back to him and waited.

There was a mirror on the cupboard so she saw him anyway, fumbling with the buttons on his shirt. But she was caught by her own reflection, naked under underwear, lit by the candles on the dresser and in the mirror. Her skin glowed gold. Damon in the mirror was taking his socks off. She unhooked her bra, wriggling out of it. Black: for bad girls. She smirked and looked at her breasts, sticking her chest out. Orange and beautiful. Electricity pulsed through her, tingling.

His face appeared behind her shoulder and she turned around. He had a good chest. Nice arms. She kissed him and their nipples grazed and she felt his erection pressing into her through twice cotton. Both of them pushing, her above and him below. Reciprocity, thrusting and yielding. She shoved him by the shoulders and sent him falling willingly backwards. She pulled his shorts off, flicking them from his toes. As she climbed onto the bed she hooked a finger into her own panties and slid them away. She knelt above him, straddling his body. Lowering herself, thighs tensing, she engulfed him.

She closed her eyes and felt like the universe, enclosing this thing, this man, in her infinite folds. She wrapped herself around him, enveloping him—warming, smothering him as she heaved up and down. His hands crept around her waist and she opened her eyes.

It was Perry. Perry beneath her, looking calm, detached. Perry like a mountain: steady, dependable, unshakeable. But a glass mountain: smooth as obsidian, no cracks or flaws or fissures or anything to keep hold of. And cold, cold as granite in his heart. Her fingers slipped as she threw herself against his stony face, trying to cling but falling instead. Toppling through space as he uprooted himself and wandered away, not caring, leaving her uncaring too. Falling through a flash of white...

She landed with a jolt. A chill crept through her, stabbing between her legs and spreading inside her. The lower half of her body felt numb, paralysed. She looked down and it was *him*. A corpse, naked and bloodied, frozen and purple and encased in ice. Dead eyes staring. Jake. She bit her fist to stay her silent screaming. Her legs refused to move as she tried to scramble off him, *it*, tried to dislodge the icicle wedged into her. Her skin stuck to him, *it*, stretching painfully as she tugged. Her tears hardened into hailstones and lodged themselves in her eyes. She flailed her arms in despair and swung her fists into the frozen head. It shattered with a sickening sound, crunching like an ice sculpture, spraying shards in all directions. She held up her hand, stared in disbelief. Her fist was bleeding, red seeping between her fingers and running down her wrist. Blood dripped onto the corpse and burned where it fell, melting holes in the body. And soon the whole thing was dissolving, running onto the floor, nothing more than a puddle of water tinged pink. And she was falling again, turning over and around, hearing his cry in her ears, seeing the fir trees hurtle past and the mountains dancing a ring around her. Face first and helpless, struggling like a fish drowning in air. Until she paused, paused for a split-second, and thought: no. Then turned her body around, upright, and shot earthward through a cloud of serenity, of confidence, thinking: this time I will land on my feet.

The impact wracked her body as she landed—not on her feet, but on her knees. Close enough. And there was something beneath her, breaking her fall. Not snow, cold snow, but Damon. She looked at him, straining beneath her, and felt a rush of emotion she thought would drown them both. She lunged at him, spread herself along his chest, kissed him desperately. Then rolled him over, grabbed his buttocks and pulled him deeper into her. She looked him dead in the eye as she dragged an orgasm from him, feeling in his throes the suggestion of her own climax—too late. But close, and there was time. Still time.

Daylight came and went, and they ordered room service.

'We have to get up,' Damon said, winding her hair around his fingers.

'No, we don't,' Stacy moaned, pulling a pillow over her eyes. The world went soft.

'Yes, we do,' Damon insisted, snatching it away. 'We've been here three days.'

'But we've got everything,' Stacy said. 'Cheese toasties from room service. Real champagne if we could afford it. A big, bouncing bed. What's outside that we can't get here?'

'Paris,' Damon said. 'Paris is passing us by outside. We have to get out there. The walls are closing in and the sheets need changing. Put some clothes on and let's get out of here and let the chambermaid do her job.'

'Is this some wet patch thing?' Stacy said.

'It's a Paris thing,' Damon said, reaching to the floor and flicking clothes at her. 'Come on, let's live a little.'

The Latin Quarter, around the hotel, was as she had expected it. A college neighbourhood, full of cheap bars and cafes and life. The streets were old and the university buildings ancient, sturdy as monasteries. Students walked around looking like students everywhere, wearing suede and duffel jackets and jeans, experimenting with facial hair. The sky was blue, the air crisp and clear. It was even better than the hotel room.

Across the river, the Louvre and the green Jardin des Tuileries. Then the Champs-Elysees cut a massive rift through the 8th Arrondissement. They walked hand in hand.

'I had a girlfriend back home,' Damon said.

'You shouldn't talk about past relationships with your new lover,' Stacy said, clutching his arm. 'Don't you read *Cosmo*?'

'Only my sister's.'

'I didn't know you had a sister.'

'I don't,' he said.

An intersection of six roads cut the area into wedges. They waited at the traffic lights until the chaotic stream of cars stopped rushing from all directions. It took a while.

'Emily, her name was,' he said.

'Your sister?'

'My old girlfriend. I don't have a sister.'

'Why do I need to know this?'

'You don't,' he said.

Cars streamed in both directions, five across, gunning their engines and lurching forwards until the traffic jammed again. Scooters and bicycles darted between the gaps, kamikaze. Horn blasts and French abuse fought for airspace. The buildings were huge and old, enormous prisms of stone with glass holes chiselled out of them, laid end to end.

'She was doing Economics,' he said.

'You've got a one-track mind, haven't you?'

'I was just thinking about her.'

'Well, don't. Think about me.'

'I don't mean it like that,' he said. 'It's not like that.'

'Isn't it?'

'No.'

There were shops like she'd never seen before. Department stores, emporiums, boutiques: Chanel, Christian Dior, Gucci, Gaultier, everything. Glass and brass and marble storefronts; mirrors reflecting each other. Frozen mannequins posing, wearing what nobody wore. Perfume bottles like works of art, liquid light refracting. Jackets and flowing dresses and pointy bras. Glittering.

'Maybe it is,' he said.

'What?'

'Maybe it is like that. You and her.'

'What have I got to do with her?'

'Nothing,' he said. 'Well, everything. I mean, I want you to know things about me, about my life. Before. I think it would... help.'

'I don't care about before,' she said, squeezing his arm. 'As far as I'm concerned there is no before. There's only now.'

'There's before,' he said. 'For me, there is. In a way I'm still there. I haven't left it yet; not completely.'

She stopped, circled, looked at him. 'Do you still love her?'

'No,' he said, surprised. 'No, I don't. I hate her.'

'Good,' she said, and they walked on.

'I hate her,' he repeated. 'She sucked the life right out of me. The whole time I was with her, I didn't know who I was. We'd do whatever she wanted to do; she'd make me go to—to yuppie bars, make me think I liked it there, liked her friends. I lost myself in her. She made me wear these shirts, these fucking shirts, with—like, with patterns on them—'

'Hey,' she said. 'Hey, easy there. I'll *never* make you wear a patterned shirt, okay? Wouldn't dream of it. And you won't catch me in a yuppie bar. Okay?'

'Okay,' he said.

There were street cafes parked along the broad sidewalks. Stylish, uncomfortable chairs with silver piping and intricate patterns carved into their backs. People sitting around looking French, wearing trenchcoats and expensive clothes and smoking elegant cigarettes.

'Not okay,' he said. 'I mean, she fucked me up. I wasted so much time. All she did was push me around. I couldn't even think for myself. And I didn't mind! I didn't fucking mind! All because I thought I loved her.'

'Hey!' she said. 'What's going on here?'

'I thought I loved her,' he repeated, sounding hollow.

'What's your point?'

His eyes flashed. 'I think I love you.'

Something recoiled in her mind. 'Well,' she told the ground. 'You don't have to sound so pissed off about it.'

'Sorry,' he said. 'I'm not. I just—look, forget it. Let's go.'

The Arc de Triomphe loomed at the end of the avenue. The footpaths were getting packed; people everywhere. An immense roundabout circled the arch at Place Charles de Gaulle, fed by a dozen arterial roads. She caught a glimpse of its chaos as they strode up the Champs-Elysees. Damon was powering along, pounding the pavement, dragging her behind him. A clutch of schoolgirls carrying designer shopping bags jostled past, tearing him from her grip. He continued up the street as she shoved the shoppers aside and followed him, face burning.

'Hey!' she cried. 'Hey! Stop!'

He stopped, turned around, and shook his head briskly. 'I—' he started.

'Hey!' she said. 'Get a fucking grip, okay? You don't need to be doing this! I'm *not her*! I don't want to dominate you, or whatever you're worried about. I'm not interested in that. I don't care what you do, what you wear, nothing like that. This is totally different from that. We're totally different. It doesn't have to be bad, okay? It doesn't have to be bad!'

'I know,' he said. 'I know, look, I'm sorry. It's just—I don't want to lose myself. Again. I've looked so hard.'

'You won't,' she said. 'It's okay. You won't.'

'Sure,' he said. 'Just keep an eye on me, okay? Make sure I don't.'

'First sign, I'll let you know,' she said. 'Promise.'

He smiled. 'Okay then.'

There were no lines on the roundabout; just scattered columns of mayhem circling anticlockwise. All of the cars, scooters, vans and buses were pointing in different directions, trying to get on or off or around or just enjoying the adrenaline. Amazingly, the mass of vehicles kept moving; even more amazingly, nobody got hurt. It was mesmerising to watch. Fortunately, there were underpasses attached to the Metro station, so Stacy and Damon dived underground and surfaced beneath the arch. They watched the chaos in silence; then Damon turned and took her in his arms. She hugged him back, clinging tightly. Together, alone, while the universe crashed around them. Facing the insanity. Tighter.

Their sex that night was truly desperate.

When she awoke, the room was huge. Sunlight streamed through the window, pushing the walls in all directions. The bed had grown beneath her; from king-size to emperor-size; god-size. She stretched her limbs in all directions and couldn't reach the edges. The ceiling loomed impossibly high above her. She felt like a shrunken Alice in a growing Wonderland. Damon was gone.

She groped around the bed for him. Gone. She got up, wrapped a sheet around her, and checked the bathroom. Gone. She scanned the sink for his toiletries: razor, shampoo, toothbrush, anything. Gone. She strode back into the bedroom, searching the floor for his shoes, clothes. Gone. The bedside table for his glasses. Gone. The closet for his jacket, behind the door for his backpack, the dresser for his wallet: gone, gone, gone.

She sat down on the bed and stared into the mirror. The room was huge with his absence, huge and cold. She was tiny. She looked at herself and suddenly felt very naked. Mechanically, she put on some clothes. Jeans, T-shirt on backwards, jacket clutched around her. Why was it so cold?

Her foot brushed against something warm and soft. She reached down and picked it up, fuzzy between her fingers. It was a sock, his sock. She stared at it, turned it over, pulled it inside out. It was all that was left of him, this sock, blurring through her angry tears. She took it and flushed it down the toilet.

Paris was ignoring her. It was warmer outside the hotel room, but still freezing, still bitter. Nobody looked her way. She walked gingerly through the streets, holding herself behind crossed arms, afraid she would shatter. People wove paths around her, avoiding her only by accident.

Where?

Through the shock, she resolved to make the most of the city. Dragging herself through the streets, she watched the Seine ebb by like lead. She admired the architecture, browsed the markets and wondered why the sun could be so bright and yet so cold.

Why?

She strolled dispassionately through the Louvre. An assembly of portraits refused to meet her gaze, eyes avoiding her around the room. She almost caught the glance of the Mona

Lisa, peering through perspex. But the painting turned away and frowned an inscrutable frown.

For how long?

In the Rodin Museum, pale statues turned their backs on her. They looked like she felt: cold, hard, dead eyes staring without pupils. The couple of *The Kiss* taunted her, wrapping their stone bodies around each other, becoming one. Shutting her out.

Forever?

She left the museum and walked through the garden, crunching leaves and feeling the shadows of naked trees play across her. There were more sculptures, frozen like trespassers in a magic garden. *The Thinker* frowned and drove his knuckles into his stony chin. She sat against his base, covered her legs with leaves, and felt her body slowly petrify.

1	Een
2	Twee
3	Tre
4	Fire
5	Viisi
6	Шесть
7	Семь
8	Åtta
9	Neun
10	Deset
11	Onze

12 Douze/Doce

Ghost town on the Riviera.

The sky was grey and sullen, the streets slippery with recent rain. Seagulls flapped against the gusting winds, mewing hungrily. The air was cold and damp, and Nice was deserted.

The afternoon was dimming with an early dusk. Along the main boulevard, empty shops were closing for the night, wondering why they had bothered opening at all. Some of the sightless shutters had been locked down for days, weeks, ever since the summer had fled south and dragged the tourist season with it.

Damon cursed himself again. Dickhead. He slumped along the street, kicking the pavement, hands deep in his pockets. His hair hung in wet strands over his eyes, barring the world. He stepped in a puddle and felt the coldness seep into his feet. Fucking dickhead.

A few valiant cafes were still open, umbrellas drooping over the outdoor settings, chairs tipped against tables to drain. Damon felt hungry—or, if not, he felt the duty to eat something. He stopped by a seafood restaurant; a mosaic of ultramarine tiles led inside, curling with squid. The waiters had gone home, and the manager was sitting at a table looking thoughtful. He leapt up when he saw Damon.

'Good evening to you, sir!' he effused.

'Hi,' Damon said.

'Ah! English! I thought so,' the manager said. 'Are you in town long?'

'I don't know,' Damon said. 'I think, probably, not. But then, on the other hand, maybe.'

'Oh, but you should stay!' the man said, sounding almost desperate. 'All summer there are so many people here, I am run off my feet even with six staff. Beautiful people, and so friendly—some come to my restaurant every day for two, three months. Always people to talk to. But suddenly winter, and everybody goes away. Everyone has somewhere to go but me. I stay.'

'Yeah,' Damon said. 'It's kind of lonely, I guess.'

'Lonely.' The manager nodded and looked wistful. 'You should see it in the summer. Madonna was here. And once, long ago, Princess Grace...'

'I think I like it better now.'

The manager looked at him suspiciously, then softened. 'Oh, but it is good that you are here now! We need more like you to keep the place alive. People to talk to... but what would you like? Wine? Some fish? We have lobster.'

'Just something with cheese in it,' Damon said. 'To go.'

The man's face fell. 'Is that all?'

'That's all,' he said. 'Oh, and where's the nearest photo place?'

Son of a bitch.

The words sat in the back of Stacy's throat, nudging the base of her tongue. She tried to spit them out like gobs of bloody phlegm. *Son of a bitch.* But they stayed there, blurring into one word, *sonofabitch*. Her lips curled with the foul taste of the word, now less than a word: *snuvbitch, sumbitch, sbtch*. But she bared her teeth and grinned humourlessly, savouring the anger clenched inside her. Every time she thought of him her fingers curled into claws, her molars ground together and a wave of hatred convulsed her body. But she thought of him every time she thought.

Claustrophobic streets threw a tangled web over Sant Pere-Ribera. Elsewhere, Barcelona was meticulous, arranged in a neat matrix of squares with their corners clipped, spreading octagons into the hills. But here, in the old town, the alleys were deep, narrow and tightly packed. The buildings were grimy and ramshackle, hanging together by bent nails and tradition. A rotting stench stuck rank fingers into her nostrils, choking her. The sun poured through a haze of pollution, chiselling into the shadows.

Three o'clock was siesta time and the city was asleep. More than asleep: dead. The whole place reminded Stacy of those towns they built in the desert for nuclear testing: movie sets complete with mannequin extras, erected to be detonated. Wiped clean by the same hot wind that blew through this city; settled with the same radioactive dust. Windows shattered, screen doors hanging, sand fused into glass. Dirty streets, heat and haze, buildings tumbling and nobody around. Dark wood and blackened stone blocking the sun as she hurried through the streets, scuffing her shoes in the dust. She heard sirens in her head, blaring: *son of a bitch.*

The smell was overpowering now, the air unbreathable, robbed of oxygen. Sweat stood out on her forehead; she was burning. She swung her fist into a wooden post and it collapsed, bringing a building down with it; she punched a wall and it toppled. She had to clear some space, get the air circulating, open the slums to sunlight. So she flailed her arms, punching and slapping and scratching until the rubble piled around her. Damon appeared and she hit him, too, but her fist passed straight through him and connected with a brick wall. And everything was still dark, the sun still in hiding, the air still clotted—and the buildings still upright, cramming closer together, suffocating her. Only her fists remained bloody, knuckles grazed. She pulled a long splinter out of her ring finger, wincing.

She remembered feeling this way before. Bursting, mad with frustration, nowhere to turn. She had felt invisible hands clutching at her, tearing her in all directions, driving fingernails into her flesh: she had felt it before. But that had been then, back home, before everything, back when she really *had* nowhere to go. How could it have followed her here? Would this always happen? When she felt secure, if only for an instant, would the ground be pulled from beneath her every time? Would whoever she trusted, if only tentatively, leave the country or the mortal plane just to escape her? What was wrong with her? Was she doomed, destined, damned—forever? Of course. Of course. This was her; this holocaust town was hers. It would follow her everywhere. Son of a bitch. Bastard world.

The sun had decided not to rise. The sky was a deep, angry grey, and the clouds hung heavy and bloated. Damon collected his newly-developed photos and took them down to the sea.

The beach, when he found it, was nothing but a strip of rocks piled untidily to the water. His ankles twisted as he clambered along the shoreline, filling his shoes with pebbles. He flipped through the photos until he found her. She was standing in front of a terrace of Dutch houses, out of focus with half of her face cropped off. He stared at her blurry image, defocussing his eyes in an attempt to make her out. He traced her body with his finger, remembering. How long ago had it been? Six weeks, two months, a lifetime?

A few photos later, and there she was again. Kneeling against the Little Mermaid, looking actually not much at all like the statue. Looking uncomfortable, restless. Pleading. Perhaps it had started then, back in Copenhagen: the confusion. Or perhaps when she came back, that night on the boat. It had definitely started by St Petersburg and her drunken divulgences. Or, if not, then the night afterwards, or in Berlin, or in Prague. Or perhaps not until Paris. What was a beginning? A look, a glance, something unseen but felt? A conversation, or a kiss? Maybe the beginning was impossible to pinpoint. The end was much clearer.

Two photos; that was all. He remembered his camera, buried in the bottom of his backpack, ignored for weeks. He probably should have kept a diary as well; kept it vigilantly, every night. Surely with a record like that he would have been able to see what was happening, to spot the pattern emerging, to realise what he was doing before it was too late. Instead it had sneaked up on him while he was helpless, oblivious. Dickhead.

A fat raindrop fell onto Stacy's head, throwing it into some kind of focus. A smudge exploded across one lens of his glasses and dripped in monocular semi-existence. He looked out to sea and saw the storm approaching, angry clouds joining the water through a screen of rain. Lightning clawed across the sky and an ominous rumble swept to shore. He stuffed the pictures inside his jacket and ran for shelter.

He found an outlet spilling storm water into the sea through a broad tunnel. A bank of sand—real sand—followed the stream under the esplanade, so he sat on it and waited for the storm to come.

As the thunder and lightning danced closer to one another, he tried to work out what had happened. He hadn't been able to help leaving Paris, leaving her. Seized with the panic of a claustrophobic, he had had to escape, clutching his crazed head in his hands. This town is too small for the two of us. Irrational, perhaps, but at the same time deeply rational. With distance, he could see that. He had done the only thing possible. It was all happening again. He had searched so long for himself, and now he was slipping through his own fingers. It was too soon. He wasn't strong enough, not yet. Not strong enough to withstand her. He was like wet cement, not yet hardened, and here she was carving her name into him with a stick. No.

He traced a meaningless figure in the sand, then covered it over. Gulls screamed as the storm came closer; some of them waddled into his shelter and eyed him nervously. A piece of waste paper blew along the beach until the rain pounced on it and battered it, soggy, into the rocks. Water crashed all around him: rain whipped into flurries, waves coaxed onto the thundering shore.

But he had been wrong, a coward. No. He had been right. No.

She would hate him now. The thought chilled him. Would she understand? Of course: of course not. How could she know? Emily. Patterned shirts and yuppie bars but so much more.

Daaaaaamon, howled the wind. *I love you and everything, but you couldn't make a decision to save yourself. I swear! If you were drowning and they asked you, do you want a rope? You'd say, I dunno, what do you think?*

It hadn't been Emily's fault, of course. She was just like that. Pushy.

They're good people, Damon. They're my friends. You just have to make an effort. You do like them, don't you? Good. Now come along. They're all at the College Arms tonight.

And he had been led, shaped, moulded into an image he couldn't recognise.

I'm so glad you're doing Law, Damon. Everybody's so proud of you. You'll make something of yourself, a future. Guaranteed.

Ridiculous. What had he become? Anything?

That way, Damon. Yeah, yeah, that's good. No, move your knee. It's—move it! Good. Kiss me. Keep kissing me. Mm. Slow down; you'll—wait! Wait! Not yet. Don't—damn you!

He winced. But all he could hear was the last thing she had said.

God help me, I've tried, Damon. I've tried to—to accommodate you, make room for your ideas. I've tried to encourage you, I have! But what have I got to work with? Nothing! I feel like I don't know you, like all you do is bend to me and then resent me for it. So what now? You're going to drop out, give up your life—to spite me? The hell with you! No, go! You'll be back. You're weak. You're weeeeaaaaa...

The wind rose to a shriek, and the sky flashed and boomed at once. He scooped up a fistful of sand, watched it spill to the ground. It was getting cold; the tide was coming in and the stream was rising. Wet wind gusted into his alcove, chilling him. He stepped out into the storm.

Barcelona had woken up and was partying all afternoon. Siesta had given way to fiesta, and the sidewalks were jumping.

Latin bands danced comic tarantellas at every Rambla, floppy sombreros bobbing, guitars sized from ukuleles to double basses. There were stalls selling paperbacks and magazines, caged parrots and monkeys, wicker baskets and metal trinkets. Buskers sang, juggled, performed magic tricks and drew caricatures. And people milled everywhere, strolling the pedestrian street between the trees, circling the performers, sitting on benches. Music and colour and chatter and spectacle crammed together.

The sky shone blue and the smell dissolved. The air seemed to have lifted, now cool and refreshing. Stacy stood in the middle of the pavement and felt dazed. People drifted around her, jostling her, walking and talking and looking happy as she stared blinking after them. She felt like the only miserable person in the world, and her depression swelled to staggering enormity in contrast with these ludicrously cheerful people. She felt the ground freeze beneath her feet, looked down and saw a circle of frost expanding across the cement. People walked across her frozen patch and left warm footprints, thawing the ground.

But as she walked towards the harbour, she felt her spirits stirring, almost lifting. The music danced around her, infecting her with its rhythm. Everyone seemed so vibrant that she couldn't help feeling some of their enthusiasm as it nagged at the corners of her mood. The Spanish might have been the most beautiful of all the Europeans: dark eyes and olive skin, proud jaws and rose-clenching teeth. They were young and sophisticated or old and distinguished, wearing jeans and waistcoats and flowing dresses. Even the couples didn't bother her as much as they could have. She felt a bounce in her step and wondered where it had come from.

By the time she arrived at the waterfront she was feeling almost cheery. The water was green and clear and full of boats, masts prickling in a bare forest. Schools of shining fish surged against the current, backs lacerated by propellers. Shadows crept over the wharf as she sat on a post and looked out to sea. The breeze lifted her hair and made her eyes water. Her mind felt comfortably empty, thoughts weightless. She was holding up well, considering. She hadn't lost it, hadn't hurled herself into a snowdrift and waited to die. Not this time.

The sun set over the land, which was unfortunate, but the sea still glittered as the shadows melted together and night fell.

The next day looked better but felt worse. Clouds still covered the sky, but they were high and only faintly grey. The air was fresh and everything felt clean. But the loneliness remained, clinging to Damon like a leaden shadow. Several times he almost checked out of the youth hostel and caught the express back to Paris, thinking no further ahead than getting back to the hotel; not sure whether she would still be there and having no idea what to say if she was. But instead he walked back down to the beach, looking at the two pictures of her. The rain had done strange things to the colour and the texture, but it didn't matter. He brushed her smudged, warped and blurry face with his fingers, almost lovingly.

On top of the hill, a stony path overlooked the surreal blueness of the ocean. Even on such a dull day, the water shone an incredible azure, looking as fake as a movie matte or a tourist brochure. But real. A pile of Roman ruins lay in an ancient garden, probably a fortress or a lookout. He wandered between the worn stones, reflecting how much they reminded him of Nice as a whole: empty, abandoned, laid to ruin—at least until the summer came again.

He ran his finger along the mossy rock, cool and moist. What had she said? It didn't have to be bad. She was different; they were different. A comforting theory, complicated by the unfortunate fact that no, he wasn't different. He was the same, always, immutable as these ageless rocks. Civilisations could come and go, and he would be the same, feel the same, have the same problems. He was steadfastly indeterminate. He smiled at the contradiction. Unshakably wishy-washy, that was him. You're a good man, Charlie Brown. Just wishy-washy. Fucking blockhead.

On the blind side of the hill, a concrete breakwater jutted out into the bay, protecting a small harbour. Rocks on one side and a smooth drop on the other. He walked along it, pacing the tightrope across water bluer than the sky. The swell rose and fell, engulfing the rocks, slapping the concrete and sluicing away again. The rhythm was comforting.

He had been someone, briefly. He had been Damon. Seeker of beauty, student of angels, witness of history. Keeper of secrets, lover of jazz. But it hadn't lasted. He had become, simply, lover of Stacy. Lover of long hair and cheekbones and hidden pain. Too much too soon. That characteristic, that facet of himself, had threatened to overwhelm all the others. The rest of him would shrivel and die, starving undergrowth beneath a mighty tree. His love for Stacy was stronger than he was.

Wasn't it?

He came to the end of the breakwater and sat against the small lighthouse whitewashed there. Watching the heaving waves, he wondered whether he had perhaps made an incomprehensibly massive mistake. The more he thought about it, the likelier it seemed. He had been hasty, foolish. Perhaps.

Damon looked out at the sea. A sailboat was making its way up the coast, salt spray shooting from its hull. He thought about December and about going home, poor and humbled but perhaps different. Perhaps. He thought about November, still in its final throes, and about October, September, August, June, February. He *had* changed. He thought about last week and this week and next week, and it occurred to him that he might have done something monumentally stupid and that there was nothing, nothing he could do about it.

Stacy was climbing Gaudí's temple of the Sagrada Familia. The stairs were going on forever. She must have been in the stratosphere by now, spiralling through the rarefied air as the breath was sucked from her. She trailed her hand along the inner wall as she climbed, always turning to the left, anticlockwise. Turn, turn, turn. She felt giddy, disoriented, the constant twisting motion mixing with her vertigo and sending her mind spinning. The circles were getting tighter, the ceiling and floor creeping together, the walls squeezing against her. Still she climbed.

Windows flicked past her as she gathered speed, throwing

patches of sunlight against the wall. She tried not to look at them, to pass them without looking down. But every time she turned there was another one, flashing a new image. Mostly the windows just revealed blue sky or the pale stone of the opposite towers. But there was more. There was—the Lake Placid General Store, Jed & Marsha Box, Proprietors. Doorbell jangling. She blinked and it was gone. Blue sky—then Chet's Diner with windows of its own, figures hunched beneath lumberjack shirts, pert blue uniforms like the one she'd worn. Gone: pale stone. She slowed, shaking her head. There was nothing there; she was disoriented, that was all. But she had to be getting near the top; not long to go. So she lifted her pace as the slit windows flicked past like the slots in a zoetrope. The truck stop, neon buzzing, big rigs and beery men. Blue sky, pale stone. Jake. Jake Rogan, smiling. When did he ever smile? A few times, yes. Now and then. She took a deep breath and set her jaw, knowing what was coming. White sky, dark stone. Snow-laden clouds. Blizzard, everywhere white. Then a dark shape falling, frozen in every window, dropping minutely like successive frames of film. Somebody screaming. Red sky, red stone. A room, a dim and dingy room with no windows where she had stayed for weeks, lost from life. Black sky, black stone. A ticket, an airport, a plane, a future. Blue sky again, and pale stone: she blinked in the new light. Canals and a mermaid and Damon, and Perry. Bright sky and pastel stone: green and blue and yellow. Damon again and a darkening sky, stone the colour of flesh. Fire and ice and snow and mountains and falling and screaming and cold wind and rocks and bare trees and Damon and Jake and Perry and love and sex and death and pain and memory and silence.

The stairs ended. A dead end, steps closing in on the ceiling. That was all; that was as far as she could go. Anticlimax. Only a crack in the stone, the tiniest of windows, and through it a patch of blue sky.

1   Een
2   Twee
3   Tre
4   Fire
5   Viisi
6   Шесть
7   Семь
8   Åtta
9   Neun
10   Deset
11   Onze
12   Douze/Doce

13   Tredici

Venice was flooded. More so than usual, even. Damon tried to leave the youth hostel and found that the courtyard, which had been dry the night before, was under a foot of water. He had to climb around the outer walls to escape into the street, which was also submerged but was serviced by a wooden walkway balanced on trestles. The planks bounced as he walked along them, wondering what was going on, whether anyone had noticed that the city was still sinking.

Venice was so beautiful, so famous for its beauty, that he felt almost embarrassed about noticing it. It was all a big cliche: old buildings dropping to the water, canals winding past, stone bridges spanning the gaps. But there it was. Just like the postcards, just like the movies. Beautiful Venice.

He found higher ground and followed the drier alleys through the middle of the city. It was an impossible place to navigate: peculiar angles, irregular blocks and a mess of intersections. The buildings were so tall and closely-packed that the city couldn't be seen for the architecture. Corners were hidden, streets retreating. Every house, facade, bridge, canal, everything looked similar but different; he suspected he was going around in circles but could never be sure. The city council seemed to have been unnecessarily stingy with street names. Breadcrumbs were what he needed, though they wouldn't last long with the pigeons swooping through the canyons. A ball of silver thread, perhaps.

The Piazza San Marco stretched before him in a massive rectangular pond, lined by colonnades. Pigeons carpeted the roofs of the surrounding buildings, nowhere else to go. Columns rose out of the water in the middle of the piazza; statues stood helplessly on top of them like flood victims waiting to be rescued. Chairs and tables paddled their legs, looking surreal.

On the other side of the piazza was the sea, no longer contained by the banks of the island, encroaching through a line of moored gondolas. The whole scene reminded Damon of Atlantis, golden city reclaimed by the ocean. He wondered whether it would continue to sink until it disappeared beneath the waves, dragging him with it like a shipwreck. That would be okay, really. He would drown in the beauty of this place, this most beautiful place. It was all he had left, anyway. But it was enough. Enough beauty for anyone. It would fill him, fulfil him, satisfy him until the water closed over him and the world forgot that he had existed.

But the waters receded shortly after noon. The tide went out and Damon expected to see rainbows and doves with fig branches as he continued his wandering. The people around him grew younger, sinking to his own age, carrying satchels and dressed in jeans. Students. He soon came to the university, hidden behind old stone walls. He ducked through an archway and into the courtyard. Students milled around in groups, eating on the grass. A familiar scene, reproduced in every town with a university. He knew it well. Back home the semester would be over. Everyone had finished their exams and were busy partying. But the years were different here. Summer holidays in July; no three-month Christmas break. He thought back to college. His friends would be graduating, applying for summer clerkships, enrolling in legal practice diplomas. And here he was in Europe with three-quarters of a law degree. He could feel it, sitting there at home, calling out to him: come back, Damon. All is forgiven. Come specialise, come seal your fate. Your future. Realise your investment. Damon for the defence. He walked up the street towards the Grand Canal, just glimpsed, and wondered...

There. There, in the window. Damn, it looked just like her. He shook his head as he walked on past the cafe, waiting for his stomach to untwist. It was just the back of a head, that was all: anyone's head. But he turned around and walked back, glancing through the plate glass as he passed. Still the back of a head, long black hair and shoulders. Familiar shoulders. But that was stupid: recognising somebody by their *shoulders*? He felt like an idiot, stopping, circling and peering through the cafe window once more. He saw an ear. Her ear? No. What would Stacy be doing in Venice? He considered the question. Travelling, maybe. Being a tourist, sorry, traveller. Could happen. It had been two weeks, almost: it wouldn't take that long to cross Europe half a dozen times, to see twenty countries. She had been heading south. She could be anywhere—even here. He stopped on the pavement, staring through the window like a pervert. It had to be her, the back of her head, her shoulders, her ear. He could imagine her face, fitting perfectly in front of this back, merging seamlessly. Passing students regarded him with suspicion. Still he kept looking, looking until there was nothing left to do but march into the cafe, walk up to her and see if it really *was* her.

He marched into the cafe and walked up to her.

It really was.

'I don't believe it,' he said. 'What are you doing here?'

She looked up at him. Nothing registered on her face: no surprise, recognition, anger, anything. Her eyes were dark, unblinking.

'Sorry,' he said. 'I mean, before you say anything, let me just say this, okay? I'm sorry. I didn't mean to—God, to hurt you. If I did. I don't even know. I mean, I don't mean to presume, assume, it's just—shit. I did hurt you, didn't I? I mean, did I?'

She looked at him.

'Of course, I know, I know I did,' he said. 'And I'm sorry. I didn't mean it. I was a dickhead, I was a fucking dickhead. I should never have left you. I should never have *found* you; I mean, nothing ever should have happened. At all. No, I don't mean that, it's just—look, I can't explain it. I'm sorry. I'm just sorry.'

She said nothing.

He sighed. 'It's not enough. I know it isn't. But what can I do? What can I tell you? What? I could tell you that you're the most beautiful, perfect, beautiful person ever. Ever in the world. I was—I was lost, truly lost, lost in a world of bullshit until I met you and you were like this light, this beacon, just shining. And I feel I was always meant to meet you, like I would have found you anywhere in the world. Anywhere. I mean, look! We're both on the wrong continent, half a world from home, and we found each other. And it's because we're the same, you and me; we are. We're wanderers; we're trying to find ourselves and lose ourselves; we're both on this journey and we'll *never get there* but it doesn't matter because the journey is the important thing, the travel, even if that's all there is and all there ever will be.'

Such dark eyes; such dark, unfeeling, expressionless eyes. Deep and dark enough to drown in, engulfing him with their stare.

'Exactly!' he cried. 'That's what I'm getting at! I don't *know* what happened! All of these things, I felt them all from the beginning, since I met you. But even then I also knew, without realising, that we could never be together, that it would never happen, *could* never happen. We were always, never, always meant to be together.'

Her jaw seemed to be setting firmly, clenched with some contained emotion. Perhaps her teeth were grinding.

'I *know* it doesn't make sense.' he said. 'But it does, as well; it does. All my life I've been doing things for other people, *being* things for other people. It was so important to me, so important to do good by others. My whole—my whole *being* was wrapped up in it. It was like I *wasn't*, you know, I just was *not*. A person. Myself. Anything. But since I've been on the road, just me, and me the only constant thing—pretty weird—since then, you know, it's like I've been—solidifying. But then you came along and it seemed like the same old thing again, and there wasn't just me anymore, there was you, *you*, and more you than me. More you than me.'

And maybe there was something in her eyes after all: some indignant pain, something inquisitive.

'I don't *know* why it has to be that way,' he said. 'I'm not even sure if it does anymore. All I'm saying is that's what I thought, and so I panicked, and I had to get out, I had to run away while there was still any of me left. I'm so sorry. So sorry. And the first thing I realised, almost straight away, was how—how miserable I was without you, and I couldn't bear it, couldn't bear what I had done. And I thought: okay, I'm me, but I hate it. I hate being me if it means I can't be with you.'

He stopped and breathed deeply, drained. She said nothing, staring like a waxwork.

'Look,' he said. 'All I'm saying is, I love you and I want to be with you and I don't care what that means. And I'm sorry that I've ruined any chance of that happening, I truly am.'

She blinked for the first time, then again.

'Say something,' he prompted.

She looked at him curiously. 'Do I know you?'

He stepped back. What? It wasn't her at all. It was her twin, her Italian student doppelganger, or he was going crazy. He screwed his fists into his eyes and looked again. It looked so much like her. 'I'm sorry,' he said, completely bewildered. 'You look like somebody I know.'

'You're fucking crazy,' she said. 'You know that, Damon? You're a fucking head-case. Goddamn, I don't know why I waste my time listening to you.'

'You hate me...?' It was a statement, really, bending into a question as a last resort.

'I don't hate you, Damon,' she said. 'You're too fucked-up to hate. You're too fractured, too... I don't know. Too humble, maybe. That's what we have in common, you and me. That's why we're the same.'

She seemed almost tender. Her eyes were misting, and not from anger. The corners of her mouth were wavering, lips trembling.

'So where does that leave us?' Damon asked softly.

She turned away. 'I can't do this,' she said. 'I can't talk about this now; not now. Let me think, let me go home and think. I'll meet you tomorrow, all right? Tomorrow.'

'Of course,' Damon said. 'Sure, of course. I'm—I didn't think there'd be a tomorrow. Tomorrow's fine, great.'

'Okay,' Stacy said. 'Ten o'clock in San Marco at that column with the flying lion on top. Tomorrow.'

She brushed past him and stumbled uncertainly out of the cafe.

'Bye,' he said.

He didn't sleep well. The dawn taunted him, refusing to break as he lay awake in his bunk. The dorm was full of other travellers, sleeping around him, breathing in overlapping waves. But he was alone. He slipped in and out of waking dreams: he was locked in an iron box, a coffin, suffocating—but there was a chink in the wall, an opening, his only chance. A one in a million shot—but crazy enough to work? He pondered the odds, sweating, twisting. So much depended.

He lay in the dark, thinking about himself. It was getting easier. He was Damon, thinker of thoughts. Climber of heights. Finder of self. For months he had been many things together, which meant one thing, one person. There was constance in him, consistency.

He was Damon, lover of Stacy. It wasn't all he was, but it was a necessary part. And it was a part of *him*; it was his. It wasn't about her. He could claim it as a part of himself. It could make him whole.

If morning ever came.

The San Marco piazza was flooded again. The water seemed deeper than yesterday, rippling grey across the square. He stopped on the walkway and cursed. Their rendezvous was in the middle of a lake. It was going wrong already. He looked over to the column, dropping into the water like a mangrove. Only one of the steps circling its base broke the surface. Stacy was standing on it, leaning against the only rock in the middle of the ocean, looking like a castaway. The churches of the Giudecca island raised their spires across the water, and the gondolas bobbed against their wooden poles. And there she was, rising out of the water like a statue, like Venus. He came to the end of the walkway and stared helplessly at the stretch of water separating them.

'Hey!' he shouted. She raised her head and nodded at him; he couldn't read her expression. 'How'd you get over there?'

'I walked!' she shouted. Her voice skipped over the water like a flying stone.

'On water?'

'*In* water. Don't be a wimp!'

He sat on the edge of the plank, took his shoes and socks off and rolled up his jeans. The water was cold as he dangled his toes experimentally, even colder as his feet touched bottom and he waded across the square, water sluicing around his legs. He felt his calves cramping, goosepimples cramming his skin. His jeans were wet already.

'That's more like it,' she said. 'Beautiful, isn't it?'

'It's *cold*,' he said, teeth chattering as he climbed onto the column and shook the water from his feet. 'You know, we could have relocated.'

'Not for anything,' she said. Her jeans were rolled up too, knees purple. He looked at her legs, smooth and glistening, and swallowed. She picked up her shoes, laces knotted together, and slung them around her neck. 'Come on,' she said. 'Walk with me.'

They splashed out into the middle of the square. The resistance felt strange against his legs and he was reminded of home, down at the beach, walking in the ocean. This was like that, only colder and immeasurably more surreal: instead of sand dunes and beachfront parks there were churches, palaces, a bell tower looming like an oil rig. Not sand beneath his feet but stone. No girls in bikinis but Stacy in her peeled-back jeans and jumper and jacket.

'I was thinking,' she said. 'A lot, actually. It was a...' She looked down and searched the water for a word. 'Shock... to see you yesterday. I thought it was over, everything, and I have to say I'd gotten pretty comfortable with that. But when you came back and started saying all those things you said... well, they sounded really familiar. Different, but familiar. Like, I can relate. You did hurt me, Damon. And maybe you don't even know how much. You left me; you were a coward and you ran away. And I was ready and willing to fuck you off just for that, and I almost didn't turn up today. But I remembered, and you've got to remember, that everything you did, I did it too and I did it first. I left you too, back in Denmark. Without much of a warning or an explanation, as I recall. And things weren't... developed, back then, but if what you're saying is true then it can't have been much of a picnic for you regardless. And I did feel... stirrings. Which is as much why I ran away as anything, I suppose.'

'I wondered,' he said.

'Yeah.'

The colonnades around the square dangled their stocky legs in the water. Cafes and boutiques stretched along their inner walls, closed and flooded. Mannequins sat forlornly behind plate-glass windows and doors tragically not watertight. The columns stretched towards a vanishing point as they walked past the shops. Everything was awash, everything grey and rippling— and they were strolling through it like trainee Messiahs, like divers exploring a wreck. It was another world, transformed.

'So, you think maybe we're even?' Damon said.

'In so many ways,' Stacy said.

'Good.'

She moved towards him, splashing his knees. He rubbed her shoulder, not sure what else to do. She looked at her shoulder and flashed a surprised grin.

'What was that?'

'It's a hug,' he said. 'It's a guy hug, a bit like this.'

He made a fist and gave her a gentle chuck on the chin.

'God, you're going to start calling me kid, now, aren't you?' she said.

'I might.'

She looked away, then turned back and stared into his eyes. 'Well,' she said. 'You hug your way and I'll hug mine.'

The shadow of a smile flashed across her face as she put her arms gingerly around him. He looked over her shoulder, hands dangling, then hugged her back. She wasn't letting go. She pulled him closer, squeezing him with all her energy. He buried his face in her hair and held her as they rocked gently. For an instant he felt a sensation of complete comfort flood over him. He closed his eyes and floated in the contact, holding and being held, utterly secure. His mind darted through the darkness like a firefly, experiencing fleeting glimpses of perfection, happiness, a new life. A second chance. Then they overbalanced and fell into the water.

It took a split-second for the coldness to rush through his clothes and tear along his body, freezing his blood. His mouth gaped with the shock and he roared silently: *haaaaaa.* Sitting up, he saw her lift her head above the water, hair hanging in black ropes. She was blinking, winded. A dripping grin spread across her purpled lips.

'Fuck,' she gasped. She swept a tangle of hair from her face, leaned over and kissed him on the mouth. The weight of her body pushed him underwater, encasing him in ice. But warmth spread across his face and through his body: her lips were warm, her tongue warm, her breath warm as it flowed into him. Her fingers warm in his hair. Her body warm against his. Warm as he pulled her to him, dunking both their heads, grinning and choking and spluttering as they surfaced.

'Are we a postcard or what?' he said. Wet, sopping wet, as wet as it was possible to be. But happy, coursing with adrenaline and relief.

She wrung her hair, sending rivulets into his face. Her clothes were clinging to her body, becoming less like clothes and more like skin. Naked with chequered skin she sent eddies swirling in the water around him, splashed his face and followed him beneath the surface. Everything was texture, his nerve endings flayed and sensitive. Her lips against his, the smoothness of her skin, wet bulk of her jacket, tightness of her jeans. They made chaste, drenched love on the submerged concrete of the piazza while saints and angels and winged lions looked on, smiling to each gold-plated other and remarking that this, ah yes, was Venice.

The number 5 ferry chugged around the island, then took off across the lagoon towards the island of Murano. Everything had been tinged with a pale blue. The water was blue all around them, foaming blue beneath the boat's hull. The sky was blue, the clouds wispy with different shades of blue. The buildings of Venice faded to blue as the main island disappeared in their wake. To the west, the sunset drew a thread of gold across the horizon, but it too was becoming blue.

Damon and Stacy sat on the stern with their arms around each other, riding the rhythm of the boat. A line of lanterns stretched into the distance, hanging from wooden pilings. The sea grew choppy as they moved away from land, waves slapping spray into the air. The wind wrapped them in a gusting blanket.

'It's no gondola,' Damon said. 'But, you know, it's not without its charm.'

She snuggled into him. 'Who needs some pole-carrying wise-ass in a stripy shirt to watch over us, anyway?' she said.

He ran his fingers through her hair, trapped by the wind-blown knots. 'That reminds me: where are you staying tonight?'

'I'm staying with nuns,' she said. 'Can you imagine?'

'Can I come stay with them too?'

'Of course not.'

'Why not?'

'Well, you know, you're...'

'What?'

'Well, evil.'

He laughed. 'They've brainwashed you already. As soon as we get back to the island we're picking up your stuff from the nuns and you can come stay with me. I've got a youth hostel that floods in the mornings.'

She smiled. 'Don't tempt me.'

'Why not?'

She patted him on the chest. 'Nuns tonight, Damon. And tomorrow we can go somewhere else, get on a train and just go.'

'Rome?'

'Ah,' she said. 'There's no place like Rome.'

'Rome, then. You sure you'll still be here tomorrow?'

'Yeah. You sure you will?'

'Yeah.'

'I've heard bad things about these Italian trains,' Stacy said. 'This girl in the youth hostel had a friend who had her bags stolen while she was sleeping. She woke up and everything was gone, even her money belt.'

'I've heard worse than that,' Damon said. 'They pump gas into your cabin and send you into such a deep sleep that you don't wake up even if they take the clothes right off you. I met a guy on a train who told me he knew someone whose friend it happened to. They woke up naked with nothing.'

'So what are we going to do?'

He looked thoughtful for a moment, patted his pockets and started digging through his backpack. 'Here, I know.'

She raised her head and watched him as he produced a length of rope, wound it three or four times around the door handles and tied the ends to his backpack and to his foot.

'What's that?' she asked.

'Travel insurance,' he said. 'I'd like to see a bunch of luggage thieves get through *that*, gas or no gas.'

'You're so... resourceful,' she said dreamily.

'Want me to tie it to your foot too?'

'I'll take my chances.'

'Okay.' He gave the rope an experimental tug. 'Let's sleep!'

They tipped the seats back and arranged their luggage into a platform of footrests. He wedged himself into a corner and she lay against him, head on his chest. His heartbeat was slowing down, their breathing becoming synchronised. The Italian countryside flashed by outside, blurring into warm colours.

'How much distance do you think we've covered?' he asked, voice bouncing off the window. 'How many kilometres of train track; how many hours?'

'A lot,' she said sleepily.

'Amsterdam to Copenhagen, to Stockholm, to Helsinki, to St Petersburg and back... they all took all night. That's, like, two, three days on the train.'

'Or the boat,' she mumbled.

'Yeah,' he said.

'Or the train on the boat.'

'Yeah. Anyway, then—'

'I didn't go that way,' she said.

'What?'

She opened her eyes and looked up at him. 'I didn't go that way. Stockholm, Helsinki, that way. I went to Oslo, Bergen and back, and right over the top of the world. That took forever. Days...'

'You got to Helsinki in the end, though,' he said. 'Then St Petersburg and back, then Berlin: that took two days and a night.'

'Stockholm,' she interjected.

'Yeah. Prague, another night; that was so slow... Paris...'

His voice was slowing, dropping in volume. She closed her eyes again and listened to him mumbling. The steady percussion of wheels grinding rails drummed her into a lower state of consciousness. The afternoon sun grew soft through the window as she drifted on the edge of sleep.

She felt his arm relax around her, muscles easing one by one. The carriage shook but they didn't, held in comfortable suspension. She felt her thoughts bend away and reflected that there were moments, split-seconds in every lifetime, when everything seemed perfect. When an instant of contentment banished all memories of the past and worries for the future, and the universe was at peace. Moments like this.

'Gas...' Damon said, trying to struggle into wakefulness.

'No gas,' Stacy mumbled. 'Go to...'

Her mind was jerked from sleep before her body had a chance

to catch up. She flicked her eyes back and forth, trying to wriggle her limbs out of their paralysis. For a chilling moment she thought that she must be back in the snow, in the dream of snow, frozen in ice. But it was more like being wrapped in cotton wool: a comfortable anaesthesia under which any movement was just too much effort. But something had torn her into consciousness. She shook her body awake and looked up. The door handles were rattling angrily, the rope dancing. A robber was trying to force his way in: a blue robber with a peaked cap and name badge and a ticket punch, knocking on the glass and rattling again.

'Damon,' she hissed. 'Wake up!'

Damon paid no attention, so she reached over and jerked on the rope. His foot kicked air and he leapt into sprawled alertness. 'Thieves!' he stuttered.

'Untie the rope, scout boy,' she said. 'We've got company.'

He fumbled with the knots until they came loose. The guard made an about-time face and slid open the door.

'*Biglietti*,' he barked.

'What?' Damon said, rubbing the sleep from his eyes.

'Three guesses,' Stacy said, rifling through his day pack. 'Where's your ticket?'

'In there,' Damon said, pointing. 'No, there. In that pocket.'

She unzipped the pocket and pulled out his Eurail pass, adding it to her own and handing it to the guard. He punched them gruffly and handed them back. She noticed that Damon's pass was full up; all of the flexi-days had been filled in. Today's date occupied the last box, and not in erasable pen either. She folded it up and stuffed it back in his bag as the guard moved on.

'I wonder where we are,' Damon said.

She glanced out of the window, thoughts elsewhere. 'Italy,' she said.

'That's good,' he said.

She turned and looked at him. 'Where were you planning to go after Rome?'

He stared at the countryside. 'After Rome...' he said. 'Home.'

'Home to Australia?'

'Home to Sydney.'

'And you were going to tell me about this... when?'

'I told you just then.'

'Only because I asked.'

'Yeah, but I knew you would. It's all people talk about around here.'

'So what if I hadn't asked?'

'Then I would have told you...'

'When?'

'As soon as I'd admitted it to myself.' He turned towards her, sincerity glistening deep in his eyes.

'Great.'

'My railpass has run out,' he pleaded. 'I've been everywhere in Europe now. Just about. I'm running out of money; I haven't worked in months. My plane leaves from Rome...'

'When?'

'In a week. But I can change it,' he said hastily, seeing her expression. 'I can put it back until I run out of money. Qantas, you know. World's best airline.'

'A week,' she said, riled. 'A week. So let me ask you this, okay, Damon? Why did you—why did you *bother* spinning all that *garbage* to me? Two days ago, *two days*, you stood like an idiot in front of me and babbled your teen-angst bullshit until I believed you. I believed you! And all the time you knew, you *knew* that you were going home in a week anyway. So why bother? Why not just walk on by, go about your business, kill time for seven lousy days and then disappear? What's the point?'

'I thought—' Damon said. 'I thought, you know, even a short time would be better than none.'

'You've been listening to too much commercial radio,' she said.

'I just couldn't leave things how they were.'

'Things were fine! *I* was fine! I get over things, you know. I'm getting pretty good at it; God knows I've had enough practice.'

'Things weren't fine with me,' he said. 'I had things to fix up.'

'And you thought I'd care?' She felt her lips curl around the words and saw him flinch as each one found its target. Poison filled her mouth, then seeped down her throat and into her gut. Son of a bitch.

'Look,' he said. 'Let's not fight, okay? Please. We've got so little time already. Let's just make the most of it: let's have the best week anyone ever had. And I'll postpone the flight and we can keep on going for as long as we can—only let's make it good, okay? Let's make it perfect.'

'Yeah, sure,' she said. 'Whatever.'

The sun passed behind a cloud, darkening the carriage. Low thunder rolled ominously. She looked out of the window and saw that the sky was blue and cloudless, the trees undisturbed by wind. But it was dark all the same; so dark...

She tried to be friendly as they arrived at the central station and dived underground to the crosstown Metro. But their exchange remained terse.

'Where are we going?' Damon asked.

'To the youth hostel, I suppose,' she said.

'Which one?'

'There's only one.'

'You don't want to stay with nuns this time?'

He smiled weakly. The poor guy, a part of her reasoned. He was obviously struggling. What was wrong with her? Couldn't she just—

'No,' she said.

The train was too crowded for conversation anyway. People crammed around them, hanging to straps and complaining at the bulk of their backpacks. She used the throng to raise a barrier between them. It wasn't hard. Breathing was hard, talking below a shout impossible—but stony silence was easy.

Everyone piled off at the Ottaviano station, end of the line. Emerging into the sudden sunlight, Stacy and Damon wandered around the intersection until they found the bus stop for northbound 32. A straggling queue was already waiting, so when the bus arrived they were packed aboard like anchovies. The standing passengers all fell over as the bus jerked forward, but they didn't have far to fall. They apologised to the people behind them and cursed the driver in good humour.

The bus powered up Viale Angelico and Stacy managed to manoeuvre herself around in the throng of overbalancing flesh. She looked forwards and saw that Damon was even more entangled. His backpack seemed to be in everyone's face, and the arms of three or four people wove around his, reaching for poles and handstraps. He looked confused and immobilised, trapped by the crowd and his luggage. The men around him smiled at him and he frowned, suddenly uncomfortable. For a moment he looked like a worried Siva, arms coming from everywhere, caressing his body. Then the bus stopped, the arms retreated and three men burst through the middle doors and pelted away down the street.

Damon looked ashen. He reached inside his jacket, then inside from the other direction. He plunged his hands into his front pockets, withdrew them and slapped his back pockets. He staggered and looked like he was about to fall over.

'Stop!' he shouted. 'Stop! Halt! Arret! Uh—' He faltered, searching. 'Fermi! Oh stop, stop...'

His voice faded to a moan. Everyone was looking at him, staring as he held his palm to his forehead and closed his eyes.

'Those bastards stole my wallet!' he cried. 'Stop the bus! They stole my wallet!'

A man standing next to him laughed, actually laughed. 'And you think you can find them again?' he chuckled. 'You English have no idea.'

'I'm Australian,' Damon said. The man laughed again and shook his head. Stacy wanted to march up and punch him in the face, but she had no room to swing. Damon was looking bewildered, eyes darting around the bus, searching for some support in this crowd of strangers.

'My wallet,' he said. 'My money, my—fuck, my Visa card! My addresses, my phone numbers. My collection of foreign currency: my rubles, my francs. My condoms...'

Stacy pushed through the crowd, knocking people aside with her backpack. He saw her and looked at her with eyes devoid of hope.

'Are you sure?' she urged. 'Jesus, Damon, are you sure?'

'I'm fucked,' he said. 'Fucked. What am I going to do?'

'You're not fucked,' she said. 'It's fixable, okay? We'll fix it. Just—stay on the bus. We're almost at the hostel.'

'You have to *pay* for hostels,' he said. 'Jesus, you have to pay for everything. I have to—fuck, I don't know *what* to do.'

'I'll pay for the hostel,' she said. 'Don't worry about it. I'll even buy you dinner. We'll get there and we'll sort it out; it'll be okay. This kind of thing happens all the time; there are, like, measures...'

He nodded, staring with vacant eyes. The bus began to empty out as it drew away from the city centre. The river appeared to the right, following the road like a dolphin speeding beside a ship. Trees flicked past and the falling sun cast a golden haze over everything. But Damon stared like a zombie, slumping into a newly-vacated seat and looking utterly beaten.

'You know what I'm going to have to do?' he said hollowly. 'You know?'

He looked up at her with pleading eyes. She shook her head.

He said, 'I'm going to have to call home.'

She stood by him at the youth hostel's public phone and waited. She could almost hear the distant ringing tones, amplified inside his head. Each a pair of pulses, a heartbeat coursing through a fibre-optic vein, bouncing through space and echoing on the other side of the planet. Four, five, six couplets. He looked at her and smiled nervously. Eight, nine. He shrugged, then—

'Hel—' he said, interrupted. 'Oh.' The operator would be asking if they would accept the collect charges. She wondered how often people refused. No, go to hell, leave *us* eight months ago with nothing but a note and not so much as a letter since? I have no son—click. Sometimes, she supposed. Not this time.

'Hello?' he said again. 'Dad? It's—'

Dad must have got in early; it was hard to interrupt on an international call. Damon stood and listened, making a weary face.

'I know,' he said. 'No—look, I left you a note. Did you read the note? I tried to write, but—no. No. I'm fine; I've been fine. I'm in Rome. Italy. Yeah. I was in London, working. What? Just in a bar. No, I've been all around Europe. Holland, Denmark, Scandinavia—look, Dad, there isn't time for this. You know how much this is costing you? No, I *couldn't* pay for it, that's what I'm trying to say. My wallet got stolen.'

He jerked the receiver away from his ear and held it out it to Stacy. A tinny voice was barking from the earpiece. He shrugged and returned it to his head.

'This afternoon. It was a pickpocket, Dad, three of them. Right out of my pocket, my inside jacket pocket. Zipped up and everything. I don't know, it was on a bus. Everything. Money, Visa card, everything. No, that's in my bag. And the ticket. I've still got them. It's just money; I need you to wire me some money. Ring the bank and cancel the card; I'll report it in the morning. No, Dad, it's night time here. Okay? They can't get at the account. Well, yeah, they could, but Visa wears it. I'm pretty sure. But I can't get at the account either. No, it's an Australian bank, they don't have branches here. That's why I need you to wire me money. It's easy. Just go to Amex— Amex. American Express. No, you don't need to write it down, it's—'

He sighed. An expression of great fatigue was tugging at his features, as if the telephone were draining the life from him, sapping his strength from across the globe. His hand was quivering.

'He's gone to get a pen,' he told Stacy before his attention was drawn back to the distant voice. 'Okay? Go to American Express, and say you want to buy traveller's cheques in my name for me to pick up at Amex in Rome. The main one. I dunno, enough to live on for a couple of weeks. Five hundred dollars, say. No, come on, I'll pay you back! I tell you, there's money in the account; I can get it as soon as I come home. A lot! What? You opened—that's confidential! It is, those statements have confidential written all over the envelopes. You can't—*eighty-five dollars*? No way. I *know* I've got more than eighty-five dollars. No, you can't get a balance here, but— when *was* this? *Yesterday*? But I took another fifty *out* yesterday. It was stolen! Oh, man. Oh, man, thirty-five dollars. Well, please, just lend me a hundred bucks, okay? Two hundred. My plane's in a week; you've got to lend me enough to survive a week. You can't let me *die* here. Just a loan, okay? I'll pay you back; I'll get Austudy again. Yeah, I am. Yes! Yes, father, I am going back to university. I think. I don't know, I was inspired; it's very inspiring here. Yeah, I've decided. International Law. You know, human rights, United Nations stuff. I'm not really sure. Yeah, I'll find out when I re-enrol. But it won't happen if I die here, will it? Okay, thanks, Dad. Two hundred. Plus the thirty-five in my bank account; I'm good for that. No? Okay, whatever. For the phone call? Very funny. Thanks. No, I'll be okay for tonight; I'm with a friend. Okay. I'll see you, Dad— I'll see you soon. I'll see you in a week. Sunday morning, I think. No, I'll get a taxi. No, really. I don't know; call Qantas. Right. Bye, Dad. Bye.'

He looked at the handset for some time before replacing it in its cradle.

'Well,' he said. 'That could have been worse.'

She stared at him. 'How?'

He shrugged. 'I dunno. He could have told me he'd just murdered my mother with a nail gun and he was coming after me next.'

'Well, if you put it like that,' she said. 'But didn't I just hear you mortgage your future for two hundred dollars in traveller's cheques?'

'My future?' he said. 'Oh, that. No, I've decided. That's what I want to do. I just thought I'd use it to my advantage. It may as well make me some money now; God knows it won't later. No jobs for international lawyers. He wasn't too happy; I think he was hoping for securities and investment, or advanced corporate fascist law, or something. But he'll get over it.'

'So you've got yourself a direction now,' she said. 'Well, that's pretty cool, I guess. At least you've got something to go back to.'

'It's only a provisional plan,' he said. 'But it sounds okay for now. And, hey, the UN meets in New York so I'll probably be hanging around there half the year. So we can see each other again!'

'Swell,' she said.

'No, really,' he said. 'I'll meet you there in five years. That should be long enough. Say, noon on the winter solstice, underneath the Australian flag.'

'Enough talk,' she said. 'Let's go to bed already.'

She took his hand and walked with him to the dormitory, thinking with some confidence that for a while, a short while, everything would be all right. It wasn't long, but it was all that mattered. Long enough.

Rome was more than a city: it was a terrarium of history. Half a dozen epochs wound through the chaos of its streets, built on top of each other. The rise and fall of an empire was charted in its architecture; the ebb and flow of civilisation undulated with its seven hills. Scooters chugged through its cobbled streets, and the carbon monoxide of a million Fiats ate at buildings displaced in time. Markets arose where markets had always been: resonating halls of vegetables and fruit; leather jackets and stolen watches where togas and amphoras had crowded the stalls an eyeblink ago. Policemen, not centurians, rode clopping horses through the streets and the Romans did as the Romans do, eating and drinking and shouting and gesturing and singing and painting and driving too fast and carrying on like an empire that could fall again at any moment and was frantically enjoying its decadence while it lasted.

Stacy walked through the ruins of the Forum and the adjoining Palatino, following where the streets must have been. Strange to think that there had been Romans here, ancient Romans, wearing these paths twenty centuries ago. Standing on street corners and debating the law and planning their utopia, or whipping their mules or playing in the gymnasium or whatever they did when they weren't being eloquent. Her feet tingled as she walked, and she heard the faintest murmur of the echoes which had bounced between these ruins forever. She walked through the memory of a wall and found herself in the inner sanctum of a temple. She felt like a ghost, ignoring the streets now and wandering wherever she wished. But she was not the only one: there were ghosts everywhere, cramming the courtyards, lingering in the remnants of their homes. She heard the shuffle of their sandals in the silence, felt them brush past her. And occasionally she saw one: an orphan shadow playing across the grass; a curve of the light obscuring a statue for a moment. Glimpses of movement, snatches of sound to remind her that she was not alone. There were recent ghosts, too: she seemed to collect them. Foreign ghosts, American, Canadian, Australian: tourist ghosts come to marvel at the architecture and the plumbing. But they were no more corporeal, no more persistent than the Roman ghosts, and as the sun rose higher they melted away with the shrinking shadows and left her alone. Alone with an Australian who looked like some of the ghosts but was real: a real Australian, poking around the necropolis looking for headstones or skeletons or undiscovered treasures he could sell in order to be with her.

'I mean, it's nice and everything,' Damon said as they walked across the piazza of the Vatican. 'Well, it's stunning, let's be honest. Unimaginably... nice. And there's nothing like a cathedral for peace and a sense of well-being. Except those fucking tourist churches, of course. But it's, you know, nice.'

'Oh, unquestionably,' Stacy said. 'I just wish...'

'...They'd come up with some new themes?' Damon said, nodding with her. 'Yeah. I mean, God!' He looked around in mock guilt. 'Uh, whoops. But it's the same thing over and over. It's like rock music, only instead of love it's archangels and the Virgin Mary.'

'Baroque and roll,' Stacy said.

Damon looked pained. 'Shut up,' he said. 'Anyway, Michelangelo's Renaissance. Renaissance and roll.'

'Still,' Stacy said. 'I can't believe I'm getting bored of Europe.'

'When you're bored of Europe, you're bored of life,' Damon said sagely.

'That's what I'm afraid of.'

The columns of the Basilica San Pietro curled around the piazza in triple rows, looking like an optical illusion. A line of buses were parked next to the fountain, and a group of monks filed out, arranging themselves into twin files as they marched across the courtyard, habits flapping. A group of Japanese tourists intercepted them and demanded they pose for photos. The monks broke ranks and grinned in the flashbulb lightning, then pulled out cameras of their own and snapped the tourists, the fountains, the columns, and each other. It was impressive, no doubt about it. More than enough to make even a monk lose his composure. But she'd seen it before. The same statues were lining the roof, looking down on her like old marble friends. The same baroque dome loomed; the same columns shuffled their feet. The same wrought iron lamp posts hung their multiple heads towards the pavestones. Europe was worried that it would lose its heterogeneity to America's cultural imperialism. But even America was more varied than this. America had slums; filthy, unattractive cities, towns where people stopped only for gas and cigarettes. In Europe there was beauty around every corner, and it was getting tedious.

'So what are you going to do?'

'Hmm?' she said.

'Now that you're bored of Europe.'

'I don't know,' she said. 'Go somewhere else, I guess.'

'Come to Australia?'

'What is there in Australia?'

'Everything,' Damon said. 'It's an amazing place; really. You don't realise until you go somewhere else. The country's beautiful. There's mountains and rainforests and deserts and beaches and everything.'

'I don't know,' Stacy said. 'It's a long way away. But maybe some day.'

'Where in the meantime?'

Good question. 'Home, I guess.' She shrugged. 'I'm about out of money too. You don't save much working in a diner. So I guess I'll go back, see how everyone is, let them see how I am. That'd be okay, I guess.'

'Back to Smalltown, USA?' Damon looked dubious. 'Back to three thousand max? You could handle that?'

'For a couple of days, sure,' she said. 'After that—I don't know. Maybe I'll go to the city, take my backpack, look for a job in Manhattan.'

'Three thousand to eight million,' Damon said. 'That's some step.'

'I think I'm ready for it now. I've seen a lot of cities these last few months. Put them all together and they're even as big as New York. Kind of.'

'I don't know if I want to go home at all,' Damon said. 'I've changed so much, you know. Learned so much. I just hope I can hang on to it back there. I hope I'm strong enough.'

'You're strong enough,' she said. 'I have a feeling this is the big one. This change, this travel change—I don't think you can go back.'

He stopped halfway across the bridge. The Tiber ebbed past below, and leaves scratched the river banks. He looked into her eyes. 'I'm going to miss you,' he said.

'Yeah,' she said.

Contemporary Rome was, of course, as contemporary as anywhere else. The traffic was psychotic, streaming along the newer, vehicle-friendly roads and squealing through the old alleys, cornering on two wheels. Squat buildings rose from the pavement, hiding the streets between them. The urban planners of history's various Romes had clearly worked from different premises, and the city was in chaos. A few rectangular blocks fell along accidental grids, but everywhere else the streets twisted into a labyrinth. Some echoed the curve of the river, some radiated from central points, some sketched expanding triangles or curled like an architect's signature. In between, the buildings crammed into whatever space they could find, carving shapes in negative space: empty wedges, alleys leading nowhere, irregular expanses of concrete and flagstones. Getting lost was an adventure: every corner revealed something unexpected, tucked away and discovered by accident.

The air buzzed as Stacy and Damon wandered through the streets, chewing on their squares of pizza. This new Rome was as enchanting as the others. Strange how they could all coexist so amicably, fading seamlessly into one another. Perhaps their relationship was symbiotic; each demanded the other. The old Rome had been doomed, of course, unable to support the weight of its own empire. But new cities had sprung from its ashes, building on its ancient foundations. The memories, the ghosts of the past infused the present and would continue to support the future. Nothing had been forgotten: history was still conspicuous; clearly too persistent to be escaped. But it had been built on, its power tapped, its energy harnessed. Life from death.

The Spanish Steps raised a staggered slope from the Piazza de Spagna to the church of Trinità dei Monti. Their broad ripples climbed to a landing, almost a square in itself, then split and rejoined at the entrance to the cathedral, using its obelisk as their rendezvous. The steps demanded to be sat on. Crowds of people had already succumbed to the temptation: Damon and Stacy sat down, watched and were watched.

'Tomorrow,' Stacy said.

'Don't remind me.'

'What, you'd forgotten?'

'Forgotten what?'

'Wise guy.'

He put his arm around her, leaned into her and tipped his head against hers. 'I can't bear it,' he said. 'It's all I can think of, all I can feel. This loss.'

'You're not gone yet,' she said.

'One more day,' he said. 'Don't you feel it too?'

She searched herself, trying to distil single emotions from the morass that had gathered inside her. Strange cocktail. She knew this loss should have been a major ingredient, but it wasn't. As she tried to seize on it, it slipped through the fingers of her mind. No: not loss. Not exactly. There was a faint current of elation, of victory. She felt like she had won some profound battle: for her sanity, soul, something. An impatience coursed through her, a determination to get *on* with it, to get back to her life, to implement whatever it was that she had learned or become. There were trace elements of a distant sadness, humming like background radiation—but transformed, dispersed, banished to memory. Anticipation burgeoned. But here was something like loss, some distant relation. She felt like she was basking in the last rays of a sunny afternoon, a golden time drawing to a close but perhaps, after all, not too soon. From the body pressed against her she felt warmth, comfort, security, a pulse of passion. From the mind floating somewhere inside it she felt closeness, understanding, an inexpressible sensation of beauty. She knew she would miss him when he was gone; knew that it would be painful to think about him and impossible not to. She knew life would be harder without him, but knew too that she would manage, alone but no longer lonely.

'Yes,' she said.

'I'm glad about everything, though,' he said. 'I mean, obviously. I'm glad I met you. All those times.'

'Yeah,' she said. 'Me too. It's enough.'

'Well, it's not enough,' he said. 'But I guess it's all we get.'

'It wasn't a bad deal, really.'

'No,' he said. 'And there's no-one we could have complained to anyway.'

'Good thing we're just a couple of satisfied customers, then.'

'Satisfied,' he said, tasting the sound. 'Yeah, that's the word.'

Shadows crept up the steps as the sun fell and the sky deepened to a rich blue. From the twilight came a distant rustling and a flock of birds, birds in their thousands, swept across the square. They sailed through the sky in some implicit formation, crowding into a mass of shapes twisting, spinning, stretching in the air. She watched the airborne sculpture shift before her eyes, watched the shapes giving birth to each other. No meaning unfolded in front of her; no image. Just forms, ripples, waves, enchanting her with a silence too deep to be disturbed by the sound of the birds. The thankful silence of a mind finally at rest.

They lay together for some time, caressing each other languidly, breathing as quietly as they could. Poised and waiting, bursting with contained fervour, they wondered whether anybody else was due back at the dorm. Maybe there was nobody; or maybe whoever was left had met someone and found a better place to have sex than a youth hostel. The breathing in the room grew slower and more regular. Somebody snored once, twice, then stopped. Stacy's heart pounded like a metronome, marking each half-second. She felt his blood coursing through the veins beneath her fingers, pulsing in syncopation.

The last guest in the dorm arrived so quietly that they might not have heard him or her creeping across the floor, might not have registered his or her painstaking footsteps, if their nerves had not been sped into alertness, their senses heightened into sensitivity. But they heard the last intruder climb into bed, heard the bunk creak minutely, heard the sleeping bag settle over his or her body with a gentle breath.

Damon's bunk hid emptily below them.

The only bed left was theirs.

Their eyes, accustomed to the darkness, saw everything in blue. Damon shifted his weight, testing the effect of his movement. The bunk's wooden slats complained quietly; at least there were no springs to disturb.

'Shh,' she whispered.

She felt the warmth emanating from his grin. He pushed her T-shirt up around her neck, ran his hands over her breasts, kissed them soundlessly. She reached for him, raked his back with her fingers, pushed away his underpants as he did the same to hers. She wriggled her legs free, felt a sudden chill over her body and pulled the blanket back over both of them. She pulled him towards her, slowly, cautiously, parting her legs and clamping his lips to hers to stifle any sounds they made as he entered her. They wrapped their arms around each other, holding each other as tightly as they could. She locked her heels against his calves. They were a statue, a sculpture, fused together, rigid, silent and immobile apart from the slow and rhythmic thrusting of their hips, the controlled clench of their thighs and buttocks. A bed of fire encased in stone, that was them. Unseen and, more importantly, unheard as they breathed into each other, sweating silently. She felt like she was screaming, bellowing with all of her being, whooping and laughing and moaning into the night. Maybe everyone was awake, awake and listening, getting off on the sounds of their focussed passion. But the blue silence of the room pressed against her; the waves of breathing and occasional snoring lapped over their joint bodies, and she knew they were quieter still.

Everything was happening too fast. The subway train had felt like it was breaking the sound barrier as it rushed towards Roma Fiumicino; her eardrums had burst, her equilibrium shattered. The airport clock had spun with a face full of second hands as the queue had dwindled and Damon had checked in, heaved his backpack onto a conveyor belt and watched it disappear towards the belly of a jumbo. He looked suddenly strange without it, and she realised why. He was no longer a traveller; he had handed in his badge and was heading home. She almost cried, but didn't.

'I was trying to work out something to say to you,' he said. His voice quavered. 'Some speech or something, something to tell you that this whole travel experience has been the greatest part of my life and you've been the greatest part of that. That I know I've been a dickhead for a lot of the time we've known each other and you didn't have to put up with me but if you hadn't I don't know what would have happened, what sort of person I'd be now. Because I really feel I've grown, you know; I've grown and I've changed. I'll never forget you and I owe you more than you'll ever realise. And I know it's ridiculous to talk about love at a time like this so I won't, but I think you know how I feel so it doesn't matter. I wanted to tell you all that.'

'So what happened?'

'I guess I couldn't think of the words,' he said.

'They're pesky like that,' she said. 'Words.'

'Yeah,' he said unhappily. 'I had so many, too. So many words for you.'

'I have one for you,' she said.

'Yeah?'

'Yeah.'

'What is it?'

'Goodbye.'

She looked into his eyes and felt her heart break.

'Yeah,' he said. 'Oh, man, the plane leaves in four minutes.'

'I know. Say goodbye.'

'I can't.'

'It's easy. I'll help you.'

She kissed him on the lips, cradling the back of his head. She flicked her tongue into his mouth, tasting him for the last time. Then she mouthed the word *goodbye*, guiding his lips around the syllables. They parted.

She smiled sadly at him and shrugged: nothing else to say.

He smiled back; then his face fell and his mouth dropped open.

'My God,' he said. 'I can't believe it. I don't have your address!'

She looked at him, nodded: I know.

'Well, quick, give it to me!'

She shook her head, once: no.

He looked confused, but an expression of understanding crossed his face and he nodded miserably.

'Three minutes,' he said. 'I have to go. Thank you.'

The corners of her mouth crinkled upwards, then downwards, undecided. She waved him away.

He stepped backwards onto a moving walkway and was sucked away from her. She watched as he dwindled before her, watching her back. A tear broke free and slid down her face; she left it to hang unattended from her chin. He almost fell backwards as he reached the end of the line and the carpet started again. Waving to her, he rounded the corner and disappeared towards the departure gate. Gone.

She waved back, uselessly, then raised her hand before her face and stared blankly at it. The tunnel he had disappeared down stretched to infinity. She stood and watched it, wondering how long it would take before something came to fill the emptiness yawning inside her.

All she knew was that something would.

More quality literature from Hyland House ...

The Crystal Messenger by **Pham Thi Hoai**
This extraordinary novel has been described as the 'renaissance of Vietnamese literature'. Winner of the Frankfurt LiBeraturpreis and acclaimed by the French daily *Le Monde* as a 'startling, beautifully written book', Hoai's magical portrait of post-war Vietnam is now published in English for the first time. ISBN 1 875657 71 1, $19.95 jacketed pbk

Tusk by **Bill Reed**
'A lonesome dove in the current wash of Australian literature ... it is a novel infused with that lost notion—craft.' *The Australian* Bill Reed is a great Australian original. This moving and innovative novel has been praised for its exceptional imagination and emotional depth. A psychological thriller about the links between fathers and sons, it is a unique and memorable achievement. ISBN 1 875657 86 X, $24.95 jacketed pbk

Crete by **Dorothy Porter**
Short-listed for the NBC Banjo awards, this collection is one of the most popular works of Australian poetry published in recent years. Erotic, thoughtful, packed with wit and risk, *Crete* is another masterwork by Australia's most popular poet. ISBN 1 875657 68 1, $19.95 jacketed pbk

The Monkey's Mask by **Dorothy Porter**
'I am so knocked out by the startling unlikeliness and originality that I barely know how to begin this review.' The Times (London). Porter's revolutionary crime thriller in verse is now an international bestseller. Arguably the most successful work of Australian poetry published since the Second World War, it has been translated into several languages and has won many awards, including the *Age* Book of the Year and the NBC Banjo award. ISBN 1 875657 43 6, $19.95 jacketed pbk